NO GUN'S IN LITTLE CAVERN

Craig Sholl

Book Cover created by "SusansArt"

Printed in the United States of America

First Printing: Dec 2017

2nd Edition

ISBN: 9781729130698

"In the room the women come and go talking of Michelan-gelo."

- From the "Love
Song of J. Alfred Prufrock" *by* T. S. Eliot

To Miss Emily Sholl and her Diaries

1

Not so long ago and not too close to the present there lay a town in the Midwest on the Wyoming frontier called Little Cavern. This was back before people went around in automobiles and planes were flying in the air. Back before many of the things needed by people during the present but before things hastened by those of the far past, roughly ten or so years just before the turn of the nineteenth unto twentieth centuries. This was when cowboys rode on their horses matted by a leather harness and spurs on their suede leather bound boots. Their clothes were often colorful and patterned intricately as things were meant to last as time weathered on as it often did. The town of Little Cavern though consisted of several stretches of dirt roads often covered in equine from horse hides and even worse when the bulls came through harnessed in rows to their wagon counterpart's.

Fashionable stores though were embanked on either side selling various products such as clothing and pantry items as well as various foods and sweets. Children would go in and out of these stores daily and Mrs. Cannerville's sweet shop was as popular to the young ones as the saloon at the far end of the town was to ornery cowboys coming through to deliver goods as well as sharp shooting young and older men slightly more polished than the average swagger in town. The town of Little Cavern overall was prosperous and more popular to stay in than most being along that part of the open range but no town is without a common theme whether among the people or the look of the town itself or most often both. The theme of Little Cavern was not uncommon in those days though and had been repeated before in other parts, but, above all, there were no guns allowed in Little Cavern and to bear a firearm except for the local officials in charge of the public and responsible for the common good was an offence punishable by imprisonment or either force of disarmament, but either way, to carry a firearm was to carry an injustice.

The presiding deputy sheriff was Jeff McCormack as the last one had recently died of old age during his sleep. The old sheriff's name was Bob Morris but the locals had referred to him often as "Bob Cratchit" or "that Cratchity, old Bob" or whenever out of his presence which was most often preferred since he was something of a repressed soul and not very witty, but unanimously considered, a complete asshole of a sheriff. Nevertheless he was a good man as any a Bob Cratchit could be and it had been rumored among the town folk that his last words for the night he had come to pass on were, "I'm tired. I think I will go home now – Goodnight," although how his eternal rest was not unwelcomed and now at least the town folks would no longer have to whisper their decree towards him. The new sheriff, however, to be blunt was something of a real asshole and was much more witty and joking and splendiferous in his remarks when it came to knowing about other more modest ones similar to old Bob. The locals at the moment did not take to offense though and welcomed his fair reign over their bestowing town of Little Cavern, Wyoming. People still moved the same way and hurried by the same as before when crossing the dirty roads or strolling along the porch of the street shops. Women still basked in their glory with their voluptuous hats and fitted in their dainty, garmented skirts careful not to walk near any horse droppings upon the rode and the shops they frequented as men escorted them tall and thinly producing a wake of aura suggesting Sunday worship and godliness and straight folded linens placed in rows on a solid oak, dining room table and all the things one alludes to when thinking of hypocrites straight from hell, the devil sitting on his thrown and with a knowingness. Nobody knew this better than the sheriff Jeff McCormack though and how he basked in his fruits of knowledge similar to that of the devil and with the same intent. Late at night one would find him sitting crooked in his chair at the sheriff's desk beside him a few empty jail cells ready for intake and saying something to himself like, "*I piss on their God*," or, "*Justice is Mrs. Taylor, alright*," who was the most promiscuous woman in the town, for the matter, and also the most bodacious and healthiest of looking women around thirty, always carrying her white parasol and dressed in white just shy of a bride to be although she was very much married and the day she walked down the aisle to collect her gold ring was long gone as she was given away at the age of fifteen to the best man in Wyoming passed the age of thirty five, his name being Mr. Nelson Taylor. To be honest hardly anyone wound up in jail next to Jeff McCormack's desk and chair except for a few occasions involving vagrancy along with some minor theft as well as an alcoholic whom drank up at the saloon and was not accompanied by many but shunned by most. His name was Wyatt Cobb but he was mostly quiet and kept to himself as a drinker. Wyatt was young around thirty like Mrs. Taylor but not unkind unlike Mrs. Taylor. His hair was parted and longish and light colored, but not too long and his black suit jacket wore over him thinly but often giving the effect of looking squeamish at times. He was by no means a pugnacious character or a slobbery type of drunk. His drinking had grace and he was not undignified and when he walked it was not overbearing and in line even when he drank. His problem though was not to create disorder for the town or to impede the public good. His problem was himself, and he was given to bouts of melancholy and a quiet binge of stagnation so that he would be placed in the jail cell out of bafflement and concern rather than the notion of hurting someone else but more for the notion of possibly hurting himself and to see him in need of drink or with drink came with a kind of pity or scorn. He was also an avid writer and had worked for the local newspaper at one point adding his own serials and doing some editing alike. He liked poetry too and had published a few short stanza poems about the town but the verse never took too well and most of the others never took notice. Other than that there wasn't much to Wyatt and no one else nearby seemed to know what his past was or what was ailing him and one could only speculate what it was like for him in the jail cell all night next to the sheriff. Only the sharp shooting sheriff could utter some of his brassy wisdom to define Wyatt's plight and without a great deal of sympathy, mind you. Indeed, the night would whistle on into the late as Wyatt lay in his cell without a sound or peep except for some heavy breathing which subdued eventually. In the background one could hear some humming every so often coming out of the sheriff that suggested something calm and relaxing so that Wyatt could hear as the wit of a sheriff leaned back in his chair fully knowing he was listening and uneasy in his cell. Yet Wyatt never gave into his minor tirades in his numb state of being. Instead he would just lay there with half a smile on his face and looking straight above from his cot fully knowing that hell and the devil resided in the town of Little Cavern, Wyoming, of all places, and that he could hear him humming some of *Old Sweet Loraine.*

Nevertheless, the rest of the folks didn't pay it any real heed although there had been some minor ramblings about Wyatt among the older male gentry, but nothing ever came of it and things went on the same. Little Cavern was a fairly small place with big headed people and old Christian zeal and values. It thrived on its own virtues and truth was scarce and rarely beckoned on but often put away so that one could stumble on it another day or a few decades down the road. But the truth of the town of Little Cavern be told now and the way it was as I unlock the keyhole to its thick and heavy door as recently I had unveiled a few diaries of my Great, Great Grandmother as she had resided in Little Cavern as a young woman and were put away in the attic so that I had found them while trying to find an old typewriter that I had stowed away for quite some time and forgotten where I had put it. As for the diaries they were slightly dusty wrapped in an old garnet hidden in a closed cabinet but I knew they existed before although never assuming the desire to go through them as I recently did. Although the grandmother of my grandmother had passed on long before my birth and we had never met I knew her name well from my own grand-mother's utterances of her or when she spoke of past memories of her up-bringing in the west, although far from the town of Little Cavern as she had been borne much further north someplace else and given the name Emily. Her grandmother's name though was Mildred O'Leary but people knew her and called her "Millie" and the name Millie is in quotation marks on the front cover between the first and last name or as in print:

The Life and Daily Happenings
Of
Mildred "Millie" O'Leary

Almost every entry of the journal is dated and written with an elegant hand, nicely put down I can only assume from a quill pen dipped into an inkwell with few blotches of ink on the page. The diaries are in fairly good condition even inside and a little smaller than a regular size notebook, but enough entries to fit three books all the same kind.

Shortly after finding them I set down to read them in my den as I sat in my arm chair cross legged, my desk lamp providing most of the light that was just bright enough as my desk is situated a few feet from the chair. For I was then in a fugue state and very inert and had been for a while melancholy but the look of the forgotten diaries suggested a time that I did not know and did not live in as if their might be a kind of truth in store within them as they were begotten glimpses of the past, perhaps, of what one loved and wanted and what was and what was not. Yet, there was also the feeling of infringement and a caution upon opening the books as though a privacy would be broken.

Nevertheless, this only prompted me further in my trapped state of being to go into the unknown. As I read the entries though upon the page I realized that the diaries were intended to be read and written for that purpose, a kind of vague revelation or a kind of passing on to someone else to know of course that they too had lived felt and pained and that they were passionate enough to write it down and let fate bring them to another's hands. After reading them I felt a strange peace that came as a relief in my isolation and numbness and decided to set down on paper of what had been passed on to me so that a certain respect would be shed and a certain feeling of kinship would be instilled in what I had written and perhaps over time a truth would be preserved. As for the town of Little Cavern it is now a relic of the past, a ghost town of the old west, but I think in a way, a modulation of what is. So, when I set down and began to write the story of Little Cavern and its peoples, I thought not of myself and what I wanted to see but rather what I wanted to show so that a deep reflection could be carried to a lowly observer in search of something or rather a belief, and to believe in something even is strongly conjectured so that people will spit at your feet for it, or just something different than what is accepted or opposing, is sometimes better than not believing in something at all.

My Great, Great grandmother lived in a house on the outskirt of Little Cavern with a low rise front porch and white, washed boards nailed and sank to fit sturdily by the hands of a wise and proficient carpenter one can scarcely think. The quality of the house she lived in was above average during those times and in those parts but far from nobility but not entirely immodest. Her parents were not unpopular and went to Sunday prayer like most everyone in the town with the exception of a few such as Wyatt Cobb who was never to be found around at that time other than up at the saloon on occasion as well as those just passing through such as the new cowboys and cattle pickers in town and of course the sheriff Jeff McCormack who was busy with keeping the law in his sight and making sure there were no unwarranted outbursts in the town which was his dutiful excuse.

One would sit in the Protestant bearing church listening to the passions of the priest in his words of God being bestowed unto oneself as Jeff sat at his desk and upheld the common good one cartridge at a time as he would pluck them from his peacemaker with its iron clad handle in and out whistling *Old Susanna* bits of hay and cactus bushels blowing in the dirty road outside and down the town where no guns were allowed for posterity.

The priest of the church, which was lap strake and white as snow, and having a small steeple in the front with its declarative bell hanging inside was something of a harsh man in his lessons of religion and chastening's from his tall, and whitely painted pew, the altar of God upon his shoulders with the old testament in front of him strewing out his blowing fathoms of the protestant faith, needless to say talk of the devil was vindictive in temperament and his blasphemy unforgiven and without any blithe. The priest's name was Father Coleridge a moderately sized man having snarling eyes and black hair with no mustache or beard but only some minor sideburns cut trimly with a trim haircut and orderly looking though he could put the fear of God in you just as Mrs. Taylor could spell out among some of the married men in town with their sheepish looking wives courting them from not afar.

Mrs. Taylor like everyone else, except for the few others mentioned before, would go to church on the Holy Sunday and listen to Father Coleridge up on his pew as she sat up highly in the first row next to Mr. Taylor now a much older looking man having dark, greyish hair strewn roughly around his iron, face head and always dressed in formal clothes with a black suit jacket and dark tie to match his black trousers. In point of fact, Mr. Taylor was a rather harsh man himself as was the priest in his sermon but Mr. Taylor was far from moved in the priest's reproaches about fellow sinners and their due punishment from the heavens above. Instead, Mr. Taylor would sit there fully knowing that if what the parson said was true than he would just disappear like that and be taken down to hell's grave the church in flames and clouds above it in a storm with thunder and lightning coming from the heavens. Mr. Taylor was not concerned though with Father Coleridge's minor ramblings about such things but instead looked unto it so that everyone else would be in fear of such exaggeration of the lord's upkeep regarding sinners and their petty ethics, and how they were moved for the unknown:

"Ye that use the sword and live by thee shall perish in blood by it. A sinner's paradise is such and must be cast away and burnt like a burial at sea. Live with God and repentance shall set you free. For God is your friend and your advocate to eternal rest and paradise - " Father Coleridge professed in his deep and bold voice of conviction as the older women listened intently and with their full approval as the younger and more vulnerable ones just listened, this bundle including my own ancestor Millie O'Leary whom possessed the most sense and the most clarity and righteous sensitivity among the younger and even older women in the town, but would listen to the religiosity of Father Coleridge and all that went along with it with a kind of ferment and a sense of relief that the Sunday bickering's in the church would be over soon with each syllable said by the father and every diligent minded observer gesturing their approving looks and small curtsies to. At the time she was only seventeen but young and pretty with brown hair and a freckled face but not overly appealing like that of Mrs. Taylor or some of the more eager and younger women getting ready for their budding jakes. Millie wasn't anything like that though. She was young and firm and just as truth was her main aim in life, although her apprehension for it was sometimes muffled and left in a confusion with it. She loved life and she loved the seasons but had never come upon a love of her own and that empty feeling of sorrow among the young was at her feet at all times so that her face was modest and her dimples were shallow as her face was a blank sheet of ponderings and a longing for love that was tucked away in the presence of others but looked upon by herself when alone.

So when church was through and finally done those Sunday mornings in the white washed house of prayer and Millie had gone home with her parents on their horse driven carriage that was matted by a single horse she would be by herself and in her own world of thoughts and with such notions as chivalrous love and her woes for it and what it meant to her. In other words, Millie was passionate and loving and respectful as well as talented and intelligent. Yet she had few friends in the town except for one other girl who lived not far from her own home down the water creek that lay beside it her name being Stella Parsons. Stella would occasionally come by to fetch Millie and they would go off together to roam the pastures nearby of corn and wheat or even go into town to groom the stores filled with things they found enticing and an enviable longing for things they didn't have.

One Sunday morning then in the later summer when school was out for Millie and the other young people alike she and Stella had gone into town to visit the priciest clothing shop for women that was owned by Miss Purcell, a fragrant and elegant looking woman with a slight Parisian accent and always with the knowledge that her dresses in the window were the best in those parts and that women would kill to own one or two of them. However, Millie had seen a white dress that looked fitted for her and very elegant and that she had wanted a while now for the town gala where all the young people would gather and have a dance which had been a tradition in the town and county it resided in, or Governors it was called, for some years and that the other young folks from different parts of Wyoming would come to participate in likewise.

Just before the two young girls went in the store they stopped for a few moments as Millie viewed the dress from outside the store front through the glass, a sleek white dress and sewn with silk that she thought would show her up well. Her friend Stella around the same height as Millie, but brasher looking with short blonde hair and blue eyes stood aside her grazing over some of the other gowns in the showcase window. A few moments later the shop door was opened by Stella as Millie followed her from behind and as the bell hanging above the door jingled. Miss Purcell was the only one in the store as she sat behind her counter and had been writing something down with a feathery looking quill pen in hand and a pair of frameless but elegant looking eye glasses that were resting on her prim and delicate nose as they were attached to her upper garments by a chord of string. Beside her centered on the counter, was an old nineteenth century, solid metal cash register ready for the day's business and raring to go. The store was very nice inside and velvety with various dresses hanging about along with various fabrics and a few sewing machines for quick preparations and a wide satin rug that covered the boarded and nailed down floor. Nevertheless to get a dress from Miss Purcell meant a great deal more than just a dress as she was a cornerstone of the town gossip and one whom was respected among the older women hens and busy talking about everyone else's business. Millie had been to the store with her mother other times before to pick out some fabrics as Millie was accustomed to having her dresses sewn up by her instead as her mother was very skilled with the needle and thread herself but it was on one of these recent occasions when Millie had seen the white dress in the window and soon began to covet it like nothing else.

"Ah, young mademoiselle so I've seen you've come back," Miss Purcell exhumed in her thinly laced Parisian voice and as she removed her spectacles from her face so that they hung down across her torso and silky gown.

"How may I help you?" Millie was a little hesitant to speak at first as she stood there momentarily with Stella aside her.

"I would like to buy the dress in the window – the white one."

Miss Purcell just looked at the young girl for a few moments as she began to get up and come around the counter near Millie. Then standing in front of her she said,

"I see you have a keen eye, mademoiselle. That dress happens to be one of my best. But for you, I will be generous and ask only twenty dollars for it, although I'm sure you have some money saved for it. *Am I not right?*"

"Yes. I have almost ten and a half dollars saved, but I can get the rest from my parents." In those days ten dollars was much and the money Millie had saved had taken her a while to gather. Miss Purcell just waited a moment but then in a rather raspy tone replied,

"*Alright.* But if it needs hemming though I will ask for little more, of course." Glancing over Millie she continued, "But, I don't think it will."

"Oh – Thankyou, Miss Purcell," Millie went on exuberantly.

"You're quite welcome – young lady. *And* for what is the occasion?"

"Well, I was going to wear it to the upcoming spring and gala County dance." Miss Purcell paused.

"I see. But, of course. I suppose you'll want the dress soon than?"

"Well – Yes, if that's ok?" asked Millie in her modest tongue.

"I should think that not be a problem. Do you have the money you saved with you now?"

"No, but I can come back with it tomorrow."

"Very well then. That will not be a problem. If I may ask though, how did you save so much?"

"Well, some money I've saved from my chores, but a few days a week and on Saturdays I've been going up to Judd Mare's farm and helping him."

Judd Mare lived up the creek from Millie, a few miles away, having a chicken farm and a crop of corn but he was a colored man unlike anyone else in Little Cavern. He rarely went to town and was far from allowed in the Saloon, but wouldn't have cared too much for it anyway. In Judd's mind the only thing worse than hating everyone else in town was hating everyone else in town drunk. He was pretty smart too and it was well known that he was fairly literate and a good speaker but he was not challenged easily or would be easy to outwit, especially by some of the patrons up at the saloon. Only Millie could withstand the outward scornfulness that Judd kept at his side for most of the day although Judd Knew that Millie was different and not like other girls and was fairly impressed by her pureness of the mind so when she asked if she could be of help one day when school was finally out and after gathering enough nerve to go up to his farm to ask him Judd was intermittently accepting of her and said she could but that he couldn't pay her much. Nevertheless Millie was ever relieved and said that would be fine and would go to his farm with only thoughts of the dress she wanted and would wear to the dance and the young man who would see her in it and in time court her.

"How long have you been doing that for, if I may ask again?" Miss Purcell said in her snootiness.

"Since before the summer. After I had finished with school."

"I see. He must pay you much, then."

Millie just stood there with her friend next to her but to this she just replied somewhat pretentiously.

"Well – he says I've been a big help to him. But, I suppose."

"Well, then," the mademoiselle went on. "I hope to see you tomorrow when you come back."

"Yes, I will."

"Very well. Goodbye then, and to your young friend too."

"Thank you again Miss Purcell," both girls, young Millie and her friend, curtsied, as the two went out the shop door, the bell above chiming again on their way out. The mid – evening was now approaching with the eventual lighting of the torches and lantern wicks then to commence and light and make clear the walkways along the store fronts for folks to stroll, and when the dark would sweep over, as it had before, the town of Little Cavern.

2

The next day Millie rose from her bed and from the gallant night time dreams she had of wearing and possessing the dress in Miss Purcell's window. Her mother, Kate O'Leary, a delicate looking woman with her red hair all in a bonnet and having a Bonnie sounding Irish voice, was busy downstairs preparing breakfast to commence the day with. Flap Jacks of flour and milk with sheddings of butter dripping off topped with syrup oozing down layer by layer could be smelled all the way throughout the house and into Millie's nose upstairs. They were placed in the middle of the garmented oak table beside the display some pieces of ham next to it. Mr. O'Leary or Benjamin was busy outside in the small stockade barn that lay closer to the creek cutting up some timber for the coming cold months as now it was almost the end of summer into August, nearing September soon.

Millie came downstairs to have breakfast that morning with a promise and grace to her. Her mother was still in the kitchen waiting for her presence but as soon as Millie saw the layout upon the table inside the dining room she sat down eagerly. Her mother came out of the kitchen a few moments later holding a large pitcher of coffee with the steam coming off it like a chimney as she set it down on the table between both the flap jacks and the dish of meat while her mother sat down after on the other side of the table Millie looking up at her with her brightened eyes. Just then she asked, "Isn't father going to come?"

"Not hungry he said," her mother replied. "He's outside in the shed. You can go out and help him after Breakfast if you want."

"No, I don't think so. I'm going back into town today to buy the dress I wanted for the dance. Miss Purcell said I could have it for only twenty dollars."

"*Only* twenty?" her mother said with some facetiousness, but then asked, "Are you sure I can't make a dress for you? I could make it so very nice and I would hem it myself. *The other one...*"

"No," Millie cut in. "I want the one I saw. The white one."

"Alright, but if that's the one you want then I suppose your father and I can manage it."

"Thank you, but I've been saving for it. I have over ten and a half dollars already. I started saving ever since I've been going up to Judd Mare's farm and helping him."

Her mother looked worried to this and said, "Millie, I really don't like you going there. They say he's -"

"It's alright," Millie cut in again. "He's not mean to me or anything like that. I think in a way, Judd sort of *likes* when I'm there."

"Well, when school begins again just please tell him I said you can't go there anymore."

"Alright. But, I really don't mind him. It's funny, but for some reason, I think *I* even like him now."

"*Please*, Millie," her mother came in abruptly. "Now when summer ends and you go back to school you'll have plenty more work to do and here too. Your father's getting older and I can't do everything by myself. Your father is having trouble enough with his legs the way they are, and I'm afraid *he'll* -"

"Alright, mother," her daughter came in again. "I won't go there anymore. I promise."

"Be sure to now," her mother affirmed. "Anyway, I suppose if that's the dress you want for the dance then I'll give you the money for it and you can keep what you saved. I want you to have the dress you wanted." Hearing this Millie just replied in a sigh of grace and said, "Oh, Thank you mother."

Nothing more was really said after this though as the two continued having their breakfast at the table. As for the father, Benjamin O'Leary, he had fought as a soldier in some Indian skirmishes when he was younger and had been wounded below the waist and now suffered arthritis in one of his legs giving him a slight limp. He was a mellow kind of man and more modest than most and knew what the taste of battle meant. Millie looked up to him though and as an only child did not have to compete hard for his attention although even at this it could be hard at times to talk to him as he could be quite introverted and not easily accosted by others.

Nevertheless, Millie was always in his thoughts and he loved her much holding her image highly although he did not always show it openly as affection from him was hard to give. Millie's mother knew this well and it was hard for her too at times to receive comfort from the other but she had a firm temperament and was strong willed and did not let herself come victim to his conspicuous lack of open feeling for both Millie and herself. So, whenever she felt dismayed by it she would pride herself in making clothes or her knitting which she was also very good at and had embroidered many detailed designs and patterns. On occasion these pieces she would sell to people that had seen them in town or whenever they had come up to the homestead.

As Benjamin was now past the age of fifty about ten years older than Kate his poor legs and immobility was increasing. Up to that point he had worked as a blacksmith but was now becoming tiresome work and their main source of income was more out of his pension from the army. At this they were becoming more and more dismayed for the coming years, although they would try not to bring Millie into it, but just as well she knew of it and would obey what she was told more than regarding her own wants and needs.

After breakfast Millie went back up to her bedroom and put on an old dress her mother had made as she was still in her nightgown. Shortly after she came back downstairs and asked her mother on her way out for the money to buy the dress. Her mother went and got the money she promised out of a small metal box sitting openly on a mantle above the brick fireplace that was in the other room but taking a few cents more to give to her. After this she went back over to Millie now standing near the front door waiting to go out and handed her the money along with the extra few cents more and told her to buy a pound of some ground coffee and small parcel of cornmeal from the stationary store with it after she had bought her dress. Millie said she wouldn't forget and kissed her mother on the cheek upon leaving as she went out the door. Her father was still outside though carrying some wood he had cut that morning in the shed to put next to the chimney in the house. As Millie passed him he stopped her to ask where she was going but she just told him that she was going back into town to buy the dress she had seen. To this he gave a benign look and said very well as he continued his way into the house.

The way to town was not far, but, nevertheless, took some time to walk to on foot as Millie made her way along a dirt road that led to it. The trail was better to walk on than in town as it was covered in much less horse excrements, but as she made her way a carriage and wagon passed and hurried her by from in back matted by two horses with two men in front escorting it. As she glimpsed at the men upon turning her head she noticed that one of them wore a badge and had a gun around his waist. This stood out to her naturally as she knew no one else wore or were allowed to wear a gun in town except for the sheriff or as well as his assisting deputy partner Joe Collins. Joe was much younger than the sheriff but very attentive of him and regarded the sheriff with a kind of looking up to as he thought he had much to learn from him and his seeming innate wisdom and sharp tongue. The sheriff himself didn't mind very much in his deceptive egotism and looked unto Joe as his protégé and welcomed his scrutiny. Joe was far from the sharpest tool in the shed though and it was easy for him to become under influence of the sheriff. He also possessed a slight stammering of tongue at times especially when nervous or if the other did not like what he was doing which would unnerve itself out of fear. As indicative he had an unapparent sense of caution when dealing with the sheriff and could seem at times possessive of him and entranced in his presence, but still was able to keep his own for the most part.

As Millie approached the town with the money in her purse her eagerness to buy the dress in the store front window of Miss Purcell's was heightened with her face in a frame of delight. Upon entering the shop she gave the white dress in the window a quick glance as the bell above the shop door jingled like last time. Millie looked inside for a few moments but to her dismay she could see no one was in the store or Miss Purcell for that matter. Instead she saw a note made out on top of some yellow parchment paper as the Madame would do when leaving the store for a while and without locking up. The note said she would be back later in the day as Millie read it to her disappointment knowing she would have to go to do Judd Mare's farm later and couldn't come back that day. As such she left the store down trodden and slow paced as the door jingled again on her way out. It was near noon and the town outside was busy with many wagons and townspeople making their way to various shops and some of the days business. Millie stood outside in front of the store for a few moments more knowing she would have to wait to buy the dress and feeling somewhat disenchanted and discouraged but then remembered the coffee and cornmeal her mother wanted from the stationery store which was near the other end of town past the precinct and sheriff's office. A covered wagon was going through then as she waited for it to pass to cross the road. After it went by she cautiously walked over the wide road, careful to avoid the obvious as she got to the other side and continued to make her way along the planked out walkway passing one establishment after the other and folks dressed up as it was Saturday and customary to look dressy during the weekend break as most officious business was out then, especially in Little Cavern. As she did this, however, a sudden sense of disillusionment began to settle upon Millie and from what she saw of the town that day as it looked of an augmenting monotony of pretension and untrue appearance that she seemed to have felt before, although unlike other times not as concentrated as she had been in town many times before, but now it was becoming much harder to bear its phoniness and underlining hypocrisies that she knew were present just as she had really known all along. The townsfolk that day were nothing more than the same people she had seen before but there mannerisms and gestures were as if now a drum beating inside her of syncopated time and beat as though meant for slaves trapped and chained in the hull of a Roman vessel. This circumstance as fetching as it may seem would deplore itself unto her and others as a battle on the mid horizon was now approaching.

As it happened the men who had passed Millie while she had been walking to town earlier on and who she had glimpsed at were actually carrying another patron with them in the back of their wagon who was covered up and bandaged so no else could see his presence. He had been wounded several weeks before by the men escorting him and steering the wagon in front chiefly by the man wearing the badge who put a slug from his colt Winchester rifle through his left shoulder. The man who had been shot though was part of a renegade in those parts reprehensible for the murder of most of a well-off family and some others whom had been traveling to another town and having much loot and valuables in their possession.

His name was Colby Jenkins but he had been called a variety of names before some profane and others more coined but he was good with a pistol and dangerous and vehement in his ways so that his name would be synonymous with others in history one to recollect and quite mysterious, Jack the Ripper, but blood followed wherever Colby went and bullets zipped through the air like small infinitesimal swamp flies festering a dead pigs hide.

Having longish dark strands of hair running down to his shoulders and always wearing his guns round his waist and easy to get out having a sort of crookedness to them yet sitting firmly in his leather bound holster, he stood six foot two his western cowboy hat suede and with a small goose feather sticking out from the side, but resting evenly upon his grimacing and often malarkey face and head. So when he was finally apprehended just before dawn one week before between that of Little Cavern and another town called Bison that lay further south near the Wyoming Nebraskan border, as they had been trailing him for a few days by foot and horseback even with an old and wised Indian tracker and a nose more sensitive to smell than an average mutt, a sigh of relief was in store for the law bearing and upholding men in those parts as the ones who had originally helped capture and wounded him now had a grinning smile inside of them wide and deep – Or like in the crest of a thunderous and crashing wave breaking on the shore of some Hawaiian Island.

The reward for his capture had been great and some others had tried their hand at it but wound up either dead or close to it. The man who had shot him though and wearing the badge was someone very respected by other law men and called by the name of Joe Clemens but now would likely be granted a seemingly well – deserved promotion for his capture. The other man next to him up on the wagon was from the town Colby had been brought to after he was shot where a doctor was summoned to save his certain brief and wondrous life and all he had to offer before what would be his trial and with little luck in verdict his execution. As it happened they had decided to bring Colby up north though where they knew none of his gang or any of his enemies were around and thinking that few would come to break him out or either come to kill him. There was another reason, however, for this as it was known that a girl was still missing from the family that Colby had murdered down in Nebraska en route from the East and that an uncle of hers had been informed the outlaw had been shot and caught and was being taken to Little Cavern now to be jailed where he would be meeting him to find anything he could about the girl's disappearance.

All this had been taking place on the other side of town as people had now gathered to see what was happening, though some had already speculated and were passing on to others that Colby Jenkins the known and infamous outlaw and killer had been put in one of the barred jail cells in the sheriff's office.

It was passed noon now, but as Millie turned the corner to the other side of town she could see the lingering crowd in front of and near the precinct which she had never seen before and was instantly curious to see what was going on and why so many were gathered around. The people seemed to be mostly men although some women were present looking rather beguiled and apprehension in their faces with a touch of fright. To Millie though the men in back of the crowd were like a wall to which she could not see through others nearby trying to look onward into it as well.

As Millie continued standing there in her bewilderment and curiousness for the gathering a carriage could be heard then coming through, passing her in back, as she turned her head like the others to look, and as it calmly wended itself down the road and through the crowd, the people parting themselves in half in almost equal parts.

The carriage itself was tall and elegant looking and not like most and suggested a certain opulence as the man sitting and steering in front was more dressed up than average and Teller like. There was a brief hesitation at first when the carriage stopped as then a man with a cane in hand made his exit stepping down and off the carriages step. He looked of an older man and bearded with grey hairs and wearing a cashmere looking hat with only a very slight bend of the rim. His pants were dark and his jacket was dark too but with minor tails in the back down to his legs. As he made his way up the steps to the precinct his walk was slow paced and learned so that there was still fair silence in the air around even when he walked with only a few whispers here and there being passed on. As soon as he reached the precinct door it was opened from inside as the mysterious visitor entered the townspeople lauding back into talk and loudness and Millie still standing in the same place as she had been but with an intrigue and distinct yearning to know whom the man was. For his unusual demeanor and modest seeming disposition were admirable to her and in envy of all the things that in her mind went along with it like riches and jewels and a sophistication to oneself that the man seemed to possess.

By then some of the crowd began dissipating and men and women were leaving the area to continue whatever it was they had been doing before. As for Millie she continued her way to the stationary store to pick up the coffee and cornmeal for her mother though rather hazy still of what occurred.

The owner of the store was a stout looking German man and spoke with a Kaiser accent but his name was Dixon Von Stoltenberg though everyone just called him Dixon or Mr. Dixon. Of course Millie had gotten things from the store many times before and was quite familiar to the shop keeper standing behind the counter. The store itself was an array of open barrels holding various materials such as ground wheat and flour and nuts or anything not self-contained in those days like the cornmeal and coffee Millie needed. In back of the counter on the wall were various chocolate bars and boxed candies as well as an array of cigars and chewing tobacco or any kind of tobacco or smoking substance one could think of for that matter. When Millie entered the shop door a bell jingled above like Miss Purcell's as Mr. Dixon was standing alone and behind his counter as usual and waiting for the next customer.

"And how can I help you today young lady?" Mr. Dixon asked spritely and in his German sounding tongue.

"May I please have a dimes worth of coffee, and a small bag of some corn-meal?"

After Millie had asked for the items Mr. Dixon came out from behind the counter and over to the coffee barrel on the other side of the shop to scoop it out into a straw bag. As he began doing this though another man wearing a badge had come into the shop. To Millie the man looked like a stranger as she had never seen him before in the town though men were coming and leaving often, but the way he carried himself was unusual even amongst the ones that would just come through. He seemed rather cocky looking to her and wore a tan camel hair looking hat but his step suggested a certain confidence as he stood away from her and taking in the store. Just then though, he looked over sharply at young Millie as she had been looking at him the whole time since when he came in. Tipping his hat to her then he said, "How d' you today ma'am?" Nevertheless, Millie was not used to this as she was still young and older men did not accost her in this way, but she replied back to him in a quiet voice and said,

"I'm fine, thank you." The strange man just kept his eye on her as he stood in the same spot.

"Pleased to hear that," he requited. After this though Mr. Dixon chided in as he was scooping out the coffee and with his back still turned.

"How can I help you, sir?"

"I'll be needing some of those Cuban cigars you have," the man replied. "And maybe one of those bars of chocolate you got up there. You know one of them imported Belgium ones."

"How many cigars?" asked the shop owner as he was tying up the bag of coffee.

"I don't know," the man answered with an inner sarcasm. "Why don't you give me the whole box. Maybe I'll just keep some for myself."

"Oh?"

"Yeah, it doesn't matter anyway. I'm not paying."

"I see."

Mr. Dixon went back over to behind the counter carrying the two small bundles of cornmeal and coffee for Millie and then to get the cigars down from the shelf but then the man spoke up again.

"Yeah - they want it down at the precinct. Seems that guy came off that fancy carriage was a relative of that family that was massacred a few months back by the Colby Jenkins gang."

"I don't know. I was in the store," Mr. Dixon said uninterestedly.

"Yeah," the man continued. "They got Colby himself in there and every-thing. He's all laid up and shot in one of those jail cells of that Jeff McCormack. Some Joseph Clemens down from Bison brought him in and shot Colby him-self. I just happened to be nearby coming up myself when Joe caught up with me. I guess they'll be wanting more law men around here now that Colby's in Jail. Anyway, I think that man's niece is still missing from that family he mur-dered. Maybe trying to get Colby to talk about it for some cigars, a little pow-wow. I don't know but that Colby sure is a sore sight."

At this Mr. Dixon handed over the box of cigars and a chocolate bar he just took off the shelf.

"Well, I thank you very much for that. You can just put it on the sheriff's tab," the man told the shop owner but not without turning to Millie after and tipping his hat off to her again. "Hope you have a nice day ma'am."

Millie just stayed hushed though and was still standing in her same spot as the man left out the store door holding the chocolate bar and cigars under his other arm. As for Mr. Dixon he handed over the straw bags to her then while she had been looking at the door where the man had left out of.

"That will be fifteen cents young lady," Mr. Dixon said almost intrudingly.

Millie just looked at him though and handed over the money thanking him afterwards as the shopkeeper gave her a nod with his iron clad face making her way out the shop door then holding the two bundles in her hands.

When she was outside she carefully crossed the road again and started to make her way back to the other side of town and then back on to home though without her coveted white dress in Miss Purcell's window. As she passed the precinct though on the other side she almost stopped to look at it as she was quite intrigued by what the man in the store had said, but then hurried along briskly with thoughts of the family that had been massacred or what she had just overheard in the stationary store. As she would make her way however, a strange feeling of fear would ascend her as though she knew something was going to happen but somewhere within knowing her adolescence was slowly dissipating and fleeting like a sand castle on the beach as if being swept over by the coming tide. But what would this be, and when?

3

Inside the sheriff's office Jeff McCormack sat at his desk with his legs stretched out in front and his hands folded at his belt looking quite calm, his badge gleaming and attached to his flannel buttoned down shirt snugly and wearing his hat slightly crocked forward as he leaned back into his chair. His young partner Joe Collins and the other man who had been sent by Joe Clemens and having the name himself of Pat Thomsen and who had bought the cigars from Mr. Dixon were standing aside near the closest cell to the desk or the one they put Colby in as he lay there bandaged on the cot making little sound, but with his eyes shut only opening them a few times, though more conscious than he had been. Also present was the Mayor of Little Cavern or the all bestowing, John Whitcomb, a heavy, plump looking man and having a white powdery face with white greyish hair to complement. Nonetheless, he was a man of few words and did not open his mouth to speak as readily as others, even despite his position and what office he held, but rather stood aside for the most part in his unassuming and benignly manner though giving and leaving to the lamented misfortune much to be said by the opportunistic Jeff McCormack; at the moment he just stood there like the others next to the sheriffs desk looking over at Colby.

Not too close to the cell, but not too far from it the man that came off the carriage and requested the cigars sat nobly and looking elegant still holding his cane at his side and even in the present setting of iron bars and shabbily used cots and locked up guns in metal cabinets all in the pristine presence of the apprehended Colby.

Indeed, the gentleman wanted the cigars in hopes of being able to make the outlaw talk and try to find out where his missing niece might be, a young girl who would have been about sixteen by then, and whose parents and older brother had all been killed by Colby but to see if she was even still alive. Her uncle sitting in the chair and bearing the name Alfred Arrison Alcott, was brother to the nieces' mother and in law to her father as he was the inheritor of several silver and coal mines, but very rich and regarded as an aristocrat to most and those in politics.

The name of his niece was Marie having the last name of Russell, a rather fragile thing and easily made nervous lacking the ferment opulence and sequestered knowing of privilege of her much older Uncle. For this though he loved her much and a hair harmed on her head was a source of discomfort so that her disappearance would undoubtedly bring harsh and unmerciful due punishment to whomever involved.

As the rich entrepreneur sat in a chair placed in front of the cell Colby opened his eyes laying on the cot and looked up at the man lifting his head forward and then setting it back down. At this he sort of chuckled to himself in his languid state. Then the gentleman began to speak in his learned and lightly toned voice.

"I have no intent of saving your life. You are a murderer and have killed many and you must pay for taking the life of my sister and as well her husband and my nephew, their son. Instead I offer you a chance of repentance and to tell me where my niece is being held."

A moment went by but then Colby opened his mouth and spoke, his eyes shut and head still set down and in his cocky voice although weak and sluggish.

"Well, hell. You must be that rich Uncle of hers she has... That infamous Alfred Alcott. The slave driving coal miner himself."

"Is my niece alive?"

"Sure she's alive. Alive and living."

"Where is she then? Is she safe?" the gentleman asked again despairingly.

"Supposin she is?" Colby said still lying there.

"Where is she?"

"I don't know. She must be somewhere around. I know sure as shit she's not in this place. And come on in here to kiss my ass before I tell you."

Colby was very vindictive and rude at times and cussed much and with the polished and eloquent man sitting away and looking at him lying there through the iron clad bars of his cell his behavior must have come uneasy and quite different than what the cleanly and finely trimmed man was used to. So upon saying this Jeff McCormack spoke up from his calm demeanor and still sitting in the chair at his desk.

"Shut up. You be rude again and I'll come in that dank cell of yours myself. So shut up and answer the man."

"Like hell," Colby uttered.

"Answer him," Jeff recoiled.

"I don't know where she is. And if I did, why should I tell you? Ur gonna hang me anyways."

The gentleman paused for a moment.

"Perhaps you could remember better if you had a cigar or two. Or, if you like, perhaps something else."

"I don't want no cigar or yours or anything else," Colby jeered out. "I'll tell you what though. You get me on out of here and from this town free and clear and shoot these three in the head, I'd might be willing tell you where she is."

The sheriff looked quite unhinged at hearing this and looked to the other two standing by to go in then and rile Colby, but the sitting gentleman would just put his hand up to stop this and say, "I can't do that. I am not the law and your punishment will be up to the judge and jury. Instead, you can redeem yourself in God's eyes and tell me where my niece might be. If not you get nothing and then you will hang as I'm sure the verdict will show."

Colby lifted himself up in his bandages to an upright position on the cot.

"Well if that's the way it is then I might well just hang. God never really did me alright and sure as hell some of those slave coal miners you's got worken' for ya's, or those ones that aren't dead yet from all that dust they breathe in. I reckon I better just sit tight right here and let you guess where your niece is. But those Wyomin' mountains sure are big and since the winters comin, gonna be real hard to find her with all that snow gonna come down on em. I don't mind too much myself."

"I see I'm not going to get anywhere with you. Your manner is most vile. I will wait then for your plea and I suggest you do. For if not, hell will await upon your death."

After this Colby didn't say anything more and still looking weak from his wound lying there. As for himself, the gentleman just rose up from his seat and cane still in hand and went over to where the Mayor stood silent as ever and Jeff McCormack was sitting in his chair as he stood looking down at the sheriff for a moment to say, "I trust you know where to find me if he changes his mind. Or anything at all. I want to be the first one to know."

"Don't worry Mr. Alcott," the sheriff said and knowing Colby was listening. "You have my word. You'll be the first one to know. I'll tell you myself, although I'm sure he'll be willing to cooperate at some point. Who knows? Maybe even tomorrow. Either way, he'll be staying in that cell of his and since I'm not planning on feeding him anything too good, or maybe not even dead, he just might share a few words with us. I'll even let him piss in his can later to help him remember. But, I promise to tell you if he does."

Colby just sort of laughed to himself knowing that Jeff could do whatever he wanted really and that he probably wasn't too God fearing himself and quite full of shit just like him.

After the sheriff spoke though the gentleman, or Mr. Alcott just put his well – tailored hat upon his head with a rather disconcerting look giving the Mayor a brief glimpse and left the precinct out its door as the others were now alone with Colby.

"Well, you know where to find me if you need me," the Mayor wearily said to the calm looking sheriff while taking out his pocket watch to see the time.

"Sure thing John," Jeff answered back. After this the Mayor just tucked his watch back into his vest and said, "Evening men," as he went to go out the door. It was, then, though when Jeff got up from his seat and went over to Colby's cell close to the bars as he looked at the outlaw with a cold sneer, although saying nothing while the other two lawmen standing away from him looked at this with an unsuspecting apprehensiveness. Only after a moment more, however, as Colby gleamed at him from his half shut and angrily outlaw eyes the sheriff would speak up again.

"We'll get him to talk, alright. I'm certain we will."

What was Colby in for, and how long would it be until he would, finally, *talk*?

Craig Sholl

4

As soon as Millie got home she went in the house and put what she had bought in a cupboard in the kitchen. After this she went to go upstairs and to her room but her mother, Kate, was quietly sitting in the den doing some embroidering, though Millie did not notice her in the darkened room and stopped her just before she was going to make her way up the stairs.

"Millie?" she said. Her daughter hesitated at the sound of her mother's voice as she was about to make the first step but she answered.

"Yes, Mother?"

"Did you happen to get the things I wanted?"

"Yes mother."

"Did you get the dress you wanted?"

"No. Miss Purcell wasn't in when I got there." Her mother looked inattentive looking down at her sewing as Millie went over to her in the other room.

"Well, I'm sure you can get it another day, then."

"Yes, mother," Millie said with a sort of sigh.

"Is something wrong Millie?" her mother asked with her head still down in her sewing.

"No, not really."

"Oh?"

Millie was hesitant at this point, but in her sense of apprehension from what occurred she went on to tell her mother what she had seen during her stay in town and all about the outlaw now supposedly in the towns jail, including the stranger that had accosted her while in Mr. Dixon's and the one whom she had overheard all of this from, or what she now knew, though all of which now were beginning to come to surface in her mind and feeling the need somehow to release them, but just the same unsure of what her mother would say as she thought her mother did not always understand her as readily either.

"Well – When I left Miss Purcell's store to buy the other things there was a big crowd of people in front of the sheriff's office. But then, when I was in Mr. Dixon's, a man came in and said they caught this bad man named Colby Jenkins. The man in the store was a law man and said that the other bad man had murdered an entire family and even some others and that there's a girl still missing. He said they put him in jail next to in the sheriff's office." Her mother responded in a mild tone.

"Well, don't be worried. There were plenty bad men before him and I'm sure they'll be more after. At least he's in jail now. I'm sure they'll be hanging him though for killing all of those innocent people."

"Hang him?" Millie replied. A fear stirred up then inside her as the sound of death was something still elusive to her. "But why?"

"Well, it's only natural that they do. They must take his life from him as he did those people. Otherwise they will never rest. Father Coleridge would attest to it."

"I suppose," Millie went on though glumly. "If you say so, mother."

At this her mother felt something uneasy inside her daughter though more strange to her than understood. So, finally looking up from her sewing and over at Millie she asked,

"What's wrong with you? You look pale. Are you sure nothing else happened while you were in town?"

"No," her daughter answered, "Nothing else happened."

"Well, you be sure to tell me if anything did." Millie sighed.

"Alright mother."

There was a brief hesitation but then her mother remembered and told her she was making up a custard pie to have after dinner which she knew was a favorite of Benjamins.

"Oh, I'm making a pie for your father to have after supper tonight. A custard one – your father wanted it." Then she asked, "Don't you have to go to that Judd Mare's later?"

"No. I don't think I will today."

"Well, I don't know Millie," her mother said, "But I think you should, if he's paying you to. Don't want him to come round here to look for you."

Millie sighed again.

"I see. Alright, I will mother."

"But be sure to be home for dinner. I know your father wants you to. You know he's really very fond of you. Even if he is hard at heart."

"I know," Millie assured.

"You going to change now?"

"I will. Soon."

"Make sure you do. You shouldn't go there in that dress you're wearing, of course."

After talking to her mother Millie walked away feeling still unnerved though she knew her mother meant well even if she didn't understand her own feelings at times. As she made her way up the stairs and to her room the sound of her footsteps were oddly even and monotonous and hinted at a melancholy of discouragement. Her yearning for love was at its peak but her concept of it was becoming more and more disillusioned and becoming misshapen like that sand castle on the beach with its tall towers and rounded out mote becoming much more of a lump and cast away by the inevitable retraction of the sea. In this case, the sea to Millie were like the hypocrites she had seen back in town and the stranger tipping his hat to her in the store and telling of Colby Jenkins and all the blood left in his wake and the missing girl as well as Colby's own fate. Finally there were her own parents as she still loved them, though their ineptness of her was now feeling more concentrated like a beam of light drawn from the sun and slowly coming together. All these things were tugging at her and suggesting a dismal fate of inconsistencies but somehow knowing or even feeling that in all these a consistency would eventually emerge but that its meaning might be too much for her to bear. Whatever would Millie do then?

After changing out of her dress and into some overalls she headed over to Judd Mare's farm up the creek passing through various fields and wending stone walls shaded from the early evening sun by apple orchards hovering their droopy and stretched out bows above.

Judd lived in a small but sturdy looking log cabin next to his farm and chicken coop. As routine Millie would always knock on the cabin door to tell Judd she was there as he was often inside in a state of dictation and self – satisfying thoughts. But when she went up to the door this time and knocked there was no answer though she thought it strange as Judd would usually open the door for her. Thinking that he wasn't home or nearby she decided to stay anyway and begin to feed the chickens as she would usually do then to clean out the coop after.

The chicken coop was next to Judd's cabin a couple of yards away. There were about eight chickens he had all quietly pucking away to themselves in the coop having a metal wire screen keeping them out of the feeding area. Millie went over to it then opening up the screen and taking a handful of chicken feed or a bunch of seedlings that were in a straw bag on the dirt ground in front of it. One by one the snowy white chickens entered the feeding area with their oblong necks sticking out and bopping up and down and that Judd himself would eventually cut off after they had served their initial purpose. Millie went and tossed the seedlings upon the entrapment in her hand with the bag in another as the small flock of chickens began pecking at them for their daily nourishment.

Just then Judd Mare had been standing in back of Millie with her back turned to him though his silence made her unaware of him. Suddenly Judd startled her and began to speak as a shrill went up her spine and to her pure and now melancholy head. Upon this she instantly turned around as she could see Judd just standing there. His face was black as night but rather thoughtful of course and deep looking and always wearing a thinly rimed but finely woven straw hat on top of his head. His beady eyes were focused on Millie as he spoke in a cordial yet subversive manner.

"And how do you do today young lady?" asked Judd.

"Fine," she replied.

"I see you've taken the liberty of feeding my chickens. Their usually quite hungry this time of day and in the mid evening, though, I must say, they consume little and offer so much more. Don't you think so *Millie*?"

"Well, yes. I suppose."

"Well, if you suppose than *they must*," Judd replied.

"I tried knocking on your door, but you didn't answer."

"No, I'm afraid I did not. I was having a touch of sleep and feeling tired from the day's wrath. The day is quite lovely now though. Would you not say so yourself?"

"Yes."

"Yes, it is lovely?" He said trying to uplift Millie. At this she answered flustering.

"Well, yes. It is. I mean, its lovely today."

"Yes. And I'm sure it will be your last time here undoubtedly now that you will be continuing your education and now that the summer is near its end."

"Well, yes. I'll have to, and my mother said I'll have to help more at home, so I wouldn't have any time. I hope that's alright, Mr. Mare?

"Ah, So I believe I was correct. And how is your mother doing? I should hope your mother would be in good health and just fine. Am I not right of this, too?

"She's fine."

"Ah! I believe I'm correct again. It just confounds myself sometimes I know of such things. I must say, I certainly are adept to intuition. "

Judd sounded of an inner sarcasm though Millie was still submissive of his unsound demeanor as he had never talked to her with such equivocation of tongue. At this Millie just stood where she had been standing the whole time as the chickens were still puckering around her and her face looking rather hazily at Judd's.

"Tell me," he went on. "Did you happen to get that dress you wanted, from that French ladies store in town? I believe her name is a Miss Purcell as you had told me."

"No, I didn't. I went, but she wasn't there."

"Oh, that's too bad. I must say to hear that just aches at my kindred spirit. But, they do say those Parisians do take long lunch breaks. Sometimes for hours on end. But I'm sure you'll go back to buy it another day. Perhaps even tomorrow then."

"Miss Purcell won't be there tomorrow. She closes on Sundays." There was a moment of hesitation as Judd continued.

"Tell me, mademoiselle. Did you happen to see anything else in town when you went to buy the dress? Were there any trifling outbursts I mean or any foulness amongst the denizens? Of course, that might be hard considering the towns barter on firearms. Though one never knows what hostilities may rise up even without such things."

"Well, I don't know. I suppose. But, there was a big crowd of people when I went out in front of the jail. They put this outlaw in it. His name was Colby Jenkins."

"So I see," Judd said as his eyes got wider. "I must say that does seem inordinate. But then, I don't go into town often since all its frivolity might be too much for myself. Did you hear by chance what this Colby swine did?

"I happened to hear he murdered this family and that there's still this girl that's missing, but I don't know too much about it."

"I must say, he does seem rather unkindly. Was there anything else you saw?"

Millie began feeling unnerved but went on anyway.

"Well, no. Except for this man that came in on a carriage and went into the sheriff's office. It was very nice looking and when the man came off of it he was all dressed up and seemed so calm, but sort of gentle, and everyone else got real quiet."

"Is that so? Who do you think he was?"

"Well, after the man went into the sheriff's office everyone started leaving but I went into the stationary store after and this other law man came in, but that's when I found out about the missing girl and about the man that he said murdered her family. I'm not sure but the lawman in the store said something about the girls Uncle being in the sheriff's office and trying to make Colby talk."

"But I bet that man that came off that carriage was real different and that you liked him."

Millie was getting agitated.

"I suppose. So what if I did?"

"Oh, I should hope there is no distastefulness from my questions. Is there?"

Millie just stood there at Judd's recant and said no.

Upon this, similarly as before when she was with her mother, she felt another fear coming from within as Judd sounded of devious intent which she disliked. So in a sort of fluster she felt the need to leave the farm just then uttering,

"I think I'd like to leave now, if that's ok?"

"Are you sure our conversation isn't bothering you?" Judd asked obtusely. Millie just said no again but then Judd continued in his relentlessness.

"Then why should you want to leave?"

"I want to," Millie answered back firmly. "And I don't like the way you're talking to me - Goodbye."

After saying this she just dropped the bag of chicken feed on the ground and began to briskly set off the farm through the hobble of chickens. As they dispersed aside, a few of them even flapped their flightless wings to get out of the way but she then stumbled and fell in her escape. When Judd saw this he gave a hint of concern as Millie glimpsed at him while getting up, but then, unhesitatingly, continued her way off the farm and down the road fast and running.

As soon as she had gotten home her father was outside on the porch sitting in a chair near the far end as she entered the house without even hardly looking at him as he noticed she looked silent and upset of something. After Millie was in the house she went upstairs to her bedroom to lay down though she was still very disturbed from the prior feelings she had and happenings during the day from hearing about the killer now held in the sheriff's office before the disappointment of not buying the dress up to the recent account with Judd Mare. All of it seemed like a discouragement of profound despair as though that sand castle on the beach had been utterly wiped out by the sea. She only lay there, still, not making a hindrance of sound with her stomach turned down and her back facing up and stretched out head to toe her head on the pillow turned slightly away and her arms near her head.

It was only a few moments more until she heard a knock at her bedroom door though it was her mother again as her father had relayed to her that Millie seemed rather strange upon entering though he didn't know what to make of it and never having great lucidity of what his daughter's thoughts were anyway.

After knocking Millie's mother went on to ask her if she was alright although her voice was muffled from the door.

"Millie, are you alright in there?" At this Millie didn't move on the bed or say anything.

"Your father said you seemed in a hurry," her mother continued. "Did something happen to you while you were up at the farm?"

Finally Millie answered.

"No."

"Are you sure?"

"Yes. I'm sure."

"Is anything else wrong, then? Is it about the dress?"

"No."

"Well, if you want you can come down and help me in the kitchen. I'll be done with that pie soon but you could help me with the rest of it. Only if you want to, you know."

"I know," Millie said. "I'll be down soon. After I change."

"Alright, Millie. But make sure it's soon. I'll be in the kitchen."

After this Millie's mother left her door and went downstairs to finish whatever she was making in the kitchen. Millie could then hear some distant words being exchanged between her mother and father but not sure of what they were saying. As she lay there on the bed her spirit was still sunk and her attitude still in the sorrows of the day without the benefit of knowing what would happen for her next though she knew a part of her had faded and that to go on meant to accept this. To say this to her mother before would have been too obtrusive to this acceptance as she knew her mother would not understand swiftly of her feelings and knowing her words would seem quite vague to her as to produce a well of questions inside her mother of worry but with no way of answering them. To Millie she felt now alone and that her womanhood had come upon her and now her reliance on herself was greater than ever though the prospect was depressing and overwhelming.

At this she thought about writing in her diary as she had done up to that point with her weekly chronicles but now it seemed useless and its purpose had lost its luster and been revealed to her as a pointless act as it was now all wound up with all of her other worries. If she did write in it she would have written little and a confession of an existential despair having little faith in the towns white washed church of prayer and that she had gone to before along with her parents and the others, but just the same her feeling of God was not utterly hesitant but rather put in view before her in a faraway place. Whereas before she had thought of God closely but quite dismissive of his existence she would now think of God less but with a very vague unsurfaced need at times to see how others, though with much more intimacy and the omniscience of her own parents whom saw in him what she did not and that their belief in him had to be carried with a kind of stride in order to receive love from them, or to love either of them herself.

So with all these things stirring inside her she decided to take grasp of her own will as she lifted herself out of her bed and changed into the dress she had been wearing earlier and out of her overalls. After this she gathered herself making her way from her room and down the stairs and then to the kitchen to help her mother as she had told her she would.

As she entered the kitchen her mother was just then removing the pie out from the oven she had made while Millie was up at the farm. The oven was wood burning, of course, and charcoal black and made of solid iron that could heat up to a temperature almost hotter than halfway to Saturn. In other words, a pie cooked rather fast inside it or anything else that needed cooking for the dinner they would have that late evening. Millie looked rather dull and unfeeling in her sullen face but when her mother looked at her as she come in the kitchen she perceived her daughter and how she carried herself with a sort of aloofness and with an undoubted misconception of her. For if she knew the real dilemma being stewed about and kept behind her daughter's eyes she would have been in a kind of shock leaving her deeply overwrought. But this notion unnatural as it seems was not something Millie did not presume in her mother so that she would continue to conceal her emotions from the other, though just as well she had mostly kept them to herself before her new and profound angst. So, with this in mind, instead of her mother asking her daughter why she felt and looked a certain way she merely gestured at it and asked,

"Are you feeling better now?"

"Yes," replied Millie though without any resonance.

"Well, I'm glad of that," her mother recapped in sigh of relief. "You can go ahead and make the potatoes on the stove. You know what to do."

"Yes, ma'am."

Millie still sounded down to her mother as her deeply affected daughter went over to the stove next to the oven that had a beef stew cooking in a large metal pot fragrant of a rich and saucy aroma and next to it a pot of cut up potatoes in some boiling water and that steamed a white puff of cloud when Millie removed its cover. Her mother stood off to the side still handling the pie that she had placed on a wooden rack to let it slowly cool in its piping hot state. Looking down at the pie still she asked her daughter again about before. "Your father was very worried about you. He said you looked scared when you came in before. Were you?"

Millie didn't say anything but then her mother raised her head from looking down at the pie and over to her daughter. She asked, "Did you hear me?" Oddly Millie didn't respond still. "Millie?" she asked again. Her daughter looked of surprise and slightly distanced to her but finally she responded, whence turning away from the stove as she had been stirring the potatoes in the pot.

"Yes?"

"I said your father is worried about you. Didn't you hear me before?"

"Well, no. I don't think I wasn't listening." Her mother looked of concern again and asked,

"Are you sure you're alight?" but Millie just answered back,

"Yes."

After this her mother didn't say anything more even though her daughter's seeming lack of consternation with her dull appearance was still odd to her. But after they had finished in the kitchen preparing and the stew had finished its last phase of cooking Millie's mother and she set out the main course in nicely decorative china ware and ladles on the dining room table outside. All this was done quietly but shortly after the table had been set Benjamin O'Leary appeared into the scene as the daughter and mother sat down at either side as the father finally took his own seat up at the head of it. While they were all seated a moment passed by in the presence of the prepared dishes now steaming through the sides of their porcelain lids with their ladles sticking out. Then all three bided their heads to say a very brief grace which was always orated by the father with just a few humble words.

"We thank you our blessed Lord for this supper. Ever after. Amen."

After speaking this all three raised their heads though Millie's face showed a hesitation to the ritual as now of course her disillusionment toward God's grace was in her hidden despair and her displacement though unseen by her parents was visible only to herself or anyone else able to discern it.

In a little while once they had finished the main course Millie's mother went back into the kitchen to get the pie off the rack. A moment later she came back with the dessert setting it down on the table with the rest of everything else that had been laid out before. Then, after her mother had sat down again, Millie said she didn't feel like having the dessert asking to be excused but her mother looked disagreeable at her after saying this knowing that her father wanted her to stay and that he had been looking forward to it. Benjamin just told her mother or Kate that it was alright though as Millie looked rather ardent on leaving to go back up to her room. Upon her father saying this she stood up tucking her chair under the table leaving her parents as she proceeded over to the stairs and up to her room. When she was back in her room she now felt the full burdens of her plight and her angst was now real to her. A monotony surpassed her as she looked into the future and leaving her in a frustration and the anxieties of knowing how to be around others. She knew in order to go on meant to accept their ways and that her own feelings though far more mellow and modest and even with a kind of contempt for others would have to be kept close to her and not let loose towards them. She wondered how she would do it, and for how long?

5

The next day Millie woke from bed feeling numb and suppressed. The day upon her was the beginnings of her torrent and seemed to stretch out, the hours and the passing minutes like the vision of a clock in her mind bleak and the hands of it moving ever more slowly.

As she wandered the quandaries of her mind further and as she lay there in the cotton sheets of her bed, she saw the faces of the people she knew looking at her with a tension of both despair and dread. Some of these faces stood in front of her laughing in chastisement but others looking unto to her with a pity as though her appearance would be unsound and fearful to others. She felt as though an enigma to whomever came her way but just the same a scorn for those that saw her as this.

Millie rose from bed that morning with a new life in front of her and one she would have to somehow find meaning in. The white dress she had wanted badly for herself only just the day before and that had stood out in Miss Purcell's shop window was now a faded desire and seemed ever more unimportant to her as though it were a remnant of her childhood fancies now in the past. Even the coming dance she had wanted it for was like this and instead was now a thing to be worried of as she knew her mentioned indifferences would be almost entirely in contrast to her own peers.

So, keeping this in mind, Millie or the young woman she was now, Mildred Annabel O'Leary, came downstairs that morning with sounding steps of loss. Her face was now far from immodest with a dim complexion to it and her gaze was more deepened and mindful. Breakfast that morning had not been made either yet and she had risen quite early as compared to many other mornings when her mother would be up before her and her father outside.

It was a calm and strange morning outside and the dawning light showed through the clouds with a strain and lack of arrival to the land below. Millie herself went in the other room where she had spoken to her mother about what had happened in town and the day before, but it was only to look at herself in the mirror below a mantle on the wall.

As she stood in front of the mirror looking at herself she knew she was different and that she was now facing what had come as her fate, and somehow no longer did she see what was once a brightened image and, instead, had turned to what was really there or of what she thought was the truth. After looking at herself she then decided to go outside onto the porch and look out into the distance as the creek could be heard over the quiet landscape. For a little while she sat in the rocking chair at the far end where her father would sit, but she could feel herself blend into everything with ease and knew that her life was now up to hers. A little later her mother would come downstairs and go into the kitchen as Millie was still out on the porch looking out over at the shed, but her mother did not notice she was outside. As she was in the kitchen though getting the breakfast ready she heard Millie come in quietly through the door but slowly she came out and thought it strange that her daughter would be up so early.

"Are you alright?" her mother asked as Millie started her way back upstairs. Millie just looked ahead though and didn't say much.

"Yes," she replied.

"Would you like anything to eat? I could make some..."

"No, that's alright," Millie cut in.

"Alright, then," her mother said looking at her as she hesitated before making her way back up the stairs to her room, but not before her mother said her name again so that she stopped once more before continuing. All her mother said though was not to mind her with a look of puzzlement.

When Millie was back in her room she went over to get her diaries out of a chest at the end of her bed though she did not know what she would write in them. They were the same diaries she had always kept but in her hands now felt like a foolish thing or something naïve to her but as she handled them in her hands she slowly went over to a small vanity and chair to write in one of them or where she left off just a few days before.

Aug 4, 18--

I woke up today and did not hear the birds outside or anything. I just heard myself like so much sand falling through my hands. I feel everything is bad and something is going to happen, but I'm not sure. I feel as though I've lost something but I don't know what exactly. Yesterday there was a big commotion in town and everyone made me feel sick except for this one gentleman that I saw coming off a carriage. He seemed so much more clean looking than the rest, but I don't know about this either. I talked to my mother about what happened and a man they put in jail where everyone was gathered but it didn't help very much. I think about that man and in a way I almost feel bad for him and what they'll do to him. I know he killed all those people too and that there's this girl still missing, but it all makes me feel awful inside.

The white dress I wanted doesn't even seem important now and the dance I'm afraid of. I hope it never comes, but I know it will. I don't know what I'll do either but I think I'll just ask my mother to make me up a new dress instead of the one in the shop window. I know whatever happens now though will only be one more thing for me to get through, but I'm afraid as I've never been before.

After putting down her reproach she put away her diaries again and undressed and put on some clothes to go back down in. She had no plans on going back to town and as she had written down just asked her mother later on that morning if she could sew up a dress for her although her mother was a little confused by this but rather came of a pleasant surprise to her that she could do this for her. Nevertheless she said she would and that it would be one of the nicest dresses she had sewn for her as her daughter listened to her mother's regale with more ease than usual. The rest of the day and the days to come would be ordinary and Millie's parents would not see her as being unusual as they had been almost more accepting of her quietness and rather aloof way. However, things would not last like this and Millie would soon be confronted by another incident that would make her new nature more unveiled and her parents more estranged.

* * *

Colby Jenkins sat upright in his jail cell and had been ever more at ease from his wounds urinating into the can Jeff McCormack had given him just as he had promised. As for Jeff he sat almost in the same position as he had when Mr. Alcott had come to question the inmate though looking more attentive of his presence than usual. As soon as Colby finished his business he put the can back down on the jail cell floor and laid back in his cot.

"Well, I'm finished taken a piss," Colby exuberated. "So, whenever you're ready you can come and get it."

Jeff didn't say anything at first, but no one else was around except for them, which was rare, though after all there were supposed to be more men coming to help and that had not arrived yet. Joe Collins had gone out earlier and Pat Thomsen was on break but the scene was quiet and the two men's acclamation for one another had grown and now that Colby had his very own piss can and was being fed enough food to sustain him, and not too bad either. The sheriff wanted this, however, and for Colby to feel more at home although he was behind a whole bunch of bar cells lying on a cot in bandages and knowing sooner than later government officials from the East and even abroad were coming to commence his trial with a most needed and certain hanging in store for himself.

The only thing the Sheriff had on his mind though was to make Colby talk about where the man's niece might be, but hardly for the benefit of the girl to say the least, or even Alcott's sake in this, and instead, for his own selfish ends knowing or at least figuring on that Colby had still the loot and other valuables held up with some of his comrades cross the border, and was with the intent or interest of somehow getting his hands on it and taking all for himself, and with no other than the very leader of the gang, or bug eyed Colby he was looking at then to lead the way. For now, though, he was only trying just to get Colby comfortable enough to make him talk, and knowing he didn't have much time, either, which would not be easy, and then, if all went according, to have Colby released for the sole purpose of finding the niece which in the meantime, he would then somehow and by someway have to come up with another plan to find it necessary to breakaway from whatever lawmen he brought with him during this excursion. All of this was something he could hardly think of now though if he were in the first place, to even get Colby to talk and out from his cell which for him was the bigger of tasks at the moment. So, with all this precipitating in the back of the sheriffs scheming and plotting head, and knowing time to make Colby talk was going fast he simply sat back in his sheriff's chair at his desk while Colby lay in his cell with his eyes tightly shut, almost as if asleep looking, but the sheriff without any indication about to speak, suddenly uttering something to him in his cynical and sarcastic air of voice as Colby listened ~

"Nice night out. Wouldn't you not say so Colby?"

Hearing this Colby didn't move and kept his eyes shut to the sheriffs comment, but just replying to him, "Well, if you think it is than it might be. But I prefer it when there are more stars out. Anyway, I wouldn't know since I'm in a jail cell, but I can still hear the June bugs out and that is fine."

Colby sort of riled himself up with his words but the sheriff just kept sitting not saying anything. After a moment though he lifted himself up from his seat and went over to Colby's cell ever so slowly.

"You know what I think Colby?" the sheriff asked.

"What's that, sir?"

"I think it is a nice night out. I think there are many things nice about it and the stars are out, although I know you're in your cell and you cannot see it but they are out." Colby just kept laying their as the sheriff spoke.

"*This is* a nice night," he continued, "Because tonight you're going to tell me where that man's niece is and if you don't I will not be nice to you anymore."

"Well, hell! I didn't even *know* you were being nice to me," Colby replied.

"Sure I am. I like it that you're getting better now. Especially since you're going to be riding with me soon and to find and give me all those nice things you've got stowed away." Colby opened his eyes and sat upright on the cot with his legs to the floor as the sheriff had been talking.

"What you mean?" he replied. "I'm gonna and show you what?"

"You're going to show me where all that money you've got and everything else is or I'll drown your head in that can of yours."

"Why should I tell you where it all is? How would you get me out of here anyways?"

"I will. But first you have to tell me where that niece is and I'll find a way."

"And if I do what's in it for me. Would you let me go?"

"Sure I would Colby," the sheriff answered. "But if you don't tell me than you'll hang either way."

"How do I know you'll let me go?"

"You don't. But I just might be able to figure one out if you get me to that treasure chest."

"Well, you must be out of your mind," Colby said. "But if you can figure out a way *than...*"

Just at that moment the assisting deputy Joe Collins came in with Wyatt Cobb looking drunk as ever as Jeff turned to the two with half a grin knowing his talk with Colby was more than inappropriate. Joe himself looked a little sheepish looking at the sheriff and then over at Colby keeping his head lowered and holding onto one of Wyatt's arms as the veteran vagrant showed no sign of making a getaway knowing there was nowhere else to go.

"Picked up this one here over near Tom Callaway's place again. Say's he was going out for a stroll, but his breath gave him away as usual. How's that Mr. Cobb," Joe said sort of laughing.

"Is that so," the sheriff picked up chidingly. "Well – hell. I think you two should meet. Mr. Colby this is Mr. Wyatt Cobb. Let me know if you two want to shake hands. Joe you just put Wyatt at the far end of the residency here where his usual cabin is."

"Yes, sir," the deputy replied. "I'd sure like to see these two get along," he continued. "How 'bout it sheriff."

"Yes," Jeff came in. "I believe that would be something to see." Colby just kept quiet in his cell the whole time but Wyatt barely gave out a peep as Joe went and put him in the far cell. When he was finally inside as Joe closed the bars on him Colby just said,

"What the hell is he supposed to be? Some type of nut or something?"

"Don't be rude now Colby," the sheriff retorted. "Mr. Cobb is our best customer yet. Isn't that right Mr. Cobb?"

Of course Wyatt didn't say anything but knew that he had come back to hell and that the devil was with another patron. Joe just sort of went over to the sheriff's desk and stood there for a few moments as Jeff was standing too and looking at him but then candidly enough asked,

"And how is Mr. Callaway this night, or don't you know?"

Tom Callaway was an old southern Confederate and fought with Robert E. Lee at the battle of Gettysburg and may have been one of the few lasting survivors from that side of the battle, his age, and on that day. He was given to drink like Wyatt and sometimes Wyatt would go over there to drink with him as he would listen to some of Tom's ramblings. Mostly Tom was inept when with Wyatt but Wyatt would keep him company at this and listen to him more kindly than others. He always kept a blood hound around too that was old and crinkly looking and that smelled something awful, but Tom didn't seem to mind and nothing really seemed to bother him but after all he was old and still dismayed that his side had lost the war and that he thought the nation was *still* in peril.

Nevertheless Joe answered the sheriff and said, "Well, he was out there on his porch sipping down his whiskey, and you know that old blood hound of his just stinking up the place. I saw Wyatt down the road walking back stiff as a board, but he looked as he does now so that's it. Just plain drunk."

"Is that right?" The sheriff snarled back.

"Sure is," Joe said. Then he asked, "Do you think any more men be coming to help us now that Colby's with us?"

"Sure they will," Jeff assured looking over at Colby. "They should be here quite soon. Just got a wire yesterday they would. Should be here in the morning matter of fact."

"How many men coming? Did they say?"

"Should be two more about," the sheriff answered back though sounding distracted knowing it would be much harder to talk to Colby with all those men around.

"Well, we'll sure need 'em."

"We certainly will," the sheriff went on, but only standing over near Wyatt's jail cell without sounding suspicious and Wyatt just lying there as he had done before with that grin on his face and listening to them with a knowingness and Jeff McCormack looking over at him and grimacing himself.

As for the saloon at the far end of town that late evening it was at the height of its nightly charades and men and women some from town others passing through were busy drinking and playing card games and listening to the piano player and singer as though tomorrow would never come. Men smoked cigars and women smelled of perfumes fragrant of a rose garden.

There were not as many concubines in the town or up at the saloon, as the town was much more proper than most and would not easily tolerate such a thing, but there were some women still more promiscuous than others. Mary Mulligans was one of these women and was sought by the younger men much more readily than any of the others. Mary had lightly tinted red hair and wore a colorful dress and drank anything that her escort could buy her which was much more than less most of the time. Mr. Taylor himself had seen Mary on occasion and it was well known or at least to the other higher brow men around that she was more a mistress to him than anything. In fact on that night Mr. Taylor had been seen with the woman again and one could imagine all the other women hushing their pursed mouths at hearing such degrading and malevolent behavior and towards his wife but there were times when even Mrs. Taylor was known to commit to such unsound vice.

That night Mr. Taylor had seen Mary though more over something than to see one another and as she was now with child and likely pregnant from his past courting's with her. Max Singleton a bald headed man who served behind the bar knew of the relationship they had and had suspected something inordinate between them after seeing them that night as the look on Mary's face was more sullen than usual and suggested more than a usual meeting between them. He was behind the counter getting a glass when a young fellow sat down across from him on the other side.

"Hey how 'bout a drink?" the young patron asked the bar tender or Max as he was shining up the glass with a white cloth.

"What will you have, sir?" Max asked.

"Give me a whiskey straight up."

Max went over then and got a bottle of whiskey off the liquor case and filled half a glass setting it down on the counter for the young man.

"Anything going on tonight?" asked the man.

"No, sir," Max answered. "Nothing unusual. There's a good poker game going on over there if you're interested."

"Oh?"

"Yes, sir."

"I don't really play poker. Never liked the chances. I reckon you haven't seen anything unordinary yourself. Have you?"

"Well, no sir," Max replied, though with some apprehensiveness and leaning up against the bar counter.

"So I see. Or perhaps you wouldn't know about a Mary Mulligans and her rich friend the illustrious Nelson Taylor." Max tried to look aloof but just said,

"Well. I wouldn't know sir. Not really."

"What d'you mean not really. You know he went and got that woman *pregnant*. I'm a friend of his wife's. She's pretty upset herself. She doesn't even know, but she thinks. Haven't you seen them at all?" the man asked. He was wearing a tan cowboy hat and looked dark with some sideburns but on the smaller side and wearing some spurs on his boots below.

"Well, tell you the truth I did," the bar tender said. "But I don't know anything about all that."

"Well, what did you see? If you don't mind telling me."

"I just saw the Miss with the man coming through here but that was all."

"Yeah, I see. But, you didn't hear anything?"

"No."

"If I gave you a few dollars would that help?" Max just looked down at the bar with the cloth in hand to wipe it and just said,

"No, sir."

"Well you be sure if you change your mind on telling me. That wife of his wants to know."

After saying this the man just finished his drink with another sip and took out a coin to pay for it as he placed it on top of the bar and began to leave. The looker of a man had seen Mrs. Taylor before more as a friend than anything and was known to others as a Clarence Booth but now she was having him try to find out what her husband was up to with the prim looking debutante. As he was leaving out through one of the swinging saloon doors though he was suddenly met with a hard punch in the face by someone on the other side as he went flying backwards and into the arms of an older looking white haired gentleman sitting at a nearby table as everyone stopped suddenly even the singer and piano player who were in the middle of a light ballade to look at the stranger entering.

As it was one of Colby's enemies was in town and had come to avenge the murder of his friend supposedly gunned down by the outlaw. His name was Juan Julius Pugliano – the third, a Mexican, and very ardent on killing Colby himself. He was a bit heavy set having a curly mustache and wearing a sombrero and dressed quite well although quite indifferent looking to anyone at the bar scene as all the others looked unto him with a kind of bafflement of what he would be doing in their quant or now becoming less quant town.

"My name is Juan Julius Pugliano," ~ he declared with his high pitched Mexican voice, "And I have come to avenge the death of my slain friend Jose Velasquez Velez whom was gunned down by the man imprisoned here in this town. I am here for this purpose."

The distinguished looking Mexican was also wearing a gun which was against the city ordinance of course but a young boy outside had noticed the man and gun coming in on horse and had gone up to the precinct to tell the sheriff what was going on as the sheriff was now on his way walking down to the saloon after he had told his assisting deputy Joe Collins to stay behind to guard Wyatt Cobb and Colby who was now rattled a bit and very anxious from overhearing the news.

The Mexican continued though.

"A drink to the man who helps me do this!"

At this everyone kept hushed still and there was no way anyone would have helped the red skinned Mexican in vanquishing Colby, needless to say, but all of a sudden the sheriff himself came in behind and shot the man straight in the back with his loud .45 colt as he fell to the floor dead.

No one made a sound except for some women trying not to scream but then the sheriff went up to the Mexican he had just killed lying dead on the saloon floor as he stood there looking down at him. Upon this though he immediately started carrying the hombre down and out of the bar to the side of the road where he put him face down next to the horses all in a row and strapped to a long dock of wood in front of the saloon. A few of the patron's even started coming out or by then to look at the dead assassin as the sheriff could be seen walking back to his office and down the half lit road as the torch light poured on to his back glaring here and there between the shadows and darker crevices as he made his way. It was then though when the men and women who had just bared witness to the bloody killing would begin to feel the encroachment of what was happening, or the aforementioned battle that was now playing out as though a ball, strange as it was, had been rolled in their direction, but one they would not be able to stop nor knowing just either where it would roll over or to what, as it grow bigger and bigger by the day, and regardless to the towns own sense of once self-assuredness and distinction in rule and manner, all now beginning to see something foul and horrendous on the horizon.

6

It was a day or two later and by now the word on the Mexicans death was well – known and everyone knew what had happened even Millie who had overheard it from her parents while they had been talking as her father had just come back from town while getting a new chisel for some work he was doing in the shed or some wood work which he was also apply knowing of. By now the man had been taken off the side of the road and given over to the mortuary or undertaker for and to be buried. The man who ran the service had the name of Randall Farnworth but he was a white curly haired man and heavy set with a plush face but unaccustomed to such vile dead folk as the Mexican or even one that had been killed by the sheriffs own hands.

Farnworth had made up a coffin though much more modest than for anyone he had made one before or whomever had died in Little Cavern. Usually he would make up such masterpieces of antiquity, but for the seemingly lowly Mexican did not produce anything too like this. Instead it was made up of just a few boards of wood and nailed together snug as a bug where the dead man would rest inside with his eyes shut and his roundly rimmed sombrero resting on top of his chest for whatever funeral would occur.

As it was young deputies Mike Taverns and his friend Will Blake who had come in overnight from another town in Wyoming further west and were now present at the sheriff's office had taken the dead man in to the other side of town near the sheriff at Farnworth's parlor as he stood outside in front looking meager as ever and almost in a fervent fear of his coming duties as undertaker.

"We brought you this here's Mexican mister," Mike told the sheepish looking undertaker as he rolled up in front and tugging at the horses. His younger and inexperienced partner and friend in back and uplifting a cotton terrycloth the bandito was underneath added,

"Yeah, he's got a bullet hole in him the size of a grape fruit and everything."

Farnworth just stood there though looking at the dead man like he was a sleeping tiger about to wake.

"See," the young kid went on and pointing with his finger, "the bullet hole's right here."

Farnworth just kept looking at the dead man and just trying to not to faint but then just noticed a small book next to the dead Mexican's arm.

"Well, what is that?" He quivered to the two young law men as he pointed to it.

"Oh. We just found that in one of his boots," Mike Replied. "We don't know what it might be and it's all written up in Spanish."

"Hand it over here," Farnworth said as Mike picked it up and gave it back to him.

As the undertaker handled it in his hands he saw no title on it except it was a black book and looked like a bible or small prayer book. Upon opening it though he saw that it was far from either although he could not read the Spanish script but besides that there were some sketches or map like drawings on the first few pages but he could not discern what these might be either.

"Can you make anything of it Mister?" Mike asked and squinting at Farnworth.

"Well, I don't know," Farnworth replied. "I'm not sure."

After looking at it a moment more the undertaker decided to put the book in one of the man's dirtied coat pockets and asked the two others to take him off the wagon and put him in the back of his parlor for further cleaning up and to get him ready to be buried. After all Little Cavern may have been a high brow town but it would have been less than Christian to give the bandito a less than proper burial.

Millie herself wondered why the Mexican had come up just to be killed by the sheriff but she was also in her own mindset still, and did not look unto his death with any lengthy thought or any more grief than what she had overheard from her parents. To her it was just one more bad thing that had come and was now at her feet leaving her feel vulnerable to whatever fate would bring.

Her mother by this time was rather opposed to her daughter going back into town and did not want to see any possible harm to her so she was more than pleased that soon she would be going back to school for her last year and that she wouldn't have too much spare time to wander around the unpredictable borough with all her housework as well. For the time being though she had given Millie some embroidering work to do and was trying to teach her some newer things but she was far from as good of sewer as her mother although she had knitted a few humble designs before.

"Are you almost finished with the pattern you started the other day?" her mother asked her daughter as they were sitting out on the porch while Kate was making some finishing touches on a design herself, or which was actually of the quaintly porch view. Millie was looking out, just then, over at the countryside where some of the creek could be seen glistening in the later evening sun.

"Well, not quite," she answered picking her head up from gazing out. "But I should finish soon I think."

"You should. It's been almost two days now since I showed you."

"I know mother."

There was a pause for a moment but then Millie's mother went on.

"You certainly do take your time with things I must say. Your father says so himself. I wonder if..."

"*Please*, mother," Millie butted in grasping for relief. "I know I have to finish with it," she continued. "I have to finish a million things, and then maybe I can be left alone and no one will criticize me again. Not you or my father. No one." Her mother could see she was shaken after saying this and put down her sewing as Millie had never projected herself unto her before in that way.

Still, she tried to be firm with her.

"Millie," her mother bolded out. "Please try not to get so angry. You must..."

"Alright, mother," Millie resounded. "I will try not to do so, again," she went on though looking trance like. Her mother just sat back down in the rocking chair after this but said,

"That's good, Millie. I should think you won't. I wasn't trying to be reproachful. Just that you should finish something sometimes. I'm sorry you're upset, but I was only trying to be helpful."

Her daughter looked of an inner frustration building up. A few moments went by but then she finally said in a mild and dull voice, "I know mother. I know you're only trying to help. I know you are. I must try to finish."

Millie looked and sounded unfeeling as she spoke but her mother didn't press on it and did not see the full sense of what was happening to her and her frail state of nerves as had been observed.

Instead, she sat there looking at her daughter concernedly and sewing as Millie continued looking out from the porch with a dour yet sullen like face, her soft red hair being blown about by the mild breeze and her eyes fixed on the coming sunset.

Just then the father came out onto the porch from inside and gave a look to Millie though she did not look back. He had been repairing a chair in the wood shed and was making his way to it but it was only the other day when he had gotten a chisel from town and had found out about the shooting and told it to Millie's mother afterward while Millie herself had been listening from upstairs. After looking over to his daughter he looked in front and just said, "Gonna try to finish with that chair today." Nothing more was said but then stepping off the front porch into the sun he went on – "Sure is hot these days," though Millie did not react again as the mother kept looking at her more acutely.

A short while later it would be near dark and the sheriff's office back in town was now becoming ever fuller with the two new assisting deputies now quartering it and helping with the guarding of Colby. By now the outlaw could walk fairly well although did not need to do so in his confining jail cell but the sheriff looked unto this with ever more inner promise that now he could take him to wherever it was they needed to go or where he thought the loot would be.

On either sides of the town there were signs held high up and nailed down to boards that no guns were to be carried in Little Cavern by anyone and that this would not be accepted which had been well procured by the death of Colby's assassin. Still, more and more people thought something strange was coming in all around and there was a great deal of talk about the sheriff and suspicions were being raised so that anyone passing him would have a tinge of fear and try to avoid any type of accosting with him. Nevertheless, the killing of the Mexican could only really be seen as a necessary thing as his reason for being there was made quite conspicuous, but now people were beginning to question the sheriff's abrupt sense of duty – was he as well – meaning or was he more in common with the assassin himself? Nonetheless the secret between him and Colby and of what they had spoken was still lingering between the two and kept at close guard. As for Wyatt Cobb he was now free again and was released the next day as he usually would be to continue on his trodden life. As it was he had not produced anything for a long while or written anything new and had been trying to just stay sober enough to go back to the newspaper although inasmuch having this recent setback. He stayed in an older woman's house actually on the outside of town who took him in more as someone who could help her around the place and also outside in the garden as she was now getting up in age and becoming difficult for her to walk. Wyatt would do this for her although knowing he could not give her much in money but she was more understanding about this than most would be and possessed an older woman's wisdom and would try to look passed his faults. Lately she was even sometimes trying to get him to write. She was quite literate too and had read many books and had taught when she was younger at the school house as Wyatt had even been one of her pupils. She liked Wyatt for who he was rather than the others in or around the town that saw him less than appealing and knew he knew much more than what others thought of him.

So, when he had come back the next day from the sheriff's office he tried not to make too much noise coming in as he passed by the old woman's room and to his own that was upstairs at the end of the hallway. Thinking she was asleep she caught him anyway as her door was slightly cracked open.

"Is that you Wyatt?" the woman asked in her frail elderly tone. Her name was Evelynn Jones but Wyatt would just call her ma'am mostly. At hearing this though Wyatt just turned on back removing his hat and opening her bedroom door further as she lay in her bed in the darkened room.

"Yes ma'am," he replied in his ruffled voice. The greyish haired woman just sat up then a touch and looked at him as he just stood there with his hat in hand.

"You've been gone again," she said.

"I know. I'm sorry ma'am." She just tilted her head a bit though at hearing this but then said,

"I could use some help in the garden you know. Perhaps, in a little while?"

"Well, I will, but I would like to rest for a while yet. If that would be alright ma'am."

"It is," she recurred. Wyatt started to close the door and go to his bedroom but then she said as he turned his back to her, "Wyatt - You've been drinking again." Wyatt slightly hesitated before answering.

"Yes, ma'am. I'm afraid so."

"Were you with the sheriff?"

"Yes, I was."

"You know how I feel about your drinking. You have to try to fight the urge. You mustn't for yourself. You were one of my best students too, and with such promise. You must find it in yourself not to."

Wyatt didn't say anything more but after a moment implied, "Yes ma'am," as he put his hat back on his head closing the door gently and then going down the hall to his bedroom.

When he was in his room he looked around for a few moments and then sat down on top of his bed that seemed to have a small end table next to it as he lit a kerosene lamp that was resting on top neath a cotton lining by using a match he took out from a drawer in one of the upper compartments. Once he had done this he took out from the same drawer then what appeared to be a plated portrait or early daguerreotype of a woman he had known when he was younger as he look down holding onto it as he did, though as it was she had gone away and now the aging Wyatt Cobb only had the plated image of her face to remind him of what may have been once an innocent love and on the back of it as he turned it over was the name inscribed,

With Love
Yours Truly,
Sarah

But who was she, and where had she gone?

7

I t was next Sunday and everyone including the Mayor himself would soon be up at church as well as Millie and her parents. Soon the high priest would take his command over the town's people from his tallish alter and seek to understand the Mexican's death and through his own words amend the act or what others felt of it.

Everyone would show up on their carriages and wagons or even some on foot just to hear the sermon. Father Coleridge had prepared a special and theological case for the recent accounts which he would undoubtedly bestow to everyone listening that morning, but the sheriff, as always the case, not to be found anywhere around the white washed church and steeple, and instead, back at his precinct along with the other lawmen, busily there, as was his usual dutiful excuse and with the guarding now of Colby.

Everyone going to church that day looked entrapped within their ideals and morals than usual and was eager to hear what the Father had to say so that women did not smile as much and men looked more vulnerable to uneasiness than usual. As for Millie she looked quite still in her face and would no longer hardly be able to tolerate the Holy gospel as she had before, but now would have to sit there in one of the white paneled pews kneeling to what she could not see in as to what others did.

Mr. and Mrs. Taylor were sitting in the front row as usual though Mrs. Taylor did not look at all pleased with the knowing of her husband and the other woman whom had taken her place having a rather impatient expression on her face but the Mister just looking on with a little more conviction of anticipation of hearing the priest's words. Suddenly then everyone bowed their heads as Father Coleridge looking bold as ever came out from in back of his alter and then making his way up its steps.

"O' Father our blessed Lord, we give thee thanks," he renounced as everyone raised their heads back up and said, "Amen." Then, looking out into a seemingly distant point that did not look to meet he began his fiery and

unlamented sermon meant to upheaval any unreason to the recent and nefarious incidents taking place in town.

"Well," he uttered over everyone listening. "Is there not enough overwrought and disdainfulness in the rest of the land than to come here and mark
our loving town with such indignation? Is there not enough people either to
bring fear to others in places unlike our own. Do knaves come to us with such
spilled blood flowing red like the sea parted by Moses where he picked its fruits
and drowned his pursuer's in its frigid tides so that his escape and his breth-
ren's too could live without its rulers who shed their blood and drink it like
wine. For I am uncertain of what these men are guilty of or what they have done
to be feared so, but I do know that their evil ways lurk beyond than here and
beyond where they were derived from. They come here to show this, to show
that evil can proliferate wherever men shall go. This is their purpose and why
they are meant to be."

After making his opening recant the priest told everyone to take out their
hymn books as they rose from sitting and began singing one of the more life
celebrating hymns. Millie felt still inert after hearing the priest's words and all
that was said with her flattened face and in her dulled nervous state. Her parents stood aside her as they sang along with the others but Millie just stood
there with her lips more pursed and hardly letting out a syllable and knowing
that she would not be able to keep up in such a state of being and that she could
only last for so long.

Just then, during the hymn, a woman had entered from back of the church
through one of the redly painted doors as everyone suddenly looked in back
and stopped singing. The name of the woman was a Lena Perkins who never
really went to the church and was better known as one of the few aforementioned saloon girls, but she was a young woman near thirty having good looks
with a somewhat shy disposition and a close friend to Mary Mulligans. That
morning, incidentally, she had discovered her friend and Mr. Taylor's notable
mistress dead in her bed as she had taken her own life the night before, but
young Lena had showed up at the church in a state of grief and knowing that
Mr. Taylor had likely been the cause of her friend's dire act.

Mr. Taylor just kept forward, however, not looking back unlike the others
as young Lena Perkins started to suddenly speak in her weak and weary voice.

"I know you all know me. I know what you all think of me too. A whore, and
a friend of that Mary Mulligans woman the charlatan of the town herself. I
know what you think though. You've all come down here to listen to your priest

and bid your heads to what you think is the lord's way. I don't know too much about it myself, of course. I don't know too much of anything," she continued to say as she almost tripped over but grabbed one of the pews to hold herself up. Then, looking up towards where Mr. Taylor was seated in the front she said, "I know you too Mr. Taylor. You don't even look at me but I know you know me and why I'm here." She paused. "She's dead. She took a whole bottle of ether to do it."

Everyone hushed at hearing this but the unfeeling Nelson Taylor still kept his back turned.

"I've come here to tell you that, and the baby she had in her is dead too. But I know you and I know why she's dead."

At this point the woman was looking quite frail and began crying as one of the older women standing next to her took hold of her and walked her out of the church side by side as the shaken young woman let her do this.

Mrs. Taylor was almost broiling inside though standing next to her husband and just took her white parasol that she was holding and shoved it into Mr. Taylor's arms as she proceeded out of the church ferment as ever and quite different than when she had walked out of it on her wedding day some years before.

Needless to say church that Sunday morning did not go as planned as Father Coleridge stood up there on the alter and looked on with the rest with almost equal befuddlement trying to grab hold of what was happening. Mr. Taylor however started to walk out the church himself having a calm and slow step and still holding his wife's parasol as everyone hushed again and looked as he made his way to the back and opened one of the doors to make his way out.

The Sunday church proceedings did not last any longer after this as everyone was furtively disenchanted with what was happening but the last words of the priest only harped on what had been seen by saying,

"Please do not let these few bring no more down than what has come to them. For they come to us as only as those in need of our love and we must serve them with such. Their sin can only relinquish themselves of what can be replaced by the goodness in us. We pray for thee our Lord and in the Holy Ghost for them and for us."

Upon finishing everyone bowed down their heads once more as the processions had finally come to an end and as everyone started to leave the church through the same set of red painted doors in the back. Millie had even seen her friend Stella leaving with her parents as Stella noticed her first but Millie did not seem to notice her as much. Nevertheless, Stella looked and said, "Hello, Millie," as she was leaving. But to this her friend just turned shyly and replied hello as though there seemed ever more distance between the two than had and similarly, like strangers were parting, and although the two girls knew one another there seemed no need for anymore words to be said.

For Millie the rest of that afternoon would be spent mostly in the woeful thoughts of her growing and afflicted outlook on her own life as it had not still been fully surfaced to her parents yet. She would sit there on the porch of her home as before and think now of what she had seen at church that morning and of hearing of how the woman had taken her life and her child's and all of the discouragement it produced within her grabbing at her own soul like so many hands dragging her down and now the deathly image of a grave stone was marked in her mind, but oddly enough as she continue to look out into the day somewhere she could see herself slipping away and a feeling from within as though her own grimly finality was somehow out there on the horizon.

It was now a few days from the disastrous sermon undoubtedly filling the town with more gossip of what had happened, of Mr. Taylor's affair and the rest of the scandalous things heard. Another night was presently sweeping over the cumbersome though, more and more, ensnared and gradually stirred up little western village as men and women walked along the street porches and as one by one each of the lantern wicks above had as custom been getting lit. The man who lit them every night had only one arm having the name of Sonny Pickens but he had lost the other arm during the Civil War fighting for the union and may have been one of the wisest of men in all of Little Cavern. He was an older, quiet man but not completely without talk and bided the men and women that passed him by with a pleasant side of face as he held his tall lighting torch in his hand with the only arm he had left. Just as he had been doing this, however, another man suddenly came through on horseback down the long stretch of road wearing a gun in holster as Sonny immediately saw this while he momentarily looked back at the man with his distinctly wizened and furrowed older man's face. The man on horseback seemed to be a younger person than himself, his face hidden by his ink black cowboy hat titled slightly over his forehead as he rode on through looking unaffected by anything and having a sort of pretentious decadence in dress as he wore a black leather vest over a white terry cloth shirt with some frills sticking out along the chest and a pair of some black slacks with a pair of brown leather boots on below and some spurs attached and harnessed in his horses stirrups.

The man's name and face was unknown to anyone in those parts and his uncanny demeanor and silent presence was quite different to that of having to do with Little Cavern so as he rode through his very sight would have been distinct to his surroundings of colorful shop signs and spindled ornate columns sweeping down below the low top store front roofs, and, of course, the few people walking along the procession who intermittently turned their heads to look at the stranger as he passed through, although not without a kind of enigmatic look in their eye, either, sensing as well he was far different than anything they had seen. Nevertheless, he continued his way down the road on his slow paced and darker haired Stallion, only eventually, stopping with a slight tug of the harness as he patiently made his way down off his fiery looking horse in front of what was a white glazed window Inn or known as Mrs. Ruford's Parlor.

The mysterious man, or whomever he was, only went to tie his horse off then in front of the cozily looking Inn similarly to the vacant horses now sitting in front of the saloon which was on the opposite side of the road down a few stores away where men and women could be heard rustling and carrying away as usual through its saloon doors though the stranger did not seem to look at this with any interest but seemed to be in his own prerogative and didn't even so much as look at the loud establishment with his clef in chin and straight angled face.

After this the man began to pace over to the parlor door opening it and closing the door behind him as he made his way up to the empty counter where a registry book and push bell sat on top next to each other. When he got up to the counter he waited a moment but then pressed down and rang the bell to summon the maître de or Mrs. Ruford who was then in the back den rocking in an arm chair where she would usually go when business was slow so that she was surprised when she heard the bell ring up in front thinking that no one would come that night. Upon hearing this though she got up from her rocking chair and gathered herself abruptly to go and greet whomever was there.

The door of the den was half open as she went over to it opening it a little further so she could get through while she had a benign smile on her face and hardly looked up at first to see who it was. She was an elderly woman with short red curly hair and wore a trim petticoat dress over her plump and roundly figure though she was not unkindly or overly imposing like some other women of her type in Little Cavern or like that of Mrs. Purcell needless to say.

As soon as she looked up, however, after making her way to the desk and reaching for a pair of spectacles in her dress pocket placing them on her flushed red nose she was immediately taken back by the stalky presence of the lone gun carrying stranger his eyes still shadowed by his tipped hat and undiscerning look on his face. Seeing this suddenly the smile on Mrs. Ruford's face herself turned to a kind of nervous and awkward expression as she thought the stranger in front of her much different than her usual clientele who did not hold arms at their sides, as in Little Cavern, and were much more average in their demeanor or personable so that to say hello would not seem a trifle. The man before her though was one that hardly suggested the described, bother to say, and so instead Mrs. Ruford looked unto him with a sort of perplexed timidity as though he were an embarrassment to his surroundings which could hardly complement him, although he seemed not to notice the indifference or the old woman and Inn keeper's incumbent manner.

"You can just sign here, if you please sir," Mrs. Ruford said shakily as she held out a pen that was sitting in a well of ink next to the registry book which she pushed towards the man trying not to be unkindly. At this the man just took the pen in hand and wrote down a thinly and stiff looking "X" on one of the vacant lines down below as Mrs. Ruford's face just turned a pale, white while she saw him do this and could plainly see the letter of the "X" written down as she was looking. Upon this she turned the book back to her afterwards still in a timid manner to put down the time and date of the visitor among the other previous signed names and arrival times and dates of her recent guests, or as the log may have looked in print:

Name	Arrival Time	Arrival Date
1. _John P Toml_	-	-
2.		
3.		
4. _Buddy Tucker Clarnal_	_3:5_	_8__ 10_
5. _X_		

Taking hold she turned after this to get down a skeleton key from behind her off a row of hooks and other similar keys mounted on the wall and then turned back to the inimitable stranger and said, "If you'd come with me please I'll show you to your room."

Mrs. Ruford just lifted the side mount to make her way out then from behind the front desk as she slowly put it back in place and as the man began to follow her from behind at a close distance, his tall stature overshadowing the old woman who was looking up to him still in a quivering way. Slowly, grabbing a part of her dress, Mrs. Ruford began then to make her way up some satin lined stairs as the man continued to follow her from behind. Just before they reached the top one of the steps squeaked but Mrs. Ruford just said chidingly, "I have to get that one fixed soon," as she turned her head, although the stranger just looked onward but Mrs. Ruford only prompting her head back herself after. Then, no longer holding her dress the Inn Keeper went over to a small table halfway down the dim lit hallway with only a small lit kerosene lantern hanging above it as she took a candle and holder resting on top of the table and lit the wick from the flame of the other lantern above by removing the sconce while the man kept close to her the whole time. After this she made a few more steps towards a side door holding the candle in her hand and the key in the other as she unlocked the door from the outside opening it and walked in as the man followed her from behind.

Mrs. Ruford went over thereafter to another small kerosene lantern hanging off the wall removing the glass part and lit it with the flame of the candle she was holding as she turned the wick up from the side of the lantern and as the room and bed began to get brighter.

"Well, this is it," she went on while the stranger just looked around ever so coolly. "It'll be two dollars a night and breakfast and dinner is three dollars more a week, if you're planning on staying."

The man just kept on looking and listening to her as he took out a large bill and gave it to Mrs. Ruford while her eyes just widened and with a slightly surprised expression on her face. "Well, I hope you'll be alright here, mister," she continued as she began to make her way out of the room but not without turning to the man again to say, "And let me know if you need anything, of course."

The newcomer didn't look back or say anything as Mrs. Ruford closed the door behind her now leaving himself alone in the lantern lit room, the yellowish incandesce light pouring onto his back, as well, throughout the rest of the cabin, with its warm and pastel colored glow but with the question still looming underneath it all – who was this stranger, and why had he come?

8

The night had gone by and the man had not been seen since and one could only assume he had been kept away to his room, although few knew the stranger had even come to their malingering town anyway as his presence coming through had been abrupt. The day was half through already with the mid evening sun above and people dispersing over the town. Up at the precinct the sheriff Jeff McCormack and Pat Thomsen along with the two younger deputies now were sitting down in their chairs as though waiting for something to happen and Colby in his cell quiet as usual. Suddenly the sheriffs partner Joe Collins came in rattling along as he would and disquieting the scene in his nervy way.

"Boy I say sure is hot today," he went on as the others didn't even look up at him. Mike Taverns was just then sitting in his chair and polishing up a rifle he had gotten from the gun cabinet while the sheriff was sitting in his same manner with his legs stretched out resting on his desk and his hands folded at his belt with his hat crocked forward. Joe just went over and looked at Colby a moment wiping his brow with a small linen before saying something.

"Heard some people saw some man comin through last night."

"Yeah, so?" Mike Taverns replied as he stood up and went over to put the rifle back in the cabinet.

"Heard this one was wearing a gun," Joe continued.

The sheriff didn't do anything and hardly twitched but Pat Thomsen who was playing cards with Will Blake suddenly looked up and said, "Who saw *who* wearing a gun?"

"I don't know, but someone found out from some Mrs. Ruford the Inn Keeper down there. Say's he gave her the willies, but he's been staying up in one her rooms and hasn't shown himself since."

"Well, I say we should be checkin' into that. How 'bout it sheriff?" Pat Thomsen went on looking at the dubious Jeff McCormack though he hardly moved again and remained in his same posture. Then, slowly lifting the front of his hat to uncover his forehead he finally replied,

"I reckon we will, boys. I reckon soon as he comes out we'll go and seek out this mysterious man in town."

A moment went by, but then Mike Taverns said looking over at Colby, "Do you think it's for him?" At this the sheriff just looked up at the jailed convict though without lifting his hat.

"*How bout it Colby?*" he said. "Is this one of yours?" but the outlaw didn't do anything after except to turn on to his side.

"Did you hear what his name was by chance?" Will Blake went to ask Joe looking over at him and still standing up and leaning against a post with his arms folded.

"No, I didn't," Joe answered back. "Except to hear he signed with an 'X' or something."

"Well, you ain't kiddin?" Mike Taverns said looking over to the others. Pat Thomsen though just spoke up again concernedly from in his own seat.

"I say we should go get him right now instead of waiting round here if you ask me." But the sheriff didn't say anything more to this except, "I wouldn't worry too much. I reckon we'll have plenty of time to go out and get this nameless man. Just wait until it gets dark and we'll have ourselves a nice meeting up with the mister then."

Strangely no more words were spoken afterwards, as Pat Thomsen just looked on confusedly and just as anxiously with the others, but the sheriff contrarily calm and relaxed as ever, sitting at his desk in the same way. The deputies would stay on with him in the precinct until night, when the man in question, would finally come out of his room and make his way along and down the torch lit boardwalk, as others nearby could see him walking with his gun still visible and quickly fleeing, or hurrying on in fear, as if innately knowing somewhere within that something was going to happen, and whatever it was that it would be more sooner than later.

The night was well on its way now, and over at the precinct the sheriff and his deputies were still sitting around waiting to make their assault while the sheriff remained in his same position with his hat crocked forward.

Suddenly, though, Joe Collins came in, as like last time, only not saying anything for a moment, but then opened his mouth to say " - That man finally stepped out of his room. I saw him walking down along the boardwalk headed over down towards the saloon. Had a gun on him just as I had heard."

"Well, that's it then," Pat Thomsen spoke up as he took out his sidearm to check its load. The sheriff still didn't move, but Pat just went on " – Looks like we finally have our chance."

After though, the sheriff only kept at sitting there at his desk when, then, he finally removed and took his legs down from off it as he pushed up his hat. "Well, boys," he said. "I reckon we do."

"How are we gonna take him?" Will Blake blunted out standing next to his young deputy friend.

"Looks like we're gonna have to get 'em in the saloon I guess," Joe answered looking at the sheriff, but to this the sheriff just stood up tipping his hat back as he looked back at all four of them to say, "Well, I guess that's that boys. You all just follow my lead. I reckon we'll disarm this lone gunman yet."

It was then, ten minutes passed eight as the hands on the ornately wood carved clock hanging above the equally finely built and solidly looking saloon bar were at their farthest distance and stretched straight out from one end to the other. The nameless stranger stood in front of it with his head hidden down and his hat covering his face and his gun hanging plainly at his side. Max Singleton was, just then, placing a glass of gin on the bar front as the stranger had asked for while the meek seeming bartender moved away cautiously knowing trouble was probably coming. All the rest of the men and women more quiet than usual were looking wearily up towards the bar and noticing the gun bearing stranger and waiting for something to happen. Suddenly the saloon doors were opened as the piano player and singer in the back stopped playing, almost similarly to when the Mexican had come, as the four assisting deputies all entered having their side arms on them and one holding a rifle though the man sipping his gin at the bar did not notice and hardly looked up. Only a few women made some sounds trying not to scream but it was then when the stranger looking ahead at the bar turned and could see to his side a rifle pointed at his head along with three other guns pointed at him ready to shoot.

The sheriff or Jeff McCormack was the last one to come in through the saloon doors though he was not raising his colt in the air, and instead, looked at the stranger with a gleaming eye keeping his hands tucked in his belt at his side and looking calm. Only, after a moment, though he began to speak in his blunt and maniacal way.

"Looks like you didn't see the sign outside Mister about there being no guns allowed in this town."

The stranger didn't say anything but just kept looking at the sheriff as he spoke.

"Or then again maybe you did see it," the sheriff continued. "Maybe you did see one of those boarded signs coming in. I reckon, you just can't *read* is what I mean mister," the sheriff went on.

Everyone kept hushed but the quiet and pensive stranger still didn't say anything.

"How 'bout that," the sheriff said. "Maybe you just couldn't read that big old sign out there."

Again the man just kept standing there only lowering his head down slightly but hardly moving as the other deputies just kept their firearms pointed at him.

"Now how about given over that gun of yours? Don't want any trouble, of course, considering you just couldn't read and didn't know any better. Just give it over nice and calm."

The man hesitated for a moment before doing anything, as he slowly reached to undo his gun belt unbuckling it and slipping it off carefully as it dropped onto the saloon floor. After this Joe Collins lowering his own gun just went over and picked up the gun and holster while the sheriff continued looking at the man with a sneering grin.

"Now that's real good," the sheriff snidely said. It seemed at that point everything was alright, but then, coming up to the stranger as he went to get close the sheriff sort of whispered to him.

"Now, see. If you knew how to read like everyone else this would've never happened."

The man and stranger just kept standing there as the sheriff went to turn back. But, the ruthless Jeff McCormack, as was his nature, had all along no intent of letting the nameless newcomer get away and in a quick motion upon turning his back suddenly back handed the man, now defenseless, as he hit the bar spilling his glass of gin over and landing onto the floor while all else remained quiet, except for the sound of another woman trying not to scream. At this point though the pugnacious sheriff in so many words began kicking the tar out of the man as he kept trying to get up and as Jeff knocked him down with each thrust while all else looked on at the helpless victim.

Finally, the nameless character tried to get up one last time as Jeff back handed him again so that he fell down from his knees trying to hug the saloon bar but no one made a sound still or even the sheriff's deputies standing by.

"Get 'em on out of here," the sheriff or Jeff McCormack said to the others with his back still turned to them and looking down at the man as the others looked on hesitatingly though the two young lawmen Will Blake and Mike Taverns finally went over then and picked the bloodied man up off the saloon floor from head to toe and started removing him and walking him out of the misshapen and disturbed drinking and gambling saloon.

Following from behind out through the saloon doors were the other two deputies and the sheriff in his calm step feeling very satisfied of what he had just done and looking snide.

"Hold on their boys," he said to the other two still holding the man up.

"Get that mule over here," he told Joe Collins as he went and got this jack assed looking mule off the horse dock although looking apprehensive and unsure of what was happening.

"Now what d'you say boys," the sheriff continued. "Put him on up there and he'll be haven himself I nice trip."

The two deputies holding the stranger just looked at each other for a moment but then hoisted the man onto the saddleless mule as he sat up their barely hugging its neck and still very languid and stooped over.

"Now all you gotta do is give a good kick to his behind and he can get on his way," the sheriff hollered as Mike Taverns standing next to the four legged sight looked over and gave the mule a sharp slap to its behind. The mule immediately took off after while the ravaged stranger on top hobbled off and down the dark road with the man until at some point they could no longer be discernable, the torches in their procession on either side and in line with one another giving off their fading and burning wicker glow.

"Well, I think we're finished here boys," the sheriff said in his conclusive way as the others just looked onward in silence but although it seemed no words were necessary somewhere within the other deputies, in one way or another, was summoned a strange feeling that they had just done something wrong and that they would somehow come to regret it, so as young deputy Will Blake turned to go back to the precinct with the rest of the others he couldn't help but to look back again as he stare, once more, into the darkness.

* * *

The next day's to come went by uneventful after what was now the second incident to happen up at the saloon, although people went on doing their usual business considering it just another blemish to mark their fragile but now tainted town of sin as whomever had witnessed the bludgeoning of the stranger at the hands of the sheriff that night would not speak of it and kept their thoughts to themselves or in their stride as a certain feeling of shame could be felt within of what had been observed, but the sounds of a whisper here and there still could be heard every so often. As for Millie she had been staying close to home still and had not gone into town just as her mother had wanted and neither one of the parents knew of what had happened at the saloon either as Benjamin had hardly been to town himself nor Millie's mother for that matter. Instead it was another afternoon and Millie sat in her room in front of the vanity looking out the window and wanting relief from all the things that were grabbing at her mind. She thought of her friend and the way she felt of seeing her after church and the distance she felt now with all the rest. Her mother at that moment was busy downstairs in the beginnings of making her new dress for the dance but Millie was not thinking of this with too much anticipation naturally and hoped her mother would just finish it off soon.

"Millie!" Her mother called from downstairs. "I need to measure you."

Upon hearing her mother's call Millie gathered herself and went downstairs trying to look unaffected. As she turned at the bottom of the stairs she could see her mother in the other room with fabrics of white and blue ribbons strewn about and in the middle an upright woman's torso and chest having different pins and needles sticking out of it.

"Yes, mother," Millie said.

"Oh, there you are," her mother went on. "I need to measure your shoulders. I haven't in a while and I'm sure you're a little bigger."

"I see."

Her mother took a measuring tape out of her sewing box that was laid out on the floor and went over to her daughter as Millie stretched out both her arms and as her mother wrapped the tape around her shoulders.

"Well, I'd thought you would be bigger, but you're almost the same," she said looking at the two ends of the tape. Millie didn't say anything, however, but instead just kept looking over at the torso.

"I think this will be the nicest dress yet," her mother continued. "I'm sure you will like it when I'm finished. I'm making a blue bow tied sash to go around the waist and you'll look so nice. I'm sure you'll be..." Millie's mother could see her daughter wasn't listening again, and instead, just looking over at the torso. Frustrated by this she asked, "Well, what is wrong with you? Every time I talk you seem to be going off. Aren't you looking forward to the new dress? I'm sure they'll be some boys at that dance that you'll see and might come over."

Millie looked in a daze again but just said,

"Sure their will mother. I'm sure." After this her mother kept looking at her as Millie began to leave and go back up the stairs.

"Millie?" Her mother said once more.

"Yes, mother?"

All her mother said though was, "Never mind," as Millie continued her way back up the steps to her room.

That same evening the sheriff had left his office to visit the more recently notorious Little Caverns saloon to meet no other than Mr. Taylor as had been requested by the cattle baron himself while the sheriff stood silently as ever and hovering above, but joining Mr. Taylor in drink as he sat with his head down on a stool next to him. There were only a few others in the saloon at that time or some old worn out looking cowboys as they sat away from the bar sitting alone and drinking at some tables while the piano player could be heard playing a Chopin nocturne in the background at his old and honky sounding of a keyboard over in the corner. Mr. Taylor had actually sought the sheriff through one of his cattle hands, although the sheriff did not drink often nor would be considered a drinking man and hardly touched his glass the whole time they spoke.

"I supposin' you know like the rest of this prissy town my wife's leaving me," Mr. Taylor told Jeff leaning over the bar as he looked down.

"Well, I'm sure sorry to be hearing that," the sheriff recapped.

"I bet you are," Mr. Taylor rallied back. Then, after taking a drink he leaned back down and said, "I guess you don't have any idea why I've sent for you." The sheriff just stood there and waited a moment before replying.

"I don't reckon I do."

"We'll," Mr. Taylor said. "I want you to find where that Alcott's niece might be." The Sheriff looked attentive just then.

"I didn't even know you knew about the despaired Miss Russell," he said. "How did you find out he's been looking for her?"

"I have my ways," Mr. Taylor replied. "And know a few other peoples around."

"We'll, why do you want me to find her? Don't tell me she means anything to you?

"No," Mr. Taylor requited. "Actually she doesn't. But, I'm thinking I want that Alcott to know I helped save her."

"And how do you figures on that?" the sheriff asked.

"Cause I have a good idea on where she is." The sheriff looked interested all of a sudden.

"How's that?" he went on.

Just then Max Singleton came out getting ready for the coming crowd and started to wipe down the bar though still looking very weary of the volatile sheriff, as well, the now much tarnished Mr. Nelson Taylor as even he was quite aware of what had happened at church just a few Sunday mornings before when the other woman of the saloon, or that of Miss Lena Perkins, who had shown up to demark and make her case as she had. Mr. Taylor just looked at him though and said, "How do you do tonight Max?"

"Very fine, sir," the bar tender replied cautiously.

"The sheriff and I are just having a chat," Mr. Taylor continued. "How about giving us another round. If you don't mind Max?"

"Certainly sir," Max pleasingly said as he went and got another bottle off the liquor case removing the cork and poured a shot of bourbon into each of the men's glasses. After this he put the cork back into the bottle and put it down next to an empty one that was already on the bar near Mr. Taylor.

"Thank you, Max," Mr. Taylor said to him uncannily.

"You're very welcome sir."

"Max?"

"Yes, Sir?"

"I can always rely on you," Mr. Taylor went on. "Am I not right?"

"Well, yes sir," the old bar stool replied.

"I knew I could," the other pranked on and raising his glass to his face as he drank it down with one shot. "Now how about letting us talk for a little here. The sheriff and I will make sure of it there are no outbursts."

Mr. Taylor just looked over to the subversive Jeff McCormack sitting next to him with his drink in hand.

"Sure we will," the sheriff affirmed with a grin.

Max went off over to the other side of the room then to get a broom and started sweeping as the piano player stopped playing his nocturne and started playing a more lively and fast pace piece getting ready for others soon to come in.

"Where is she then?" the sheriff leaned in. "And why do you want me to know?"

"I told you why. I want that Alcott to think I helped you."

"And why is that so important?" the sheriff asked again.

"Cause I'm lookin' to make out a little profit myself from the little coal mining tycoon if I can. And this would be a good reason for it. Don't you think?" The sheriff hesitated before replying looking slightly jostled from Mr. Taylor's answer but went on anyway.

"Well, I'm sorry," he said. Taking a sip of his drink as Mr. Taylor smirked himself he continued. "So where is she then? Is she with one of Colby's gang?"

"No, she isn't," Mr. Taylor sharply recapped.

The sheriff just kept looking at Mr. Taylor as he kept his head down at the bar while Mr. Taylor, finally, answered as the sheriff went to fill up both their glasses full of bourbon.

"She's with and old Indian chief down in Nebraska. In some cabin a ways from an Indian reservation near a Fort Brent." The sheriff looked beguiled after being told this but asked,

"We'll why the hell is she down there with this Indian?"

"Cause this old Apache saved her life," Mr. Taylor went on, "And found her in some cave nearby where her parents were killed by that Colby. He has some name like, Rolling Tides or something, but he came from some half dead Indian tribe livin' out on some reservation down there."

"How do you know about all this?"

"I found out from a man who saw the girl with the Indian. He said he knew it was her after hearing about the massacre and reading about the girl in the papers, but she's been with this Rolling Tides ever since."

"What was the man's name?" the sheriff inquired and just as Mr. Taylor was looking down at his glass as he reached for a bottle of bourbon to fill it up again.

"Scott," he replied removing the cork from it. "Scott Terence."

"Who's that, if I may ask?"

Filling up his glass then Mr. Taylor answered.

"Happens he was a friend of the woman Mary Mulligans. The one I'm sure you've heard about. How 'bout it?"

The sheriff just sat their smiling at Mr. Taylors retort, but to himself only thought of telling of what he had just heard to Colby in order to make him talk and that this would be a way to get his hands on whatever money or loot he thought was stowed away by Colby's gang.

"We'll I'll be sure to tell that Uncle what you told me. What's in it for me if I help you?" the sheriff went on. Mr. Taylor just stood up after this though and said,

"We'll I don't know. Seems I could do something for you, or don't you know already?"

After saying this Mr. Taylor put his hat back on his head and began walking out of the saloon with a pleasing grin on his face as the sheriff sat there with the two empty glasses and empty bottles on the bar looking back at him. As Mr. Taylor was going through the saloon doors though another man came in and passed him by only stopping then to look at Mr. Taylor's site as the well suited and scandal imbued cattle owner just picked his hat off his head again and said coolly, "Good evening," though the young straggler did not respond and just kept looking at him as he went out of the saloon. As the sheriff continued to sit there the piano player was still playing his old fashioned saloon tune and soon men and women would gather around in the smoke filled caravan of card games and drinking and lively discussion, and to once more listen into the night to the ballades and various harmonies among the other requested tunes during that evening when, as many a night before, the darker side of the mild mannered town would take place once again.

Since Mr. Alcott's meeting with Colby in the sheriff's office the opulent gentleman had been staying at a plush sort of Inn between that of Little Cavern and another town called Montclair that lay further north east of Wyoming. One could see him drinking from a kettle of tea and his teacup in hand sitting at a lounging table outside with his cane in one of his white gloved hands and reading a newspaper flattened on the table waiting to hear if any words had been spoken by the jailed outlaw of his nieces disappearance, or whatever come of what last was said during their meeting, his face still disconcerted and his body stiffened from his unapparent grief.

It was morning now and just then a young boy or porter with cap and wearing a grey uniform came out to his table and handed the proper gentleman a telegram as he reached into his coat tailed pocket to give the dispatcher a small nickel for his services.

Then putting on a pair of reading glasses he took out from another inside coat pocket and resting them on the edge of his nose he looked down to read its message:

> From Sheriff **Stop**
> Now know more on whereabouts of niece **Stop**
> Please come down to see me soon as possible **Stop**
> **End**

After reading it the jacketed gentlemen stood up with his cane and began making his way back to the Inn. He felt a relief that at least he would know about his niece either way but still a fear that she was in great danger and only to get to the sheriff's office right away. So without hesitation he decidedly left the hotel in the same carriage that had taken him to town and when he had first come as everyone had stopped hushed to look at.

The trip would take half a day to get to the town but by now the loathsome sheriff or Jeff McCormack had his plan well worked out and his hands ever closer in his palms of the outlaw's loot and whatever he thought was being confiscated as he felt this coming feeling all over and up his spine and beneath his badge and shirt where his cold heart was beating faster and faster, and although the deputies surrounding him at the precinct were of good intent he would have gotten rid of any one of them to get what he wanted.

That same morning of that day the bunch of them had been all standing around quietly inside the jail although ever more tense now from what had happened to the slain stranger up at the saloon still having the branded image of the man in their minds riding off on the mule down the dark and irksome road though they could not be certain why the man had come, but almost hoping, even in their silently doubting thoughts that it had not been in good faith as the sheriff had conducted himself unto him in the way he had, but still, no one speaking as to it, either way.

As for Colby he was laying in his cell on his cot without any chance of being spurred, but just as expected, neither one of the other deputies knew of what had been told to the sheriff by Mr. Taylor as it was most certainly the sheriff who had sent the delivered telegram to Mr. Alcott, although had kept this detail to himself so far and going according with his plan.

"Why don't you boys go out and take a break," the sheriff suddenly said breaking the silence in the precinct as he was sitting in his usual seat at his desk.

"You sure sheriff?" Will Blake spoke up over in the corner.

"Sure I'm sure boys," the sheriff went on. "And I'll still be here when you all get back... Won't I Joe," he said looking over to his old partner. Joe just sort of smiled and said,

"I reckon you will. I think I wouldn't mind myself getting a bar of some that chocolate at that Mr. Dixon's."

"Sure thing Joe," the sheriff went on in his auspicious voice. "You just get some of that chocolate for yourself."

With only these last words having been said from the sheriff the others started making their way out following Joe from behind, though thinking nothing of it and even not before Joe Collins himself in his good spirits and with his same smile had turned to ask, "You want anything sheriff?" The plotting Jeff McCormack just looked ahead though and said, "No. I think I should be alright here Joe. But, thanks for asking anyway."

Joe didn't say anything more, although he only continued his way out the door of the precinct along with his fellow deputies following from behind him leaving the sheriff alone now at his desk having his legs stretched out as usual with no other than Colby still hushed laying in his brick and iron bar cell over in the corner. Slowly, however, after the others had soon left the sheriff got up from his seat and went over to the outlaw's cell as Colby stayed still, even when the sheriff was standing in front.

"You got something to tell me?" Colby suddenly dashed out with his eyes still half closed and without even moving.

"Sure I got something to tell you Colby," the sheriff said.

"Well, I wonder what that could be?" the other went on candidly.

"Seems like you're not the only one that knows where that girl is."

Colby opened his eyes wider then though but still not moving.

"Like hell they do," he uttered.

"Seems someone saw that niece not too long ago staying with an old Indian man down in Nebraska. Say's this old squaw found her in some cave nearby and knew it was her from reading about the girl in the paper."

Colby lifted himself up after hearing this to look at the sheriff.

"And who the hell might this be?" he asked.

"I don't even know myself," the sheriff answered. "But, it just so happens a Mr. Nelson Taylor here in this town heard it from a man who saw her on down there, and he went and told me about it."

Colby got up off the cot then and went over to the bars of his cell closer to the sheriff.

"Who the hell is Nelson Taylor?" he asked.

"Some well to do cattle rancher round these parts. He was seeing some other woman in town that took her life, but she was supposed to know the man who saw the girl with the Indian."

"Well isn't that just peaches for you."

"Could be," the sheriff went on. "But I figured to tell the rest and that rich Uncle of hers you told me where she might be."

"And why the hell don't you ride down there with this Nelson Taylor and get her yourself?"

"Because then I'd be missing the charm of your company. And besides, I don't plan on finding the girl. I want you to tell that Francis Alcott she's in some other place so we can ride off where you can give me some of those nice things you got stowed away and we can make ourselves a little trade."

Colby just looked up at the sheriff from his cot with an unsure and curious expression but asked, "What about that Nelson Taylor?" All the sheriff said to this though was,

"Never mind about him. I'm not planning on telling that Uncle anything about that. Just tell him you think you might know where his niece is and I'll get you on out of there. Otherwise you'll hang."

"Well, thank you very much," Colby rasped. "I'll be sure to do that then."

"Good," the sheriff said. "Incidentally, he should be here later on this day," he continued. "I had a telegram sent to where he's been staying at."

"Don't worry, sheriff. I'll do what I'm told."

"That I believe you will... That I believe you will," the craftily and conniving Jeff McCormack kept saying out loud as he went and sat back down at his seat over by the desk and resuming his position. Colby, however, just went and leaned back on his cot knowing now or at least thinking he would have a chance to get free, but always knowing too that the sheriff just as volatile and vehement as himself could side swipe him at any time.

Things were as usual in town as the daily on goings of people coming and going were always a mix of newcomers and various wagons holding different products as well as horses making their way through and down the entrapped and muddy roads. Soon the mid evening would pass over as most business would finally conclude for the day but it was during this time when the mysterious Alfred Alcott and his carriage could be seen wending itself through the towns traffic as others walking along the street shops glanced to look at it as they had remembered it just few weeks before when it had first come and the elegant carriage only stopping again in front of the sheriff's office while the others nearby wondered if it was carrying the same gentleman in it and with the question of why he had come back.

Slowly the man ascended himself off the carriage and into the office like the last time and as the door opened in the same way. Standing inside was the sheriff and his deputies and, of course, Colby himself sitting bent over on his cot in his cell.

"Seems we got our Mr. Colby to talk about your niece after all. Isn't that right?" the sheriff said looking over at the inmate. Mr. Alcott went over to his cell as Colby sat there looking at the wall straight over from the sheriff's desk.

"So I see you've decided to speak," Mr. Alcott went on. "What can you tell me?" Colby acted a little reluctant to talk at first but the sheriff just looked over at him.

"Speak up now," he bolted out from his desk and seat. "Man's talking to you." Moving his head towards Mr. Alcott then Colby finally opened his mouth.

"Well, I have's an idea of where your niece might be."

"And where is that?" Mr. Alcott asked although Colby hesitating again before answering.

"I figures on a place I know of down in Nebraska," he finally said. "Where some of my boys are being held up. Just a ways over from some old half abandoned mill town used to be around down there."

"How do I know you're telling the truth?"

"Well," the outlaw continued, "I'm only telling you on where she might be at. *But...*" Before going on Colby was suddenly interrupted by the sheriff as he stood up from his seat coming over to his cell near Alcott.

"Well, I don't know," he intruded lifting up his hat. "But being that's where he says your niece is I'm thinking it would be best if Colby here came down with us just a precaution. Seems to me he can help us find her if he says she's where he thinks she is providing of course, we keep close guard on him. If that's alright with you, Mr. Alcott?

The studious gentleman waited a moment before answering as he kept standing there next to the sheriff although looking slightly hesitant about the whole thing. "I see," he finally said though looking down at the precinct floor. Then, as he looked up at Colby he continued, "I am glad you have spoken up. And, I will grant the sheriffs request to ride with the others. But should you cause anymore disruption to the finding of my niece I trust you shall not live long and I will leave it up to the sheriff of your own fate."

Turning to the sheriff afterwards he asked, "How soon can you leave?"

"Well – we can head out on in the early morning," he answered. "Soon as we get cleared by old Mayor Whitcomb." Pausing then he turned away to continue, "It might take some days to get down there, but, we'll cover as much territory as necessary."

"Very well then. I want every possible precaution taken and I leave it up to you to see to it that the finding of my niece may be expedited swiftly as possible."

"I wouldn't worry Mr. Alcott. We'll find her – if she's to be found."

With these last words from the sheriff the uncle looked grim in his face and hesitated a moment before proceeding out the jail in his same slow paced manner, but having more than certain doubts to whether or not he would see his relative again or if she would even be the lovely niece he had had known before her kidnapping. After this then one of the other young deputies or Mike Taverns spoke up standing aside next to the other to say, "How are we supposed to take him with us?" as he looked over at Colby in his cell with his bandages still in sight and laying on his cot.

"Don't' worry," the sheriff said with a grin. "He shouldn't be too much trouble."

"Will we really be leaving in the morning like you said?" Will Blake jarred in.

"Sure will," the sheriff affirmed. Looking over at Colby who just lay there looking back at him he added, "Bright and early."

Joe Collins on the other side of the room standing next to Pat Thomsen suddenly came in and said, "Well, I guess I should start waterin' down the horses and getting 'em on ready to head out then seems we don't have that much time." But after hearing this the sheriff just came over to Joe real slow and went on to tell him something in this rather phonily though sympathetically sounding tone.

"Uh, hold on their Joe," he said lowering his head as he spoke. "It just so happens you'll be haven to stay here while the rest of us go down and try to find the little lady ourselves. Sorry Joe, but we'll be needing someone round here to carry on with the usual business."

Nevertheless after hearing this Joe just looked at the sheriff disappointedly and replied to him in his timid tone and trammeling a bit as he spoke. "Well, Jeff," he said. "I didn't know. *I* – I'd just thought you'd be 'a taken me with you on this one. That's all."

"No, Joe," the sheriff went on. "Sorry, but as I said we'll be needing someone to stay behind here. I'm sure you can appreciate that though. Right, Joe?"

The long time sheriff's partner and protégé just kept looking down trodden and disheartened but still managed to reply, "Sure, Jeff," just before he went and sat down in a chair over from the sheriffs desk looking quiet and subdued. After this Pat Thomsen standing aside like the others just put his hat back onto his head as he said,

"Well, I think I'll go down and get a cigar before we head out tomorrow."

The others didn't say anything though but Mike Taverns spoke up then and said, "I'd think I'd like to join you in that, if that's ok?" Pat Thomsen just looked over at the young deputy as his younger friend next to him went to say, "I wouldn't mind some of that myself."

To this the sheriff just looked over at the others, then, as he was making his way back to his chair but said, "Alright boys. You go down there and get some cigars for yourselves. Take your time at it if you like. I reckon myself and our Mr. Colby over there will still be here when you get back. And, maybe bring me back one while you're out." Upon this the three began heading out of the precinct leaving the sheriff and Joe still sitting in his chair in the same way as the sheriff leaned back in his own with the same distant look of eye in his face and peering over at his partner saying nothing. Some time passed, but then, Joe finally got the nerve to ask,

"I'd think I like to go out now too if that 'a be alright, Sheriff?" as he kept facing straight ahead without even looking at him.

"That should be fine, Joe," the other replied. At this Joe just stood up still avoiding the sheriff but quietly began to leave the precinct himself, the sheriff following him with his eyes as he went out the door. Once Joe had left though the sheriff turned his eyes back over to Colby still laying down on his cot as he took out a cigar from his desk of all things and lit it. Colby just lay there with a sneer on his face while the sheriff sat in his chair puffing on the cigar and grinning as he stare back at Colby through the bars of his confining cell, as the two conspirators knew at least their plan was already being carried out, but despite the proposition set forth the little crooked trust they had for themselves, or as to what the other really had in store ever more in peril and remaining still yet to be foreseen.

9

It was several days later and the venerable Mayor Whitcomb, had, indeed, given his consent that very same evening in the sheriff's office with Mr. Alcott to have the prisoner escort the sheriff and his deputies to where his niece was being held though as all the rest most unsuspecting of what the sheriff had in store or what his real motives were. Across the pristine view of a prairie range the three deputies and sheriff including Colby himself cladded in iron hand cuffs and riding on a white spotted mule with a rope tied round his waist and attached to Pat Thomsen's saddle riding in front with Will Blake in back on his own horse could all be seen prancing along the Wyoming mountainous landscape, the morning sun hovering above in the white clouded sky.

"- Alright boys. I think we'll hold up here for a little," the sheriff uttered riding and leading the others in front as he came to a slow stop tugging on his horse slightly while the rest just looked around before stopping and getting off as well their own horses to take a rest.

"Get on down from there," Pat Thomsen said looking up to Colby still sitting on his mule with his rifle in hand and holding the rope the prisoner was attached to as he had just unfastened it from his horses saddle. After hearing this the handcuffed Colby slowly just descended himself off the small horse next to the cautious deputy thumping onto the ground with the last step being in his awkward position.

As for the sheriff he stood off to the side looking out into the distance with his sharp stare but Will Blake and Mike Taverns had already sat down across from one another in the shade of a branchy tree as they took their hats off to wipe there brow.

"Don't get too comfortable now. We still have a ways to go before it gets dark," the sheriff embarked still looking out into the distance in the hot cindery sun. "I sure am tired," young deputy Will Blake yawned from under the tree he was sitting. To this though the sheriff just turned his head back then taking a step towards the others and without even looking at the two young

Craig Sholl

deputies glanced, "Why don't one of you take a look and gather some firewood around. Maybe we'll just have ourselves a little meal before we head on out again." Looking right at Colby afterwards without resisting one of his remarks he snared, "You wouldn't mind that. Right, Colby?" The outlaw didn't show much expression though with his sneering and feigning face as he just stood in the same spot next to Pat Thomsen who was still holding his rifle as he cradled it in both arms.

"I'll do it," the older of the two deputies sitting neath the tree or Mike Taverns spoke up standing to his feet briskly as he started to set out. His friend Will though, just looked up to him, or Mike, once he had risen, but only eventually lifting himself to help join in. "I guess I might as well look on with you," he spoke up as he set out along with the other as his friend just minded him.

A little while later the bunch including Colby would all be sitting around a small fire the two deputies had forged some wood and kindling for as Colby heartily ate gracious spoonful helpings of hot beans from a twisted looking metal plate he was holding while Pat Thomsen stood aside the outlaw with his rifle and keeping guard.

As for the sheriff he and Pat had already had their meal while the other two deputies were still eating along with Colby as the sheriff just sat off to the side picking his teeth with a small piece of twig and having a faraway look. Then, looking over at Colby as he ate without hardly lifting his head the sheriff scathingly asked, "How are those beans, Colby?" The prisoner didn't say anything to this, of course, but just picked his head up finally and stopped feeding himself as the sheriff got up after a moment and went over to a not so big but not so small black iron pot that was sitting out on the dying fire and that the beans were being stewed in as he took the ladle in hand that was sticking out of it and poured another generous portion of beans onto Colby's plate.

"Here, we don't want you to starve to death before you get us to where we're goin', of course," the sheriff belated. Colby just sat there looking down at his plate and began to take his spoon to his mouth again as the sheriff went and sat back down looking over at him and continued picking his teeth. Leaning back he spoke up again and said, "...That's it. Eat up boys. Be a while yet until we have our next course."

Colby sort of gave a sort of timid look as he ate almost hesitating and knowing much more unlike the others the sheriff was damn well full of it. Young Will Blake on the other hand just asked ever more in his naivety, "Where is this place we're goin' to anyways?" as he lifted his head from his plate.

The sheriff didn't say anything at first, but instead, just looked over at Colby who still had his head down stuffing away his beans as he finally replied, "I wouldn't worry too much. Our well – fed prisoner here be leadin' us soon enough to our destination." Throwing his piece of twig away after he slithered, "Isn't that right, Colby?" though the apprehended escort just turned over to the sheriff without saying anything and having his lowly look as the other just looked back at him with a flat pan face.

"We'll I think Colby's finished their Pat," the sheriff suddenly came out as he looked up for a moment towards his deputy. "Now you just go and put on those handcuffs of his," he continued as Pat Thomsen set down his rifle away from Colby on a log that he was sitting upon and reached for the pair of solid iron cuffs out of his back pocket wrapping them around both of Colby's wrists and locking them up with a key he took out from another pocket.

"You two can get on ready yourselves," the sheriff told the young deputies finishing up as the two would just set down there plates, then, and stand up to stretch with Will Blake pouring some dirt and sand over the near dead fire with a shovel sticking out of the ground next to it while the smoldering smoke from it slowly dissipated. Once Colby was put back up on his mule, however, and re-tied to the deputy's saddle the bunch would set out on their way again as the afternoon sun continue to shine down while wending through the wooded and grassy terrain as they had and resuming their pace. It would be another day and a half until they would be over the border but the deceiving sheriff Jeff McCormack still waiting to make his next move when at last he would take off with Colby and somehow, or, by someway lose the others, but still unsure for that matter of how he would exactly carry this detail out... *But, just the same he knew he would...*

Back at home Nelson Taylor had been growingly becoming aware that the sheriff had not informed Alcott what he had relayed to him up at the saloon just a few evenings ago or about his knowledge of where the girl and niece was staying. Instead, one could see him standing out on his white columned porch starring out into the distance and having a small gleam of eye, though only the nerve rattled cattle owner aware of what could be afflicting him.

As for Mrs. Taylor she had already left Nelson to make other arrangements by this time and was presently staying with the shady Clarence Booth character and who had prior been asking about town on her behalf as to her husband's recent activities, and as to his egregious affair with the deceased Mary

Mulligans woman, but was at the moment planning to make it to California with the young swash bachelor as he himself was not completely without funds, and more or less, living day to day off what he accrued from his own family name, but having his plan of striking it rich with the recent gold mining that was going on out there and trying to see if he could cash in on the profit.

Mrs. Taylor, or by her maiden name of, Isabel, was not against the notion, but went along and indulging in his fantasy to the extent that she could, although in the back of her rather vengeful and slandered mind planned at one point to come back and lay claim on what she could and in some way or another get back at her husband for what he had done to defame her half goodly name, even if it meant lugging back the freshly minted gold they would find under arm and by foot, or even in the form of loaded guns and live powdered bullets just to do this.

Regardless of what Mrs. Taylor thought, however, or what his present circumstances and worries were, it had just so happened that the cattle boss's reason for coveting the missing girl to be recovered had nothing to do with gaining any of the Alcott's business interests in which to make a profit for himself like he had told the sheriff, though, instead, his real reason for wanting her to be found was something much more personal to him and reprehensible, and if put in the wrong hands could fatally be indicting, pertaining to something the girl may have actually had in her possession, and that could be construed as evidence of Mr. Taylor being responsible for an intended murder that he had hired someone else to commit for him. Not by coincidence, the name of this man was Scott Terence, the same one who had been a friend, or more appropriately put, former lover to Mary Mulligans, though this detail like the other was not shared by Mr. Taylor with the sheriff when they had spoken. As it was Scott had been a cattle hand of Mr. Taylor's, and had gone around with the Mary Mulligans woman for some time though it was not well known by others except by the cattle owner himself and some of the more wrangling ranchers, alike, but it was Mr. Taylor who had actually sought out the young and not so lucrative cattle hand himself and quietly proposed to him for a certain fee to go down and seek out a man who he saw as a threat and could lay part ownership to his ranch that Mr. Taylors father, this being Nelson Taylor Sr., had willed to the other just before he died as he had worked on the ranch when Mr. Taylor was still young and only a foreman. As it happened, Mr. Taylor's father had taken a liking to the bright and freshly spirited worker and upon near his death had put in or added as an amendment to his will that he was to be part owner and inheritor of the ranch next to his son, though young Nelson himself was hardly accepting of this nor did he like the other and had gradually built up an inner jealousy over the years toward him and knowing his father greatly liked the boy further lacking and feeling his own fathers affections.

The terms of the will were given as such that the other party would not inherit his half until his thirtieth birthday for reasons, unknown, but at the time of the father's death the cattle hand was only nineteen and it would be some time until he could assume his share of the ranch although he had been given and still retained a copy of the deed which at the time was made out in secret with the only exception of knowing its existence, being the fathers son, or now chief inheritor of the estate Nelson Taylor.

After the inconspicuous arrangement had been made, however, the cattle hand soon came under bad company as young Nelson made it clear his presence was not warranted and making his work unbearably hard through his bitter treatment of him though the other fellow workers were always partial towards the boy and liked him. Nonetheless, the worker and hand knew he was not liked by the obstinate rancher and had suspected this all the while but finally had become fed up with his contempt feeling no other alternative than to leave the ranch although just the same promising he would return to lay claim to his part of it when he could as Mr. Taylor listened to his plaintiff without saying anything but just the same knowing he would come back.

Time would pass by and Mr. Taylor had not thought much of the young man since. Not so long ago from the present, however, he had overheard from some of his older ranchers still about the place and who had been around at the time of the man's leaving that one of them had last seen him down in Kansas and had said something to the other about coming back up to Wyoming although he did not say what for. As for Mr. Taylor he had gradually become more and more unhinged after hearing the news at knowing of the man's eventual return and also remembering his vow to implement his share of the ranch within the boundaries of the secret fathers will made up years before and that the man also retained a copy of it in his own possession. With this in mind Mr. Taylor had concurred to one of his cattle hands, or this being Scott Terence, that for a certain profit which Mr. Taylor would pay to him after completion of the job and also with the promise of being made foreman one day he was to carry out the underhanded and grim mission of going down and finding the adversary or soon returning foe where at once upon finding him he would either kill him or stifle the man from coming up further anymore, though Mr. Taylor knew that the later would hardly be expected. He had also told the young cattle hand that if he did not carry out what he wanted or declined to go he would be let go and in danger himself without hardly any prospects of finding another suitable position in those parts.

The ambivalent worker was not adamant about accepting the job, however, but Mr. Taylor as usual got his way and swayed him into it as he also knew he was an admirer of Marry Mulligans and was now in the frame of mind of having thoughts that at least he would have enough money earned from the job to wed the thrifty and ambitious lady providing she was accepting, of course, and with the promise too of eventually be made foreman of the ranch.

It would only be a matter of time upon taking up Mr. Taylor's bargain when Scott would catch up with the man he had agreed to hinder, or only after riding down to where the man was supposedly staying at in a small town in Kansas called Newberry and that Mr. Taylor had overheard the name from the other ranchers when they had been talking. Only after Scott had become acquainted with the man himself which was done through a series of seemingly friendly and innocent enough exchanges between him and the other as he had intended he eventually got the man to let Scott accompany him up to Wyoming telling him he was headed that way himself though was really with the intent of fulfilling Mr. Taylor's wishes of somehow discouraging or even harming the man as to not letting him be able to continue. By then, however, Scott had also developed an unsurfaced liking for the newly met stranger as he did not have many other friends who he saw as trusting and that he could comfortably talk to or even his own boss, needless to say, but as their journey progressed was now more and more becoming unresolved to what he would do knowing he would have to confront the issue eventually when they were alone and he felt it was safe for him to do this as the two made their up from the plainly midwestern states.

One day as it happened, though, Scott finally came out with his plaintiff and attempted to dissuade the man from returning to the destined Wyoming Ranch in a quick and unexpected frenzy. To this, however, the man just became confused and apprehensive as to why he thought he should not return but then Scott not knowing what to do finally told him the truth about himself and how he was another cattle hand of Mr. Taylor's and that he had been sent down by him to disparage the man from coming up, even if it meant killing him. Upon hearing this the other became immediately solemn in demeanor and hardly said anything except that he was going to go up no matter what thinking that the other didn't have it in him. At the time they were alone standing next to the tall drop of a cliff with the distant sound of a flowing and sweeping river at the summit below as Scott was holding his gun to the man shakily but then told him to turn his back as the other stood off near the edge of the descent. Slowly the man turned having his own gun still down below his waist as Scott kept his held up at the man's back and ready to shoot. Suddenly though the man reached for his gun and in a quick draw as he turned around managed to shoot Scott in his side near his waist although Scott still managed to fire at the man wounding him in his left shoulder as he fell from the cliff down into the river.

As for Scott he had already fallen flat onto the ground at the time of being shot and was on his back with his leg slightly bent up. For a few moments more, he lay there as he slowly took his hand to his wound, and then, just as slowly brought it up in front of his face as he could see the blood stained onto his skin as his face began to quiver with fear. In a natural reaction he quickly lifted his torso up off the ground and pushed himself over by kicking his feet haphaz-ardly to the wall of a large rock in back of him looking down the whole time at his wounded side. Then, almost as soon as he did this he looked straight out to the edge of the cliff where the man had gone over and having a look on his face as though he had seen a ghost. As he got up off the ground slowly keeping his hand to his wound he staggered over to the edge and looked down at the river but could see nothing of the other man thinking he must have been swept away by the current. The only thing that remained of the others though as Scott turned away and looked in back of him was the man's horse standing slumped on the side next to his own as he started to make his way up to it taking the horse by the harness with his unoccupied hand. Deciding to reach into the horse's satchel then to see what was inside a deplorable feeling was felt within knowing that he had just killed a man and taken another's life, but vaguely and not fully understanding what it meant nor hardly being able to realize what he had done himself. As he looked, however, there were only a few things in the satchel though, or possessions of the other man, including a beat up looking tin canteen along with some chewing tobacco, and a not so ungenerous amount of money he took out from a separate leather pouch and laying loose in the satchel though he paid hardly any mind to it as he put the money back almost as soon as he had removed it. Strangely, then, he took out what ap-peared to be a small, but, still sizable, and peculiarly looking box made of some darker hard wood and with a pretty gold leafed trim even on the outside as he opened it up to see if anything was inside. Upon doing this though he was met with that timely but old familiar hymn of *My Darlin' Clementine* as he looked down and could see the turn of the gold-plated reel oscillating from inside. After listening a moment more he closed the box again and put it off to the side on the ground next to him, but then, thinking nothing else was left inside the satchel he reached into another small flap as he felt around to pull out what was a folded and old looking piece of paper or some type of formal document. As he unfolded the paper though he realized what it was as he read the fine and bold looking script written down on it even in his half illiterate tongue and could see that it was more or less a kind of will or deity claim, the very same one that Mr. Taylor's father had made out years before between himself and the cattle hand he had just killed and the same reason why Mr. Taylor had wanted to get rid of the man in the first place.

Still feeling shaken from what had just happened and knowing the piece of paper was important he strangely decided to keep it and folded it back up as he picked up the music box off the ground next to him and opened the lid again as its simple tune began to play. Then, instead of placing it inside the box he tucked it into a fabric lining on the bottom of the lid where it had been torn for some reason thinking that it would not be noticed as easily. Still, he knew he had to get rid of the horse and all that remained upon it so after putting the music box and will in his own satchel he went and undid the satchel and harness of the others as he carried both over to the edge of the cliff and threw them down into the river as well. Going back over to the horse now with its bare back and standing behind it he would give an abrupt hard slap to its behind, then, as he waved his arms about while the horse slowly and rather eerily went away up into the steep surrounding brush and hills. Once back on his horse as he sluggishly got on to his saddle he took one last look around and set off knowing he needed tending to his wound fast though just the same knowing he could not stop and that the trip back to the ranch would be a ways.

As he made his way over the next few days though hardly stopping except to rest for a moments of relief and with the slug still in his side while bleeding more and more, and his clothes where he had been shot soaking in blood, he finally collapsed one day from off his horse onto the ground in a field of some tall grass as he lay there next to it with the breeze and wind blowing over him, and through the grass, also, strewn around his head and body. Still slightly conscious he would lay there some more as the afternoon sun shone down on him in the plain light of day. It was after this though when the small and stoic figure of an Indian man dressed in animal furs and jacketed in deer skin leathers came on through, as he noticed the man, or Scott lying there half dead on the ground, but the Indian himself hardly showing any signs of startlement from the site of it.

The Indian dismounted from his calmly paced horse, nevertheless, walking up to him a few steps after having knelt down to see if the young man was still alive as he approached him carefully, but upon seeing that he was he would then by himself manage to rig up a small, but, still yet, efficiently assembled pulley as for the use of bringing back Scott to his own homestead which he would attach afterward to the young man's sedentary horse, still hovering nearby, as it slowly drag Scott off with him back into the woods and forest. It would be a few hours after that, however, until they would reach to wherever the Indian was taking themselves to, but by then Scott on deaths door and barely awake. Not so incidentally though the name of the Indian riding in front and who had found him was the one called, Rolling Tides, but the same one that Mr. Taylor had spoken of. He lived in his log cabin fairly nearby just as Mr. Taylor had said and not too far from the old Indian reservation where he had found the wounded young stranger while he had been out hunting that morning and mid evening to bring back food and nourishment for the coming months.

Upon arriving at his hut or small cabin situated somewhere quietly in the woods with only the presence of a small stream running through, the Indian, or Rolling Tides, descended from his old warrior horse and quickly got Scott from off his woodsman pulley as the door of the modest wood structure was opened by someone hidden from inside and darkly lit with the only promise and slightly glare of a small fire coming from within as smoke could be seen as well coming from a jutting piped chimney outside on the roof.

Rolling Tides carried Scott over his shoulder, then, to the door and into the dark cabin as it was closed behind him by the same person who had opened it from the inside. After this he put Scott down on a small bed or cot that was not too far from the sound and warmth of a crackling wood burning fire on the other side of the room. Seeing he was shivering now and sweating all over the smoothed moving and pensive Indian checked his forehead for fever as he placed his hand over the top of his face. Feeling that his head was burning up Rolling Tides looked to his wound afterward as he removed his blood soaked shirt and jacket around Scott's arm and could see as he had thought that the young man had been shot and knowing too that the bullet was still in his side.

As the wearily Indian continued looking down at Scott for a moment with his straight gaze and war painted head he went over to the fireplace taking out his knife from his side and stuck it in some red burning coals on the edge of the fire. Then, turning to the other person he was with, he said something in his poor English enunciation telling them to get some water from the small stream running outside not too far from the cabin as whomever it was went and took a bucket sitting over in the corner and proceeded out of the cabin through its door closing it behind them on their way out. A few moments went by but then the Indian went back to his knife still embedded in the fire and took it by its handle as he brought it back over to Scott's bed kneeling down beside him and placing his hand above the wound with the knife in the other. Although Scott was hardly conscious he painfully squirmed as Rolling Tides stuck the scalding hot tip of the knife inside the wound to remove the bullet. As the knife brazed the skin the sound of it could be heard along with some smoke coming out of the wound while the Indian felt around with the tip. Turning the knife slightly angled as Scott continued to show discomfort the Indian finally managed to locate the small piece of round levering it out of the wound with the knife as a blood soaked cartridge was repelled from Scott's side plopping down onto the cot next to him. After this he took the coiled metal in hand as he stood up and scrutinized it holding it to his face to see its shape and if it was intact. Seeing that it was he put it aside near the fire and went back over to Scott taking hold of his arm but still seeing that he was in great discomfort though his eyes remained closed. The cabin door was suddenly opened then as the person who had gone out came in carrying the bucket now filled with cold water over to the Indian as he took it from out of their hands setting the bucket down on the floor next to the cot. Making a gesture with his hand then he told the person to get a piece of cloth on the other side of the room as they went over and brought it back to himself as he took the rag in hand standing over Scott and soaking it in the bucket. After wrenching out the rag he took it and placed it on top of Scott's forehead as the Indian or Rolling Tides took the other persons arm and hand standing behind him and brought it over to hold the rag in place while he went back over to the fire and stuck the knife into the hot coals once more as he blew over them so that they lit up brightly red and making the blade of the knife scalding hot. As Scott kept laying there, however, he suddenly opened his eyes looking up at the person who was holding the rag to his forehead, momentarily becoming conscious, but seeing the small and shadowed figure of a young lady looking back at him with her long and lightly stranded hair and face slightly illuminated by the fire as her still and placid eyes stared into his own. Now getting more and more faintly though, Scott reached for the young ladies arm but fell back down as soon as he had lifted it while the old chieftain came back over to the young man's side with the knife in hand. Then, telling the other to keep the rag to his forehead, he took the side of the scorching hot knife and put it to Scott's wound in an attempt to sear it closed as the sizzle of the burning skin could be heard and as Scott could barely contain himself just lying there and yelling out from the pain with his face straining and tightening from it.

After the wound had been seared and Scott lay back in the cot enmeshed from the pain and just weak from the ordeal the Indian went then and got a small stool somewhere in the cabin for the girl to sit on and apply the rag to his head soaking it in the bucket every so often as Scott continued to tremble with fever. As for Rolling Tides, he boiled some of the water by the heat of the fire, or that he took from the bucket using various fragrant smelling herbs and lentils he took from out a small pouch in one of his pockets and gave it to the girl to give to Scott as he sipped it down little by little from a clay bowl she held in her hand. As she did this the red skinned native stood over the two and began a lightly chant with his deep and mythic ritual sounds while holding an ancient totem in his hand meant to ward off evil spirits or apparitions that might be near, but Scott barely opened his eyes after that as he lay there in the dark and musty shelter and as the Indian and girl continued to tend to his life much unlike the one he thought he had taken just a few days before.

10

The rest of that evening had gone by uneventful as to Scott's condition but a few days would pass until he would finally come to and open his eyes again. It was late now, almost dusk, and the cold damp early spring weather of March could be felt permeating outside as Scott lay there sweaty on his cot with a fresh cloth around his wound while the girl who had been wetting him down with the towel and having the rag still clenched in her hand lay asleep on the chair next to him, and her back up against the cabin wall. After a few moments then, Scott suddenly opened his eyes wider than he had, or ever since the Indian had first found him laying out in the field so that he could finally see where it was he was being kept at, although not knowing how long he had been there.

As for the Chief he was asleep himself on a cot against the other side of the wall, near the fireplace, with the dim glow of some burning ambers entrapped and radiating from out of its stone trove. Only a moment more passed by until the girl was awakened in her slouched position sitting out on her stool and could the see young man's eyes fully open, and more conscious than he had. Upon this she stood up to look at the stranger with her own undiscerning eyes, hesitating, as she went over to waken her Indian companion still sleeping in his cot and lightly snoring. After she tug at him he was quickly wakened though and rose up from his cot just as smoothly and unhastened as earlier on only going over to Scott as if to perform another remedy, but with his same Indian clad, wrinkled face showing little expression. As for Scott he just lay there looking back at him and not saying anything but the hovering Indian over him going on to just gesture to the girl standing aside as the young man looked over at her momentarily. As he lay there, however, he couldn't help but think he had seen a girl or young lady like her before, as her demeanor and the way she carried herself was oddly formal for the setting but suggested a well - rounded education and bringing up though he was not sure where or in what way he had.

After coming back from the fire then with some more of the hot water and some of the Indians herbs she came over to Scott with the same clay bowl she had used earlier on as he could now see her close up but herself helping him drink down another sip of the brew while he looked up at her the whole time in an odd enough way, knowing now he had somehow once seen her, but still not placing where it was. As he looked, however, the young lady shied away seeing the look on his face as if about to tremble but the Indian just took the bowl out of her hands, sensing this and said something to her in his Native tongue, so that she quickly went out of the cabin, although Scott not presuming why.

As the Indian gave him another sip of the steamy liquid he suddenly began to speak to him in his very poor English trying to place the words he wanted to talk the whole time as the other listened in his weakened state but able to discern what he was saying enough. At first he told him his name, but only in his own language, and then what it meant in the white man's English as he went on afterwards to say what tribe he was descended from, or the Winnipeg as he called them by name – a lower tribe or descendent of the Pawnee, who, by then, had given over most of their land, or, more or less, lands to the present government and those stationed at the nearby Fort Brent now under their jurisdiction, but went on to say that he had been a distinguished warrior though did not wish to live where the rest of his fellow tribesman or what was now left of them living out on the land reservation that had been dealt to them by the white man, or just as young Scott was himself. As he was listening, however, the young lady came in from outside with some more wood in her hands for the fire that all the while during the Indians discourse had been slowly dying as the girl placed the split timbers into the mouth of the stone furnace for more warmth and now that the young man was coming to, and perhaps, even getting better. Still, he had lost quite a bit of blood and did not seem well enough to get up as he just glanced over at the girl who was now traversing over to her cot as she climbed into it while the native could see this. Turning back to Scott, then, as he glimpsed the girl himself the Indian or Rolling Tides went on to finally tell his wounded white man of how it was he had come to find her as Scott listened to his more somber spoken words thus far, though eventually, realizing, or to his astonishment where it was he had indeed seen her before – "She has been with me. Young girl I found - Now stay here along with Rolling Tides. Took her out, hiding in small cave not far from where white man had come and kill all – Her mother, father and brother. She did not do anything for a long while, and would not *see* with her eyes," he said lifting his hand to place both fingers over his eye lids. "– Blinded by those who take from her. But now she can see as before and does only want to stay here and be with me. I am not alone now, but she must go back to her own one day, unlike myself apart. And I then, a lonely warrior rolling along the tides."

For a moment Scott turned his head away from the gravely sounding Indian as he had been speaking to him lying silent on his cot but was sure, or at least surmised, who the girl was now and that she was no other than the same prestigious young lady who he had heard and seen about in the papers a while back reported to still be missing and whose parents had been murdered by the bloodied Colby Jenkins gang. As Scott turned back afterwards to look at the native the tribesman continued in his simple and broken English, though with a slight look of caution, "...You too may return to your kind soon. The bullet was not deep. But – had lost much blood. Better to rest now I think," he went on as he stood up from the man's side and went out the cabin door in his calmly manner. Now that he was gone Scott was still sort of apprehensive about the Indians aforesaid refugee and if she really was who he had thought she was, so after a moment or two more he somehow gathered enough strength to rise up on the cot. Then, rather slowly and keeping his hand over his wound while he did Scott gently walked over to where the girl was laying as she was now asleep underneath some bearskin looking blankets as he stood there gazing at her head that was sticking out into the light of the fire. Suddenly her eyes opened though as she could see him gawking at her and giving off a frightful, yet, stern look of eye, as he made his way back to his cot and laid down again, but she being just as fearful almost of him as he was of her. Nevertheless, the girl just resumed to lay there in her bearskin made up bed, similarly, and fell back into her sleep shortly. As for Scott he was fully sure now as he lay there that she was, in fact, the same flaxen haired girl who he had seen down in the papers, but just the same, in his precarious state of what to make of it. Amid all of this, however, Rolling Tides had only been outside smoking his pipe and of all things going through the young man's satchel that was still clung to his horse on the other side of the cabin. Just as he was or had been a simple Indian warrior though he was far from a fool, and, had known for the most part that the man inside of his cabin and that he had saved from certain death had come to him by means of some foul play, and was most likely the guilty culprit himself. Still, he knew Scott would not havoc anymore and even though he was wounded in a physical sense his bigger wound was within so that to think him causing anymore danger than he was to himself would be unnecessary at the moment. There was not much in the satchel though that he could render as means for any reason of misconduct or suggested it but just a few rounds of ammo along with a deer skin canteen that was well empty, and, of course, the music box Scott had taken with him having Mr. Taylor's will obscurely tucked inside. As the Indian handled the unique looking box in his hands admiring it he opened the lid up momentarily, but, could hear then the lightly music it played as he took it closer to his ear. He closed it though shortly after still puffing on the small Uncle Ben's type pipe he was smoking, but oddly, just before he went to put it back had decided he would hold on to it and bring it inside with him to give to the girl as a present, or gift, but not before replacing it with his Indian war knife he kept at his waist as if a small token or worthily trade for it. As he opened the cabin door slowly at first with the music box still in hand he looked to see if Scott, or the young man could see him coming in or if he was asleep though he was not and had merely just turned away with his eyes shut in his deranged and paranoid state trying not to incite the Indian. The other, however, went over to the girl now asleep and placed the music box underneath the skin pelts though she remained to be sleeping as the Indian went over to his own place of retirement and laid down removing the pipe from his mouth as he settled and resting it next to him on the side. Time would go by, or almost over an hour until Scott himself would get up again thinking everyone else was asleep as he had only been waiting to make his next move and leave the Cabin away from the girl and Indian and then to continue and make his way up to Mr. Taylor's ranch, but hardly now with the intent he had started out with or before from the shock of killing the man and then being rescued from death by the Indian accompanied with the girl that he had recognized and along with the rest of the calamity he was presently steepened in.

He stood to his feet with all this mind, regardless, and slowly, then, by trying not to disturb a flee in the whole cabin started making his way quietly out the door but not first without picking up and taking his boots along with him that had been removed by the girl and Indian next to his cot, as well, as, his raw hide cowboy vest which was hanging from a small hook like splinter that seemed to be sticking out of the cabin wall and still stained from his blood with the bullet hole in it though his much more blood inundated shirt and undergarments had already been taken and burned up in the fire. The wisely Indian just as well opened his eyes now facing away from Scott himself as he could hear the door creak open as Scott made his way out then, and as if Rolling Tides knew he would intuitively go, but, of course, that there would be no reason to stop him and that he was only wandering helplessly between the winds the warrior, and native, and those like him intrinsically worshiped. Closing the door then, thinking he had escaped without detection he quietly went over with his arm still tucked in as before and looked in back of the cabin to see if his horse was there. Although it was very dark without hardly any light except for the half – moon above showing through the clouds he could see his horse standing upright next to the Indian's. For a moment he looked back to the cabin door to make sure he was clear, but then, turned again to his horse and proceeded over to it in his weakened manner trying not to make the horse or the one next to it flinch or startle them. As he took the reins of his horse with his good arm after giving a few strokes to the nuzzle he put his naked foot in one of the stirrups not even bothering to put on his boots as he held onto them while he carefully mounted the animal as not to make any sounds precariously using mostly his good arm to do this. Once he was on top he was nearly content he had almost gotten away without the others knowing but could see the Indians old war horse translucent and foreboding eyes staring back at him as he waited for a moment before strolling off with a look of fear and trepidation written on his face. As he pulled away from the rural homestead the clouds overhead began to cover the half shaped moon more and more as a storm would soon be encroaching but Scott hardly knowing himself of course nor showing any slight concern for the coming forecast, but instead with just thoughts of getting back to the ranch and interrogating Mr. Taylor once and for all regardless of how long he had to live, or if he would even make it, yet somehow knowing he would if just for that much.

It was much later but the storm that had promised to come had already bestowed itself throughout the night as Scott had been unrelentingly trying to ride back to make his return. Now drenched and soaked to the brim as he rode upon the country scape without stopping once to break he was getting frigidly cold and close to exhaustion and without the help of his side and in his weakened state was only making him more and more vulnerable to sickness. The night was slowly turning over to the early morning hours as Scott got closer and closer to the cattle baron's ranch and was in near reach of it by early dawn though it was still dark out with the storm gradually dying down, finally, but Scott well sick now and close to having pneumonia.

As for Mr. Taylor that night and early morning he lay asleep in his bed next to Mrs. Taylor and had steadily been sleeping when suddenly he was woken by something though he did not know what and woke without being startled, but instead, slowly opening his eyes having a feeling something had happened as to make him get up nor without waking Mrs. Taylor. Then, quietly putting his bathrobe on he went to make his way out of the room and down the upstairs hall as he descended the steps of the stairs holding onto the white spindled railing along the side. At first he looked over in the far den hesitating just before looking in and only seeing what was there by using the bright and sharp pulses of lightning that were coming from outside through the tall frames of the draped windows, but only leaving shortly after to look elsewhere or outside somehow knowing something was lurking in his belated manner. After going back over near the stairs, however, and looking in another room on the other side he could see nothing there either, but finally decided he would go out onto his porch as he opened the front entrance door and crept out. Outside he could feel the cool, dampened air around him as he looked into the distance as just another flash of lightning came from overhead, though he still did not notice or hear anything to suggest something was there. As he went to turn back though he heard something again coming from a large shed that was on the side of the estate between the cattle ranch and hut where the workers were fast asleep and all slumbering from the last day's hard work. As he made his way over to the obstruction though he could not see anything or anyone at first in the darkness as he looked side to side to see what had made the queer noise. He was about the turn back again when another flash of lightning came overhead, but as he looked he suddenly saw the cryptic figure of a man before him his pants and jacketed vest worn and torn looking and the man bent over slightly, his heavy breathing easily discernable from the air he was heartily puffing in and out across his face. Looking as if about to go for a gun in one of his bathrobe pockets Mr. Taylor went to utter the words, "Who goes there?" but before getting the words out he was interrupted by a familiar voice knowing at once who the man was, or no more than the young cattle worker he had sent to do his dirty work a few scores ago as Scott Terence had indeed made the whole trip back to the ranch never minding the elements against him to face his boss Nelson Taylor for what he knew would be the last time as Mr. Taylor stood there helpless but to feel shocked from his sight.

"I've come back. Don't you recognize me, Mr. Taylor?" Scott lamely uttered in his thinly voice and trying to gather breath to speak as the other stared back at him trying not to look too shuddered to his appearance as Scott hugged his waist looking as if he was about to drop dead. Mr. Taylor just kept playing along, however, trying not to bring any more attention to the scene and with intentions of just getting Scott into a concealing area before anyone knew he had returned and in his horrible state knowing it would be fatal for himself as well. So, in spite of all this, Mr. Taylor just stayed calm and spoke out in his seemingly kind and amiable voice as Scott continued to stand there next to the wood shed he had been leaning up against while Mr. Taylor had been speaking.

"Sure I recognize you – *Scott*?" he said. "I was wondering when you'd be getting on back," Mr. Taylor continued as he approached his limped and sickened cattle hand slowly trying to sway him.

"Like *hell* you were!" Scott said sort of beguilingly to himself and still leaning up against the shed with his back to it as Mr. Taylor had come over in front holding him up now, but the cattle owner looking ever more anxious of possibly causing any attention to them. With this in mind he decidedly took Scott into the shed by holding him up himself by the side as the other shrieked at first from his mended wound, though Mr. Taylor replied just to hush up and not make any noise as he took him into the shed which was spacious enough for them to both fit in where he laid Scott out on the floor next to some barrels in the far corner. As he lay there Mr. Taylor just took off his bath robe and covered the young man and now that he was shivering and getting sicker. Mr. Taylor stayed at his side though listening carefully to what would be his final and weakened words trying to find out what he could of what had happened to him or whatever he could tell him.

"Looks like you've been shot there Scott," Mr. Taylor kindly pointed out as if he didn't know it himself while he lifted up the robe slightly to look but could see the blood stained vest underneath as he knelt over Scott in his night clothes.

"*I was shot alright*," the other painfully jabbered from his lips. "... I was shot and this Indian came and found me," he sluggishly continued. "That's why I'm still *livin'*."

He laughed a little similarly to before as he finished the phrase, but looked solemn in his face right after. Mr. Taylor didn't say anything looking down towards the young man but began asking him and wanting to know what had happened to the one whom he had sent to get rid of, or if he had even met up with him though he knew somehow he had.

"Did you happen to take care of what we had talked about?" Mr. Taylor asked innocently enough though Scott didn't speak up at first just laying their gasping for relief.

"Sure did," he finally said. "I reckon I went and *killed* that man you wanted me the find."

Mr. Taylor hovered over him barely giving out a grin as his face almost glowed.

"How, uh, you figure's on that Scott?" he asked in his morbid inquisitiveness.

"Cause I shot him myself," Scott barely got out. Then, almost looking of dread again he continued, "- Fell off a cliff and *everything*. Right down into the river."

Mr. Taylor just grinned to himself after hearing this at least knowing now that his adversary was most likely gone and even dead and would not be returning to lay claim for his part of the ranch, but knew still that if anyone saw them, just then, or knew that Scott had returned in such condition, the two would undoubtedly be implicated as to all their murderous and blood shed business as he, instead, just continued to listen to the young man lying there and looking up talking in his gibberish language, as Mr. Taylor was almost contemptuously waiting for him to breathe his last breath, only to get rid of him after as fast as possible so no one would find him.

"Well, that's real good there Scott," Mr. Taylor remarked in his unremorseful candor though Scott knew just as well his boss was as far from good as the word itself. Scott just sort of smiled a strange grin though as Mr. Taylor could see him and inquired why he was.

"What's the matter, Scott?" The cattle owner asked smiling himself.

"I know why you wanted me to go down there and kill that man," Scott said in a firm and devious sounding whisper as Mr. Taylor's face looked inept again. "I found that will made out to him in his satchel," Scott went on trying to gather breath. "I brought it all the ways back with me, over in the horse shack on top of my Colt."

"Well, now. That's good to hear their Scott," Mr. Taylor kept on complimenting him. Looking as if he had a great secret to tell Taylor Scott reached out and grabbed his underclothes as he said, "Hid it inside the seam of some music box he had, along with the will – just in case. *You know?*" Letting go of his boss Scott went silent again as Mr. Taylor kept at his side looking down but really with the earnest intent of just wanting to see to what he had brought back with him.

"You just rest easy for a moment now Scott while I go see to that will," he said reaching for his bathrobe and tucking it over his deeply sick assassin while Scott lay there profusely shivering in the cold. Standing to his feet then, Mr. Taylor came out of the shed though it was still slightly raining with shades of lightning here and there as he went to look for Scott's horse where he figured it would be over in the horse shack that was on the other side of the ranch next to where the men were sleeping. As expected he was very quiet as he made his way trying not to wake anyone but knew the men were hard asleep, and a few even loudly snoring as he entered the shack when just another flash of lightning from above could be discerned. One by one he passed by each horse kennel some occupied and others empty but only looking out for Scott's horse to see what was in the satchel. Again, it was very dark inside but Mr. Taylor was reluctant to light one of the lanterns hanging about in fear of creating or drawing any attention and just as well knew his way even in the dark as he had been in the shack for many a time before and relied on his other senses for sight. Feeling that something was ahead of him he stopped for a moment before continuing when the head of a darker haired steed appeared in front as he could see its red glaring eye looking back at him while coming up to it trying not to arouse any excitement by taking it from the long strands of its mane and stroking it keeping the horse firm in his hands. Then, turning his attention as he noticed the satchel mounted onto his back he looked at it with focused eyes to see what was inside feeling with one of his hands as he held the reigns of the horse in the other. At first he could feel something but wasn't sure what it was as he took out Scott's canteen and strapped it over his shoulder as he continued feeling inside and, then, of all things, took out the knife Rolling Tides had put in place of the box, but hardly knowing what it was at first and not understanding why he would have it. After this, however, he decidedly went to get a match near a lantern as he walked over to get it down from a shelf of one of the horse docks and then walked back to light it as he swiped carefully away from the horse and took the small flame to the knife as it appeared to be an authentic Indian dagger with a holster made from buffalo skin and having an animal bone handle as he looked at it in his hand for a moment more before tucking it underneath his night clothes and looking inside the satchel one more time with the light of the match but seeing no music box, as young Scott had said.

Almost as soon as he had lit it though, Mr. Taylor blew the match out bringing the horse inside the dock it was loose from and closing the gate gently behind. Then, still having the knife tucked in and the canteen over his shoulder he went back over to the other side of the property as quietly as he had come and back over to where Scott was but hoping like anything he was still alive. When he got back to the shed he saw Scott was still lying down in the same position as Mr. Taylor carefully walked in and as Scott opened his eyes barely.

"Well, you look like that Indian went and found me," Scott belched from the shed floor looking up at Mr. Taylor with his bleary eyes seeing that he was dressed at the moment in his ridiculous outfit as a shade of lightning flashed upon him and with the knife and canteen he was carrying. Mr. Taylor didn't say anything though having the same look on his face as when he had just been with him earlier on coming over to his side bent over.

"Uh? 'Bout that music box, Scott," Mr. Taylor spoke. "I looked in your satchel where you said it was, but there was nothing in it except for this here's knife and canteen."

"What d'you mean?" Scott said gathering more breath as he turned his head to the side for relief.

"Had it with me when I left," he went on. Scott had a puzzled look on his face, then, and set his head back as though a bad joke had been played on him though eventually realizing that the Indian must have taken the box after going through his satchel and that he had left his knife in exchange for it instead.

Almost with a grin now with some inextricable thought going through his mind while he lay there and knowing he was close to his last onset Scott spoke as Mr. Taylor listened uneasily, and now also knowing himself the will and music box were not with him.

"Well, I guess I didn't come through after all there Mr. Taylor." Scott paused with a cough and rolled his head some more before continuing. "That totem chief must've took it for that knife you've got under there."

Mr. Taylor didn't find any of this funny, needless to say, and just kept there at Scott's side looking down and with the thought of only trying to get out of him what more he could before he either did away with him himself or waited for him to expire though the way his partner looked the later seemed more promising.

"Hold on their Scott," Mr. Taylor said as he unstrapped the canteen from his shoulder and removed the cork from it. "Why don't you have a sip of water," he went on taking the canteen and pouring a small bit of water out onto Scott's faded and shivering lips as the water ran down Scott's chin and neck swallowing little. As he did this he asked, "Did you happen to get the name of that Indian man by chance?"

At first it was difficult to think but Scott managed to remember it as his eyes opened wide placing the name and seeing the image of the Indian in his mind.

"Yes," he finally came out. "Said his name was - Rolling Tides." Mr. Taylor tried to look calm and understanding but now hoping like anything he knew where it was the Indian had taken him to, or at least where it was he found him.

"You don't happen to know where this Rolling Tides took you?" he asked Scott frayingly. Scott just closed his eyes again but not before reopening to answer.

"Brought me up to this cabin he lived in. Supposed to be close to some Indian Fort down there," he said as some spit roll down his cheek. As Mr. Taylor saw this he just gave Scott another sip of water though the water running down his cheek in the same way. Seeing Scott was slipping off he then asked,

"You don't happen to remember the name of that Fort? Do you, Scott?"

The young man just thought for a moment trying similarly as before to place the name.

"I reckon – a, Fort Brent that Indian told me," Scott finally said. "Next to where all his people said they lived," he went on. "On some Indian reservation."

As he got closer to Scott Mr. Taylor asked him another question but in a more softened tone knowing Scott was going fast. "Was he alone when he found you? What I mean is, did anyone else see you with him?"

Scott opened his eyes again as he answered, distinctly remembering the familiar girls face by the firelight he had seen with the Indian man.

"Yes," he said starring out as he went on as Mr. Taylor leaned in to listen. "There was this girl with him."

"Girl? Mr. Taylor asked. "What kind of a girl?"

Scott still had his eyes opened as he spoke.

"I had seen her before," he said turning to Mr. Taylor slightly. "It was the same girl I'd seen in the papers down on back," he continued drawlingly. "Wouldn't be surprised if that Indian gave her that box with the will inside as some present – But her rich parents..."

"Yeah?" Mr. Taylor asked noticing him slipping off.

"Gone and all killed by that Colby Jenkins gang." Mr. Taylor settled back in his face as he heard this, though Scott closed his eyes again. Turning his attention back to Scott he asked, "Anyone else?"

At this point though Scott looked to not answer, but, instead, took one last gulp as he looked up to Mr. Taylor next to him with his last thoughts belonging to the woman whom had been his main reason for making the trip in the first place though fatal it had proved for him as Mr. Taylor would calmly listen.

"Do me a favor?" he asked his cattle boss opening his eyes for one last time. "My Marry told me she was pregnant when I left. *You*..." and before he could finish the sentence, his head turned out, with his eyes withdrawn as Mr. Taylor could see he was no longer breathing and had stopped shivering, also, as he looked down at him with undiscerning eyes at his still face, and sensing he had finally slipped away. Upon this he immediately got up but not before covering the body with some loose hay strewn about, or that Scott had been laying near in back as he knew now he would have to get rid of the body somehow and taking all precautions to do this quietly as he could, knowing if anyone saw him doing this it would mean almost certain death for him. Hurrying along then, he went out the shed door looking around as it was still dark outside, though he could not see any signs of anyone around still, or awake other than him, as he made his way back up the steps of his front porch to open the entrance door and quickly as possible proceed to go back up to his room while trying not to wake up Mrs. Taylor, only to gather some clothes then to bring back with him to the shed where at once he would begin getting rid of Scott's tired remains. As he came through the door, however, in this most indicting way, he was met upon turning around by the glow of the chamber maid's lamp, as she held it in hand looking at Mr. Taylor with stern eyes and as Mr. Taylor looked back trying to look unsuspecting. Mainly she was Mrs. Taylor's porter and household accessory, but she had a room to herself in the back somewhere on the lower level of the household as she was usually called by the name of, Nanny, by the two though she was hardly partial to Mr. Taylor, or even Mrs. Taylor at times for that matter knowing well of their petty misdemeanors and that they were, in so many words, a pair unto themselves.

"Well, where have you been now?" she asked in an impetuous tone as Mr. Taylor stood there in his under clothes trying not to look guilty.

"Went outside cause I thought I heard something before," he said. "Figured it must have been raccoon somewhere."

"A raccoon?" she asked bluntly after a small moment's thought. "You were out there a long time for that if you ask me?"

"Well, Nanny," he underscored. "In that case - I would say, it must've been a *big* one −" though only trying to get rid of her most uninvited presence to make his way. To this, however, she just gave him a snug look and recanted her way back to her room carrying the lantern she was holding still in hand. Nevertheless, as expected Mr. Taylor started his way back up the fancy columned stairs and down the hall to his room where Mrs. Taylor was still asleep in her bed as he waited for a moment before entering making sure of this by opening the bedroom door slowly and entering the room after, closing the door just short of all the way behind him in the darkened room. Then, after looking over at Mrs. Taylor who was lightly snoring and turned onto her side he began creeping over to what was his tall and bourgeois looking armoire standing up like the shadowy abyss it was in the far corner of the room and opening up one of the cabinet doors to remove a shirt that was more rugged from his formal type wardrobe and that he would wear when working with some of the cattle hands on the ranch. As he closed the cabinet door then he could hear Mrs. Taylor turning over on her side facing himself as he looked at her sleeping face hoping she would not wake up. Seeing that she wouldn't he then opened up another bottom drawer to remove a pair similarly worn dungarees but looking back over at Mrs. Taylor again as he closed the drawer, though just short of all the way before making his trip back to the bedroom door, but not after Mrs. Taylor turned again to the other side as he looked at her with a small grin making his exit by slowly reopening the door only planning to go back downstairs and then to get his boots out of the den where he usually kept them.

As he was doing this he was very quiet, again, and looking out for the chamber maid the whole time, though he thought she wouldn't summon her presence anyway but making sure she was not around by looking over his shoulder as he got his boots that were laying out on the floor sitting upright next to a bureau along one of the walls of the den as he then began to make his way to the door. Nonetheless, as he looked over the railing of the stairs to make sure she was not there and seeing that she wasn't in fact, he made his way out of the entrance door with the clothes and boots in hand and started his way back to the shed where Scott was still lying dead on its open bare floor. It was fairly dark out but the early morning hours were soon going away when first signs of light would be dawning, although he knew the workers would not be up too soon either since it was there day off and had spent the night in town carousing up at the saloon and drinking steadily, but still knew he only had so much time to dispense of Scott's body and get back in time as to not be seen. The lightning that had been occurring earlier on had also abruptly, gone away, for the moment, as Mr. Taylor entered the shed stealthily holding his clothes and boots and seeing his dead partner with the burgundy colored bathrobe covering him and in the same position with the bits of hay on top as he had done just before leaving him.

Briskly, he put his clothes on not even bothering to remove his night-clothes, and then, his boots onto his bare feet. After this, he went over to the body as he gave it one last look just before he would drag it over in front of the shed door, and then, planning to prepare to make his way to the horse shack again so in order to straddle back, not only his own horse, but that of Scott's tired and lamed one laying down now in his kennel where he had left him. Providing then that he thought no one would be wakened and looking out for anyone that might be outside of the worker's hut, though he knew it would only be to go to the nearby stall or outhouse next to it, he would somehow have to get them both back over to the shed, nor without being detected or waking anyone.

Going along with his plan once getting back to the shed he could still hear the snoring of the men coming from inside but felt confident no one would wake as he entered in the same way like last time by opening the stable door half way, and then, going over to the kennel, or one of the first ones in the row to open the gate to get out what was his own finely clipped and freshly groomed mount while steadying the animal by keeping it firm. After reaching, then, for his saddle which was on a lower shelf between the outside of the kennel he reached down to only start strapping it in place by buckling up the leather flaps hanging off the saddle as the horse could be heard neighing and puffing a bit, Mr. Taylor trying to hush it with some strokes of his hand. He then took one of its reigns and loosely tied it off to the top of the gate gently closing it back up all the way trying not to make any sound. Feeling his horse would not move he knew he had to get Scott's horse next out from his kennel in the back as he sneakily did this knowing he was almost halfway through with his plan as he passed over each kennel again just as he had done before to get it out.

Just before opening the kennel gate he would give the horse a sort of de-ceptive look though as the resting equine came over to him eventually without hardly any coercing of his own. Keeping his eye on the horse then he closed the gate slowly locking it in place with its latch nor needing to put the saddle on to its back unlike his own horse, of course, since it had it on top still this whole time or when he had put him away earlier.

After though he took one of the straps or reigns of the horse and started walking down to the other end as he let go of the other to undo the strap he had tied off, and then, taking both of either straps in hand as he walked the two to the end of the shack stopping just before heading out with both horses and opening the gate all the way while making sure it was safe for him to start back over by peeping his head out to see. As he listened he could hear no one or most certainly see no one was up as he went to go back for the horses, tugging them out from the shack, knowing if he was going to get caught this would be the time, but always as was his luck making his way with both of the horses undetected and back to the shed. As the two stood quietly enough aside one another he then went on into the shed as he began and without wasting any time to drag Scott's tired body over to the door along with his red bathrobe on top still as he set him up in front of the entrance preparing to lift him up onto his shoulders. Before doing this, however, he took hold of Scott wrapping him up further with the bathrobe so that it draped most of his body, including the head and most of the legs, with the exception of the toes and boots that he had on as he started to lift him up by his torso though he could feel some stiffness as he did this, but by using most of his ardent strength, managed to lift him up onto his shoulders and then slowly opened the shed door to make his way out. After this he would then carefully slip the body onto Scott's horse as it slightly neighed but which he knew would not cause too much ruckus as the shed was a way's from where the men were sleeping and there even being a lightly fog setting in by that time to hide him. Only then, after, he would go back a moment more into the shed to retrieve a small shovel on the side for the carrying out of his dirty work, but while coming back to his horse to fasten it to his satchel, he could hear something back near the workers hut as he listened while a shrill of tension went up through his unnerved and derisive spine though it was just one of the workers coming out of the outhouse as he could hear the faint sound of its attached wood door shut, but sensing that the worker was well back on his way to his cot to resume his sleep hearing the hut door shut abruptly on after him. Being consoled by this and his face refraining from the fear of being caught he resumed his grin as he got up onto his horse and took the reign in hand of the others with the body of Scott wrapped in his bathrobe, and hanging off head to toe on both sides, as he gently set off into the foggy girth away from the house and cattle ranch, and into the nearing woods where he would continue his way deep within them until at one point when he thought it was safe enough he would take the shovel he had brought with him and start digging a most vacant and shallow grave for young Scott as he dragged him off from the horse and dropped him inside the small pit un-ravelling his bathrobe he was wound up in as he did it. After this he removed the saddle down from Scott's horse, or by his unusual name of "Curtain" as he had called him though the horse neighing and kicking his heel a little just as he did this but Mr. Taylor removing the saddle and satchel anyway and placing it over the body and then going on to shovel in the dirt on top of all in his hasty manner by using both the shovel and his own hands. Still, making sure that there would be no chance of others stumbling upon it and reassuring himself of this he took some nearby leaves and branches afterward and laid it here and there on top to give it an inconspicuous effect. Finally, though, there was Scott's horse, Curtain, standing bare backed and hardly moving as Mr. Taylor stood upright himself and giving the old honcho once last look as he stared into its cold marble eyes knowing he could not bring him back to the ranch, although unsure of what to do at this point and that there would always be the chance of him returning to the ranch regardless. As he looked around him in the densely wooded area the morning light was beginning to peak somewhere out in the far sky and the birds were chirping all over with the sound of a dis-tant crow or two as well. Unresolved slightly of what to do he had thought of shooting the horse at first by using a cloth wrapped round the leaver to hide the sound and withdrew his weapon almost with a reticence as to what he was about do and his face nervous with the callousness of the act, but before he could even make up his mind the sound of a hovering owl in one of the trees nearby could be heard hooting about, as Mr. Taylor looked up around himself and hesitating to commit to his plan. Suddenly, whatever it was swooped down through the trees with a loud wings and flustered on out as the horse kicked off, almost simultaneously, before Mr. Taylor could even go on with his devise, as Scott's horse fled without warning leaving Mr. Taylor alone in the empty darkness of the subliminal woods and where he had just dug Scott's craven grave as his own horse standing alongside looked to jump off as well, but the cattle boss managing to keep it from fleeing and calming it enough so it would not. As he looked around, however, he could not help but feel his own darkness not only of the woods but from within, as he started to gather up his shovel, and then, tucking into his satchel the dirtied bathrobe. Upon this he would begin to head his way back to the ranch as he would arrive just before or most of his other workers would be up and Mrs. Taylor for that matter. He went back though thinking it just as well the horse had fled, though he knew the distinctly cattle stamp of his ranch was still emboldened into its rear, and bearing the sign of one his workers horses should it be found, or either coming back by itself to the ranch and without sign of poor Scott with it. Whether he would return or not as horses often do to their owners time would only tell, but instead, for the present he was gone as Scott would be for all time onward, though unlike himself the question of whether he would come back unknown.

As for Mary Mulligans it was, indeed, Scott's child whom she had been with all along, unlike the stories told of Mr. Taylor's involvement with the unmarried and carefree sally it seemed, or as to the question of this, but instead, it would be Mary Mulligans finding out of Scott's true fate, or at least her own speculation of it the night she took the ether, that would cause her ill fate when Mr. Taylor's efforts of keeping her quiet of their affair was hardly met with ease, and after having gone and asked him vainly for money to help with the child. Nevertheless, Mr. Taylor would be the one she would learn this detail from, and in the end the truth as they say too much for her to bear, only eventually realizing Mr. Taylor for who he really was in their triangle of deceit. Still, the truth as seen by others, or to what really happened would go unknown just as that of Mary and her unborn child, but in the end, truth, the unlikely foe itself, and claiming all despite.

11

In turning back to the present to those other certain shenanigan's that were transpiring elsewhere to do with the sheriff, as well, as, the other lawmen and all the unvirtuous plotting that was taking place, it was, in so many words, the tolls of virtue and purity that continued to taunt Millie back at home with her parents, although quite differently than the crooked ordeals and circumstances of the previous. Instead, each day had gone by the same as the last as her own Internal psych more and more began to weigh her down waking up to the contemptible mornings, and then the slowly paced afternoons, but with the only relief of night that the other two had gone by. Millie's mother had already by then finished the dress though her daughters reflection of it after showing it to her one day could hardly been less satisfying but the young lady almost untruthfully admiring it like an act put on for her mother, but her mother carrying on the way she did just as distantly and as misunderstood as she felt of her.

School was now beginning again with the end of the summer months and Millie had returned for what would be her last year down at the small Little Cavern's one roomed school house somewhere between that of the town and her own homestead or place where she lived as it was a short enough distance to walk to, which she had always done before, but far enough still so that it would be a tiring enough distance each way. She would make her way, regardless, upon the dirt road and then crossing over some patches of woods following some worn and old grassy paths that led up near the school which was a tall and large cabin like structure with its tin piped chimney sticking sorely out from the middle almost like the Indian's own cabin as the children of all ages, some old as Millie and others young as seven and six from that area one by one made their way inside. Unlike all the other first days of school years before Millie's father Benjamin had driven his daughter to the school house this time in the small carriage they had as he knew it was her last year and hoping she would be surprised for his offering as he knew she was now becoming a woman and in his way trying to show his affection towards this by making the uninvited gesture. Nevertheless, she would accept the favor with as much vigor as she could muster but just answering with a simple, "Alright," to her father after he had asked her if he could do this for her in the early morning shortly before making her way out the front door.

Very few words were spoken for that matter between either of them which, of course, was not inordinate, but Benjamin just uttering a few words with his face starring out straight ahead and minding the reigns and horse the whole time going on about how she was now old enough to accept the custom of being driven to school instead of her usual long way of hiking and that if it were fine with her he would be willing to take her in the morning and even so much as to bring her back at the end of the day when she was through though Millie didn't say much to this other than, "Yes, father."

The name of the teacher that headed the school house as her younger and older pupils listened intently to herself standing up in front of the chalkboard during the age indifferently mingled classes was known as a Mrs. Motts – a slightly shrewd and single minded lady in her sternness during her teachings and giving out whatever assignment, and also having a slightly unsteadied voice as well so that her wit was matched with her intellect as if having a fragile bond.

That first day Millie had returned to school Mrs. Motts greeted her mentee eagerly as ever before as her well regarded and brightly promising student stood momentarily holding her notebooks up in front of the school house just before taking her seat in the back along with the other students her age including her friend Stella, who, like the others, had already been sitting for some time as class was about to begin. The teachers name or that of Mrs. Motts was written plainly on the board in a distinct descriptive style for those younger students who were not accustomed to her yet and those new to the school house.

As for Millie her response to Mrs. Motts was not as receptive as had been previous times but instead similarly to her parents she replied passively to the teachers reproach as she curtsied a little and proceeded to take her seat in her same subdued manner. As she continued to sit, however, just as Mrs. Motts went on to introduce herself to any of those that might be unfamiliar with herself or the young ones for that matter Millie had an uncomfortable feeling come over her in her silent state of being but as though sensing the eyes of those around her glancing over as she sat there at her desk and just the same somewhere within having the feeling or at least suspecting she knew what they were thinking. As she sat some more then she could see Stella out of the corner of her eye upon turning slightly looking to her side in back but easily could see her acutely and attractively featured face sharply pinned on herself though she quickly turned back to look up towards Mrs. Motts who was now writing something in her cursive style up on the chalk board, the younger children taking out their small chalk easels from their desk as the older ones started copying what she wrote in their notebooks using their ink pens.

Mrs. Motts had spoken to Millie by that time on more than a few occasions about continuing her education after finishing her last year at the school house or whatever more she could possibly show her and had even once suggested to her parents that she should go out East to a better suited college or even a University and learn to perhaps one day become a school teacher like herself or either invest in her literary and writing talents that she knew she had as well (And lending out many of her books or whatever she could give to her throughout the years at the school house). But, in the end it would be up to Millie what she wanted to do and although the prospect of fulfilling Mrs. Motts aspirations for her were once an enviable thing she no longer now saw anything having to do with continuing her education or becoming affiliated with the East as something worthwhile having difficulty enough deciding what she would do moment to moment and all her other worries coming from within.

As the school days and nights went by the last day like the next Millie was more and more becoming unresolved as to what she would do as she came into class in the early morning and went home feeling the same and the other students her age rarely speaking to her or making the gesture or even her friend Stella for that matter. Soon the dance she had increasingly been undesiring to go to and had, by then, built up a kind of firm inner fear of although she knew it would be almost approaching and finally taking place with only the winter recess and few colder Wyoming months ahead, as it had always been held and taken place during the last week and month of April, but Millie, contrarily, overhearing from the other students her age here and there about who would be going with, who, or which boy would dancing with which girl as they were so much more looking forward to it than herself and seeing this in their temperament and delighting faces as they made their small gossip in and out of class.

One day, as it happened then, her father had been driving her back from school as he had been doing almost every day since, but unlike other rides before after picking her up from the one roomed school house he seemed to be more astute to his daughter and in high gear towards his fondness for her and saying how it was good now that he could drive her and that he was gracious that she was accepting of this, thinking that there relativeness to one another had somehow deepened and carrying on towards this sentiment as Millie was hardly listening, but instead, just looking ahead and to the side of her with her troubling eyes and her gazed expression showing little apathy to her father's words as though thinking of something else. Nevertheless, it was then during that ride home when Millie began to feel her dilemma to point of separateness of what was real and what had been standing in front of her for those long and torrid months of acute anxiety and was now and had been almost completely replacing itself ever since with that reality. So, instead of coming off the carriage once it had stopped and once Benjamin had already gotten off she keeping with her mood and expression stayed dormant on top with a distinct stillness in her poise as her father came around as he would to see her off the buggy although his face and demeanor remained the same unknowing or ever unsuspecting of his daughter or her indifference.

After this, however, he went inside of their country house as he opened the door to enter while Millie followed him from behind and went up to her bedroom though uncannily it was as she would usually greet her mother first who was then busy in the den doing some of her knitting while Benjamin came in and took off his old and brawny looking wool coat to put and hang off the rack on the wall the opposite side of the stairs.

When Millie's mother or Kate saw Benjamin come in the room she barely looked up at him but just kept at her sewing like usual. Lifting her head momentarily though to look at him as he had his back turned to her now just then looking out the window she lowered her head back to her sewing and said, "Have a nice ride home?" Benjamin just kept looking out the window but seemed to be off in an aloof way almost admiring the day. Just then the mother gently spoke up again as she noticed him looking out.

"Benjamin - I was speaking to you?"

He answered back finally as he turned and became astute again.

"I reckon," he said seeing her sitting and with her sewing. Then, he started in suddenly about his thoughts regarding Millie and reminiscing slightly as he put his hands in back of him clenching them.

"I believe she's coming of age now, that girl," he said in his gruff tone.

"What do you mean?" Kate asked having an amused sort of expression to his reflection but knowing still something impressing was on his mind.

"Oh, I don't know," he replied with a thoughtful expression and lowering his head as though trying to express something he couldn't. "Just seems to me we should be thinking more about her leaving us soon. Goin' out East to be a school teacher like that Miss Motts told us," he went on turning to the window again. "That girl seems to be made more for than just out here." To this Kate didn't say anything at first but just stopped sewing and looked to the side as she raised herself and went over to Benjamin giving him a sort of look of finality as she knew deep down within something was going to happen and that they would somehow have to face it which through their own soft speculations would be that surfacing of what they already knew as truth.

"Now you know we don't have the money to send her away like that. How are we going to provide for her and where will the money for that university come from? We can barely keep up with things here the way they are, and I'm not sure if she could handle going out East like that Mrs. Motts thinks she should."

"No," Benjamin came in abruptly. "She has to. She can't stay here, Katie. You know that. She has to go out there and make up her mind what she wants to do, even if she'll be needin' to provide for herself to stay at one of those big schools they got once she's out there. That teacher of hers said she has the brains for it, and she can get that special grant she told us about so she can go and get herself an education. We can help her with some of the rest, but she'll have to go east first if she ever wants to come back and stay here with us. There's nothing else here for her if she stay's."

Millie's mother began to go back over to her seat to resume her sewing after hearing the father's remonstration trying not to say anything more in her apprehensive state. As she took up her design again and needle in hand she looked of thought for a moment but then realized Millie hadn't said hello to her after coming through the door which was odd, and then knowing she would go to the kitchen to have something to eat out of one of the cupboards as she didn't even hear this.

"That's strange. Did Millie come in before?" she asked Benjamin now getting his pipe out of his coat pocket that was hanging on the rack.

Hardly thinking about it he looked to her to answer.

"I reckon she did," he said. "Well, what's wrong?" he asked not knowing why she thought it strange and still seeing her unclear look to her.

"She didn't come in before," she said. "She always does," continuing, "And then right after to the kitchen."

Benjamin just stood there not saying anything and lighting his pipe as Kate went back to her sewing, but still thinking it odd.

"I think I'll go put, Marybeth away," he said, or what was the name of their horse as he went on puffing his pipe only while the mother had just lifted her head again seeing him leave. As soon as he had left out the door to do this though Kate was now left sitting alone with her embroidery, but shortly after had set it off to the side then, having an unsatisfied expression to her deciding she would go up to her daughters room once and for all, but to see what she was doing. As she got up from her lofty sewing chair she began heading over to the stairs looking up just before making her way one by one up the steps with her head peering ahead the whole time. When she reached the top she looked down the hallway to Millie's room hesitating just before going over to it though still suspecting something was wrong again but just the same unknowing of what could be afflicting her daughter or to why she did not come in to see her before. The door was slightly open as she looked cautiously to enter, but upon creaking it open as she slowly did she saw Millie at her vanity seemingly writing something down in her notebook she thought might be some of the abundant amount of homework her teacher would assign her, but seeing her calmly way and unnerved posture made her mother think little of her behavior as she would usually see her or always starring at something or concentrating on something she knew not what. Still unsure of what she was doing her mother asked as Millie turned to her nonchalantly,

"I'm just checking on you. Seeing if everything is alright?"

"Yes, Mother," she answered. "I'm – *fine*," she continued though with a feeling of strain behind the words.

"That's good," her mother replied passively, unsure of her tone and own passivity towards her question. Going on to leave as she was about to close her door as much as she had opened it she said, "Supper be ready in a little while. I'm sure you're hungry."

To this her daughter didn't say anything except, "Alright, mother," as she looked to go back to her writing though the despairing sound of her words only audible to those that knew what she was about to near do and why. Closing the door, then, the mother went back down to the kitchen feeling helpless herself to her daughter's lack of temperament, but carried on as she knew that was all she could do. As for Millie she was now by herself in her room as she looked down to see what she had been writing on a piece of paper from school. It read in blotched and dreary Ink:

"Forgive me for what I have done.
I cannot go on like this anymore.
Everyone has made me sick,
and I know I am not liked."

And underneath her name, or plain **Millie**, signed in the same dark blotchy ink – blackened as her soul.

12

Supper went by uneventful without hardly any talk from either of the parents keeping their thoughts quiet from their daughter or anything having to do with their previous talk about her although at one point Millie's mother pointed her head up towards her daughter and went as if she was about to speak. Benjamin seeing this though just looked to her, instead, and shook his head, deciding then that it was not the right time to bring up the matter trying to afford Millie of any early responsibility to deciding whether she would go east as her father wanted for her, or what this would mean for both her parents and herself as well. In spite of this, however, Millie performed just as unscathed as earlier on when her mother had come in her room as she was almost noticing of the indifference to her as being the opposite of what she had seen so far and carrying herself so impartially to her as to her behavior before, never suspecting what would come next, or what her daughter was about to do and what would be her dire act, or at least what she thought what would relieve herself once and for all of her despondent grief.

Later that night as Millie's mother was washing up the dishes and clearing the plates of food from out of the dining room and after Benjamin had settled down himself and was sitting in his rocking chair in the den their daughter had quietly gone back up stair's to her bedroom though neither one of the parents had said anything more about earlier on when they were in the den. Instead Benjamin was just trying to meditate to himself as he would and alleviate the tension or whatever thoughts he had of seeing his daughter leave from there homestead and knowing he would be without her for a time but taking his mind off of the uncertainties of all this.

It was still slightly light outside in the early November month as the dying sun was quickly going down, Benjamin gently looking out the old and rustically wood framed window from his rocker hearing the sound or two of a distant coyote in the background and Millie's mother in the kitchen still faintly washing the dishes or whatever else needed to be washed. As he continued sitting, however, almost as if unexpectedly he suddenly saw Millie walking out through the door as he hadn't even heard her coming down the stairs and as he sat there looking at her with a hint of surprise in his expression.

"Millie?" he said as she was about to go out. To this his daughter just slightly stopped as she was about to do this, but turned to him slowly though hardly looking at her father as she took her hand away from the door to open it.

"Yes – father?" she replied with her face still shadowed aside from the den.

"Where are you going out to now?" Benjamin asked as he remained seated in the rocker with his legs folded and pipe still in mouth. As for Millie she almost hesitated before responding as she just kept standing there between the doorway and stairs.

"Nowhere father," she replied without much effort as her father just kept in his same pose looking at her hidden face.

"Well, you must be going somewhere?" he retorted removing his pipe and as a puff of smoke ascended from his mouth. Millie, however, just stayed silent for a moment.

"I – I'd just thought I go out for a little while on the porch," she finally answered, but with a sort of imperceptible sigh.

"That's strange. I've never seen you go out at this hour," the father unassumingly enough uttered only returning his pipe to his mouth after but still resting easily.

"I know," Millie said almost just as sharply afterward. "But, I wanted to go out to see the sunset. That's all," she continued without hardly any strain in her words though a strange sort of sigh still present.

The father just turned his attention to the window as he was looking himself up at the deeply hued clouds of pinkish red through its glass his face settling back.

"Yes. I have to say myself it is some pretty thing to look at," he went on reminiscently and looking away from his daughter.

"Yes, father," Millie sighed again as she went to open the door again, and then began making her way through but not first without placing her hand in her dress pocket as though she had something in it. Seeing this as he had turned to her again Benjamin just said, "Millie?" as she suddenly stopped.

"Do you have something there?"

There was a hesitation before replying but she finally answered.

"... *No*, father."

"I see," Benjamin replied dismissively in his tone. "You go on head out now," he continued. Millie for a moment looked as if she was about to stop, but then decidedly carried on only to say, "Yes, father," before opening the door to finally let herself out while the fading light of the sunset poured onto her face and then closing the door behind her after as Benjamin sat there looking out into the clouds and resuming his trance. For all his reverie though, he could not possibly know that Millie's departing to him was about to come ever closer than it had before, or would ever possibly come again.

As it was Millie's father had retired early that night after rocking in his chair but now that it was late Kate had thought her daughter had been in her room the entire time and did not even know she had never come back in after going out onto the porch to watch the sunset as she had told her father. Instead, she was about to retire herself and had already been done with the dishes for some time and was settling in herself in her room as she sat in front of the mirror and combing out her hair with brush. As she did this though a feeling came over her something may be wrong, but strangely, not knowing what it was and trying not think it. Nevertheless, as she sat there brushing her hair she almost turned around for a moment to look at Benjamin in the bed who was then lightly snoring but decided not to keeping herself straight as she then got up from her chair and looked back to Benjamin seeing he was well asleep and not wanting to wake him. Then, taking her small lantern wick out on the dresser she could still feel something was not right, but instead, went out the bedroom to look down the hall at Millie's door. She could see that the door was closed all the way and thought Millie might be asleep though she did not say goodnight to her like most times thinking she had already gone to bed. Looking as if she was about to turn back to her own bedroom, though, she began making her way to Millie's door stopping just before she had reached it having an apprehensive look on her face or not knowing why she thought she had to open it to see what her daughter was doing. At first she knocked but then abruptly opened the door as she pointed her candle to Millie's bed seeing that she was not laying in it or any sign of her in the room and as she started frantically to worry where she could be going on back to her bedroom to wake Benjamin. Shrewdly tugging at him and as the mother said his name only once Benjamin woke with the words, "What's wrong?" as he looked up to the mother herself worriedly replying, "*I looked!* Millie's not in her bed..."

Shortly after this the father briskly got up out of the bed saying nothing but trying to stay calm as the mother started going out of the room and calling her daughter's name and all the way downstairs as she looked in the kitchen and turned then up to Benjamin who was just coming down the stairs himself still dressed in his underclothes and having an unsure look in his face.

Nonetheless, the mother kept on looking at him with her feigning face and in fear of wherever her daughter could be at as Benjamin went outside onto the porch and began calling Millie's name out loud. As he stood there on the porch for a moment more and looked around he could only see what was the black night in front of him and the few shining stars above as he raised his head to look up at them knowing something was very wrong but barely understanding what could have happened.

Upon this as he looked straight out he decided to go look in the wood and horse shed though not seeing why she would be there either, but just the same afraid of what he'd find or if anything at all of his daughter. As he hastily entered he could sense no presence of anything or anyone that would be inside but just went over and got down a small lantern from a shelf over by the wood stack and lit it by getting out a match and striking it to the box it was stored in laying on top of a barrel next to it. Then, raising its light to see he scoured over the inside of the shed from one side to the next as he went over to their only horse, or Marybeth, quietly tucked away to herself in the back and lying in some hay. Seeing that nothing was there as he kept the lantern high he almost thought he had just saw something out of the corner of his eye and to the side next to him up on a tiny loft but realized it was just another shadow as the lantern revealed nothing but an empty crevice. Finally satisfied, but ever more still weary of Millie's disappearance he went on out of the shed holding the lantern in hand and started making his way back up to the porch seeing Kate now standing off to the side as she just looked at him with her terrified eyes and hushed mouth waiting for him to say something to her but unsure of this either way.

"She wasn't in there," Benjamin finally spoke as he continued walking into the house past Kate. Relieved from this she took her hands away from her mouth just then but like Benjamin was still worried and perplexed as to where her daughter was as she clenched a post of the porch and held onto it while Benjamin went on inside.

After some time as Kate kept standing there out on the porch Benjamin returned to her holding the lantern still in hand, though she was unsure of what he was doing and could see he had as well his old union rifle with him from his soldier days but asked as he was passing her on by again, "Where are you going?" but Benjamin just replying – "Over to the Parsons, to see if she's there," as Kate stood silent without much affect and looking back. Nevertheless, Benjamin kept on making his way into the shed to saddle up the horse and preparing to head out to the Parsons, or the parents of Millie's friend Stella, which was not too far from their own homestead, or a little further down the creek between the town and their own place.

Hurrying along as fast as he could Benjamin eventually got up Marybeth who was still nestling in her back area of the shed, but getting her up quickly enough and out the barn doors, needless to say, and then mounting his saddle to her, or the same one he would use when going into town to get supplies or what errands, as he put his lantern to the side and gun to do this, though she didn't give him much trouble with this detail. Watching away in the dark from the porch stirringly Kate looked on as Benjamin rode away at a quick trollop having his gun tucked neath his saddle and holding onto his lantern in his hand not even bothering to tell Kate when he would be back, the two knowing something had happened but somehow having the feeling there daughter was in danger and not knowing or even conceiving of how they would see her or in what form next.

* * *

The next day had come and the night had gone by, but Millie had still not been found and no one sought by Benjamin including the Parsons knew of where she could be nor anyone speaking up to this but just the same a small search party had been collected during the night this including Millie's father, of course, but also, Noah Parsons, or the father of Stella along with the help of some other men that the two were able to muster in order to do this though with the darkness of night and hardly knowing where to begin looking for her other in the near area or in some vacant fields closer to the O'Leary's, they knew their chances of finding her or anything else would be much less than that of during the light of day. By now Benjamin had gone down to the precinct even and told the sheriffs partner or Joe Collins who up until then had been at the office and upholding the law every day, or since the others had gone looking for Alcott's niece, that other missing girl of around Millie's age, as Joe would speak to Benjamin standing there next to the father with his unamused and grieved face staring back.

"*Another one?*" Joe said almost sounding ironic. "We seem to be gettin' a lot of those lately." Benjamin though said nothing after, but just remained standing there with the deputy for the moment knowing by now that help to find his daughter would certainly be limited, and especially with the unassured competency of sheriffs partner Joe Collins at the forefront to this recovery, but would leave the office with the same pained face feeling for the first time, or at least more penetratingly to the notion as if somehow it was his fault in part for his daughters disappearance. Still, he could not understand nor know why this would be, or lacking precisely of what he had done. Why had she gone he asked?

It was still early morning and on a Saturday now and with the light of day a new search was being conducted not only up and around where the O'Leary's lived, but men in other parts, as well, on the other side of town, looking and scavenging up and down cornfields or what not and in any crevices or holes that they might think she could have gone to, although no one finding any remnants of her yet, or making any headway as to locating her, or even suggesting where she might have gone to. Not by some coincidence though, but still not too far away, someone, or somebody rightly familiar enough to those parts had been strolling along himself in one of the nearby tall grassy meadows, although one of which was not visited as much, nor frequented than the others, as its quiet and aloof setting was one that made it so, consisting and surrounded by patches of thick and shady woods on either side and a small rock wall cutting through on the edge as if almost hidden away from the rest of the world, or the town of Little Cavern, for that matter, and for only those privileged few to stumble upon it. As it would turn out to be, enigmatic and more often rebuked man of town Wyatt Cobb was one of these people and had a fondness for the place and serenity it offered to this as he would go there once in a while to sit down or either walk in the weeds if just to forget the things that nuanced and bellowed at his soul for the solace it offered the few moments he was there. Tall and lanky, dressed in his usual outfit and with his black hat he complemented his surroundings with a departure of seriousness and humbleness in his face that made him stand out from it as though the unlikeliest of person's to be found inhabiting or admiring its simple beauty.

He had only been there for a short time during that part of the day, how-ever, as he continued to look out upon the sunlit clearing and as he had been sitting most of the time upon the stone wall, which was mostly shaded from the surrounding brush and forest behind him where even an old and tired cob-bler tree with the colors of red and orange in its fall leaves stood not afar from its end. Just then, as he was doing this he could hear the moans of something nearby as he looked to his side calmly to listen but not sure of what he was hearing, although the faintly audible sounds suggested the presence of some-one near, or similar to that of or almost like a girls. As he got up and went over to look for whatever he heard at the moment he could not see anything at first but was still sure that something was there as he carefully climbed over the wall to the other side, as he could see then the arm of a girl sticking out as the moaning became louder and more yawningly. Making his way up to see who it was the severely weakened and stooped over figure of a girl came into full view as he looked down and could also see in plain sight a half empty bottle of what looked like some old and left over Iodine lying next to her hand as she sat with her back against to the wall and her eyes wide shut while the other hand was wrapped and placed over her stomach, but Wyatt easily discerning she was in a dire state of being. At first upon seeing this he no less picked up the half full bottle off the ground placing it inside one of his jacket pockets and without much hesitation at all he then bent down to cradle the young girl in his arms as he lifted her off the ground as she moaned again. More importantly, how-ever, or as to the point of all this young Millie had at last been found though not by those others whom had been looking for her all the while, but by what might be thought as the strangest of hands to do so, or those of Wyatt Cobb's as she had pawned the small bottle of iodine from a cupboard of one of the drawers in the household to take with her and that which was in her pocket when she was talking to her father on her way out to commit what she thought would be her last fatal act after making her way to the reclusive wooded area during that last evening in order to fulfill it.

As Cobb made his way on out of the clearing and then down what appeared to be a openly enough but narrow pebble and small rock path as it was situated in the midst of some swaying grains, wavily blowing back and forth from the chilly autumn winds, but leading up to where it was he was taking her to, the ailing girl in his arms or that of Millie, kept making moaning and some pain noises, so often, but Wyatt continuing to make his way along the shortened road, regardless, though keeping his head upright ahead for the most part as he did. Soon to come, anyhow, the country portrait of what looked to be a whitely painted and short picket fence in front and next to what seemed to be the summer remnants of an old and burnt out tomato and small vegetable garden but all of which slowly began to emerge out in the distance and up ahead of what was the elderly woman's or Mrs. Jones' own plantation and home, which its seeming immodest size and look for the country area and place could be almost mistaken for a sort of boarding home. Getting closer as Wyatt approached, Evelynn herself could be seen sitting on the wide gape of the porch in her wood framed rocker and looking down to be reading a book of some type, but eventually, looking up with her modest and reflective old womanly eyes to see her once protégé and mentee holding in his arms of what he was about the present her with. Calmly lifting herself from her chair, then, as Wyatt made his way up to her and passed the fence and open gate Evelynn remained on her porch looking down to the apparently gravely ill and sickened girl as she immediately took hold of the situation and showing concern for the girls welfare and telling Wyatt in her graceful yet unshaken manner to bring her inside after touching her hand to the girls lower arm and then opening the tightly woven and porches bent in screen door as Cobb went through first with the girl and as Evelynn followed from behind. After this Wyatt continued his way up the stairs that were ahead of him and then down the hall to his own bedroom as he settled the girl down on the old goose feathered mattress while Evelynn stood aside and looked down. Removing the bottle he saw along with the girl then he showed it to Evelynn though she only looked at it for a moment before leaving the room to extract some linens and what not and prepare to care for the moaning and groaningly girl as she tossed and continued to grab at her stomach and in her clamed position on the bed only trying to get relief from the pain.

A few moments later, as Wyatt kept at the girls side and looking down at her with his set of sharp, yet innocuous eyes he took off his hat to set it off on the side, but resting it on top the chair next to him as his keeper, or that of Evelynn, had finally, returned with the things she was rounding up as she went over and placed a porcelain wash bowl out on the bureau next to Wyatt's bed and pouring some water into it from a separate basin. After dampening a piece of cloth then and ringing it out a few times with her hands she began to pout Millie's forehead as the girl fretted slightly while she did this, but Wyatt silently watching from the side. Evelynn just turned towards him though as she continued wetting her forehead as she went to say - "You have to fetch Doctor

Treadwell, you know." As she turned back to Millie's face after with the girls eyes still closed and squirming she continued. "She's looks very weak... I'm not sure, but somehow I think she'll be alright, though."

To this Wyatt replied nothing always his quiet way except to pick his hat back off the chair as he placed it onto his head in order to set out on his way again and retrieve the towns or local doctor as Evelynn had told him.

Upon making his exit from the room he only gave Evelynn one last look before leaving though there was nothing else to be said between them as their always seemed to be a intuit between themselves or knowing of what the other intended, but a certain passivity towards one another, regardless.

The doctor's home, or where it was he lived was not as far, but, closer to town than Evelynn's as Wyatt made his way at a quickly step and like all other places he went to, or frequented, did not make use of horse, nor either so much as owning one.

He made his way, regardless, after a good saunter that took him the better part of thirty minutes give or take and to where the doctor lived with his older wife in his more lucrative settlement with its pop out bay window in front over on the far side and the lap strake siding coming down, along with some crown molding shown above the porch, the front having an array of light blues and pinks strewn throughout with its pretty and warmly design.

Cobb made use of the mounted door knocker upon walking up the porch steps as he waited patiently in front of the doctors home for someone to answer, though shortly after Mrs. Treadwell, a woman of around seventy or more, and exceedingly old looking to say the least having a white shade of thinly and parceled strewn hair on top of her tiny head to indicate this and crinkly face to go along with it soon came to the door as she opened it from the inside to see who had made use of the knocker or whomever was calling.

"Yes, who is it?" she asked mildly looking at Wyatt with her poor woman's sense of sight and wearing a pair a thick glasses over them though she knew right away who it was as Wyatt stood there in front of her distinctly as only he could while she turned back to her husband or Doctor Treadwell himself who was now coming through knowing something must be inordinate as to Cobb's calling on him.

"What's happened?" the doctor asked in his more gruffly sounding tone as Wyatt took off his hat to reply and then removed from out of his pocket, as well, the half empty bottle of Iodine to show to him. Nevertheless, he would go from there to simply tell the Doctor in front about how he had found the girl or young Millie during that earlier part of the morning with the bottle of Iodine lying like herself next to her, and that he had carried her back to Mrs. Jones where she was at that moment.

"We'll!" he responded almost jolting over after listening. "You must've went and found that O'Leary girl. She's been missing all this time – the whole town's been searching for her since last night goin' on now this morning." At this he just went back to grab his hat only as efficient as an old spruce doctor could just before leaving though not without telling his wife he wasn't sure when he'd be home and not to wait for him knowing he had to get there quick and fast to revive the girl not knowing either, of course, how bad off she was. Mrs. Treadwell stopped him, however, just before he was about to step out to say, "Aren't you forgetting something?" but the doctor hardly so much as winking an eye to remember stooped down then to grab his black leather medical bag as his wife watched him continue out the front door next to Wyatt with her weighted expression and just in fear of the girl after having seen the amount of Iodine she had swallowed from the bottle.

The Doctor made his way to Evelynn's ranch, nevertheless, as he knew the way well from the helm of his horse and buggy as Wyatt sat next to him though rare the exception was, but the doctor blatantly insisting, and trying not to waste any time. It would not be long, however, until the two would shortly arrive and Doctor Treadwell just as hastily making his way up the porch steps with his medical bag and inside of the country house, as Wyatt nearly followed him the whole time continuing his way up the stairs, and then, down the hallway where the girl lay just as deeply sick, Evelynn still at her side and wetting her as she had.

Just as quickly as he came, and in a hasty attempt to assess Millie's state, the earnest Doctor Treadwell didn't even bother to remove his hat, nor roll up his sleeves, as he lay his medical bag onto the bed next to the girl, and then, as he opened it up to take out what was his stethoscope to listen for the girls innards, setting the ends of the listening apparatus into the pits of his ears and placing the head onto Millie's chest as he looked away to determine her pulse and rhythm of heart, though all of these were weak and barely audible like the girl herself as she lay there continuing to sweat, her skin almost just as white. Then, placing his hands with his other overlapped he pressed onto the girl's chest and stomach as Millie groaned out while placing his hands on her lower abdomen. Taking a syringe out from his bag as Wyatt stood aside watching the doctor with his hat in hand and Evelynn still seated by the girls side, the doctor took the needle end and stuck into a small vile containing some kind of early day substance, or suppressant, as he withdrew the end and then removing the needle once it had absorbed all of its content as he tapped the needle a few times and some of the fluid sprouting out as well. He then took the syringe still in his hands and finally stuck the needle end into Millie's arm holding it in place with the other as he looked down at the girls face, though there being little reaction except some brief setting of the eye lids as a drowsiness within her and sedative effect was beginning to overcome spawned from the drug and laxative he injected her with.

At this Evelynn or Mrs. Jones just looked up to the doctor to ask, "She will be alright, Doctor Treadwell. Won't she?" as the physician in resuming his stiff head and straightened posture only replied to the hopeful sentinent by saying, "Well, I can't be sure, but from the looks of that bottle she took in and from what I can see here there's no guarantee." Glancing at the girl with a slightly irresolute look he continued his bluntly dictation. "All I can say at the moment now is time will only tell. But, I can only imagine what drove her to commit such an act, and as you can see, she is nearly completely exhausted without hardly any response or movement." Chuffing his stethoscope back into his bag as he looked away he idly added, " – Almost as if *comatose* I would say..."

Evelynn began wetting Millie's head again, nevertheless, even with the doctor's unpromising words, but he just gave her a sharp look as she did this as Cobb was still standing away with his hat in hand and looking at the two. "I think I'll go straight over to the sheriff's office for now," Treadwell spoke out to her short windily. "Happens the girls a, Mildred O'Leary. Live's with her parents on the other side of town. They'll be glad to know she's been found though, and in someone's good care. She's been missing this whole time."

Upon hearing the doctors plaintiff and about her parents Evelynn kept on doing as she had but the Doctor just turned to the all so transparent Wyatt Cobb as he bid his head down to ask in his thoughtful minded way, "I don't suppose you'll be needing a lift to town, would you?" though Wyatt kindly answered back to the small favor and putting his hat back onto his head as he did with a simple, "No, Sir," the doctor turning away from him again with his bag in hand. Then, as he looked like he was about to withdraw he directed himself to Evelynn once more though she was already looking away to the girl and tending to her as she had.

"Mrs. Jones," he said pointedly. "Do you think, or, would I be able to have a word with you? That is, if it would be alright?"

"Well, yes. Of course," Evelynn cooperatively replied as she turned to look up and then rose from her seat, as the two proceeded outside into the hallway to speak, Doctor Treadwell opening the door further to let themselves out in order to do this.

When they were finally standing together in the hallway the doctor went on to discuss with herself about the girl in his frank though non infringing discourse as he recommended that given her condition and mental state, providing she would even be alright again once she had maintained a steady realm of consciousness, it would be better for the girl to stay and occupy her present room as not to disturb further her faculties or trauma she had sustained beforehand, and that he'd rather see her rest there for the time being thinking it would not be a good idea for her parents to see her just yet. Evelynn, or as he knew her Mrs. Jones, was naturally agreeable to the situation trying only be as obedient to the doctors wishes as she could and asking when he would return again which to this he said he would be back either himself or with the girl's parents, Benjamin and Kate, as well in the next coming days, but that the girls faith in recovery would depend on her gentle and kindred care and urgently warning her not to move or startle nor to provoke any change that could deepen her illness being unfamiliar to these matters in part himself and unsure of her prognosis as to recovery.

After giving over his orders to her, however, and shortly after once he had left, Evelynn went back to caring for Millie as Wyatt went out of the room to let her do this though staying close and checking in once in a while for the remainder of that late and early morning and into early afternoon to see how the girl was doing. As for the doctor he had made his way to town likewise just as he said he would so he could tell the deputy partner, or the head chief at the moment, Joe Collins, of the girls recovery and where she was being kept presently, and that she had been found alive, however saying she was in a severely ill and depressively, almost incoherent way, nevertheless, but only telling him this to prepare to make their way over to the O'Leary's afterwards with the escort of deputy Joe Collins which he requested of him in order to inform them of what had happened.

Without hardly any delay as to their plans Joe went with the adamant doctor to deliver to the parents of what had just been told to himself as they made their way up to the residence, Joe leading the way on his horse up in front, and were soon to be both inside the O'Leary household as Benjamin stood in the den and as Millie's mother, Kate, sat in her sitting chair with her mouth open and listening to the doctors assessment while Joe listened as well on the side the two trying hard not to be overcome and just struggling to understand what he was saying. Shortly though as he spoke it was not long until he mentioned the bottle of Iodine Millie had nearly completely swallowed and that she had been found with, but Kate giving a second of reflection after hearing this suddenly remembered the bottle she had tucked away for some time and that she thought she had gotten rid of by then, but then looking to Benjamin as he gave some inaudible figment of puzzled expression went on to say that he had not discarded the bottle as she had told him and had in fact kept the solution in the same place the whole time, or in one of the pantry drawers of the kitchen where Millie must have found it in thinking it would never wind up as it had or be used as in the case of his daughter. Upon giving his deliberation and whatever he felt they needed to know or what solace he could offer, the two grieving parents, both Benjamin and Kate and without little impunity of being denied, asked the doctor then how and when they would be able to see her though they were unaccepting of the doctors wishes and advice of having them wait if even for the moment, but almost insisting that they see her at once and not giving in to his concerns but just wanting to see their daughter no matter what condition she was in.

Unable to stop the parents at their pleading request Doctor Treadwell took the two to see their daughter, finally, with Joe Collins following from behind that of the physicians own carriage with the parents seated next to himself as they anxiously made the trip and hoping nothing worse had happened thus far though they still did not quite know what to expect and in fear the whole way. Upon arriving, however, Cobb was sitting quietly out on the porch under its shade from the mid afternoon sun as he greeted both of them in his unimposing manner trying to be as courteous as possible as the parents stood aside while Doctor Treadwell let himself in and asking Wyatt if anything else had happened while he was away though Wyatt just told him, "No, sir," as he went up with the parents then and down the hall again as he had before where Evelynn sat at their daughters side though knowing who they were just the same upon seeing them and the saddened, guilt ridden expressions on their faces as they glimpsed Millie for the first time since she had left. At this her eyes were shut and she had been resting easy for the time being as the Doctor went up to her in the bed and took her pulse again like before. Standing aside as Millie's parents watched Benjamin had clenched his fists tight having, as well, a certain bitterness to his sobering face, and Kate, with both hands to her mouth hushed next to him as he look down at her daughter, and then, finally, Joe himself in the doorway with his head bent down silenced from the sight.

Once the two had seen their daughter though and understood better of her predicament and how she was Doctor Treadwell brought them outside into the hallway leaving Evelynn to resume her post with Millie but the elderly woman saying little to the parents as she passed them except to say that it was a privilege to be able to take care of their daughter and that she had not caused her any trouble neither, but instead, telling them both to try not to worry and that she would care for her as though she were her own. Benjamin and Kate were ever relieved upon hearing this and ever obliged saying little to her though to show her this being in their state as they left with the doctor to go back downstairs to talk some more and what he thought would be best for her or what he had told Evelynn earlier on outside in the hallway. At the moment, however, Millie was out of harm, without saying, and in the encouraging hands of the warmly old woman, or that of Mrs. Jones as well as having the endearing Mr. Cobb to help her with whatever she needed. Her parents although rather undecidedly and reluctantly went along with the Doctor orders, but were just as perplexed and unascertained as to why their daughter or young Millie would come to such a thing, instead, leaving the ranch with the Doctor almost as confusedly and disheartened as they came just trying to come to terms with what had happened, and unsure if they even could. For the rest of that most eventful and trial some November's day it would be just as sunny as earlier on but with the darkness of night falling over the day ever promptly from the nights before, or since, and now that winter would soon be on the horizon. Only once would Millie open her eyes, however, after night had already arrived, as she turned her pale head to Evelynn by her side but with her pouty and tired lips went on to ask for some water as Evelynn called to Wyatt standing nearby as he was about to leave down the hall after checking in. Regardless, he brought up the glass of water she had asked for as Evelynn helped her sip it down and raising her head to do this as Millie turned away to her side and continued resting after while Evelynn looked up to Wyatt standing in back of her and with a hint of relief in her face sensing now that she would somehow get better seeing her request as a small act of will which she knew she now had. Whether this evidence of Will or unconfirmed desire would be strong enough to lift her up and go on would come to be tested next, but as Wyatt stood aside looking down at the fragile and disaccorded O'Leary girl that he had carried back in his arms just the same morning before, he knew, similarly to his older friend and acquaintance Mrs. Jones, somehow it would – and only *he* of all people.

13

The sheriff and his fellow deputies had been on the trail, all the while, and had made it down near the Wyoming Nebraska border, and were at the present moment crossing an obstructing ridge of some steepened cliff or crag looking down into a gorge of thickly pine wood trees and colored foliage below, although the sheriff had chosen the route as a short cut rather to get to the other side while the men and prisoner Colby sat up on his white spotted mule with good old Mike Taverns in the back clutching his rifle for ready use in his arms and the rest being led by the sheriff up in front.

"– You men just take it easy for a moment," the sheriff suddenly halted as the others stopped riding to take a rest, though remaining seated up on their horses without moving much except the two young deputies in front of Colby but only to take their hats off as they waited quietly on top of the steep em-bankment while the sheriff went up ahead to look over the next corner seeing if it was safe enough to cross. Making the bend on his horse, nonetheless, he could see no signs of the pass being dangerous as he waited for the moment looking around and down into the gorge dismounting from on top of his horse as he kept one of the reigns in hand, and then, by taking a few more steps for-ward to see if it was passable. As he was about to turn back seeing nothing wrong he could hear then some pebbles or sand moving across the edge where it was most steep as he looked back though seeing little movement. Waiting then, for a few moments more, as he looked around with his vigilante face he went over to where the bit of shale had just fallen as he bent down to get closer though nothing happening at first as he left his horse a few steps behind him. Looking up to his side then, where the drift of sand had fallen out from he could tell there was a fatal flaw in the landscape, though inconspicuous, but that could be dangerous or even deathly if not crossed properly as his face glinted with his malevolent intent knowing now he would have a chance to get rid of some of the others, if not at least one for the time being.

Going back over to his horse as he got back on top he paused a moment before heading across the bend to get to the others and preparing to make his next move.

"Alright, boy's," he declared once he had gotten back though tipping his hat down. "I reckon it should be good for us to cross." Looking at Mike Taverns up near the front of the pack he went on depravedly. "I'll let you take the lead from here, Mike, and follow up the rest of you's in back just to make sure." Lifting his face up towards the deputy he finished. "That is, if you don't mind?

At this the dogged Mike Taverns clicked his spurs into the sides of his horse and started to make the bend as the others proceeded along while the sheriff backed off to the side where the edge of the cliff was drawn out a little wider and seething like anything his plan would follow through as the lead deputy made his way around but never presuming in his mind what would come next. At first nothing happened once his horse had made the turn as his friend Will kept in back looking ahead, but then, almost like a flash and as abruptly as he could see Mike Taverns horse gave way and was suddenly exhumed off the rock bluff as the shale deposits unloosened by his horses steps and just as the sheriff had observed rolling underneath the horses hooves and crumbled on after him while Mike was thrown off the tumbling beast as it twisted and turned down the brush of the embankment and landing somewhere unseen but his friend knowing that he could hardly be alive from the fall and hearing the loud thud of his body at the bottom of the summit.

Will Blake's horse jumped up trying not to be taken off the ridge along with the tattered horse of his friend's and managing to keep its ground, as Will got off then and looked down with his nervous eyes to see if anything of Mike and calling out his name once or twice, but with no answer, nor seeing any trace of him at all.

"Hold up their boy's," the sheriff halted to the rest from in back. Riding up in front at a hurried, but still steadily paced gallop he went over close to young Will as he dismounted his horse to see what he could of the fallen deputy, though much more of his victim now the young man was, while the sheriff stood apart from Will Blake who was then knelt down on all fours almost and looking on with the sheriff into the dropping slope and thick shade of Pine trees. Nevertheless, the sheriff barely twitched in his placid face as he almost grinned for a moment, but then, looking to his side at his frantically searching younger friend and partner who was still searching to see if anything of him at all he blunted, "I reckon there'll be no use lookin' for 'em now, son."

Hearing this the young deputy froze in his position and slowly turned his face up to the sheriff then with his flatly gaze unknowing of just what to feel, though just the same he knew his friend was most likely gone.

"He was just riding up in front of me," Will Blake raddled out. "But then, all of sudden the whole ground started moving, *and then...*" he failed to finish the phrase as he looked back down into the brush.

The others still seated up on their horses or the handcuffed Colby and Pat Thomsen just looked on with their indifference to the situation as Pat kept watch on his horse in back of the unsympathetic prisoner and with the same rope attached to his saddle that had been linking them only keeping his eye on Colby. The sheriff on the other hand and expectedly was more than ready to get on his way telling the rest and Will in his lowly set voice, "You be saddlin' up now like the others. We should be gettin' on closer to the other side," as he got up back on top of his horse while Will kept standing in the same pose hesitant to follow the sheriff's instructions and or wanting to depart. Just as he was about to utter something though, the sheriff gave him a sharp look and was for a brief moment unsure of what to do as he stared back at the sheriffs peculiarly complacent eyes but giving in eventually not only from the sheriffs inherit intimidation but his very own lack of words or even mere nerve to dispute the act as he saddled back on top of his horse like the sheriff had told him, although now in front of the others and leading the way. After this he quietly set off as the sheriff and the rest followed along the edge and passing the fallen debris where Mike and his horse had just been swept out, but unlike the others, only the sheriff within feeling a morose satisfaction to what had just occurred, as Will Blake continued riding through and keeping his head straight but knowing he would not see his friend again and having that same strange feeling he had once known not so long ago when another man he had seen in witness was ravaged by the very hands of the same sheriff that was leading them. Unlike before though he did not have the ability nor inclination to look back to where his friend had just gone over, but although he did not know why, strangely he could not bring himself to or as to understand what he felt, but something within despite having been his closer friend and deputy that would not permit him nor without any answer.

14

The men and sheriff had finally crossed the border and were thought to be situated close to where the girl was supposedly being held as the sheriff had made the others believe this the whole time and all along with the false directedness, and to the credit of his secretly complying accomplice – the escort and gang leader himself – Colby Jenkins. Moving along their way the distant sound of a steady stream somewhere could be heard as the men stopped for a moment at the holler of the sheriff who was now riding up in the front again and the rest dropping down from their saddles almost just as quickly and were, by then, gropingly tired from the day's ride. Deputy Will Blake had been quiet the whole time saying nothing so far after what had happened and just taking off his hat to go sit away from the others as they were in a small patch of woods near the long stretch of a larger river but unlike most of the flatly mid-western territory they were headed in, as they were still just over the border, away from the vast cornfields and potato crops that made up most of its terrain. The scene though was just the same quaintly with the trees of orange and red and yellow, surrounding the sheriff, men and prisoner as the leaves had already begun to fall from the surrounding trees by that time, and were distributed on the ground, there and here, with pockets of some sunlight peeking through overhead, and hitting the ground so that the crispness of the leaves brightened and the drifting air around them seemed to buckle and nudge at them, suggesting a longevity to the day and time giving the feeling almost, that it would go on, forever, but stay just as it was.

"I think I'll be taken here's Colby over to the stream for a latrine break gettin' on that it's been a while, if that's alright with you, sheriff?" Pat Thomsen abruptly spoke after getting the prisoner down from his horse with his rifle in hand.

"Has it now?" the sheriff or Jeff McCormack strew back to him.

"Yeah, I think the last time was just early this morning."

"Well, then I think he should be ready to go, then," the sheriff kept up as he look at the prisoner.

With these last inflicting words from the sheriff though as to his thoughts and without irreverence to him as to whether or not Colby would relieve himself or not, Pat just as well went on to get the outlaw off his sorely mule going on to undo his handcuffs as he would do, though only helping him to relieve himself and just for the sake of their irritable rub caused by the iron metal which was one of the small favors he was permitted and as they needed to keep him comfortable enough for at least himself to direct and show them to where they were headed.

"Hold on there, Pat," the sheriff intruded on the two just as he had already undone Colby's handcuffs. Then, coming over near the prisoner and deputy in his calm and cool way he continued as he mirrored to Pat first and then to Colby. "I think I'll take it from here, Pat," he said nodding his head slightly to him as he went for the pair of handcuffs in his hand and key. "You wouldn't mind that now, right Colby?"

The no nonsense Pat Thomsen just backed off at this request saying nothing, and letting the sheriff have his way as the other stood aside while the bigoted Jeff McCormack took Colby by the arm and set off with him from the rear the two then making their way out of the surrounding area and closer to where the running stream could be heard coming from, or down a shallow foothill of some overgrowth, as Pat Thomsen could see them disappearing into the foliage, their figures gradually becoming out of sight. As for young Will Blake he just sit away starring out where the two had gone in, but his contusing expression very visible and almost beginning in some way to have just as much a trepid fear of the sheriff himself, as if he could feel his snake eyed grin moving over him the whole time and in spite of what had since happened to Mike Taverns just the day before, still hearing the echoing words of the sheriff to move on up on the ledge, all shedding doubt of himself, and also, of the others, but unsure of what to make of any of it if he even could.

Stepping out as he did into the clearing Colby proceeded to go over to a fallen log as the sound of the picturesque creek could be heard more fully now with its crystalline rushing waters smoothly spilling over the rounded rocks and little ledges that made up its floor as he stopped in front of it but which was stretched out across the running water to the other side, and bending over to undo his fly to get on with his business. Just then, as he had already turned in back of the sheriff now watching with his prowling eyes from behind, Colby suddenly froze in place from hearing his loathsome watchmen's voice though tingling it was.

"So, how you feelin' today Colby?" he uttered in his arrogant jargon but Colby saying nothing or answering at first. "Well, I don't know how you're feelin'," he went on as he look off to his side where the water was to continue. "But – seems to me like we should be gettin' on with our business, if you know what I mean – that is, the way things are headed between our goodly selves?"

The gang leader and prisoner just kept his back turned as the sheriff spoke and had his hands still below his waist ready, in so many words, to go but in resuming his contemptuous and malignant face from the oppressor, he slowly turned around facing the plastered sheriff, although with a kind of grin knowing fully, too, he was in on the plot.

"And, what d'you be haven' in mind?" he squinted to the sheriff as he himself pondered up closer to the outlaw who was now waiting keenly for his reply.

Removing his revolver from his holster the sheriff made out like he was about to use it as he took it out in a quick fashion while Colby seeing this almost jumped, but, unlike himself, the sheriff had on his same entertained face making sure the other knew who was in charge and getting ready to deliver what he had in store. Then, removing the bullets from the gun as he did this in plain sight so Colby could see, and dropping them into his other hand with the revolver in another though making sure all chambers were empty as he slowly rolled the guns canister, he threw the remaining cartridges into the flowing current next to him, his face only lustering with sin as he did it.

"Now how 'bout you and me be playing a little game for the other's on back," the sheriff pronounced in an attempt to unload his simple and twisted enough scheme as Colby stood in front of him not quite sure what he was doing at first but catching on eventually to the ploy and what the sheriff was intending, or, to cheekily make it look like he was in the killers possession with his unloaded weapon. Then, taking the sidearm, the sheriff stuck it into the assassins arm as Colby reached for it taking it in hand while the sheriff stood aside and removing a small 38. Caliber from one of his boots as he lifted his leg somewhat to do this and raising it for Colby to see.

"In case you get fidgety now," the sheriff went on. "I have myself this here's little pug to put one in your side, so don't get any fast idea's there Colby." Pausing then before continuing, "That is, if you have any?" and saying this as he put the gun inside his jacket pocket for hiding.

The outlaw just stood there showing no signs of repudiation to the sheriff's plan nor any hint of making a possible break, although the notion did come to him as the lawman turned his back to commence with the debauched trickery they were about to play on the others, but the sheriff as if innately knowing this and himself being almost his equal in defilement, turned around just then to say something to the prisoner in his slightly diminutive tone and having his wizen sheriffs look as well. "I think you'd better let me do most of the talkin' when we get up to the others," he said pokily. "And, uh... make sure you be stayin' a step or two behind me until I say so." Hearing this Colby stepped down saying nothing but just made out like he had pretending not to be as afraid, as he waited for the sheriff to go on and then for further instruction as had been told.

It was only a little ways before they would reach the others and come out through the surroundings so they could be seen as Will Blake and Pat Thomsen were now both sitting down and well – unprepared for what would come next as the sheriff waited a step or two before coming out of the brush while Colby kept behind him though maintaining his obedience the entire time just as well knowing he would not get very far by himself even if he were to get away without the sheriff wounding him.

Just then, as the two deputies were beginning to almost admire the day and settle into their surroundings, the sheriff could be seen coming out of the woods where he had just gone into a little while ago along with the outlaw, but only this time raising his arms in the air though the deputies unsure of what was happening as Colby stepped out himself from behind, and with the same gun in his hand of the sheriffs pointed at his back. The other two, nonetheless, would rise up to their feet at once in a panic while the sheriff spoke out as soon as he saw them do this telling them to put down their weapons and stand down as he went on from there.

"Hold on their boy's!" he exclaimed after they had stood to their feet and seeing them go for their guns as they did and Pat Thomsen caught off guard sluggishly holding his rifle.

"Well, as you can see our here's Colby has got the upper hand on us yet," he prattled away and talking himself for the outlaw just as he said he would. "Isn't that so, Colby?" he wedged in almost jestingly as Colby stood in back saying nothing to his remark except, "*That's right...*" though in his wheezily and unmindful voice while the sheriff just sort of laughed to himself as the other lawmen could hardly think it funny and standing there in fear waiting for the outlaw to speak his next words.

"Well, just what is it you'd be wanting, now, Colby?" the sheriff spoke up trying to prompt him but the prisoner able to and catching on just fine anyway.

"One of you's give me that there horse," the outlaw demanded in his same heedless voice and holding the unloaded gun to the sheriffs back. Hearing this Pat Thomsen went to give him his own saddled up brownish and shortly haired mare but the sheriff seeing this intruded just then on what he was doing and said, "Hold on just a moment, Pat. I think Colby, here be takin' my own white haired of a sally over there. That is, if you don't mind it yourself, Colby?"

To this the con just murmured "- *Fine*," in his similarly misspoken manner as the sheriff whispered another sigh of laugh to his meagre reply, and as Pat Thomsen slowly went over and cautiously brought over the purely white and unmistakably dark spotted horse of the sheriff while Colby kept at guard and still holding his gun as the sheriff with his hand similarly still raised gave a nod to old Pat Thomsen as he then backed away with his inept face and waited for the next words to come.

"Well, I think our swine Colby here will be taken' me on for a long ride," the sheriff continued in his prompting manner. "*How 'bout it Colby...*" he bellowed out in a deep voice now that his own horse was in front of them ready to go and maintaining as well his authority to the one in back of him at the same time.

To this Colby didn't say anything as he finally reached out himself and actually took the initiative of grabbing at the horses reigns while the two others nearby flauntingly stared back at the colluding sheriff and outlaw, though their thoughts as to this could hardly be than less, and just in awing fear of what would come next, knowing that the outlaw could just as well shoot them in pieces during that very moment, almost having a dazed look to their faces and completely unsure of their lives.

"Now you boy's don't be worrying," the sheriff recapped to both just before disappearing again into the woods with the prisoner. "And don't be bothering to come on after me, either," he conveniently continued. "I reckon Colby here be lettin' me go sometime soon, enough."

As the other deputies stood there, however, bewildered in their way as to why they weren't shot dead yet, Colby holding onto the reigns of the horse continued backing into the woods along with the sheriff and having the cover of the horse now but keeping the unloaded gun to his back just as he had and that the other two had been in mortal fear over the whole time and just as well leaving them with a sort of dulling though shocked confusion that they had not been shot, their turning faces and heads uncertain of why this had not occurred.

"Well, now Colby. You did real good back there," the sheriff mocked him as he turned to Colby in a quick motion once they had gotten out of sight while the prisoner lowered his face reassuming his imprisonment. "I think I'll be taken' this back from you, now," he assuaged as he took the impotent gun out of Colby's hands and slipping it back into his holster just as briskly. Then, after he had done this the sheriff saddled on top of what was his own horse, though not before slapping on the pair of handcuffs he had taken from Pat Thomsen, but this time so his hands would be clasped behind him and not in front as the sheriff added in his whimsy, "Hope you don't mind. Just as a precaution you be ridin' in back of me." Looking back over to the very creek where they had just come from the sheriff got up onto his horse leaving Colby behind standing on the ground as he look up at him in his helplessness though very restricted from the pair of handcuffs with his hands now locked up in back of him. The sheriff seeing his awkwardness and smiling down at him from up top said, "Meet me over there by that rock stickin' out," as he set out into the brook scattering the water while Colby made his way trying not to slip and fall but managed to make his way over to the large distinct piece of ledge that impeded the flow of the distilling water almost in half, as he got up onto it where the sheriff and his horse was now set up alongside for Colby to hop on the back as the sheriff shouted to him, "Well, what's your waiting for!"

Nevertheless, Colby made his attempt landing on the four-legged right in back of the sheriff as he kicked in his heels and the horse setting off on its way, disbursing the drifting waters with its hooves, and Colby bopping side to side with his hands in back handcuffed, but holding on steady enough by using his legs though resulting in a most unusual, but somewhat farcical site. As for the sheriff his thoughts could hardly be further from this as he was determined as ever to get what he wanted and planning as soon as possible to get to where it was he needed to get as he knew he would have to rely on Colby to do this in order to show him and now that his plan had been furthered after finally making his break from the others, though he knew just as well he would have to be careful as not to fall victim to the sleuth like trickery or that of which he had just played on his very own men and that Colby would be the one who could make his move this time. Just the same he sensed they were close to wherever it was his men were at, and hoping the loot would be well stacked for himself upon arriving and then to make the unexpected exchange for the outlaw and leader he was at the moment haphazardly toting on the back of his horse. He would make his way, however, the next days and nights keeping Colby in his sight and hardly sleeping himself to do this as his anticipation for profit was more important than his need to rest and his obsession to this acquisition overpowering, giving him the ability almost to go on as such. Unabashedly to this great storm of fury, the question still remained if he would be able to get away with his underhanded plan, and then the question of what price would he settle for in the exchange, if this even was what he had in mind, or just another one of the sheriffs tricks up his spineless sleeve.

15

During all of this time Mr. Taylor had only been getting more and more unsettled about the missing piece of paper, or the fathers will and document he knew was still out of his hands, and that was supposedly tucked away in the obscure box, or at least from what he had been told by dead Scott. Although this piece of document, aside, could very well by now be construed as minuscule and in most sense well – forgotten, something, or, more importantly, some desire from within the cattle boss made it so that he could not forget its significance, not only for the material of evidence it could be used against him in the unlikely event of being accused for conspiracy to commit murder, but for the very symbolic trait it imposed on him, plainly written out and signed by his father's own legitimate hand, and that which he could not seem to part with, even if he didn't know why he felt this way. Unsure of the sheriff, or what was going on now as to the girls recovery, despite the recent conversation between the two and considering that the weather would be turning colder when winter would soon be upon the rugged Wyoming state, Mr. Taylor had, subsequently, taken the liberty of gathering a few spare men about his ranch to help go down and find for himself where it was the missing girl and Indian were, or the one named Rolling Tides she was supposed to be with. All of this, however, would only be based on what young Scott had told him, previously, or as to the Fort and Reservation he had spoken of.

As of the present, he and his men had already covered much territory, making their way down Wyoming similarly to the sheriff and his men, but had already made their visit to the Fort Brent, which had gone all the way back just before the time of the Civil War and still standing in its former glory, tall and sturdy, and just as operative as it had in the past overlooking and observing the dilapidated and worn out of a small bungalow Indian reservation in front of it, and that of which was under its jurisdiction where the girl and native were said to be living somewhere nearby. At the moment they were now tucked inside one of the elder squaws tents making up most of the reservation aside from their being a few oblong huts at the other end, as Mr. Taylor was trying to find out what he could about where the Indian in question was, or as to his more exact location and after having asked around here and there, but some fellow occupants of the allotted land coming forth and telling Nelson and his men where they might be able to find out more about this, though in exchange for a few dollars and some bottled liquor they had brought down with them, but directing themselves eagerly to the Indians tent after.

"I am chief Black Bear," the old Indian said, as he was around the same age of the man they were trying to seek, or Rolling Tides, similarly, and smoking his wood pipe in mouth as he took it out blowing out some smoke before continuing.

"These are my people, all who had died, and live, have come now to this and live in tents and shacks of white man."

His dress was simple, but more Indian like and wore a necklace of beads around his neck which draped down below his deer skin outfit.

"Tell me now, why do you come to Black Bear – for what purpose is this visit?" he asked somewhat directly and looking at Mr. Taylor though he and his men were quite out of place for their surroundings and Mr. Taylor almost feeling this as much himself being privy to his more lavish styled way of life.

"Well," he said with an error of hesitation. "You see, we're happen to be lookin' for a young lady who had gone missing sometime, ago. Happens I heard she was livin' down here with another Indian man not far from here."

"So, I see," Black Bear replied as he puffed out another cloud of smoke, but keeping the pipe to his mouth. Mr. Taylor went on though.

"Happens I heard the name of this Indian was a Rolling Tides." The bare stomached chief kept looking at him and smoking as he went on.

"And how much do you give now to Black Bear to know where this old and tired Indian you speak of lives?"

"Well," Mr. Taylor spoke almost surprised by the question of money, but went on anyway. "I don't supposin' a hundred dollars for his whereabouts would get me any where's, now, would it?"

Black Bear looked of some passive thought for a moment before answering straight facedly.

"For a hundred dollars," he finally spoke, "I would have told you anything you wanted to know about this man. But, for fifty, I would have gone and killed old and dear friend Rolling Tides, Great Spirit of water and river, and then cut from out his heart with knife to bring back to you as your gift. Tell me," he went on looking again inquisitively, "Why is it you seek this man and other girl he is supposed to be with you talk of?"

Mr. Taylor kicked back his head for a moment before responding to the Indians simple question.

"Well, matter of fact this girl happens to belong to a well to do Uncle of hers from far out East who's been looking for her all this time. I just found out about the man she's supposed to be stayin' with not so long ago, myself, from someone who had been passin' through. How 'bout it now, do you know where he's at, or don't you?"

The old Indian did not say anything at first but just put his pipe down to his side almost as if to say nothing, but finally he spoke.

"Black Bear happens to know where this man you seek lives."

Mr. Taylor just kept looking at him with wider eyes while his men stood along standing next to him on either side as he was the only one sitting like Black Bear though he began speaking up again shortly.

"He was once an old chieftain like me, but went and left here many a year ago to live by himself and did not wish to live off the remnants of the white. Hurt by those who take without give. All live now under white rule and must obey without our own way to live or money to buy and be more like the white. Nor will Black Bear take your money now, but tell you instead where Rolling Tides lives among the trees, forest and stream. He has lived now somewhere not far from here as you have said, maybe twenty-five kilometers west from the Fort Brent you have just been to in a cabin built by his own hands, and then north of the river delta. To get there you can follow the river downstream, and then to where it has always ended, and where you will come to see one of many tributaries running off. You will follow one of these and continue. He is not far from there. I would take you myself," he continued coughing slightly as he did, "but I have not been well for some time and must stay to keep watch on all. Must rest now here, Black Bear is very ill."

For a moment, Mr. Taylor looked hesitant to speak but would go on just as well.

"Are you sure now you wouldn't be comin' along with us to help find him?"

Black Bear had already returned his pipe to his mouth, but to his question just proceeded to tell him that there was another Indian man around the reservation that could go with them unlike himself, but that his tribal name was Arrow Foot and that he lived in the far tent near where some water pumps and latrine stalls were setup, and that he could not promise he would do it, although for some money he might be willing. Nevertheless, Mr. Taylor asked him again if he was sure he would not go with them and offering once more but the old Indian said nothing once again to this thought, as he rose up from his seat on the other side of the roomy tent, and silently went over to lay down and saying nothing more to the cattle boss's proposition as if nothing had been said at all.

At this Mr. Taylor was satisfied enough for the time being and left out of the tent raising up one of its animal hide flaps along with the two other men he was with to find the other man residing in the reservation Black Bear had spoken of and hoping he would not be as reserved to his proposition. Needless to say, they made their way down the reservation to where they were told this Arrow Foot lived as they could see the few dingy and rusty water pumps alongside some other form of shelter or the latrine where some elongated fountain basins and a row of open latrine fennels could be found from within and that was meant to supply most the camps water and cleaning needs. Suddenly though they could see another youngish Indian man come out from one of the smaller tents, though unsure at first if he was the one they wanted but seeing that he was not like Black Bear but looked far more agile and sharp eyed rather than old and sickly, as his face was tattooed much more penetratingly then some of the others, or Black Bears more traditional appearance, and very war like. At first, however, he did not say anything as to whether he would go along to show them, though, after telling him that they were told by the chief Black Bear he knew where the one named Rolling Tides lived. Only then after some ambivalent sway in exchange for some of the money Mr. Taylor had brought with him he went along enough just as the old chieftain had told the cattle boss and his men he would as he insisted that he have the money first before leaving with the rest, but Mr. Taylor giving in anyway and knowing at least he would be able to get them to where they wanted to go when at last his desire to reacquire the secreted will would be more fermented after making his journey to obtaining it. Still, he did not know what kind of a man it was he was about to meet, or if this Rolling Tides was as great a warrior as he had been told, and not knowing either how difficult it would be to getting back the deed and box it had been stored inside, although Mr. Taylor was not the first one to take no for an answer and as was his nature he would get it back even if some scurried force, or disagreeable bartering was necessary.

It would only take them a day's ride, however, to where they wanted to go as their native escort in his neutral compliance took Nelson and his men across the bends of the Nebraskan river and then some more down into the neighboring forest and woods it ran through, but the swift sighted Arrow Foot getting them near the old Indian's cabin close enough, before leaving Taylor and his men and not wishing to make the whole the ride, but instead, just indicating to the crew from there on in to where they needed to go, although there was little complaint to this otherwise as Mr. Taylor went along with the man's wishes, telling his own men to back off and trying to be smart about the whole thing so as not to cause a situation.

Arrow Foot would only go back his way, then, as the others were now alone sitting on their staunchly horses to go ahead though a look of caution in their eye as they started out and making sure to keep straight as the intuit red skin had prescribed and trusting him enough as to his indications to get where they were going.

After travelling on their horses for almost a half hour, give or take, Nelson and his men could sense they were finally near, and seeing ahead the same thinly line of smoke coming from out of the Indians cabin chimney, as they came to a shallow halt at the site and deducing the wood construction as to where Rolling Tides was said to have lived confident they had reached their destination. As for the two men he was with they had gone along for the trip much more to do with monetary reasons rather than anything else aside and were for the most part in thick with their incredulous boss himself, but similarly to old Scott, Nelson had picked the pair for the same reason and knowing their flighty dispositions for such a mission, which as always was the boss's nose for such people or his fellow workers.

After resuming their pace and being still somewhat at a distance to the approaching hut twisting their heads some more to look as they did though seeing no one in sight, or any sign of others that might be near beside themselves, they could then see a girl come out the cabin door as it opened up, but herself not even noticing of any of the men on horseback, or the iron fisted Nelson Taylor for that matter, as a small slope and some trees in between separated both parties. She had come out though holding her bucket under her arm and making her way to the creek as she would to fill with water and then bring back to wash with, or prepare whatever meat for cooking. Seeing this, Mr. Taylor just put his hand out and dismounted his horse while the other men got off from on top of their own and then promptly going for their rifles tucked under the saddles after, as Mr. Taylor surely knew that the girl he had just seen was the very one they had been looking for back at home, but the young lady making her way without being disturbed by any of them nor noticing the men and their horses.

Waiting then for a few moments Mr. Taylor and his men took caution as a gust of breeze picked up around them, short lived it was, while some leaves fell lucidly down to the ground below, but the men like their boss holding their rifles in hand ready to make their interrogation, or for any misdemeanor that could arise though which would come much more out of their own interest rather than anyone else to bring into the scene.

As they continued walking up to the lodge though suddenly what looked to be the very Indian man they had finally come to see, and that of Rolling Tides himself came out as his eyes immediately streamed to them almost and his shuttering face looking up at them nearing as he had just come out for the cool air and holding his pipe in hand.

Nevertheless, as Mr. Taylor and his men slowly came up to the man he made out as to stay calm, although he could plainly see the rifles they had clutched in their arms waiting for the one in front of the pack who looked to be their leader to say what it is they wanted, and unsure as to why they would come to his humble dwelling and in his simple Indian wisdom thinking that it had something to do with the strange man that had fled from his place nor without warning on that same fateful night months ago, when he had inconspicuously exchanged the fancy box he had likened for his war knife to give to the girl.

Mr. Taylor spoke out in his intimidating and direct approach, or as soon as he thought the Indian was listening while the native stood looking back but saying nothing.

"Well, how's it goin' there, Chief," he freshly greeted him with and grinning a smile though the man did not answer.

"I suppose you'd be the one they'd be callin' Rollin' Tides. Am I not right, now?" To this the Indian still did not recant or answer the man in front of him or the others, but just affirming to himself that they did not come on good terms.

"Well, to be gettin' down to business," Mr. Taylor carried on hastily, "I understand it you had a man stayin' with you some time back. Let's see now." Looking of thought and putting his hand to his face, "A man by the name of Scott Terence ring a bell?"

Suddenly the Indian seemed to have a more marked look in his black inherent eyes, but Mr. Taylor catching on to it just the same.

"Yeah," he said going on. "Well, you see, us boys came all the way's down here being that is, you might have something of mine that you took from one of my workers, or, uh – that young man you went and found shot and brought back for here yourself. How 'bout it now?" Hearing this the other two of his partners looked back at each other at that instant not sure of what was going on as to their boss's implications, and having been in the dark themselves about their fellow worker and what might have happened to him, but kept their guard despite this.

"I am sorry," the shying native answered in his deep voice. "I do not know this man you speak of now."

"Well, isn't that so..." Mr. Taylor replied sharply but as expectedly unaccepting of the Indians denial, and Rolling Tides well aware he probably would not.

"You see, the problem is or as it was told to myself – it seems you took some kind of box from that workers satchel of mine, or another." Mr. Taylor could see Rolling Tides hesitate as he went to go for his pouch to fill his pipe. "Yeah," he continued as the native did this, "To be more precise about things, I believe it was a certain Music Box you took? Well, we wouldn't want to be causing you too much trouble, but being that us boys and myself came all the way down from Wyomin' just to make the long trip of gettin' it back, it just so happens that their box was supposed to be a gift to myself, and I've come on down here and even of haven' to leave my ranch back at home, just for gettin' it. Now, of course, I'd be willing to make an offer for it if you'd like bein' that you don't look so prosperous." After saying this Mr. Taylor went up to get closer to the Indian to give his settlement. "How 'bout a hundred dollars sound good for it?" The Indian did not show any reaction or fraying to his face as to his offer, but, instead, continued to light his pipe with a small match that he had just struck and acting as though he was not in danger knowing as well what Mr. Taylor said about the box was not true.

"I am sorry, again, but old Rolling Tides knows still nothing of what you speak of."

"Now I have to say I'm getting' a little impatient for your forgetfulness," Mr. Taylor jabbed at him, but the Indian keeping his ground soundly. Upon this last pestering, however, the men and Mr. Taylor turned their heads as they could then hear something or what may have been the girl fluster back off into the woods as she could see what was just then going on, but Mr. Taylor observing this and queuing the others to go on in after her. Turning then to the Indian

Mr. Taylor looked to him in a sizing up manner as the straight-faced Rolling Tides just stood there silent smoking his pipe.

"Well, we'll be seeing about that box I came down here to get soon enough," he said while his obeying men had already mounted their horses and went on to look for the girl as they headed in the same direction that she had just gone in and disappearing into the brush.

At first as they made their way they were not sure as to where she might have gone off to, or was hiding at, although the water or nearby creek could be heard more audibly as they went. Nevertheless, the two decided to part and would go off in separate directions as they both had their rifles in hand and holding onto the reigns of both their horses careful to listen or see and notice anything that could help as to finding her.

After making his way through some thicker patch of pines one of them had eventually reached a side of the creek, although as he got off from his horse thinking the girl might be around somewhere and knowing she could not have gotten very far on foot, he could only make out the speckling glistening's of water through pockets of clearings of the embanking woods as the water reflected the mid-day sun above. Guardedly though he was as he put his rifle back into his satchel and took out his pistol from his holster, instead, and then by cocking it, he listened for any movement. As he kept walking along the side with his head lowered and ready to see the girl pop out from somewhere nearby, he heard something then or a loose branch around, but not placing where it had come from as he waited a moment before turning. Slowly though he made his way up to some thorn and berry bushes now in front of him as he pointed his gun straight and said, "Come out from there, now. I hear you's," but nothing happening nor any answer.

It was around that time, however, when something or moreover some other person in the scene had silently come up from behind the rather forceful and demanding gentleman, almost as if out of nowhere and done the duty of hitting the cattle boss's man over the head with a hard thrust by using his own gun as the man fell down to the ground without getting up and lying unconscious from the blow. Bending down then the one who had just delivered the concussion reached to get his gun from off the ground now lying loose next to the other man. After slipping it into his belt and looking to his side, he then pointed his head back over to the bush on the side and whispered, "*Psssh...*" so he couldn't be too loudly heard as the girl came out slightly from behind to see him though scared she was.

"*There's another one somewhere...*" she said to him, although he took her word for it and by using his arms told her to stay put as he went and hid again after, or behind some heavier looking trees as he laid low but relying on the uneven landscape for cover. Just then, he could hear someone coming through as he waited to make his next move, and hoping the other would come over to look at the man lying on the ground using the knocked out man as a kind of lure.

As he waited he could continue to hear the person, or whomever it was approach on his horse which by then had seemed to have stopped in its tracks, although he didn't quite know why and still not able to see who it was as he lifted his head slightly to look. Finally, though, he saw the other as his plan was going according, while the man, unlike the one he had just knocked out was carrying his rifle in hand but went over to look at his fellow worker as he stopped astutely in front of the other lying there flat as a doornail with a what looked to be a small wound or gush to the head, but trying to figure out what had happened. It was only a second longer though into his thought when the other came out from behind and said, "Drop it!" as he pointed his own gun at the man's head and cocked it. Upon this the other immediately froze and dropped his weapon as he had been told. "Now, turn around," the man went on as the other did this, his arms raised up in the air and quite scared looking.

Nevertheless, the man just reached out to take the sidearm from out of the others holster but resuming to point his own weapon at him as the man stood their shakily.

"You wouldn't be having anything else on you's by chance, now would you?" The man said but the other just shaking his head.

"Please, don't shoot mister," the boss's henchmen fearfully delayed as the other one just looked back and said, "Alright come on, now."

At this the man began to turn though knowing that the others gun was still pointed at him and now in his possession as a spiny feeling of panic went down on through him giving the captive a terrible urge just then to flee in an ill-fated escape, and in a quickened motion as he saw the other pick up his rifle, he decided to make a dire dash for it by erratically getting back onto his horse, and then attempting to ride off. Nevertheless, he was just as soon shot down dead by the other man as the horses front legs jumped up and taking a small spill itself onto the ground, but making no more than a few yards ahead in his narrow minded escape.

Craig Sholl

After this had occurred the one who had just shot him made his way up to the dead boss's worker as he looked down into his opened eyes making sure that he was not alive but even before this confidently knowing already that he wasn't, though the girl or that of Miss Russell had finally come out by then to look herself keeping clear of the other man who was still unconscious, but at the time making some moaning noises as she looked to her savior who was then coming back to her side. Seeing that the man was awakening he cautioned her, as he waited for the man to come to but seized the moment to gather his horse while the girl stand aside saying nothing but looking down, unsure of what would happen next.

"Did you see any more than these other two here," the man asked her though she did not answer right away as she looked to the dead man lying away from them.

"Yes," she finally said. "I had seen three of them coming back to the cabin."

The man hearing this just looked away from her then and turned his attention back over to the one moaning as he was almost becoming conscious again. Walking over to him he would raise the other to his feet, although he was very balmy eyed at first and hardly alert as he helped him up and told him to get moving having his gun in hand, of course, and holding the reigns of the man's horse next to him. Nevertheless, the other kept his arms out and half raised but fully submitting to the other party as he started to make his way with his head lethargically swaying side to side but walking on.

As for the girl she had already made it up to the dead man as the two passed her by, but looked away with her hands in her face, but the site of the slayed man causing her to flash back in her mind for a moment to when both of her parents and own brother had all been killed on that other horrid and night-marish trip through that part of the country, and of all had which during that interval of time been blocked out as such, but the man lying there somehow bringing back the haunting visions as though in front of her.

"You stay close to me, now," he said to the girl as she went along with him, but fearing in as much, knowing there was still another one as she look tensely around her, though unsure to herself if he had come along to look for her with the other two, but also thinking too that her older Indian companion and the very one who had found and taken her in and whom of which had been caring for her that past time since her disappearance, had possibly been hurt or was in danger not knowing what it was the men wanted of him.

They were still a little ways off from the cabin as they made their way out of the surrounding mess of forestry they were walking through, but finally reached the point at which Miss Russell herself had fled upon seeing the un-welcomed men, though the Indian and Mr. Taylor himself had remained side by side the entire time as the boss had his leg set out on small stump made for cutting wood and looking back at the Indian, though each had just as well heard the round before that had been fired and apprehensive of what had hap-pened. Needless to say, as he turned Mr. Taylor could immediately see that his man's arms were raised and under someone else's captivity as his eyes low-ered, but not making out yet the other man in back.

Just then, as they got a little closer Mr. Taylor's eyes met with the captors as he immediately recognized who it was, shocked though from his presence and the two hesitating before doing anything as Mr. Taylor was almost in dis-belief from who it was he was seeing. In a natural reaction, however, as he did the cattle boss withdrew his holstered gun in an attempt shoot the man down, but the other being well – prepared in advance for this, as his gun was already in hand and raised, fired back at Mr. Taylor shooting him in his gut as the cattle boss fell twistingly to the ground and his gun falling loose from his hand upon being shot.

Undoubtedly, but, no less ironic as to the turnout of events, or in regards to the hastened duel and quick draw that had just transpired, the man who Mr. Taylor had just tried to pull his gun on was very same one that he thought had been killed, and not by some great coincidence, the man why he had come to there in the first place in order to get back the Will which bared the man's name, and who he had been told from Scott's own mouth had fallen from the cliff into the river below. Alive though the man had made it through even after being swept along the rushing river and with the gunshot in his shoulder, but himself eventually drifting onto the calmer banks where he awakened upon the shore later the next morning. From there on in he would get up and go on to make the journey by foot through forest and over hill over the next long and tough days to come trying to get to some safe ground, or where he knew people could help him, though he was by then, headed in the same direction as to the Indian's cabin along where that part of the river turned off. As he was coming through one day it just so happened that he had seen the girl outside who was then near the brook washing her hair as she could see the wanderer out of the corner of her eye then, herself yelling back to her Indian savior for help. After coming to her call and seeing how the man was he shortly got him into the cabin as he was by now half-starved and seeing that he had been shot just as well, but his friendly and kindly way not suggesting anything wrong with him, much unlike that other young man that had fled almost a week before his coming as at first he was untold of this or knowing that the Indian had accommodated the lone killer and the one whom had shot him. Only until he saw the girl with the music box that next day of being in the cabin as she would take it out time to time and had grown fond of listening to its old hymn and *Darlin' Clementine* tune he realized then what had happened and asked with an astonished expression upon hearing the melody where she had gotten the box, but Rolling Tides himself coming forth and telling the man about the other one who he had found one day while riding in a similar condition and had brought back. After learning this though reluctant to take back the box from the girl and being that the Indian gave it to her as a gift he let her keep it just the same and was more than content to let her but unaware still of his Will that had been tucked into the seam and that of which he thought had been lost. He had been staying there those past months on after and helping out however he could as he was most obliged for their care, but also just out of not knowing where else to go and now that his horse and whatever money he had at the time had been lost, along with the most important piece or that of the deed that he knew had been taken from him as well.

A few moments later then after he had shot Mr. Taylor the Indian came over to look at him lying on the ground as the cattle boss had his eyes opened looking up to the chief from below in his restricted state.

Nevertheless, the man in question who had just done the justice of shooting him down came up to his old and familiar adversary then, as the Indian stood aside to let him talk his peace or whatever words could be said before croaking off as he knelt down beside him to do this, though not before handing off his gun to the Indian to keep guard on the man who he had brought back with him as he stood there on the side foggy eyed.

"Well, I should've known you'd still be alive somehow," Mr. Taylor said turning to him then as he waited to continue but uttering the man's name as it was in full, and that had stood out in back of his mind all those years - "... *John Davidson Simmons*," he boldly went on, and the same name made out and stamped onto the fathers Will.

"I figured it was you who came down here to do this," the other or his name of John replied as he look down knowing he had finally done the cattle man in, but still not sure unlike his word of why he had come and having made the long trip of finding the Indian at his cabin. Getting up from Mr. Taylor's side as he rose to his feet a slightly confused look was on his face but the Indian seeing this went on to tell him that he had come down with intent to have the music box for himself though at first the man was more than puzzled why he would want this and could not figure it out at first even saying this out loud as he look down at Mr. Taylor now beginning to get quieter in his breathing. Hearing this the girl that had seen everything up till then thus far had already gone into the cabin to retrieve the box as she came outside with it and opened it up herself as the tune began to play off its ribbon. Seeing this John rushed over though carefully asking for it before taking it away from her as she gracefully let him do this. Then, scrutinizing the box for a moment he could still not figure out why Mr. Taylor would want it though as he looked more carefully he then could see where the seam had been torn as he felt around the area with his hand but then by taking a small knife from his pocket ripped further the fabric as he could see the piece of paper and deed that had been embedded within it as he took it in hand and unfolded it to his surprise.

As all this had been going on, however, the others including the Indian had only had their backs turned, but Mr. Taylor seeing this had sought the opportunity then to go for his weapon or his gun lying a few feet from him. Suddenly though the Indian had seen him as he look out of the corner of his eye in back and went to take the gun that had been handed to him as he tried to point and shoot, but not before John Simmons could see this himself as he waved the Indian or Rolling Tides out of his way, and then, by only taking his own gun from out of his belt shot down Nelson Taylor to finish him off, though dropping the box onto the ground during the scurry at that as it lay there broken. While the girl only look on in the confusion its ribbon continued to play for a moment more, but then the tune coming to an abrupt stop as she picked it up off the ground peering then with her learned eyes into its innards almost revealing somehow of all her thoughts of what had happened to her so far and seen up to that point, as though bound up within a final reflection of everything. But, just when the ribbon had stopped playing it's *Darlin' Clementine* tune so had Mr. Taylor finally met his own as his former worker John Simmons stood there with the deed once more back in his hands along with the girl and Rolling Tides, and, of course, the washed up cattle man also with his hanging head staggering next to them. Nonetheless, just as the present episode had ended a new one was about to begin when at last the girl or Miss Russell would make her reappearance to the rest of the world and the society she had formerly belonged to, and those who had known of her supposed kidnapping almost a year since the incident with the stagecoach and Colby, as she knew then holding the box in her arms and looking down at its stopped reel somehow within her heart it would only be the right thing for herself to do, and that there was nothing to keep her anymore to where she had been staying at all the while, or strange Indian man who had found her and brought her back to stay in his cabin in order so she could do this someday. As for the man who had just killed Mr. Taylor, or John Simmons, he had long suspected himself that the girl was of well to do and important means and as her trust for him was just as great to that of Rolling Tides it would be him to take her up to the nearby Fort Brent and who would present them with herself when at last upon her Uncle being notified of her recovery she would return back at his side and to the people who had known her before as she had been. In addition he would also hand over Mr. Taylor's man to the authorities of the Fort and reservation they upheld and tell them of what had happened thus far and as to his killing of the cattle boss as the other complied fairly easily as to the charges and being a crony witness to the whole thing himself.

In light of everything and all that had occurred soon the girl's Uncle or the coal magnate himself by name Alfred Arrison Alcott would quickly be summoned to the Indian Fort wasting no time whatsoever after hearing where his niece was now being safely kept and once more to care for her as she was accepting of his affections, although she would be quiet for a long while about what she had seen and the mysterious Indian man who had saved her life. She would keep it to herself without ever talking about what had happened, although it would be uncertain when the day would finally come when she would eventually open her mouth and tell someone, perhaps, her very Uncle or a person other than himself, but just as dear in her words of the man who she had known, and now gone from her as his fireside intuition had proclaimed she would one day – A lone warrior, once more, Rolling along the tides.

16

In the meantime Mrs. Jones had been caring for the fragile and apathetic Mildred O'Leary girl just as she had promised to the young girls parents the same day she had first come there or more than a week of her stay and several days since, but with as much affection and her own stark sense of conviction to carry this out to the fullest extent it could, though Millie, had by then been up and about inside the household and even so much as going outside on the porch to sit for a time just to let the breeze or fresh air sweep over her as Mrs. Jones had delicately suggested to her, but the girl saying hardly anything or since that other strange man and occupant of the household the shady Mr. Wyatt Cobb had carried her back upon finding her in that awful condition as he had.

As for her parents they had been given word the next day after her coming through and notified of their daughters first signs of responsiveness, but, all the while, trying hard to follow the doctor's orders as they had learned of her progress from his own mouth, and as well, offering his due warning of having them wait to make their next visit though just the same they were in a rather quiet state themselves and had not said much of anything to one another after having seen Millie in such a condition and after paying witness to her insubstantial affect. On the other hand, Doctor Treadwell along with his given prescriptions and recommendations as to their own daughter's well-fare, had also told them that he would try to listen out, or either somehow get a doctor himself from the east who knew more about these problems of the mind and head, or a certain "Psychiatrist" as he referred to it, but that he was not sure of how he would do this or what cost it would be and the workings out of payment for such a service as he knew the O'Leary's were of modest means and did not want to vouch an estimate of fee.

Aside, Millie's mother, Kate, had by then even found the small scribbled down note her daughter had made out prior to her most desperate and what she considered to be an ungodly attempt for her life, as the piece of paper had blown off the desk by a burst of wind upon herself opening the bedroom window in front of it as the note had oddly been trapped between another. Holding onto the note after reading it, however, the mother would only sit down in her daughters chair to look out the window not knowing still of why all this was happening, or so much as having the reason to understand it.

For it is certainly just as impossible to understand the motives of another or why he or she is that way and others are not, but as to her daughter, or young Millie, and how her mother would think of her now would be rather different, and ingrained somewhere within her a feeling she could not relate nor wishing for that matter to conjure her daughter in the same light as herself. For in her own religion she could see no reason for the act, nor pardon to it, but she knew she was different and had to accept what she was and try to see in her what she could of her daughter or what was and had been in her before, though hard it would be for both herself and in her own faith.

As for Benjamin his reflections were almost similar but with a more or as much an endearing blame for what had occurred and as to his daughter's act, leaving him in an unreconciled dilemma and one he could not get over, but would do the daily chores of whatever he could to not dwell on the obvious and instead pour himself into what work or activities he could as to not think on what else was going on or the reality of his own emotions. In consequence, his hands were just as steady as they had been when chopping wood or when he used a chisel to one of his chairs or the other things he did, but inside him his nerves just as unsteady and taking the few moments he would to himself when he could no longer do what he was and to relieve himself by smoking his pipe or leave the area to only come back to it after beckoning the voices of his mind that had once more returned in the form of unresolved and ghostly spirits.

Still, yet, Wyatt Cobb was someone who would more than readily qualify as to relate to this notion of being and his presence at Mrs. Jones was something Millie was not used to, although she had seen him at other times before and just as he had observed her as well, or when in and out of town, or coming out of the saloon in his oddly uniform way unlike those others clearly affected from there drink and with their impeded in step, but also even on occasion so much as having seen himself in the very secluded place that he would go to in retreat and where he had found her days before as he had. Other school children had similarly at times either together or by themselves seen or were noticing of his distinguished and flaunted character walking by or along the road as they would whisper and pass on their own short ended gossip, or what they thought they knew of him in order to either scare the other, or just for passing the time through the superstition they could make up and imagine for himself, and which in effect was really just meant only to ward off their own lack of reasoning to deduce something they could not understand or more to the point as to face a certain reality within themselves his image brought that they could not cope.

Millie had grown up likewise in this climate and had always regarded him as someone unapproachable though a mystery to herself like others that she could not attain an answer, but more unlike the others of also having a kind of wonderment and under hidden sorrow for him that came along with her inability to do the latter.

One such morning then, she had gotten out of bed earlier than usual or even before Mrs. Jones had come in to see how she was doing, and was instead awake by herself in Wyatt's bedroom quite modest in its décor and furnishings though she knew well by then that it belonged to the same man she had always regarded in the way previously described and seeing his small desk set over in the corner on the other side which she could also see had some small pile of some books on its far side, and even some papers with writings on them she deduced came from his own hand, although she had not read any of them so far in just keeping to herself all along.

Timid at first but eventually succumbing to her own curiosities she decided she would open one of the drawers of the cabinet next to her with its small lantern light still sitting on top like before though unsure of what she would find, if anything, but listening and looking out at first to see if anyone was about to come before she did this. As she slowly open the drawer, however, with her fixed eyes waiting to see what was inside her nervous look turned to a melancholy gaze as she look down and took out what was Wyatt Cobb's tin type of the woman he would take out time to time and turning it over like he had before and in the same way as she could see herself the inscription on the back and reading the woman's name below the plate, or plain *Sarah*, as she read it.

Just then, as she had been doing this she could hear footsteps coming down the hall or the same footsteps she had heard of Wyatt Cobb himself once before slow and pacing they sounded, but putting the plate back in the drawer quickly as she could and getting back into bed and covering herself with the sheets out of fear, though she could see no one come or any hint of this as whoever it was seemed to turn around instead after a few brief moments as she lay their not doing anything and resuming her abhorrent anxieties.

After a short time, however, of lying there she decided to get up again and make her way out of the room which she had already done herself by then without any assistance from Mrs. Jones anyhow, but this time with anticipation of seeing Mr. Cobb, either out of his room or another one he had been staying in for the time being and made up for himself down at the other end of the long hallway, or, even perhaps, out on the porch as he would sit sometimes in one of the rockers situated side by side with his head slightly perched and a pipe in his mouth, but looking well kept away to himself and as though unconnected to anything else.

This time, however, unlike other times before she had decided she would make the effort of accosting him to speak and attempt to thank him for letting herself stay in his room given her courteous and gracious nature, knowing too not what to expect of him or what he would say either, as the look of plate he had and seeing the mysterious young and wholesome woman's face was something that made her want to do this and in her own secretive self could as well connect with, unsure of what the woman had meant to him, or what fate had given over to himself as to have the plate tucked in the drawer and that she had just pried into.

As she opened her bedroom door making her way out of her room in hopes of somehow trying to do this she could see no one in sight as she pass by the old woman's room seeing she was still asleep with the door cracked slightly open and tucked in her bed. Normally she had risen early almost every day to care for the young girl, but this time had neglected to get up as it was still quite before she would rise, and herself merely tired from the previous week and days to come. As she continued down the hall some more past a few doors was finally Wyatt Cobb's own bedroom as the door was closed and as Millie look at it for a second before turning to go downstairs unsure as to where he could be not bothering to knock either sensing somehow he was not inside, but thinking maybe he was out on the porch in the same way she had seen sitting in his chair those past days.

She made her way down the steps then, attentively looking out to her side for anyone but seeing no one still as she got down onto the last step, hesitating for a moment to go on as she eyed the door from the inside but going on as she did to open it as the morning sun came through and upon her, though it was a nice enough autumn day and still far off from the bitter cold winter months when the sun would hasten itself during those darker morning hours.

At first she could see no one or Wyatt Cobb rocking in his chair for that matter as she stay there standing bare sleeved on the porch in her night clothes (During the day besides her present outfit she could sometimes be seen wearing one of Mrs. Jones' dresses that she had gotten and unhidden now from the back throws of her own wardrobe, though fitting the girl rather loosely, but made more for an older person's figure. Her mother had also given by then some articles of clothing, or whatever else she thought Mrs. Jones could use and that the doctor had brought to the household himself including her own and beloved diaries that she had always kept as her mother thought it right to let her have these but the doctor giving no qualms to this and even endorsing of the idea). Nevertheless, as she stood there for a moment longer and looking out into the far horizon of breezing grains and the blue clouded sky above it the wind began to pick up then sweeping over her and blowing the strands of her hair to and fro and about her face, but with the chill in the air getting harsher than the days before and herself getting colder and deciding then she would head on back inside. As she went back through the open door to enter, however, she was met by the surprise of no other than Mr. Cobb's own presence, almost joltingly, and caught off guard for it, although he was the very person she had come down to acquaint in the first place which would be in some larger estimate and regards her second act of will, or passing over of trust to someone other than Mrs. Jones.

Shy at first the words did not come easily, but she spoke them anyway as Wyatt stood their quietly, but naturally, saying nothing.

"I... I just wanted to tell you," she said pausing before carrying on, "Thank you Mr. Cobb, sir. I mean, for letting me stay in your room and all - that is."

At this Wyatt did not respond as he stood there a moment after she had said this and as the young lady in front of him was about to turn away and go back up the stairs, but seeing this he opened his mouth to her finally, as it had been a long while since someone else or a stranger had spoken to himself in her reposing way, but went on himself to return the gratitude though first removing his hat to her to do so.

"Well, I Thank you very much for that, ma'am," he said.

Upon this Millie had looked back to him about to make the first step, but stopped then at hearing the first few words he had ever spoken to her. He went on cordially to her though. "But, I reckon you haven't caused myself any trouble ma'am, if it should be of any console to yourself."

"Well, yes. I *mean*, it is," she quickly replied trying to be pleasant, though taking notice as well his reserved and mannerly custom as he placed his hat back on top of his head. He did not say anything else to this though, as he proceeded to go outside through the half open door, and Millie turning back one last time as she continued up the stairs once he had closed the door behind him. After this she continued back down the hall to her bedroom, or more appropriately Cobb's, as she decided to cloth herself in one of her own made up dresses by her mother and that she had sent over, but as she look around the bedroom doing this there was somewhere in her mind the new vision of what she had known to be as the darkened and enigmatic man she had once seen before, and with it a new mystery to him that she could not unveil, nor surmise, but the picture of the woman she had seen somehow apart of that mystery and asking herself once again – Who was this Wyatt Cobb, really, and why had he kept the plated image of the unknown lady for all those years?

17

Somewhere in the back woods of Nebraska convicted felon Colby and the sheriff had finally reached their destination, though not so far off from where the sheriff had purposely lost the other two deputies, or the North Easterly side near the Ohio border, as Colby still had his hands handcuffed behind his back and had been riding the same way on the rear of the sheriffs horse the whole time and directing him to where he needed to go, or the small decrepit and half run-down slice of a cabin they were in front just then, the two side by side hiding quietly in the thick as they could see the thick line of gushing smoke out from the fluted chimney on the cabin's side, supposedly housing Colby's own gang and the loot the sheriff was going to exchange for himself.

Taking out his gun, then, the sheriff shot off a round into the air waiting for someone to come out though the men inside had been steadily asleep even in the late morning as it was then, but Colby and himself hearing the others getting themselves up in the meantime and making their groggy and moaning noises as they did. Shortly after, however, a big fat man suddenly came out with his gun in hand upon opening the door, almost in panic, trying to figure where the stray shot had come from.

Turning to his side he looked while the sheriff and Colby could see the man from their cover but at this the sheriff mercilessly went on to aim his gun at the helpless gang member plainly visible in front of himself on the open cabin deck as he squeezed off a shot then in his leg, the man falling to ground wailing and dragging himself back to the cabin door and yelling, "Let me back in you's yellow sonuvabitch's! I've been shot!"

The others inside were more than reluctant to open the door though even with his yelling, but one of the men from inside eventually did as he said in his grudged tone, "Hold on you poor bastard," swaying the door open to do this by holding his gun in hand and creeping out himself crouched over.

"Come on out from wherever you's are you sack of shit!" the man yelled out himself as he was doing this.

Hearing the man's vile temper, however, the sheriff took the opportunity then of shooting him in his gun carrying arm as it fell out from his hand and onto the deck, as the man fled back into the cabin clutching his arm, the door closing sharply behind him.

The sheriff, nevertheless, let the man climb back into the door way as he had, trying to merely arouse the others as much as he could before letting them know that their very own gang leader was chained up next to him and going on to make the arrangements for his exchange at the peril of Colby himself, but he figured just as well the gnarly eyed and handcuffed prisoner would cooperate with his demands and using him as leverage for the others to go alone.

"Ok, Colby," he said in his lying position next to him. "Now that I've shot some your boy's up, why don't you give a good holler to them in there."

"Hold up you all, now!" Colby shouted to them in his weary voice.

At first nothing could be heard from inside or anyone saying anything, but then one of the men spoke out.

"Is that you, Colby?"

"Well, it sure the hell is. You old crank of hoot - Tom Beardsley," he replied.

"Well, What the hell you doin' out, there?"

"Well, it just so happens I'm handcuffed with my hands behind my back you sorry bastard, if that helps you any?"

There was a brief hesitation from the other.

"Who you with?" the man or Tom asked from inside.

At this the sheriff turned to him and put his gun up against his side as he cocked it.

"Don't be using my name now," he said quietly.

"Never mind 'bout that," Colby said in compliance. "You boy's be haven the loot we got in there?"

"Well, hell, Colby. We didn't know you'd be comin' on back."

"And just what the hell does that mean, now?" Colby shouted.

There was a moment of delay in the others reply.

"Well, we spent on most of it comin' down from Wyomin' after you been caught. We thought you were dead or, somethin'."

"And what the hell you do a thing like that for?" the prisoner belted out.

"Well, sorry Colby. But, we didn't know you'd be comin' back."

The sheriff upon hearing this was quite discouraged after having made the bountiful trip, and all the plotting he had come up with as to get there but his face turning red and morose with irritable tension, and, in so many words, sticking the gun harder into Colby's side and urging him to speak up, or as to the possibility if they were holding out on him.

"Well, you sonuvabitch, Tom. You ain't lyin' to me, now – Are you?"

"No, Colby," the man said in a believable enough tone from inside. "All we got now is a few hundred dollars, but that's it."

"Well, hell," Colby replied with unsureness. "Just send out what you's got then."

Seeing now that his plan of profit was not going his way the sheriff's cynical face turned back to serene, hardly interested in the meagre payoff as he rose to his feet and then to get back on his horse that was a little ways behind him.

"Where you goin'? They haven't come out yet..." the shakily and unsure Colby said from his laying position.

"That 'a be alright, Colby," the sheriff said in chippered tone to him.

Getting back on his horse then, Colby could see that the sheriff was bitterly not pleased suspecting what he was going to do, as he began to get up and make a dash for it though the sheriff had taken a few steps with his horse and turning around as he shot Colby square in the back with his .45 and almost chuckling as he did it.

Nevertheless, Colby fell shot to the ground dead only after making a few steps over to the cabin as the others seeing this from inside and peeking out through the cracks suddenly burst outside and onto the deck shooting all around though they could not see where the one or whoever had just shot him dead was at, or anyone, as they continued to shoot in same direction, Tom Beardsley himself coming up to the slayed outlaw as he knelt down.

As all of this shooting had been going on, however, the sheriff in trying to make a clean getaway was actually hit by a straying bullet, miniscule it seemed, and in back of his left shoulder though he was not even knocked off his horse or seemed to mind the pain of it only turning around once on top and continuing his way.

By then, some of Colby's gang members had already saddled onto their horses that all the while had been stewing loose in back of the cabin trying in an attempt to get up with the sheriff, but himself well ahead of them by now, or at least far enough to evade them as he could see them riding through while he hid between some overgrowth and seeing them pass by through the trees and wood. Shortly, then, he began to ride on, though the pain in his shoulder had been getting worse now, and knowing he would have to stop at some point to mend it. As his plan had gone awry of getting away with Colby's loot, however, he now only had thoughts of getting back to town and making the trip up there even in his bereaved dilemma but at the very least knew no one could suspect him after what had happened nor could indict him, and, although now quite far off from his prior motives and plan of return he knew he would have to evade his own corroborative folly without the money or loot he thought would be his payoff and that Colby, gone and dead, as he had left him had proved less than profitable in this. Instead, he could only make the next few days up the Wyoming country with the bullet in his shoulder and fend off the night chill as best he could, but hoped no one should see him during this venture and that his next victim, wherever he lay, would surely be more than lucrative – *or would it?*

* * *

Back at home there had been a quietness to the town that had long been waited, though neither because it was so much desired, nor because people had stopped talking about this and that. Rather, it came in the wake of all the other previous noise and stir created from the inception of the towns subsequent downfall starting with Colby's incarceration, and then unto Mr. Taylor's own scandal connected to the fatal incident of the woman and child, and, finally, that of the girl, young maidenly Millie, who had gone from her parent's home one night with all those others and her own peers, and even the not to go unmentioned Mrs. Motts, herself, of the school house, but all for the most part shaken by the news.

If this banal and esoteric chatter wasn't enough though the two deputies had already arrived and returned to town to share their own knowledge of what had happened while on their way to find the girl and the supposed confiscating of the sheriff at the hands of the killer they were being led by, as well, as the death of deputy Mike Taverns, as they had been kept up in the local jailhouse along with Joe Collins still considered the head chief and now that Jeff McCormack had been detained his chances for the official position were thought to be well within his favor, grieved were the others of Little Cavern, for that matter, to know of this. Although now, inasmuch, less considered gossip than as before, a reality was beginning to shape within the townspeople and the town life itself, moreover, they could no longer afford to ignore, and one that was prevailing regardless of the rule or the towns stance on firearms, they, or the people that had come to settle its Christian way and strolling streets, and whom most had thought would censor their refuge from other walks of life regarded much less appealing to them and in their minds, but was now, without any clear reason, proving less than effective as to providing it.

Unexpectedly, following up to this contagion of numbness more talk would inevitably be inspired not only of and having to do with the town, but, throughout other parts, as well, and even in the east as the headline worthy news of Marie Russell's reappearance would be on the tips and tongues of everyone else around and a picture of her once again returning to the freshly mornings paper of both herself and her uncle in their final reunion and in the upper right hand corner her own portrait that had originally circled upon her having gone missing.

Even more than the trivial nature of the popular headline in allusion to Little Caverns people or the towns on goings, however, would be the far more reaching and unanticipated news of Cattle Boss Nelson Taylor's demise at the hands of John Simmons and whose ranch was currently being divested over to him as he was now himself being over the age of thirty as the will had specified, or thirty three to be accurate, considered the sole inheritor of the property, or in the case that no one else could show proof of another existing deed or will that Nelson Taylor or his father for the time being had made out as like the one he had, and as the cattle boss had no children between himself and that of Mrs. Taylor the odds of something surfacing were few. However, it would not be clear yet whether Mrs. Taylor, or Isabel, had a claim to either the estate or ranch, or if she had any proof in her possession as to this, but her sudden return to the estate would not be entirely certain though she would most likely hear word on Nelson's death in one way or another soon enough.

There were certainly not too many qualms either in response to this next tidbit or installment to the town's news and had come by word and through even telegraph up to the people in those parts, or as when everyone had heard the sheriff himself had been overtaken. The new owner's arrival would begin in a short enough time though, when once the arrangements had been made he would make his way up by means of his own horse to requisition the property. Unsure of what to expect though and hardly starting out in the same mindset he had of proclaiming what was rightfully his the forthright and solidly grounded John Simmons felt now a sort of reluctance to take charge of the property and assume the hard work that it would entail to keep up with the ranch as it had with apprehensive thoughts of not following through on what he had believed he wanted the entire time or when he had been down in Kansas as he had started out.

He was making the trip, anyway, to see what was left of the place and ranch he had once known and had stored in the back of his mind all that time, and what hopes he had of acquiring his share for what he had fled to the fault of Mr. Taylor's unendurable treatment of him and that would now be his in its entirety, as almost a revenge had been partaken of him. This revenge though was neither invited, nor to leave him in so complete in soul, as he knew there were worse things that one could endure having the privilege of knowing the accomplished and proper girl who he had just returned to the arms of her Uncle, and after her entire family had been ransacked and killed by a man she had never met, or would ever see again. Regardless of his own spirits though, or whatever search for meaning he required, if not his first act upon arriving at the homestead, although would certainly be close to it, and making the necessary arrangements of having to let go of Mr. Taylor's own corruptible pod of men that had worked the place, if not every other one of them he had under his command, or at least the ones that hadn't been there before his leaving or he had known himself.

After this he would certainly have to find others to take their place or whatever stations they held at the ranch, but for now on it would be up to himself to decide on, who, and what, would go on as to the workings and intricacies that the cattle ranch needed in order for it to be successful. The whole way up he wondered about this, however, although unlike before if it was the same kind of success he really wanted being reserved now to former ideals he once had of it, or what past notions of success had meant to him.

18

The sheriff had made it up, thus, half way to the town as he was now within the borders of the Wyoming State and had made it clear of Colby's gang of men chasing him prior, and had not seen any one of them since, but knowing somehow he wouldn't either. Now sitting down at a small fire of his own making he was still wounded in his upper left shoulder, but had not bothered to attempt to remove the cartridge as it would be hard for him to get access to the wound anyway, choosing to limp on, though, and instead, for now just trying to fend off the cold night around him. As he keep close to the fire to do this he put some more kindling and what small branches he had collected on the side to feed it though trying not to be too careless, or as to create too big of fire for anyone nearby to see, but if anyone remotely should.

Suddenly though he heard something in back of him, not knowing what it was but trying to listen out for whatever he could thinking maybe it might have been a lost deer or a small bird as it was quite dark all around, with the exception of the nearly full moon now in its eclipse showing up bright in the night sky, but distinctly clear and the stars plainly shown and visible.

At this, he turn around, hearing yet another sound off somewhere, or possible step of someone close as he took his gun out from his holster, and then, getting up from the side of the fire to look from behind him while his face scanned the darkness of the woods and whatever of its hidden trappings lay out in front, though his face turning back to relief just as sure nothing was there.

"...*That you, Colby?*" he uttered as he turn away almost as if a bad joke or pun unto himself and slipping his gun back into his holster.

As he look up in front of him, however, after having lifted his head he was surprised to see the face of a character coming out through the woods, but his very impartial manner and step not making the sheriff retaliate, continuing to slip his gun into his holster and even surprised that he had not heard the fellow coming through while walking his horse from in back of him and even having an odd assortment of easels, perhaps, and other apparel attached on top as he hold its reigns but without any sort of resignation as he brought it up alongside the sheriff's.

"And how do you do, my fine sir, on this clear and starry bright evening?" the man or whomever it was said in his seemingly good spirited and similarly refined voice. His face was half hidden at first and barely lit by the light of the dying fire in front of him, but he looked of an older man like the sheriff as he put his hands out in front of him to warm himself though the sheriff just going along as his ignorance to the man and situation was apparent.

Nevertheless, the sheriff did not respond seeing as well he had no gun on him and the man's dress more foreign to those parts, but rather more from the city, or the east if even this but he could not be sure.

"Well, I would have to say from the looks of it, you do not look yourself," the man continued in his strange astuteness and precocious voice, seeing the sheriffs limpid side but himself still not answering.

"I gather you are a lawman, yourself?" the other asked in his smartness, although by then Jeff had removed his badge on his way with Colby after having made the doomed exchange, or at least for him as it turned out.

Hearing this, however, he looked to go for his gun not knowing why the man would ask such a thing, although the other noticing this proceeded on to elaborate.

"What I mean is, from the looks of your horse and your own presence there is something that suggests the latter. Forgive me if I'm not right of this?"

"No," Jeff requited taking his hand back. "I'm a lawman, alright."

"Oh, yes. That is what I thought," the other assuredly replied. The sheriff looked back down to the fire before he would speak again.

"And just who would you bein' on, now?" he asked.

"My name happens to be old and true to the Christian world and time as myself, but, to most I have been called upon and answered to the name of 'William' – But, what would your name now be, or what and whom should I call on you?"

The sheriff tipped his hat hesitant at first, but hardly thinking to give out his name to the man could be a danger, although his inherit and divisive friendliness was apparent.

"Jeff," he finally concurred. "Jeff McCormack, that is, to you."

"Well, in that case, Jeff, I've very glad to have met you." The sheriff didn't say anything at first to this except to tip his hat, though using his good arm to do this.

"From the looks of it I should think you've been wounded," the man insinuated after a moment more, but Jeff McCormack ignoring the remark. "Yes," he continued as he lifted his eyes to the sheriff. "I should say, in your upper left shoulder it looks – In back."

"I reckon I'll manage," the sheriff sharply refuted as he kept his hands low to the fire.

"Yes, I should think you would," the man replied good - naturedly enough but seemingly oblivious to the sheriff's lack of feeling. "Of course, being a lawman such as yourself does come with its dangers," he added.

The sheriff tried to get off the subject and mired over to his horse.

"You a painter or something?" he asked as the oddly man looked to his side and turning away from the fire uncovering as well what appeared to be his pale white face as if having on some type of makeup or snowy white pigment to his skin.

"Oh, if you would like you can call me that, but I suppose I am, in one way or another."

"Just what's that supposed to mean?" Jeff asked sounding irritable. He noticed by then that the man sounded French or a mix of European, as he could still not place him or knowing where he had come from. The other obliged him just as well though.

"Oh, just that I am merely trying to be a painter and have come from very far away to paint what had been once described to myself when I was still a young person and that has always stayed with me up till now, or the old Western Frontier in all its glory and how it was told to myself long, long ago it seems. Whether I am a painter or you would consider me one, I do not know, though there was once another man bearing my own name who said something similar to this idea and to what question you have just addressed, or perhaps, you have heard of him yourself?" The sheriff listened as the man continued - '*To be, or not to be,*' he professed, '*that is the question.*'

"I reckon William Shakespeare," the sheriff interrupted.

"Yes," the man answered him sort of bemusedly. "So, you *have* heard of him -"

Craig Sholl

Sitting there without saying anything the sheriff listened as the man or whatever artist he claimed to be went on just as the Bard himself had written it centuries ago:

'Whether 'tis nobler in the mind to suffer
The slings and arrows of outrageous fortune,
Or to take arms against a sea of troubles,
And by opposing end them? To die: to sleep;
No more; and by a sleep to say we end
The heart-ache and the thousand natural shocks
That flesh is heir to, 'tis a consummation
Devoutly to be wish'd.'

He finished the last phrase with a sigh of diction:

"To die, to sleep; To sleep: perchance to dream."

Only upon finishing his Hamlet epitaph he would go on to the sheriff dismissively. "But," he said, "In my own indulgence or the lyrical liberty you have allowed me to share of the meaning behind Hamlet's fating words, this is all I meant when I say to you, I may, or may not be an artist."

The sheriff suddenly looked curious from his crouching position, as he put some of the sticks next to him to feed the fire that was warming both now himself and the other.

"So I supposin' even myself you would be willing to paint. That is for a price, maybe," the sheriff went on asking in his trite talk.

"Well, yes," the other delivered unto, though looking off almost in thought. "I suppose for a price so long as you and myself agreed I would paint even you."

Jeff McCormack just sat there hearing what he said, but somehow his face in one of his sneers almost amused from the thought.

"Well, I've reckon I've never had a painting of myself done. How much would you be chargin' now for that?"

At this the man looked unsure of himself, but answered his question to satisfy the sheriff anyway.

"Well," he said. "I could paint you I think for how 'bout ten dollars, perhaps. Does this sound good to you?"

The sheriff looked apprehensive, but finally answered dismissively in tone.

"Well, I don't think I'd be haven time for that just now."

"Of course, you wouldn't," the other sharply recapped. "I can only imagine you're off to somewhere important, or perhaps, on your way from somewhere. Am I not right?" The sheriff looked shy of eye for an instant.

"That's right," he said pointedly. "Matter of fact headed back to the town I came from. Happens I'm the head sheriff there." Looking down into the fire he continued in his spitefulness. "If that be any business of yours."

"Oh no, you are right, monsieur. I am sorry, for the question. But, of course, how would I know you are a sheriff if you are not even wearing a badge, although I am quite sure you have one as you very well must. Of course, you would." The sheriff tired from the man's formality and riddled talk was beginning to become a nuisance to himself more than desiring for the man just then, or William, rather, to leave.

"Well, I sure do," he said with a scowl in his undertone.

"Well, as I said of course you do now," the other answered trying not to sound presumptuous.

Raising to his feet then as he did the sheriff was finally through in his talk to the man as he took out his gun to scare him off, but in the wake of all his suspicious and obtuse questioning by the other as the man or artist if he was even this in mutual agreement quickly huddled away to get back over to his horse and move on, although the sheriff was still not sure of his face or possibly where the stranger had come from, or why he had chosen his fire of all others to warm himself by.

Nevertheless, the man took the reins of his horse with the jumbled mess on top of it and started his way back into the woods or into the same place he had just come out from, as the sheriff was content on him leaving but still left in a strange and indignant confusion – was he just a man, or was he an apparition from out of the woods, perhaps, sent to him by dead Colby himself?

19

It was during this same time frame when Millie had been growing more adjusted to her surroundings and the old woman's company, and the man who she had just accosted the other day for the first time now no longer the strange and unapproached man she once knew.

Mrs. Jones was then outside on the porch sitting with Wyatt when Millie had come out by herself, the two enjoying the last bit of bearable weather before it would be too cold to go outside, or sit a long while on the porch. She was wearing her same dress she had put on, or the day before sent over by her mother and that she looked pleasant enough in, a plain white dress it was, though hardly as detailed as the one she had picked out for herself in the shop window, the whole memory of the dress seeming like ages ago to herself.

Her expression though was much more repressive than it had, and her face now taking on a more hardened characteristic, as if no longer in the responsibility of her own self and hardly wanting to go so much as beyond the front porch. Instead, the world and what she had known was a place she could no longer trust nor look at in the same way, as her act had sealed this belief and knowing for the time being what others would inevitably think of her, or the faces she had once known up at the school house her age and younger cautious of their own reproaches to her for now on. At the moment, therefore, it was only Mrs. Jones and Wyatt that would be the only two that could accompany her, as Evelynn waited for word from the doctor on or what to do in the meantime alluding to the girls care.

As the two sat there at the far end of porch though, and seeing Millie come out Wyatt rose to his feet at the glimpse of her lost expression as he decided to go over to her where she was now standing on the opposite side of the porch and looking out. For without saying, it would be Wyatt that could see the inner beauty of her soul more readily that others, and would know more of her struggle than most being an outsider himself, but her presence in the household could not but help to have an effect on himself, as well, and seeing her just then with the mild breeze turning her hair as he went near to her, though without being ostentatious and rather more collective in thought looking, or at least what it appeared to herself.

She did not notice him, however, until she could feel someone close to her side as she turned her head to him.

"Hello," she said upon noticing his presence, though he did not react at first as there looked nothing to be said between the two, but Millie had turned back already to stare out. However, at her own will she drew her head back to Wyatt as he linger there without saying anything, but remembering then the woman in the portrait she had seen in his drawer a few days ago after she had first accosted him.

"Did you know that lady in the portrait?" She asked. "I mean, the one in your drawer?"

She could see no reaction from Wyatt at first but his face still indicating to her somehow he knew of what she spoke of.

"– I'm sorry," she went to apologize, but turning away. Finally he answered though.

"Yes," he said. "She lived around here just like yourself," he went on. "Her name was Sarah Jordans." Hearing this she turned to him.

"Did something happen to her?" she asked. Wyatt looked off slightly but answered.

"I had known her when I was a younger man. We went to the school house together, the same one you go to now. Mrs. Jones taught in those days."

Millie looked to the old woman upon her mention, although she already knew that she had taught as a teacher at one time or another, having told her this briefly when she had first come, or before reading out loud one of her books one night as she would do or in the evening.

Wyatt went on though.

"After finishing school she left this town some years ago, and married another man from out East."

For the moment, Millie did not say anything satisfied as to her question as she look out again while the breeze continued to curl the strands of her hair.

"Have you lived here your whole life?" she asked then as she turn her head to him again.

"Yes," he answered. "I had for the most part," he continued passively as he look down with his head and clasping his hands in back of him.

"Where else have you been?" she asked, although he was beginning to fray from her questioning as he lay up against one of the porch spindles.

"Once, I had lived out East for a short time," he answered. Millie paused a moment before going on.

"Well, why did you come back?" she asked. "– I'm Sorry," she said noticing him shy away again. He lifted himself up though, nevertheless.

"No, ma'am. That's, quite alright."

A few moments past by after Wyatt had said this, as Millie looked like she was about to say something again.

"I had seen you before sometimes. In town a few times when I was with my mother, and once..."

Millie looked back out across the landscape before finishing what she had to say. Seeing her discomfort though Wyatt came in to help and pay her the compliment.

"You look very nice today, ma'am," he said as she turn back to him.

"Thank you," she replied modest in her smile.

"Are you, alright Miss?" he asked to make sure.

"Yes," she said after a moment. "I'm fine."

As Wyatt stand there the two continued looking out but Millie turned to him again to speak.

"I think I would like it if you called me by my name for now on, or Millie. If you want, that is." Wyatt stood there taking in the gesture as he went on to oblige the courtesy, his pleased face looking back at her.

"Thank you, ma'am – Miss Millie," he said and tipping his hat to her.

A trace of wind picked up then as the girl tucked her arms.

"I think I'd like to go back inside now," she said as Wyatt look back at her standing there and as Millie started making her way over to the front door passing him on by to do this as he took his hat off upon her leaving, and his eyes following her through the door. As he put his hat back on to his head though, he knew there was something to the girl that was different from others and a quality of tenderness to her he had long been without or subject to. As he stroll further onto the other side of the porch, Mrs. Jones herself would only go on inside to see to the young girl like other days before as she briefly look to her old friend upon opening the door after having observed the two and even sensing herself a certain change to his step and countenance just then that could suggest the notion. Who was this O'Leary girl, after all?

* * *

It was the following days ahead when the sheriff would finally return to the familiar and subdued Little Cavern town, or, on a darkened and stormy night, almost or similar to the one that had been going on as when Scott had made it back to the ranch, as Joe Collins was at the time inside the precinct along with the other two deputies aside him, sitting off as they would do, Pat Thomsen playing with his cards to himself in the corner and young Will Blake sitting and starring out looking aloof.

The harsh rain and thunder from above could be heard plastering onto the sidewalk and drips and drabs of water coming out whatever crevices or spills were outside as Joe sat at the sheriffs desk reading the weeks newspaper and towns gazette with his feet stretched out upon it and relaxed back into the chair as the sheriff himself would do, almost imitating him, as he had been becoming more and more accustomed to his new position of being the head deputy, hardly knowing either who was about to walk in from out of the cold and dampened night.

Nevertheless, it was quite late now in the lowly lit precinct when another burst of lightning and thunder came on through as the door was opened from the outside by someone, although no one noticed or had heard anyone come in as the stealthily sheriff himself stood looking at all from the door he had just closed behind him.

In front of him was Joe Collins reading the paper and the two deputies keeping to themselves as Joe's eyes suddenly leaped over the newspaper he was reading, and to the front of the jail house where to his astonishment he could see the soaked and languid figure of the sheriff standing stooped over from his wound slightly, but his partner Joe rising to his feet upon his site.

"How you doin' boys -" Jeff McCormack interrupted and disquieting the scene as he shut the door behind him sounding ebullient as ever at seeing them again, and as only he would.

The others including Joe didn't say anything nor respond to the sheriff dripping and drabbing in front of them.

"Well, how'd you get on back so soon, Jeff?" Joe suddenly talked up and asked as the sheriff continued standing there.

"That's real good of you to ask there, Joe, matter of fact," the sheriff replied in his good humor, of course. "Considerin' all you good men here must've been worried helpless as hell and all as to my capture. Now, I'm sure you all were," he continued as he look around at the few, but still remaining seated and in their places. "Isn't that right, Joe?"

"Well, sure sheriff," he replied from behind the desk trying not to sound overbearing.

"That's what I thought Joe," the sheriff returned candid like.

The other deputies just remained silent looking away from themselves, unsure though of how he had gotten away from the gang leader that had taken custody of him. Joe could see his limped walk, however, as the sheriff came over near the desk.

"Have you been shot, Jeff?" He asked concernedly, but the sheriff just playing along.

"Well, matter of fact I had been Joe." Looking to the few around him he went on. "That low down mean dirt of a swine Colby himself wounded me matter of fact when I was trying to get away from him as my bad luck would have it."

Will Blake and Pat Thomsen did not look to the sheriff upon hearing this though, as they were still apprehensive about everything and what had happened down in Nebraska as to the confiscating of the sheriff and as well having feared for their own lives, but only seeing the sheriff's return once more to his dutiful post as something they almost wished hadn't come. Sensing this ambivalence from the two, however, the sheriff in resuming his office of power carried on by saying, "Don't you and others be frettin' now, though. I shot the poor bastard outlaw myself dead and cold in his tracks comin' towards me, right after."

The two were not sure how to react, but Joe Collins went on then to tell him how the girl had already been found, and how she had been shown in the papers together with her uncle.

"Well it doesn't really matter anyhow," Joe spoke up as to this.

"And how's that now Joe?" The sheriff said not knowing what he meant.

"Happens they found the girl after all anyway's, Jeff," he replied. "Yeah, had a picture of her in the paper and everything. Along with that rich Alcott Uncle of hers."

The sheriff became more dazed in his eyes to what he was saying as his deputy was prancing about the whole incident as was his normal enthusiasm for such things and going on to even show the sheriff the paper then with the girl and the Uncle and that had been sitting aside on the desk, though so unlike the sheriff he assisted who could have cared less in so many words.

"Well, I'll be damned," the sheriff, nevertheless, replied with as much candor as he could permit to the news.

The sheriff stood their listening as Will and Pat eyed each other for a moment.

"Happens that Nelson Taylor went down to Nebraska himself and got himself killed. He knew where the girl was and everything, with some old Indian man pent up in his cabin way out in the woods and all. How 'bout that?"

Hearing this and seeing the girl's picture in the paper Joe had just placed up on the desk, the sheriff's expression turned to a distilling look, though certainly Joe's words, needless to mention, as to Mr. Taylor's involvement of course not coming of any shocking surprise to himself.

"Well, who would be guessin' on that now?" Jeff McCormack looked to swallow to himself as the other two deputies, Joe especially, didn't think anything of this.

"Yeah, sure is strange if you ask me," his assisting deputy or Joe uttered in his naivety.

The sheriff switching gears then just looked straight to his partner Joe Collins standing behind his desk as he had conspicuously not so unlike the others as well noticed upon coming through the door of how comfortable he had grown to his temporary position as head chief.

"Well, is somethin' wrong Jeff?" His partner asked suspicious he had seen this.

"No, Joe," the sheriff replied. "Nothin' the matter here Joe – *Except...*"

"Yeah, Jeff?" his partner interrupted.

"If you don't mind..."

"Yeah?"

"I think I'd like to be gettin' this bullet now from on out of my shoulder, if that's alright with the rest of all of you's."

At this Joe's face surrendered once more to the sheriff's abrasive wit, and toughened spirit as he stood there like the others ready to step down from his present role as the towns sheriff, but rather to resume his previous position of assisting deputy chief, though the other two deputy's aside were unsure if they themselves would stay on and now that the sheriff had returned, or as they had up till then declining to go back to their more common and open gun slinging towns for sake of the mere change of it. He had come back to Little Cavern, however, to resume his command, or whatever powers that be at his disposal and his same snide grin wrapped round his face standing there familiar enough to the jail house and those around him as though the iron clad bars of the cells and gun cases beside the desk were almost complimenting and befitting of it.

20

Millie's parents had been the same at their home and as described previously as to their own behavior, or whenever in each other's presence, Kate, knitting her decadent designs as she was doing this now almost more than before, trying not to harp on the situation, and her husband Benjamin immersed in whatever he could similarly. As for the town and its own set of confectionary like folk or people either living in the town itself, or those harboring near or close to it as in the case of the O'Leary's, everyone including Millie's parents would shortly find out about the return of the sheriff Jeff McCormack and his supposed story of escape from the crutches of the outlaw that had confiscated him, as some would have their own thoughts as to this or their own hesitant acceptance to his destined return, but others still neutral as to the reacquainting either way – Was he the brave man he had claimed, or was he only a liar and the two faced suspect people had already begun to fear?

Indeed, some residents had even brought their own concerns by then over to the Mayor or the pale faced and docile politician himself, although always coming with the dismissal of their own thoughts or a kind of appeasement the Mayor, or official, would put on to dissuade the others of their own reserves, or whatever petty complaints towards the sheriff they had. Nevertheless, Mayor Whitcomb would send them on their way almost with as much doubt as they had come but not pressing on the issue further knowing they could not change what already was or could even be sure of and beyond their power as mere citizens.

As for Benjamin and Kate, it was not long from these trivial town remonstrations, nor even wanting to know what was going on about this and that, and instead, keeping to themselves, but when Doctor Treadwell would come back to their home to make another uninvited visit as he had one evening around, or just before dusk, and to inform the O'Leary's of another specialist who he had incurred to come from out east. As it was he had sent for the doctor after having had a telegram or sent teletype message delivered to the other and that he had found out about through his own means, though unsure of his own enticement to the proposition, but conveying in so many words as to their daughter and what she had done asking him if he would see her, or at least one visit for a proper assessment so long as a fee was negotiated.

Hearing that the specialist had after all been willing to come and make the trip after having received a message from the other indicating that he would, the parents were intermittently accepting of the visit, and chatted some more with the present doctor about the fee or charge as to the specialist, or the psychiatrist as Millie's parents were even using the term by then, as he called on him to be a Doctor Kettle.

Although the doctor was not sure if he would come to any precise diagnosis or more importantly prognosis as to their daughter, he told them that the details of the money could later be worked out, in any matter, even if he had to pay for the fee himself in the meantime so they could repay him whenever or however they could. He was insistent, however, that he should come to let them see her soon and had even already requested for his departure as he would arrive within the later part of the week where he would escort him to Mrs. Jones' place himself and to show him his new patient, but only to wait for his assessment then of the girl afterwards or any of his recommendations he would have for her.

As for Millie she was still in the company of Evelynn and Wyatt all along and having made her exchange the other day, or her second one so far, with the gentleman she had become preoccupied with, and as to the reflections he had made of the woman's portrait though she could not know for sure either way of the truth behind the woman and image, but for some reason and the way Wyatt had spoken did not seem to satisfy her notion of her even if she did not know why at the moment, and alone enough in her own worries not to linger on anything aside from this.

It was during that same evening though when the doctor had come to speak to Millie's parents of what he had to share when their daughter, or Millie, would herself accost the man of the household or Wyatt Cobb again, as it had been nearly two weeks going on since what she had tried to carry out and upon finding her in the way he did. During that later part of the evening though she had gone downstairs to look for Mrs. Jones as she seemed to not be around, and thinking it strange that she wasn't as she had not come up to her room at the end of the hall, or to read aloud to herself as she had done almost every night, but growing a fondness for the older woman and the learned tongue she possessed, eloquent in her reading to her of the books she too had read when she had been around her age if one could scarcely imagine it.

She would go down the steps of the stairs as before as she had done to either, go outside, or throughout the rest of country home, although she had mostly been confined to just the limits of her bedroom up till then or the porch outside, never assuming the desire to go beyond the rest of the large and roomy construct, except for noticing the room off to the stair side between the hall it overlooked coming down and next to the front entrance foyer, which by habit had one of its sliding doors separating the two areas and that Millie like others could see into passing by, or near the bottom of the steps.

This room she also noticed was mostly kept dark inside during the evening or for the most part, and not well lit except for a few candles placed around, or if they happened to be put out when she had peeped inside on occasion, and that provided most of the light. On this one evening this had been the case upon herself reaching the last step at the bottom as she turned the corner of the stairs and could see the fragrant light coming from within.

At first she was afraid to enter, but being familiar now enough with the home and as she had been overcoming her own timidities in spite of her own apathy and apparent conundrum of emotion she had decided she would finally wander in, but slowly as she did this, unsure if anyone was there as the room was still fairly dark inside, but making her way if just for the sake of seeing the room itself, or to just satisfy the curiosity that had been with her since her arrival.

She continued anyway despite her fear as she open the white sliding door slightly more so she could enter to do this. Once inside, however, she could see no one else as she look around trying to see or make out what she could there being some tables and trays assorted with porcelain trivets and whatever ornaments or similarly trinkets Mrs. Jones kept out for display, but Millie turning just then, and instead, hearing the old grandfather clock standing upright in the corner behind her as it began to chime of half past eight, or when it would do every half or on the hour so often. Next to the clock though was what looked to be a modestly framed painting fastened up high onto the wall and that she thought could have been of the old woman or Evelynn herself when she was a younger woman as Millie stood there admiring the likeness of the young woman's face for a moment.

As soon as the clock stopped its little lyric though the girl looked as if she was about to go out of the room but was surprised to hear Wyatt Cobb's own and distinctive voice as it came from the back of the den and as he had been sitting in one the arm chairs the whole time without her even knowing, although two candles as well had been up on the mantle of the fireplace and lit side by side, but still, she could have sworn to herself no one had been there.

"Are you alright ma'am?" he had asked in his somewhat somber tone, but still hidden away from the rest of the room as she hesitated upon the question.

"...Well - yes," she eventually answered to him turning at once to the sound of his voice. Upon this she looked as if to turn away again, though, and just leave the room. Suddenly Wyatt spoke up again, however, but only this time uttering her name unlike before, and in a more erudite and lightened tone to his voice.

"Millie?" he went on as he got up from his seat to look at her.

"Yes?" she replied though unsure of what he wanted as she could see him standing plainly now herself at the far end of the room.

"Would you be carin' just now as to be obliging me?"

At first she was not sure how to react as she had never been spoken to in such a way, especially by him, but seeing Wyatt standing there with his hands behind his back as he had the day before on the porch though his head rather hatless now, with his long and light colored hair against the candle light she could see no fear in staying, even in the darkened room and accepted his offer just as kindly.

"Yes, I would," she replied. He kept standing there after this though without doing or saying anything further, but upon the absence of discourse she turned her head then to look back to the painting as she look it over some more.

"Is that of Mrs. Jones?" she asked. Wyatt had still remained standing next to the chair as he answered.

"Yes," he replied.

"She looks so young in it," she carried on, as Wyatt slowly come over to her while getting closer to her side as she turned to him.

"I reckon she was twenty, then," he added. Millie didn't say anything, although she had remembered now why she had come down.

"I looked for Mrs. Jones before. But she wasn't in her room. I thought maybe she was down here."

Hearing this Wyatt stood aside and led her over to another door on the side of the room as they made their way and that seemed to peep into the kitchen area, as he creeped it open further for her, but as Millie look she could see the old woman with her white and washed out hair tuft over and a cup of cold tea sitting out on the table in front of her as she slumber in one of the cradled chairs placed at its end.

Closing the door, then, Millie followed Wyatt to the fireplace as she look around briefly her face glowing of the candlelight like his.

"Strange not seeing a fireplace lit when it's this dark out," she said ponderingly in her perceptive manner, as Wyatt looked to take notice himself. Upon the comment, however, he stepped over to take what was another long, splintered type match from out of a tin type canister upon the mantle as he struck and lit it by the side of a small match box next to it. Then, by taking a piece of crumpled paper from out of one his pockets he lit it on fire with the flame of the match as he bent down to stick the burning scrap into the fireplace which had already a few spare and charred looking logs sitting dormant within its well.

As the fire slowly picked up a few crackles could be heard, as Wyatt stood aside taking an iron poker in hand that was sitting upright next to it and fixing the wood in place in order to help it get started. As Millie stood there though she looked down seeing the fire get bigger while Wyatt finally put the poker off to the side again, and then, went to place one of his hands in a sort of resting position on top of the mantle.

"I remember sitting by the fire with my parents on long nights like these when I was younger," Millie said as Wyatt stood there listening. "It seems so long ago now, though," she continued with a sigh as her eyes lowered. "Everything I guess seems so long ago now."

Wyatt sensed her unease as he kept at the fireplace looking up to her just then.

"Are you alright, ma'am?" he asked trying to be helpful.

"Yes," she answered. "I suppose."

For a moment no words were exchanged between the two but then Millie looked over to Wyatt again to say something. She asked, "Did you have a mother or a father?"

Upon her question he just look off to the side though, finally, to answer.

"My mother had died when I was still a boy around the age of ten. But I had been raised by my father after that."

"What was his name?" Millie asked.

"Walter," he said after a moment more, as he look back into the fire now that it had brightened. "Walter Priestly Cobb."

"What was he like?" she asked curiously.

At first he did not look like he would answer the question as his face showed no expression and having his normal detached look.

"...*I'm sorry*," she replied in her fear of infringing again.

"He was a drinking and gambling man 'round these parts at one time," he finally spoke. "He died ten years apart from my mother when I was almost twenty."

Millie's face turned back to unease from Wyatt's descript, but the pensive drinking man himself lifted his head from starring into the fire after as he look at the young girls face against the flicker of the flames. As he continue to look he had on an odd entrancing expression which Millie could see then.

"Is something wrong?" she asked in her apprehension.

"No, ma'am," he replied as he look away again, but leaving her still unsure.

Just then, she felt strange standing there with Wyatt and the way he had just looked at her, as she went to open her mouth after to pardon herself, but in her attempt to do this and before she could say anything Wyatt had interrupted her.

"The other day out on the porch," he said as he looked to her again, though coming closer now to her as he continued, "You said you had seen me sometimes before, or in town."

"Well, yes," she replied. "I had."

"One time I had seen you myself," he said as Millie looked slightly anxious.

"Where?" she asked in her ignorance.

"It was in the same place, that day, in the woods, where the stone wall is. I had seen you coming home from there once. You looked then, as you did just now."

"How?" she asked.

"– Afraid," he answered her.

Millie's face only resettled back upon the remark odd as it struck her and Wyatt having the same resonance and sorrow in his voice as before though Mrs. Jones, just then, had entered the room as if by clairvoyant intuition herself knowing of Millie's own feelings, or her apprehension at that very moment after Wyatt's comment as she had been listening without their knowing, but interrupting the two in time for it.

"Are you feeling like bed, dear?" she asked in her common tone as Millie turned from Wyatt who had then placed his hand back upon the mantle starring back into the fireplace.

"Yes," she replied. "Wyatt and I were just talking."

"I know dear," the old woman answered, as she went to put her hands around the young girl's shoulders to head for the stairs.

As the two started to make their way though, over to the sliding doors at the other end of the room Millie turned from the woman's side seeing Wyatt as he was still standing and looking down into the fireplace.

"Goodnight, Wyatt," she bid him as he looked back to Evelynn upon saying this.

"Goodnight - Miss Millie," he replied as the girl and Mrs. Jones continued out of the room and the up the stairs to her bedroom as the girl went to sleep shortly after that.

As for Wyatt he stay in the den some more after having talked to Millie the little bit as he continue to look down into the fire until Mrs. Jones would come in herself after having seen the young lady to her bed, but would sit there in the open room next to her student as it had been a long while since her fireplace was with wood burning inside it as then, even so much as commenting this to Wyatt himself as she stay and meditate the lax flames with him. As for the memories that the girl had stirred and awakened within him he could not help, or Wyatt, to turn them over in his head the rest of that night onward and of things he had long spoken to anyone since, but his asking for the O'Leary girls company that evening serving himself as kind of long requited request, somewhere hidden deep in his reserved and troubled soul like, perhaps, the girl herself, and, of which, the fire like the light and flames it radiated burned of a passion he could not console without them.

21

The new cattle owner, John Simmons, or now head boss of the ranch, had finally, made his way up the Wyoming State, once and for all, returning to those parts and the county and town he had once known, but the faces of people and the look of the town different than he had remembered, and instead, mostly strangers they were to him, but others, and their families, who had settled the area all those years and back still rightly familiar enough to himself, or the local shopkeepers such as Dixon and those even partial few up at the saloon. As for the ranch some of the workers who had known of his impending arrival, or the retaking and ownership of the business, and who had known John when he was younger as a fresher worker, were now all more than pleased to hear of his new position as Boss, but certain others, or at least the ones that hadn't already left upon hearing of Mr. Taylor's death not so necessarily as welcoming as the rest. He assumed the responsibility of the ranch, regardless, or what he thought needed to be done in terms of getting it back on its feet after the duration of inactivity it had gone through and some Mr. Taylors own neglect in the wake of everything, though the question of Mr. Taylor's estate and home or what would be done in terms of this inheritance, if any, were plausible at the moment as the only one who could assume control over either was Mr. Taylor's wife, but herself, still unaware of Mr. Taylor's death, for that matter, word of it as it quickly got around even in those days eventually getting to her somehow or someway despite.

The doctor, or that of Treadwell, had also informed Mrs. Jones, by then, of the specialist coming from out east as he told her his arrival would be imminent within the next day or two where he would pick up and greet the Doctor from the train station and bring him over from there to Mrs. Jones' home by means of his own carriage, although he had told Mrs. Jones before his arrival that he wished Millie not to know just then, or at least until the doctors arrival that he was coming to see her, trying not to upset the girl further in her present state.

As for herself, or Millie, she would mostly keep away from the others for the remaining time up until the visit by the clinician, or whatever kind of doctor the man would turn out to be, but Millie and the rest of her worries now reminiscing inside her of the recent talk in the den with Wyatt, or Mr. Cobb to herself, and tucked away in the back of her mind, and what he had said to her though knowing somehow he did not mean unwell, either.

She would carry his more impartial or resounding words in stride, as all the rest among her load, and as to what he meant about her face and how he had seen her coming home that day from the same spot of which they both knew, as her reflections of his remark only made her more intrigued towards her own emotions, trying to almost understand the beginnings of what and why she was a certain way and seemed, separate, unlike others.

Therefore, without useless quivering, or needless redundancy as to the girls problems, or whatever presumptions could be made as to her mindset, it was, perhaps, in the best interest of Millie herself that the well-respected and formidable Doctor Kettle arrived at the nearby Governors County station, on a late Sunday afternoon, just shy of eight o'clock or the Seven Forty abroad from the east.

As the doctor stepped down from the train onto the station platform amid the steam and smoke of the locomotive in back of him the towns physician would wave to the more distinguished man and colleague in dress, though only among a few others much less cordial in manner and Easterly looking, as whoever after taking notice made his way over, and also carrying in one of his hands a black bag, similar almost in style to Treadwell's own, but hardly as roughened, either, or unkempt looking the man appeared in step and manner in comparison to the mere town's physician.

"Are you a Doctor Kettle?" Treadwell asked looking down at the short bearded and bespectacled man's face.

"Yes," the doctor answered in his more privy and formal sounding voice. "You must be Treadwell, then."

After abruptly making their greeting, respectively, Doctor Kettle would go on to board the carriage and horse while settling himself next to the physician, as the other quickly shook the reigns and briskly took off though on the way the two men would go on to exchange a few more words about the girl and the young lady he was about to receive, or aside from what the visiting doctor and psychiatrist had been told prior, as Doctor Treadwell hurriedly made his way trying to reach the older woman's home knowing she could possibly retire soon, but hoping to get there before this would happen.

Once they had reached the residence, as the darkness of the night did not make as easy to get to the home either, being well passed the dusk hour by now into the cold and gusty autumn month, the two stepped down from the carriage to get on with their business as the one followed Treadwell up the steps of the porch before heartily knocking on Mrs. Jones front door to let themselves in. Evelynn herself came to open the door shortly after or upon the second knock to greet both, though letting the two gentlemen inside her home, pleasantly, nor without any qualms as she had anticipated the visit having been told by Treadwell, of course, days before. As the two entered, however, the nice and charmingly quant country home of the old woman's Mrs. Jones would take notice herself of the new Doctor almost having a detached way in her apparentness towards him, as Treadwell himself could hardly catch on to her demeanor at first, but Evelynn accommodating the sharply intelligent and seemly good natured Doctor Kettle, nonetheless, even so much as offering to make a pot of tea in the meantime though he was naturally anxious to see the girl, but accepted the old woman's offering just the same while even shedding a bit of English quality in his voice and stature which the two could tell of.

At this Mrs. Jones stood aside to let the likeminded Doctor Treadwell take charge of the situation as he led the other up to the girl's room making their way down to the end of the hallway where the supposedly nervous and sickened young lady, or that of Millie, had been staying inside for the duration, as she had heard the two and Mrs. Jones downstairs talking before the few moments they did.

The door to her bedroom was then closed as Doctor Treadwell lightly knocked to enter, but going on as he did to open it seeing, upon coming in, Millie herself sitting plainly on the bed with her down cast face and her arms loosely folded as her eyes were fixed looking off at something or somewhere else no one could know for certain.

For it would be the visiting Doctor's and analysts first attempt, or at least, a mere trial of her senses through observation by using his set of specially trained eyes as to such behavior, or what other behaviors he thought had seen like it, and to begin the task of trying to locate where this place she had gone to was, or what other inherit afflictions would be affecting her as to have done what she did and be as she was then, as he go on to look her over briefly standing on the side next to Treadwell while familiar physician spoke to the girl as calmly and comprehensible to her as he thought he could possibly be, as Millie listened without hardly moving and staying in her same affect.

"Hello, Millie," he said in his kindly voice before introducing the other though he knew just as sure the girl could see the Doctor's obvious presence aside him.

"This man visiting with me is a Doctor Kettle whom I'm introducing you to now," he continued in a slow kind of speech not sure of how she was listening nor herself at any point making eye contact with him as she look in the same place. "He's what's known in our medical profession as a psychiatrist, and he's made the whole trip from farther away of coming here to see you himself," he went on seeing the young girl then look to the other doctors face, who was almost sort of squinting at her now through his pair of shortly rimmed glasses.

"I just want him to have a look at you now, or to see if he can help after – well..." he said almost pausing from his next words, "What had happened and all, and how you came to be here with us."

After this Doctor Kettle kept standing there as he had as Treadwell went out of the room, but not before conveying to his colleague, now with his back turned to Millie, or if he should need his assistance with anything that he would be near during his analysis of her, but the psychiatrist kindly enough letting Treadwell dismiss himself with ease, and considering the girl just to be another one of his patients he was observing.

As for Treadwell he only continued out the door closing it shut on his way out, but was quick to see Mrs. Jones herself standing in the hallway nearby almost as soon as he looked up from his thought unsure, either, of what she was doing there so close.

"Should the Doctor be needing anything?" she asked cordially as the other did not look to reply still concerned in his thought.

"No," he said finally. "He'll be fine for now," he continued to her though taking Mrs. Jones delicately by her arm, then. "I want to talk to you for a moment," he went on askingly but with a slight telling of look on his face, as though the other knew of what he was going to speak to her about. "If that would be alright, with you – Evelynn."

"Well, of course," she replied playing along to his ignorance almost. "The tea I had put on I should think will be ready for us soon anyway."

The Doctor just gestured to her by taking his hand to his hat and lifting it slightly as he continued to follow her down the hall, and then, down the steps of the stairs of her home proceeding into the den area, and of which during the whole time Millie had been in the beginnings of her assessment as Doctor Kettle went through his array of late nineteenth century techniques and practices.

For a moment, Mrs. Jones went out of the den upon excusing herself and into the kitchen so she could retrieve the tea on the stove she had made and that was almost ready to boil as Doctor Treadwell kept standing and looking about the peculiar room as he try to look comfortable, even now with the fireplace blazing and burning of some old and spare wood again, as had like the other nights before when Millie and Wyatt had spoken, once more finding its use, but fending off the chill of the night air quite effectively at that.

As the doctor had turned, then, almost as the young and observant O'Leary girl upstairs had done the other night herself, he could see the painting of the old woman, or Evelynn, when she had been younger, musing at it as he had remembered her back then, so long ago it seemed to him now, as he was a much older man in age like the woman, but knowing and reminded of how once they had been acquaintances, more or less, and throughout the given and uncertain years which the time had slipped by, as time itself will often be vulnerable to. Still, the site of the portrait or rendering, and what reminisce came of it only caused the Doctors face to settle back slightly and now thinking again of what he had in mind to say to the old woman, though not sure either what Evelynn herself would reply, or have to say to him after.

It wasn't long though until she came back into the den holding now a tray of some of the porcelain tea cups she had kept stored away with each resting on top of the silver tray next to what was the hot steaming porcelain tea kettle and spout, as she set everything down on a fanciful wood table, and that was stuck between the two chairs that had overlooked the fireplace as the Doctor came over to help himself and attempt to speak with her.

"Evelynn," the doctor said in his firmer sounding tone as she bent down to pour out the cups of tea lifting away after to hand himself the saucer and cup, as the steam came off the top while he held onto it in both hands. "I am sorry, but I should think this present situation with the girl has put you out some."

At this she did not say anything maintaining her indifferent expression as he stand there with her trying to attempt to tell her what he was really getting at.

"Well, it's no secret now," he bluntly went on. "But, it's my feeling..."

"Yes?" she intruded upon his hesitation.

"Well..." he said trying to go on though just seeing her look back at him with her same indifferent expression. "It's my feeling now, that after having concluded as to the young girl's diagnosis Doctor Kettle ..."

"Yes?" she asked pretending not to know what he was saying, but himself going on anyway.

"That it be recommended she'd be taken somewhere where they can help and treat her better than we."

"You mean, a sanatorium?" she asked in her forwardness.

"– Yes," he replied openly. A moment went by before anything more was said, but Mrs. Jones just kept sitting there calmly looking when the Doctor spoke up again.

"I understand you may have grown fond of the girl yourself, Evelynn." Hearing this she just sat there sipping her tea as the Doctor carried on. "But, in these matters of the mind we cannot assume that we know more."

Upon his last thoughts, Evelynn, or Mrs. Jones only went to put aside her cup as she placed it back on the tray looking as if about to say something herself as the Doctor took notice of this.

"I don't think she should be a bother if she were to stay here with me."

Doctor Treadwell only gave a snug, but apprehensive look to her more garnered gesture, or at least to himself, though replying to Evelynn in spite.

"But, what about the girls own health Evelynn..."

"Do you think she will fairer better in a sanatorium, then here?" she interrupted candidly.

Nevertheless, Treadwell looked of thought for a moment before answering, but somewhere within knew he was anything but helpless not to succumb to the old woman's sensibility regarding the issue, almost as if the memory of the once young Evelynn he had known and even may have so much as admired himself at one point had come back to stray him for that one only purpose.

"Well, I don't know, then," he said still unsure before going on. "Regardless, we'll have to wait to see what Doctor Kettle can make of it before deciding."

After he had said this Treadwell would take one last sip of his tea before setting the cup and its saucer back down onto the tray to only accompany again the rest of the chinaware laid out, as he stood there the few moments more while Evelynn remained seated in her same delicate poise with her cup in hand.

It wasn't too long, however, until the pragmatic and much more omnipresent Doctor Kettle from the East could be seen coming down then, at the end of the stairs from Treadwell's view as he turn from the fire to look in back as the doctor made his way through the open pair of doors to speak to Treadwell himself about what thoughts he had come to concerning the girl.

Upon making his entrance Evelynn herself raised to her feet as she go on to offer the Doctor the tea she had promised, but the anglophile and Gentleman amply accepting of it, as she went on shortly after to promptly excuse herself from their company thinking it necessary to see to the girl as the psychiatrist concurred on her behalf and turning to her to see her leave before beginning his talk with Treadwell.

"Well, Treadwell," the visiting psychiatrist spoke up after setting down his cup into its saucer in hand. "I can only deduce that the girl is suffering from a severe form of the melancholia or the psycho neurotic form of the illness, but I fear if she is not put under the proper supervision or placed into a sanatorium she will only get worse and her symptoms will persist. Therefore, with your permission I would like the consent to be able to do this, and, of course, with the cooperation of her parents, as I trust you must know them quite well yourself by now I'm sure." Doctor Treadwell looked slightly distant, just then, after hearing the others conclusion and as for his request of the girls custody, or wherever it was they would take her so in order to treat her, but the physician even if he did not like it beginning to now feel vague about the whole thing himself and more weary than he had.

"Oh – yes," he answered him anyhow trying to sound alert again.

"Yes," the other retorted in a kind of agreement though Treadwell keeping his hidden ambivalence to himself.

"Very well, then," Treadwell said afterwards seeming as though accepting of it while the other placed his cup back down onto the woman's busy tray.

At this Doctor Kettle looked around briefly inquiring of his coat nor seeing it anywhere near, as Treadwell looked around momentarily with him, but then, finding and spotting the befittingly and well coiffured coat of the Doctor's tucked over a chair on the other side of the room as he went to pick it up himself and as Kettle followed from behind. Picking up the coat then and slipping it onto the man's back as he did Treadwell began to speak again about the girl, or Millie.

"This sanatorium you speak about?"

"Yes?" asked Doctor Kettle in a friendly enough tone.

"Where exactly would this place be?" Treadwell asked. Looking as though the answer would be obvious Kettle replied.

"Well, of course, it would be in the East where I practice as a head doctor and councilor of one of the wards." Pausing then as he looked at Treadwell before continuing he would add, "Cederwick it's called."

"Ah – so I see," the physician said in his more plainly tone, although pensively looking down as he had spoken.

"Well, as I said I think it would be the best thing for the girl the way she is now, as I don't believe given her symptoms she will get better otherwise," Kettle went on as Doctor Treadwell seemingly concurred. "You will be telling this to her parents, though, of course, so I can make the arrangements for her care," he continued as Treadwell replied to him but only keeping in agreement with his vice the whole time without giving any of his own thoughts.

Just then, the tiny and fragile looking figure of Mrs. Jones could be seen coming down the steps of her stairs in time to see the Doctor off before departing as was her custom manner while she look to Treadwell first before the two embarking out though he did not give any sign of his thoughts as to what had been discussed.

"And thankyou again Madame, as for your hospitality in regards to the girl, and, of course, for the pleasure of your company," Doctor Kettle graciously spoke out to her as he put his hat to his head to leave though the old woman thanking him for the visit and whatever salutations could be said as Treadwell, while letting his colleague or Doctor Kettle out first, gave her one last look before heading out the door. Mrs. Jones, however, almost stopped him before leaving as he turned to say one last goodbye, but hesitating for a moment though it was unclear why, as Evelynn somehow knew what intent he had as to Millie, and feeling almost confident he would take her word over the others, and even after all the fuss that had been made in the first place just to get the busy and respectable Doctor there to see her.

As the old woman turned though after closing the door she could see the fireplace with the wood soundly burning inside as the scene suggested a certain redemption to the home and place that had not come easily, but one that only an elder woman's eyes could tell of. As she stand there a little while more within her thoughts she could feel the eyes of someone from the top of the stairs as she turn to look only to see Wyatt Cobb's face silhouetted in the dark as he briefly turn away to his bedroom, or the one he had been staying in for the time being, while she squint for a moment trying to make him out. For she could not still be sure of what Treadwell would decide as to the girls treatment nor could be sure of what the girls presence would bring if she were to stay, but as she continue to stand there she almost hoped he would decide in her favor as to not put her in the sanatorium like the visiting Doctor had blatantly recommended, but even herself slightly unsure now of what the right thing to do would be, and Fate as she knew it not always up to the one's that burden it.

22

As for the sheriff he had once more resumed his position of head deputy chief over the town as he sat with his legs crossed on top of the table reading a newspaper himself, and Joe and the others sitting around as usual waiting for something to come up. As for his wound it had been mended the few days before and by the town's doctors own hands, or that of Treadwell himself as the scrutinizing physician had also commented that bullet had not been too deep giving him the ability to go on the way he did. The sheriff sat there in all his glory, nonetheless, although having some minor bandages wrapped on the inside of his shirt barely visible, but removing the cigar he had been smoking just then, and sitting there with the paper as Joe began to speak up to break up the silence, and only, of course, as Joe himself would.

"Heard some red neck man came through here few days goin' back," he said sitting down next to Pat Thomsen who had his hat half covering his face at the moment.

"Yeah, what he'd want?" good old Pat replied with an air of sarcasm almost, but staying as he was.

"Well, nothin' I guess," Joe replied. The sheriff just kept as he was but Will Blake hollered in then, though it being rather unlike him.

"So why'd you say it, then?" he said from over in the corner by himself.

"Well, I don't know," Joe spoke up. "Just happened to hear it," he went on.

"Yeah, I guess," young Will poked at him.

At this the sheriff, lacking the humor for such antics, took notice of the young man's disposition as he continued to suck on his cigar but seeing the deputy out of the corner of the eye from reading the paper.

"Now boys," he said interrupting in his flair for arrogance. "Don't be fussing with each other like that."

"Well, hell. I'm not fussin'," Joe continued as he prattled away. "Just heard it the other day from old Farnworth back there himself. Kept askin' him about a map or something, or some type of book he figured he might've had. He said thought it had somethin' to do with that poor Mexican came up here and got shot by you yourself a few months ago."

After Joe saying this the scene turned silent again as nothing more was said except deputies Will and Pat eyeing one another for a moment at hearing the mention of one of the sheriff's victim's, but the Jeff McCormack himself doing or saying nothing, though on the inside somewhere his eyes secretly widening, sensing there was something more to this gibberish let out by his assisting deputy Joe Collins.

"Well, is that so Joe," the sheriff barged in on him as his deputy looked up to the desk.

"Sure is, Jeff," he answered amiably minded enough, but the sheriff taking one his snide grins as he removed his cigar again. Then, looking as if to sit back in his chair to continue reading, the sheriff rose to his feet in a nonchalant way.

"Well, boy's," he uttered as the others continue to sit around lazily, "I think I'll be headin' on out now for a little while myself if you don't mind, bein' nothin much is happenin' round here."

Deputies Will Blake and Pat Thomsen just kept as they had after the sheriff had said this to excuse himself, but the two for now on not surprised by anything the sheriff would do and trying to resist the inordinate behavior as they look him over with apprehensive eyes no less knowing the sheriff rarely left the precinct in the middle of the day like that, but assuming nothing they could not surmise of him.

As he made his way over to the precinct door though he removed his hat down from a small hitch sticking out of the wall just before he would head out as he went to the door then to open it. Joe, however, was standing right next to it just then but the deputy doing the honor of opening it for him in the sheriffs previously injured state and still not being able to use his arm quite as well.

"Allow me their Jeff," he said after doing this as he scuttle away from the door to let Jeff through, of course, pleasantly surprised from the gesture.

"Well, I thank you now for that, Joe," he said on his way out, but the ignorant deputy keeping his same jovial smile as always the good partner he was.

After the sheriff had made his exit Joe was left now with the other two deputies to himself who were, by now, well pent up enough in their own thoughts towards everything and the sheriff themselves, but as Will Blake continued to sit away he couldn't help but to openly remark, or at least allude to his own inner doubts regarding the sheriff as Joe listen with Pat trying not to be sucked into his own discouragements, but staving it off however he could to justify the sheriffs behavior. At one point, the younger deputy had mentioned how he had heard a different version of the story of how the outlaw had been killed and now going around after Joe had countered of the sheriffs exploit, or that the other had come to overhear from someone passing through during one chatty night up near the saloon after drinking though Joe taking the sheriffs side, naturally, but leaving him ambivalent either way as to the man who he had served all those past years in the gossiping and drifter town. Nevertheless, tired of the bickering's or whatever flares between the two had occurred, Joe finally tuckered out in one of the chairs with his stubborn look trying not to buy into what Will had claimed as to the rumor. Still, the way the deputy had shared the story to him and saying whoever it was had somehow heard by second or third ear and from one of Colby's own gang members himself of how the outlaw had been killed that day and morning right in front of the hideout cabin with others inside and by some mysterious person unknown he would be left in his own thoughts as to what may have happened, twisting almost to the point of exhaustion, and leaving himself inconclusive to the whole thing in the end as he could not face the betrayal of the sheriffs own intent easily. As to this unease he continued sitting there some more as he had looking out then the precinct window which was the only one of the whole jail, but somewhere within not knowing what to think anymore or what to believe and almost to his own irony wondering where and what the sheriff he looked up to could be doing at that very moment or if whomever he could be with, if any.

Not by some sheer audacity of the sheriff, but in answer to this doting question Jeff McCormack, had, indeed, went to go out like he said, though not to any place he would be found likely, at, or where it was he would usually take his motely hide to. Instead, he had not without coincidence found himself at Farnworth's own parlor and funeral procession, as something to Joe's words sparked a lucrative opportunity in his sordid and prowling mind having the scent for it as he did and the mention of the map Joe had briefly spoken of sparking this inner surge knowing that wherever it led that it must be somewhere important enough for the other to have made the trip of finding out what had become of it. As the sheriff entered the parlor, however, he could not see Farnworth anywhere, or in sight, for that matter, while he look around in the front of the quiet and departing mood and rapture of the parlor's waiting room with a few lanterns upon the wall giving off their somber and funeral like glow through the soft glazed glass bulbs. As for Farnworth he was only in the back room just then, or at that time of the day when he would usually break for lunch or whatever snack he was treating himself to. The entrance to the back area was through a red satin lined Velcro that was attached on either side as the sheriff lifted up one its flaps to see into the other room. Suddenly though as he look briefly he could make out the figure of the undertaker in the dark and unilluminated room having an assortment of some coffins lying about and a few chairs put out, side by side, or whenever a funeral would occur though seldom was the case in those days when the departing were given procession in their own homes after death, and then, taken to the local cemetery parked somewhere near the church in back or where the Mexican himself had been buried – his tombstone a small iron cross sticking out from the ground and with the tiny barely legible words scrawled into its metal work – "Sent from us up to God now in Heaven."

At the moment Farnworth had his back turned to the law man about to eat what looked to be a rather large and plumpish lush of a pastry or a custard chocolate éclair he had bought at the local bakesmith and sweet shop of Miss Cannerville's down the road some, as he went to stuff it end first into his mouth, but Jeff interrupting him just as he went to do this as the puffy and easily unnerved man looked to his side.

"How you doin' Farnworth?" the sheriff greeted unto him as the plumpish undertaker himself put down the stuff filled pastry he was about to ingest caught off guard by the law man as he ever was, and completely surprised from the visit of the sheriff as he stood there in his front parlor room.

"Well, just a minute, now," he abruptly replied removing the white cloth bib he was wearing as well tucked into his neck as he got up then to accost the sheriff who had gone back into the front room hidden by the velvet curtains.

As Farnworth lifted one of the flaps to get through, however, he could not see the sheriff anywhere as he look in front of him for a brief moment, but turning then to look to his side he could see the law man's face plain as day grinning his signature smile right at him, as he had just fixed to his head his pair of glasses he wore from out one of his top shirt pockets, quite nervous as to why he would make the visit, though trying not to show it.

"And just what can I do for you today?" he said to Jeff trying to seem up-front, but the sheriff knowing how nerveless he was just as well.

"Well," the other said proceeding on. "Just happened to hear something down at the precinct. That's all."

"And how would this just be concerning myself?" Farnworth said pickling at him in his husky tone.

"Well, matter of fact," the sheriff went on, "It doesn't really have so much to do with you as much as someone that came asking 'bout some book the other day round here. Let's see," he said sounding more elusive to the undertaker. "A certain book, or *map* was it now?"

For a moment Farnworth looked of thought, but just the same knew what the sheriff spoke of, as he tried to keep his act up as best he could.

"Yes," he replied finally. "There was a certain man I believe the other day who came in here."

"And just who was this particular man?" the sheriff asked.

"I don't know," the other furtively replied in his difficult manner. "He was not from here though. I can tell you that much," he continued as he stand there next to the sheriff but the lawman closing in on him, although nothing being said between the two for a moment.

"Well?" the sheriff asked.

"Well, what?" Farnworth replied pretending not to know. The sheriff straightened himself, then, to drive it out of him.

"Did you give him over the book?" he asked.

"No. I didn't," he replied.

"Then where is it now?"

"Well," he said looking frustrated. "It isn't here. I can tell you that much."

"So then, just where would this little book of ours be at now?"

"I told him..." The undertaker tried to go on but stopping.

"Yeah?" the other kept at him giving him one his wise looks.

"I told him I had buried it with the Mexican," he finally answered. "The very same one..." he went to carry on, but stopping at the obvious.

"Did this man who came to you be givin' you his name by chance?" the sheriff asked.

"No," the other replied going on reluctantly. "He didn't. But his skin was red almost like a Mexicans but I couldn't be sure of it."

"That it?" the sheriff asked.

"Yes," Farnworth answered. "*Except...*"

"Yes?" Jeff asked again.

"His teeth were awful looking. And he smelled quite foul too."

"Well," the sheriff spoke up. "If that ain't so..."

The undertaker just stood there looking rifted and befuddled, powerless to the law man as he knew he had all along talking to him, as the sheriff or Jeff McCormack with no other words said or any goodbye, gracefully made his way out of Farnworth's own parlor, but the man himself hardly content as to why he had come to ask of him what he did, or for what purpose of knowing whatever text he had buried the bandito with could serve him?

As for the sheriff he now had another plan up that mindful and resorting sleeve of his, once again, but at least would know where it was the so called mysterious Mexican's book or whatever map inside it lay, or with the very dead man he had killed himself, but any chance to profit from a possibly long lost treasure or whatever assets the map in question could lead him to not to go amiss by the sheriff's penchant for the opportunity, and to the benefit of non-other than his partners own loosely kept words and talkative mouth back down at the precinct that same day. Nevertheless, or what would come the sheriff it seemed had finally found a use for his old partner after all.

The few days and nights that had gone by nothing had come to the town or would as to change or crack open its fragile shell further than had already been cracked or blemished so far, but the towns folk keeping to themselves for the most part as life went on. The women of the town had thus far also withdrawn with their usual gossip and candor, but words could be heard so often in regards to the O'Leary girl still supposedly to be up at the Jones' place and some now even having overheard one way or another of the Doctor, or more proper "Psychiatrist" gentleman from out east who had been taken by Treadwell himself to see her, and even having so much as stayed on the night at Treadwell's own home insisting on the arrangement himself as the visiting doctor or Kettle eventually gave in, and only before making his trip back on the morning train to the east on the next day. For it would be up to Treadwell now to discuss the proposed prognosis with the girl's parents as the doctor had been diffident either way and after what Mrs. Jones herself had said during that same evening to him just before seeing to the girl herself where Millie kept at the whole time coldly and confused as to what would happen to her. After some convincing by Treadwell he and Doctor Kettle had even gone themselves to make the visit to her parents thinking it would be good to have him present at the meeting or on the next morning before Kettle's departure, although there was little time to speak in his unabridged manner. Nevertheless, hearing of their daughters descent to the east to be helped by the Doctor and stranger in front of them as he spoke openly to them was not something that could come easy to Mr. or Mrs. O'Leary or accept, while the much more familiar towns physician took notice of this just as easily, and in their faces, though still managing at that to inconspicuously keep it from the other regardless, or for whatever reason he would have in mind just then as not wanting to.

It would only be short time from then, however, until the two would finally leave the girl's parents alone, and after having heard the Doctor's assessment but to think over what vice they had been given as Treadwell went on to proffer what Doctor Kettle suggested to the two, although knowing too as he spoke down to Mrs. and Mr. about their daughter that his words were just as pointless, almost certain while he spoke what the outcome would be but going on anyway to at least oblige his colleague.

Nevertheless, the meeting ended without certain approval either way of what would happen, but leaning, if any, towards the Doctors request, or that of Kettle but having to face the fact of the matter as best they could and knowing the well – intent from both, regardless of their own quibbles or feelings towards the decision, and one that would have to be made in spite.

Treadwell brought the visiting Doctor back to the train station, nonetheless, telling him he would send definite word either way of the decision before the other boarding the train to return where he had come from or to resume his earnest presence needed back at the mental ward or whatever Institution he resided in the East, but only thereafter going on to thank him one last time for having made the trip and going over any last disputes as to the fee which Doctor Treadwell had laid out himself, though the other by no means taking advantage of the Doctors hospitalities.

It wasn't long though into his trip by carriage to Mrs. Jones home and where he knew Millie was being cared for at that very moment, but when Doctor Treadwell would make a final decision regarding the matter of her further treatment, or while he look out across the open trees and cool November wind blowing the last bit of fallen leaves about, but stopping for a moment from his carriage to look into the woods knowing soon everything would just as well be covered in snow and the drift of flakes in return blowing about instead, unlike the tossing leaves he saw in front of him. For in his unknowing or uncertainty of what to do just then, he could not help but feel helpless to his own sense of occupation, or rather to the qualms of his own profession being the conflicted doctor he was and having to make such hard and pressing choices, but as he continue to pause with the reigns of his horse in hand and waiting there briefly, eventually he could not help either but to give in to this tenuous sensation of conscious and inevitably let Evelynn have her way, somehow knowing in rather more prophetic sounding words, or that fate itself could not afford such a heavy weight of one's own soul. Only after this though the wind would pick up again as he lifted the reigns to his horse to get on his journey hoping almost that what resolve he had just come to would find its better way, unforeseeable, however, as he knew it.

23

D octor Treadwell had continued on to the home of Mrs. Jones that day to talk to her about any reservations she could possibly have or doubts of herself as to taking on the girl in the state she was, but forthcoming to him and to Treadwell as she could be about accepting the position of treating Millie, or as to what she felt she needed, uncertain the road for her recovery, although the idea of committing Millie to a sanatorium or even an asylum did not seem in the spirit of helping the girl as Evelynn had thought or saw in her, and to give into her own internal fears.

The talk itself between the two was short enough, but seemed longer to them, nevertheless, as though more had been said then really was, but Evelynn trying to reassure Treadwell that she would do her best to see to Millie's needs, or, whatever she thought could help through the girls own set of ruminating worries and whatever disconsolate emotion was keeping possession of her and most of what and how she did, or draw Millie into the more obvious futility for her life she felt and that seemed to be present with her almost at all times. Millie even herself had overheard the two speaking from up top of the stairs, near the end of the hall as she could hear them faintly loud and audible in the other room, but knowing now she would not be sent away, almost confident she had heard right but her own confidence in herself contrarily and overtly dwindled as she turn away to go back to her room shortly before the Doctor would leave.

For a brief moment, Wyatt even saw her while just about to come out of his room but closing the door after and only creeping it open slightly at her site seeing that she was listening to the two downstairs, and not wanting so much as to disturb or pry into whatever anxieties she was going through just then knowing it was not for him to act upon, or what demon's in his own soul he could not ignore.

The old woman or Evelynn went to the girl, regardless, but unaware of what Millie had overheard though her young friend, and regarded confidant by now not telling Evelynn, of course, that she had indeed been listening to them downstairs, as Evelynn went on to inform her of the final outcome, but trying to look of relief if even for the old woman that she had come to know as Evelynn took heed of this in her face and conduct hoping the girl was settled with the final outcome and relieved she would not be sent as Doctor Kettle had insisted.

As for Doctor Treadwell he would carry on then to the O'Leary household to give what would be some very well received and taken words from the trusted Doctor being in their worried state themselves as to where their daughter would stay at, and, of course, though, the two knowing the burden would be on Mrs. Jones now, but one they were told was not so foreign nor un-invited as Evelynn looked onto it as rather something she herself wanted to do despite the elements or obstacles that would or could ensue. The two at hearing what Treadwell had to speak were, of course, adamant about the whole thing but worried still of what would come but Treadwell trying not to linger on the doubts as much as the hope and what advantages the girl could absolve from the situation she was now in and faced.

For he knew no one else that could care for Millie as Mrs. Jones better, or, at least, to give her and suffice her own Will as to go on, despite the conflicts of her mind, but in leaving the O'Leary's and Millie's own parents that day upon giving his simple and judgement of vice as he ride back he could not help but think whatever her conflicts and demonic obstructions was one in all of us, it seemed, if not in relation to the girl herself, certainly, perhaps, in relation to the ones she had known and with his own hopes in the girl of those she would eventually come to know after.

The sheriff's office had not had any of its cells occupied in more than a while except for the few occasional drunks up at the saloon over rowdiness, but the few staying a night in the jail before either being hitched out of town with the rest of their bar hopping partners, or whatever horde they had come with, or otherwise heading back to the saloon where they had just come from to wait another few months, or just a matter of weeks, or days, until the same thing would only happen all over again. Aside the usual mischiefs and what minor incarcerations, but more to do with the deputies themselves, there were even fewer words now being said amongst the sheriff's men, than even before the little talk they had shared, if one could imagine this, but keeping to themselves almost entirely at this point with the background of the disputed sheriff and what was going on with him or whatever grudges or suspicions the men and town had of him coming to a standstill almost with neither side pressing forward, though it was Joe Collins his first partner and assisting deputy as only in his carefree and gullible way who would be considered his most allied source or accepting of people to come to his side of support, which was certainly not entirely unaccepted in itself by the sheriff, or would be readily contested by him, and, especially, in the reticent view of Joe's own sounding words spoken at the precinct and jail the other day, or what had been passed on.

As the sheriff now knew where in fact the book and scrawled map he hoped it contained was, the only obstacle that lay in his way, of course, was the dead Hombre whom it lay with, but beyond this being the separation of the roughly six feet of mound of dirt and earth, or whatever sod covered over it, and then, the rather more undesirable and unholy part of the prying open of the Mexican's dampened and dingy coffin, perhaps, using the assistance of a crow bar or even the very same shovel he had used to dig it up in the first place, with just then the locating of the manuscript among the corpse and body laying inside.

As it happened he had planned to carry out this more disturbingly and ghastly detail one night when he knew no one would most likely be around or too near to the church yard to get on with his business and dig up the remains of the familiar Mexican he had killed himself which his distinct and less formidable tomb and metal cross sticking out had been well known by then to mark as children around of the town and area had even come a few or more times to look and gawk at it. The tomb like the rest, though, was plainly visible from the rear of the church and easily noticeable from a standpoint, covered by a couple of old and tall oak wood trees on either side, but in the dark of night hidden away enough so the sheriff could commit the act, and even with a small lantern to provide some light for finding and getting the book and text after completing the dig and opening the coffin that was his mission.

In fact, the night he had chosen to make such a dig so as not to be seen was almost perfect and in the weekly almanac a barely half shaped moon predicted to be shown up above in the night sky and with some luck a few clouds as well passing by, if not more than few to help hide him from the rest of the site, or whomever might be nearby to possibly spot him. It would be on a Thursday though of that last week of November, around or just after midnight when he planned to commit the deed and the same night that had been predicted as such to let him do this.

It was then only Tuesday when the sheriff had seen the weather and forecast report in the weekly paper sitting at his desk and reading it, while the rest of the deputies had been out or about the town being that it was their night off, but Joe Collins coming back in eventually to assist the sheriff and the few drunken and disorderly cowhands and swingers they were holding at the moment in the nearby cells, quiet and very mellow they were, however, without even hardly moving.

"Boy, I'll say that new cattle owner of that Taylor's ranch is a real good looker, Seein' him down at the saloon the little while ago I did," Joe Collins uttered upon returning to the precinct. The sheriff hardly took notice of him as his head was still in the paper. As Joe wander around a little pointlessly though he look over to the sheriff then, but surprised he did not reply. "Well, what's the matter Jeff? Didn't you hear me alright?" he asked.

"Yeah, Joe," the sheriff finally answered him, though still holding onto his paper. "He's a real good looker. Just like you said, now."

"Sure is," Joe hoed along. Turning away for a moment then, he turned back to the sheriff seeing him still immersed in whatever he was reading.

"What's you readin' there now boss?" he asked curiously.

"Hmm..." the sheriff equated. 'Nothin' much," he went on.

"Gotta be something," Joe replied. "Well, what is it Jeff?" he asked after a moment more after having heard nothing from the other yet.

"Nothin' Joe," the sheriff said putting down the paper once and for all but starring straight at his partner as he spoke.

To this Joe could not be sure, but the sheriff would just remove his legs then off his desk afterward to get his hat off the same hitch on the far wall and go outside for some fresh night air, or what if, as Joe would be left then by himself for the time being to keep an eye on things.

"Goin' out now Joe for a little while," the sheriff spoke then about to depart. "Should be back soon, I think."

Joe would not say anything though to this as the sheriff make his way to the door.

"You be keepin' an eye on these few here while I'm gone Joe. Make sure they don't get in any more trouble now," the sheriff recapped on his way out, but his partner just keeping quiet as Jeff was not even listening.

Despite this, however, a little later Joe just would just go to sit behind the sheriff's desk once he had left always apprehensive to the sheriff now as he could be, but lifting up the paper as he did with his curious look he would read the folded page of the almanac and forecast of all things and then out loud to himself. Putting it down shortly after though he would only continue in his bafflement as to the sheriff and what he thought but still not sure of anything really either way.

24

Millie had been kept under the watchful eye of Mrs. Jones staying and helping her do whatever task or small desire in her own depression of mind and spirit came to her, but Millie unsure of what to do always nor to feel, and ambivalent of her own thoughts, or at least what she thought she was feeling during the moment, as Evelynn would talk to her or at least come to her side so often to help her through whatever doubt or anxiety she felt just then, but sharing her own older persons sense of wisdom and clarity to help her through it.

Her parents by then had been long enough kept away as to not be able to see their daughter again even in her condition, but in midst of this separation, Treadwell had arranged between either of them, the old woman, himself and parents, Benjamin and Kate, to meet as long as he could accompany them, but insisting also not for them to hope too much or to any significant change in her after all that had happened, but not to press her too hard on anything or cause her any unease or something that may make her anxious under the internal duress she was in.

As for the other man of the household, or Wyatt, he had been up and around himself as always taking his evening and midday walks, or even reading something to himself out on the porch or landing outside as Millie would take notice of him, but herself having not exchanged too many words as to their last meeting so far, and knowing, as well, she would be seeing her parents just as soon as she had been told by Evelynn herself which upon the subject the softer spoken and empathetic woman had only tried to appease the thought of it in the girl sufficiently enough so she would let them do this. As for Mrs. Jones she would only go on to tell Millie of how much they cared for her, even if she had felt hurt or embarrassed by them in the meantime for any misconceptions she could have of their intent, and for whatever they could not understand her for the better. Needless to say, Millie had been very much aware of all this herself, familiar and knowing of their concerns and affections, but without hardly so much as endowing or sharing this to Evelynn or when she had spoken to her, always in her reserved manner and the kind person she really was, although she had come to trust the woman before her almost just as much by then as any other.

This meeting between herself and her parents would arrive shortly or in a few days from the present when the Doctor would finally take the parents to see and let them visit their daughter, or since the last dismal state they had seen her in, as Millie had now been expecting this, but herself, nervous of the thought of it, as the same feelings and other despondent thoughts continue to pace her mind and stay with her almost in the same way as they had, regardless, of who she spoke to or the unorthodox care she was being given now.

In keeping with this manner though it had been, nevertheless, the same peculiarly and reserved man who had been with her there all along and whom had even found and saved her that day where he had, juxtaposing, and almost in a sense counteracting her own will with his mere presence, almost every time she would see him, either doing whatever, or even walking past her, and what she had thought always and known and understood to be true, but his manner frequently indifferent and violating of anyone she had known, uncaring it seemed of what others thought of him or might of himself, though she could not openly tell or could be sure of it either way, only furthering her preoccupation of his character by the day – He was his own person as she saw him, and to his own. Or was *he*?

It was not long from the time she had first heard her parents would be coming to see her when the actual procession of the visit had taken place at Mrs. Jones' own home, of course, or in the familiar lower den during that latter part of the week as had been prescribed, as Mrs. Jones had sought the girl from her room before the two going down to greet them, the two parents, Benjamin and Kate, standing at the moment inside the room with Treadwell himself and waiting for their daughters presence, anxiously, although knowing of what they had been told by the Doctor even beforehand, but just wanting to see Millie more than anything else.

As for their daughter, or Mildred, she had worn one of her nicer dresses to see them in that her mother had gave Mrs. Jones prior and the old woman helped her fit into, or at least so she could know how pleasing and pleasantly she looked of eye, and to make her look presentable enough so her parents would be satisfied to see her in such a nice appearing manner, even without the downcast and lethargic look of her that seemed to complement the fashion she wore almost just as effectively.

Nevertheless, she came down with the old woman behind her while leading the way as the two descended the steps of the stairs slowly, and then turning at the bottom, making their way into the den as Millie's parents lifted their heads with Treadwell to her site, and her mother standing their looking at her with ladled and fixated eyes, but Millie herself showing little expression or cause for any excitement as the father, or Benjamin kept and looked guarded to the obvious animosity of spirit and emotion within her.

"Well, Millie, what's the matter with you?" the mother hushed to herself only after approaching to hug her as her daughter shy away.

Standing aside was Doctor Treadwell as he could see this happen as well, looking on as he did with his own unoptimistic set of eyes, but interrupted just then to help proceed and carry on the visit.

"That's a very nice dress you're wearing today, Millie," he said, pausing then, as he turned his attention to Kate. "I should think your daughter looks very nice in it. Would you not say so yourself, Mrs. O'Leary?"

A moment went by though Kate did not answer at first.

"...Uh, yes. She does," Benjamin or Kate's husband finally came in huskily, feeling the need to answer, but in contrast, being able to read the Doctors intentions well enough much more readily unlike the mother.

"Ah, you see Millie. Your parents are approving of the way you look," the Doctor carefully interceded. "Did your mother make that dress herself, Millie, or is it one you like?" he asked then trying to get the girl to reply as she was still under Mrs. Jones own company standing herself to the rear in back.

"...Your mother had brought you your sewing designs," he went on after still not seeing or hearing any answer from her, but Kate standing steadily nearby holding a small sewing box with some of her own embroidering fabrics or what needle's and pins it contained as she looked unsure of anything.

"Thank you, mother," Millie spoke in response – the first one it had been from her, as Kate and the others could hear her say this.

"I brought her more than that," Kate added on almost sounding satisfied from her daughters reply, as Benjamin stood there holding a tin of something himself in one of his hands. "A whole tin full of the cookies she likes as well – Lemon and Hazel Nut Short Breads, and more of her clothes she'll be needing, I'm sure. *And...*" she went on looking up to Mrs. Jones with a fading tone instilled in her own words, "Whatever it is we can do or give that is, to you Mrs. Jones?"

"I think I should be fine for now, dear," Mrs. Jones chastely replied to the mothers sympathies, knowing herself it would be hard for both daughter and mother at the moment but Kate only confused as to her daughters lack of feeling.

"Isn't their anything you'd like to say to your mother and father while there here, Millie?" Evelynn asked the girl only trying to encourage her to say something fitting, or some showing of desire.

There was still no answer upon this, but the doctor himself spoke up after trying to assist.

"Perhaps if we all sat down for a little while..."

The parents just looked slightly inept, but the father caught on just as well again as to the Doctor's intent, "Well, sure. Of course we will," he said.

"Very good, then," Treadwell pressed on as the few sat down in one of Mrs. Jones' own chairs already set out in conjunction, and taken from around or other parts of the home just for the purpose of the visit, or whatever one it would turn out to be.

As she sat down, Kate gave a knowingly and familiar enough look or gaze to Millie as her daughter was still very unexpressive, but turning her attention to Mrs. Jones eventually sitting some small distance next to Millie.

"How long, Mrs. Jones, have you had this home?" She asked Evelynn trying to make some lighter talk.

For a moment the old woman looked of thought herself but went on then with her attributable use of wised poise and in her own choice of language which seemed to adorn the two in such a way as to give this effect.

"It seems I think, I've had this home for as long as I can remember. I was born, in fact, in one of the above rooms which had belonged to my parents back when I was only a girl, a long time ago it would be it seems now - Almost ages I would imagine. But, when I was a young this home was busy with a whole tribe of people coming and going. Not only my parents, who have been long gone. But, my two brothers Jacob and Arrison who had moved long ago from this place themselves, to go and leave with their wives and children and settle in the east. I had last seen one of them many years ago when he had come with his family to show them where he had been raised and born, but one of them has already passed on since."

"Were you never married yourself, Mrs. Jones?" Kate asked curiously as the old woman looked of some reflection.

"Yes. Once I had been married when I was very young. But, the man I had married had past shortly after. He had not been a very strong man in terms of health though unlike his Will, but he had died before I could even have children. So, I never really had a child of my own in a way."

The Doctor spoke then, himself, as he referred to the same painting on the wall with a likening of her face and portrait when Evelynn was much younger.

"I believe you can see Mrs. Jones above on the wall, there," he said, as he looked up to the frame and painting of her, along with the parents over near the corner of the wall next to the old clock, but Evelynn keeping her back turned.

"*My...* I do say she looks so young there," Kate openly remarked as Benjamin sat next to her saying little, but Millie with her back turned like the rest.

Nevertheless, the clock had just about struck half past noon when it went to play out its simple tune and chime, as the others sat listening.

Just then, however, Mrs. O'Leary's eyes deflected away from the clock at the presence of Mr. Cobb standing and looking back through the half side of the large sliding door while Doctor Treadwell had already taken notice and done the liberty of calling him inside the den so as to acquaint the girl's parents, as Treadwell had even suspected himself that he had spoken to the young girl during that past time she had been at the home, although, also out of mere consideration for aloof Wyatt himself as he came in upon the doctors invite while Kate and Benjamin sat there rising from their seats.

There greeting unto him was, still yet, a humbling one as they knew he was the very man whom had found her that day, and just grateful in their way for this even if they did not say so, but their faces and gestures almost just as indicative.

Despite their temperament the parents resumed their seats sitting back down while Wyatt stood as the doctor went on and tried to incite him to stay.

"Would you care to join us, Mr. Cobb?" He asked as Evelynn looked up his way. "Millie's parent's had just come to pay their daughter a brief visit, now that I'm sure you know she'll be staying here with you a while longer. That is, for the time being," he continued as he turned his attention back to Evelynn with lowered eyes.

There were no other chairs for him to sit in, but the doctor kindly offered his own as Wyatt replied to him though declining the offer but just choosing to stand on.

"I don't think I should be needin' to sit - If that will be fine with the rest of you folks," he withdrew in his gruffly voice while Millie's face and eyes seemed to digress towards him as her preoccupation for him grew with every accosting, or observation of him she noticed.

"Well, then," the Doctor carried away. "I should think that will be fine. *Certainly*," he continued with a nervous undertone.

Millie's mother suddenly spoke up after he had said this but expressing to Millie then about Mrs. Motts down at the school house as she had been all the while very concerned of her promising and gifted student or Millie and what had happened, but wanted badly to visit her as she had told her mother one day upon making a unexpected showing at the O'Leary place.

"Do you know, Millie, your school teacher Mrs. Motts herself has wanted to see you. She had asked me if she could come and visit you one day. She is very worried about you, of course, and wanted me to tell you she would be coming."

Millie did not look to answer but her eyes just lowered as Mrs. Jones answered for her.

"I think it would be fine Mrs. O'Leary." Kate was beginning to feel unencouraged by her daughter's lack of reply, but went on anyway.

"Also, Father Coleridge..." Doctor Treadwell suddenly interrupted before the mother could finish as she took notice and bidding her head down to move on to a lighter subject. "I should think Millie might like some of the cookies I made for her. That is, you would, wouldn't you?" she asked nervously instead as her daughter kept sitting there with her arms on either side of the chair and her legs uncrossed like the others, nor appropriate for women, or even men at certain times to do so.

She did still not answer her mother looking at her though after having asked. Taking the tin in her hand from Benjamin the mother went on.

"I made these fresh for you the other day. I know there your favorites," she said, but interrupted herself shortly by her own pouting as she put her hands to her face weeping.

Benjamin just took hold as Millie sat there looking back, but Doctor Treadwell coming in then with his own words as he did.

"It's quite alright, Mrs. O'Leary."

As for her daughter she just sat there with Evelynn in her abysmal way, and Wyatt still standing as he could see the mother's tears as well.

"Perhaps, it won't be good today to carry on," he continued as Kate looked up.

"No," she replied more composedly. "I want to stay."

"Very well, then," Doctor Treadwell noted her reply as he shy away slightly.

It was after this though upon seeing and hearing Mrs. O'Leary and Benjamin comforting her when Wyatt could realize the pain of both, as his face embellished the grief he saw as only an outsider could.

"Perhaps, I could make us some tea," Mrs. Jones suggested to enliven the scene, but Treadwell resorting to this suggestion as well.

"Yes. I think that wouldn't be a bad idea," he said in agreement to her, as Evelynn looked about to rise, but Mrs. O'Leary trying to take hold.

"No. I don't think that will be necessary, Mrs. Jones – Thank you," she said to Evelynn as the other resumed her place.

"Are you sure..." Mrs. Jones went on before being interrupted.

"No, I shouldn't want to cause you too much trouble, already than we have with Millie and all the way she is. And you must be exhausted from her stay here waiting on her the way you do. I don't know myself, but I think somehow it mightn't..."

"Yes, dear?" The old woman asked in support seeing she was ambivalent to what she was about to say.

"Well, I'm just thinking now that it just *might* be better somehow *if...*"

"Yes?" The other exclaimed still not getting it out of her, though somehow surmising and knowing what she was about to insinuate as to her daughter or the asylum and sanatorium flashing through her ambivalent mind.

Doctor Treadwell just interrupted again seeing Mrs. O'Leary was unable to finish her thought or what she was saying almost trembling with fear, but like Evelynn and even Benjamin sitting next to her with his eyes slightly repressed in some overwhelming inner thought himself the doctor took the initiative of trying to reassure her.

"Now, you mustn't worry, Mrs. O'Leary. Your daughter is still strong, and she can still get better, but I should suggest now and tell this I think to Millie herself, as I have thought the matter over myself, but that it be crucial we see some improvement as to her affect or some kind of change before we take any other unnecessary or hasty steps as to her treatment, or, for instance, the place

Doctor Kettle had mentioned prior to myself and you, Benjamin and Kate." He had leaned towards them as he said this but had been looking at the girl briefly in his regards to her but Millie still in some remote and faraway place he could not decipher. He went on regardless, as he looked back to the girl but having a circumspect expression about him: "You, Millie, Must find it in yourself to go on, regardless of what others think of you or even of yourself. It is up to you and no other to do this though. And it must be you who accepts yourself as you are now, which will be much more important than anything in the time to come."

Upon these last fermenting words from the doctor unto herself Millie just continued to sit at hearing what he had just said but her face showing a muddled confusion as to the claim of her and what Treadwell was trying to say, though she knew deep down somehow and understood what it was he meant, even if she didn't want to hear it as he had just said it, or take it as to true and accept the decree of her for what it was. For she could not be sure of anything, almost, but knew from the Doctors words the overwhelming predicament of adversity to come to her, as everyone around her could see this in her face and carriage including the oddly, but quiet Wyatt still in their presence.

"Are you alright, dear?" Mrs. Jones asked young Millie next to her seeing the whims of her anxiety stretched across her face.

"Yes, Mrs. Jones," she replied finally in relief. Doctor Treadwell took notice of the exchange, nevertheless, but prompted then if she'd like to end to the visit or rest.

"Well, I'm not sure how you feel about this visit, Millie, but perhaps it would be better if you had a rest for now, or if you feel you've had enough so long as your parents are alright with this, of course."

"Well, we hardly just got here..." Mrs. O'Leary went to say, but was speedily interrupted by Benjamin trying to allocate the doctors intent as best he could.

"No, I believe Kate and I have had our visit for the time being," he said as he stood to his feet in a sort of nonchalant manner and returning his hat to his head which he had been holding in his lap most of the time. Kate just stood up with him, however, in imitation as Benjamin turned to the doctor, and then, to Mrs. Jones looking to thank them as he bid his head and tip his hat slightly to both, as Mrs. O'Leary looked at the two herself, and, of course, her daughter Millie who was still tucked away in whatever place she was but her mother unable to understand just what it was that could be that affecting her so harsh and tauntingly as to render her as she was.

Mrs. Jones stood up with them by this time as the Doctor had already himself risen, but Benjamin handing the tin to Mrs. Jones as she put out her arms for it.

"I'll just leave this here, then, I suppose," Kate said placing the sewing box of Millie's embroidering utensils on the side or on top of the chair to rest.

"Oh, thank you kindly, dear," the old woman cordially spoke upon their parting.

"You will use it I hope, Millie," the mother betook to her with her same subtlety in her words.

It was only after a moment, but one that seemed still to last on as her nature was given to such heavy weight it seemed but when Millie gave one of her simple replies.

"Yes, Mother," she finally said still remaining seated as she had.

"Wouldn't you like to say goodbye to both of your parents, Millie?" The old woman suggested, but the girl surprisingly rising to her feet by herself to do this as her mother could see.

"Goodbye, mother," she said to Kate standing near to her as she abruptly went close to embrace her but Millie not shunning away this time, as the Doctor could see as well.

Benjamin too saw this as she stood aside like the others with reserved eyes, but unsure of how she felt of him similarly to her mother. Millie looked to him after saying goodbye to her mother, but surprised almost just as much she did.

"Good bye – father," she said as he just stood there without moving at first but finally answering.

"Good bye, Daughter," he replied, although he had never called her as such before, but in spite of all that had happened and knowing she was no longer the young lady he had known he could not help but to do so.

As the two were about to make their way to leave then it was only, Mr. Cobb who was left to bid a farewell to.

"Goodbye, Mr. Cobb sir," they said just before departing as he merely put his hand to hat, without saying anything but their faces loosening and merry to the gesture.

Upon this though the two parents made their way to the door as Evelynn followed them from behind, along with the doctor as Millie was left for a moment with Wyatt as her face looked to the side again to glimpse him, but standing there as he had with both his arms clasped behind and looking off.

Doctor Treadwell had gone out with the parents, similarly, as they had come from his own carriage to make the visit, although he would talk to them, undoubtedly, some more of not only the visit, but what time to come would bring and his hopes for Millie's recovery.

As for Millie in the brief time she had been alone in the room with Wyatt, or just before Evelynn herself would come back to her side she had thought about the words Doctor Treadwell had assumed of her as they continue to turn in her head, but with no way of knowing how long she would be able to carry out what the Doctor had meant, or at least what she thought he was implying. For she could find no avenue or desire that could satisfy her own Will, and not even with the benefit of knowing what it is she wanted most of the time, though as Wyatt stay there with her in the room she knew that there must be something more to the odd man next to her that met the common eye, and inside him something that did not equate to his own image.

In all of her confusion and observation, however, a reality was still existent within her of some deeper passion that only needed a peep of light at the end of whatever tunnel to settle through and to once more brighten and glow of her own inner promise, but Wyatt, regardless of the dark or pain he carried with him, the one in the end of all people, perhaps, to supply this tiny and weakened crack of light – A purpose in him now that could not be denied, nor pitied, and least of all unworthy.

25

The day Millie had seen her parents had gone by like the rest of the days and the last week of that November and late autumn month, but the sheriff as his intent, had gone ahead with his former plans as to apprehending the text. Even the very night he had planned to do this, or on the given Thursday at midnight had been just as predicted and reported in that week's paper as the sheriff was more than satisfied as to the forecasters expectations, and one that was not likely to have come to himself otherwise.

He had taken off that night and into the earlier evening time when everything in town was beginning to ebb out and people up and around, or, of course, the town saloon to enjoy whatever festivities as was the town's habit and spirit though without any needless mention, or redundancy.

As for Joe and the others up in his place at the jail house and precinct, there was little else going on and hardly anyone occupying the nearby cells, but the men always invigorating of themselves as Joe had told them that the sheriff had taken the night off, but the others curious enough as to where he could be or the reason for the evening off, as even a few words would come from Will Blake's own mouth like the ones he had spoken all so recently about the real colors of the sheriff and telling of what he had heard.

Ornery as he was, Joe did not bite too hard back but just waved off whatever it was he said as to the sheriff and man they served, and even going outside on the sidewalk and walking down the procession near the saloon to get away from the prattle he was experiencing as Pat Thomsen stayed on back inside the precinct along with younger Will for the most part, before hopping down to the saloon himself as he often did for either fancy of a woman, or just to play a hand of cards or two, and listen to the nightly crowd shuffling in.

As for the sheriff himself he had his own plans, aforesaid, but as the dark settled over the town the darker side of his own self grew with every fleeting minute and hour going by until it was time near to head over to where it was he meant to go and carry out his dirty work. For the barely half shaped moon that night might as well have been Full in all its glory and blood red dripping with soul, and in the sheriffs own likeness of himself, as the saying goes, as he made his way down the murky roads and eventually to the church yard itself, as few people had seen him that night anywhere else or had passed him by, although for a brief moment the towns torch lighter or the one armed Sonny Pickens thought he had glanced at him at one point after he had been woken by something outside where he lived in a small bungalow next to the horse stable though he could not be sure either way.

Regardless, the sheriff had, indeed, made his way to the graveyard, and with him holding some straw bag over his shoulder as even Sonny Pickens had thought he had observed of him, as it was just almost before midnight now when he would carry out his lowly mission, but the graveyard itself barely visible and nearly pitch black on either sides. Only lighting a box lantern then he took out from his sack as he stood between the two large Oak trees on the perimeter he would begin carefully to make his way over to the Mexican's tomb while carrying the lantern with him to light his way, although even with its modest light the dark was much. As he did this, but gripped in his other hand being of all things, was a flatly sharp tipped shovel he had removed from the bag, as well, as he continued to make his way to the Mexican's cross which he knew it to be in back of the cemetery farthest from the church.

Eventually approaching it as he did he used the light of the box lantern to distinguish the iron cross and tomb as he wave the small aperture of light side to side and just before abruptly blowing out the lanterns flame as nothing could be heard for a moment with then just the sound of the shovel hitting the ground from the sheriff's first thrust as he scoop the mound of dirt over to the side.

It was, in fact, only after about an hour going on another in relation to this when the sheriff's shovel would hit the top of the buried coffin underneath as the sound of the thud made the sheriff cringe with self - satisfaction and knowing he had finally reached his source while he now stand inside the oblong pit he had just dug knowing he would finally have his chance to pry the coffin open to find whatever book among its corpse.

At first he tried to use the shovel to do this though he could not as the lid had been tightly nailed, but knew he would have to go back to get his crowbar from out of his sack that he had hid beneath the oak trees in a large crevice in one of the roots as he picked up his lantern light and lit the wicker with a match he took out from his pocket striking it as habit across one of the spurs of his boots to light. After this he would manage swiftly enough to remove himself from on out of the ditch he had dug by first placing the lantern on top of the high ground and then cautiously getting out as he made his way over then to the set of trees as the walk was not too far or less than twenty yards away using the light of the lantern to guide him.

Upon reaching the tucked sack and getting out the crowbar, he started to make his way back when he heard another owl hooting right next to him while he shine his small lantern light to it as the staunchly looking bird looked back at him without moving, but the sheriff hardly stirred as he set back on to the trench he had dug where the coffin wait for him.

He did this quicker than before, and getting back into the grave faster yet, as the light of the lantern glimmered the sludge and dirt on the other side of the tomb as he climbed back into the hollow chamber with the crowbar and lantern and turning down the wick slighter still as he set off to the side. Only then by using his tool of the crow bar he would finally pry open the Mexican's pinewood box after some wiggle and jiggle, but taking the lantern back in his hand to see, although even his own face having an apprehensive and intrepid look upon waking the dead, as he look down at the body and face of the corpse, almost as when he had been laid the rest the few summer months back, and his pale white face with his eyes snugly shut and still dead as a doornail.

At first he could see no sign of the book anywhere among the cadaver as he flash the light about, but having a feeling it was inside the man's vest pocket as he felt for a moment around with some light touches, but feeling then something there as he slipped his finger inside the pocket and pulled out the small Bible book to the relief and his anticipation of finally having it in his hands.

Taking it up so he could see inside as he flipped it open, or the first few pages with the lantern in his hand shining upon it he could see the drawn out and Spanish notated map in front of him, but his lack of knowing any Spanish except for a few words he knew of, some by choice but others more out of habit, though unable to interpret what it was the map led to, although from the looks of it the mysterious layout promising enough as to be getting someone some- where worth their while.

As he now had the manuscript, however, or whatever it was in his posses- sion it was nearly half past two in the early morning and he knew he had to make clear of the site before anyone could see him or notice something inor- dinate, but almost just as sure no one would, especially, at that late hour, as he

NO GUN'S IN LITTLE CAVERN

turned out the lantern and set the lid of the coffin back in place. After lifting himself out of the tomb, then, to get on with the reburying of the Mexican it would not be long until he had completed this task, but far easier as he found it to be than the initial dig itself, as he took the Mexican's book with him back over to the trees with the rest of the tools he had brought and sacked everything up including the text to go along on his way.

As he went along a back road that led up to where he lived in his Sherriff's home somewhere on the outskirt of Little Cavern he could hear at one point two drunks coming down the road up in front, but hid away into the woods until they had passed him by as they walk side by side next to each other singing their drunken hymns that night in their slovenly manner.

The road itself was foggy as he continued his way with the sack, with minor clearings amid, and, in between, but as the sheriff made his way he thought he heard, or at least felt something again in back of him as he turned, although not seeing anything in the dense and thickly haze in front of him. Still unsatisfied after a moment more he uttered the words, "*Anyone there?*" but could hear no reply then, or answer to this, as the sheriff himself was beginning to doubt if anyone had been there in the first place only resuming his pace. As he sauntered along though, with the sack still hanging over his shoulder like before he could not help, but think, of a similar feeling he had felt at that moment, or when that other bespoken man and character of the woods had come out on that night on his way back to town, although when the moon in contrast had been Full and the night sky even clearer. For just as he was certain no one had been there he could not understand nor know why it was he had thought of him, but the man's chalky white face and image branded in his mind as though he had come back just to taunt him again, or in the act of the foul deed the sheriff had just committed. Had the ghost, indeed, come back to haunt him, or was it just his own darkly imagination playing tricks on him?

Craig Sholl

26

I t was a new day only upon others like it before and to come or for those at
Mrs. Jones home and that Millie had awoken to that early morning in the
same daft spirits she was in, although she had now been growing more
accustomed to her surroundings, and Evelynn's comfort at her side or what
support she could give to her, but each day that went by only a reminder of the
next to come and the same acquainted man about her new dwelling always in
the background, although she had by then grown accustomed enough to him,
or Wyatt, as not to fret when in his presence, and just being a normal part of
her daily routine.

Now a week roughly or more since the visit with her parents into the cold
December month and when Doctor Treadwell had spoken to her in the way he
had, his words had been well subdued in her mind but only coming to surface
in her most nervous and vulnerable states when she could no longer stand the
ruminations of her own lack of Will, and the doubts she had of her own being.

In all of this, a kind of inner frustration, however, had long been stewing
within her of an inability not to look down on the misgivings she had now come
to realize as a part of her character and which had become a normal aspect of
her frustrations, but could be seen in her face and manner when merely looking out the window of Mr. Cobb's room, or just by herself sitting in front of the
fireplace in the den and watching the reddening flames burning whatever
wood to slow ash, though the fire itself never completing subduing at that, as
Millie hardly move herself or look anywhere around other than in front of her.

Sometimes Wyatt or Evelynn would sit with her for a time, as well, and take
turns at this or Mrs. Jones busy with something else in the kitchen, but leaving
her young invalid (Without any irreverence towards Millie in the given sense
of the word) for the short time she would be inside, as Millie had been more
quiet the past few days than usual or even before the meeting had taken place
but the newer sense of reality beginning to shape and sink inside her, or the
everyday burdening monster she faced in the depths and horizon of her mind,

and one that was so unlike the tranquil and disconnect of the phasing fire in front of her at the moment. Still, in the face of this, Treadwell's words in the back of her mind as he had said them making less and less sense by the day, or of how she would ever find it in herself and solely in herself to go on.

Mrs. Motts her own school teacher had even come one day to see her as her mother had said during their last visit, although the stringent but seemingly good natured school teacher herself apprehensive as to what could be so oppressing her as to have done what she did, but Millie during their brief visit or encounter hardly as receptive to her as in the past, and still unsure of Mrs. Motts intent or what she had wanted for her originally in terms of what had been said as the girl sat in her chair flatly faced for the most part while Evelynn interceded every so often, but Mrs. Motts trying to be as kind as she could and just wanting to leave her with some caring words of warmness and reflection if just that much.

Nevertheless, Millie had risen one such day to face her same dilemma, once more, looking down into the fireplace during that evening and from her same chair she would sit closest to the far wall, or as in the manner described, while Mrs. Jones was then in the kitchen herself sitting with a book and sipping some tea she had made set out on the table in the meanwhile as Millie sat there in the same daunting frame and image with the door to the kitchen slightly cracked open and both her arms set out on the arms of the lounging chair she sat in.

Just then, she could hear Wyatt come in from outside to make his way upstairs, although unlike other times before she had heard him she could tell his step was not as even and suggesting an unconformity to himself that was not like his character as he was usually in the habit by now of saying hello to her after coming in, or just before making himself scarce to her, but Millie herself able to deduce and sense a disarray that was strange at the moment as she slowly lifted herself out of the chair, deciding then she would go up and try to see what the matter was, though she almost feared just as much in this venue in her desire to satisfy her own curiosity of him.

As she got up and made her way out of the den to the bottom of the staircase she looked up for an instant with unsure eyes, but continuing up the plight of steps eventually reaching the top of the stairs before stopping to make her way down the hall as Wyatt's door was now closed, though seeing hers at the end strangely cracked open for some reason but not knowing why at first.

As she put her ear to his door though she could hear nothing except for some heavy breathing and deducing there was no light in the room after looking down near the floor of the hallway and between the bedroom door itself. Looking as if about to knock, then, she decided not to nor wanting to bother him, as she only eventually decided to make her way back down the rest of the hallway to her own room and to see if he had, indeed, gone in as she had thought.

Upon further opening the door she entered her room, cautiously, or rather Cobb's that she had been staying in, as she look around herself and ponder if anything was missing, or as to why he had come in, but seeing nothing gone in sight, for that matter, and setting herself down on the bed next to the small drawer and bureau that had been his as she look to it after a moment more of some thought.

Opening the top drawer than slowly, or the one containing the portrait of the woman as she looked to see if it was still there, her face turned to slight apprehension when she saw it was gone, in fact, and closing the drawer again briskly as she look out in front, but not knowing why he had taken it.

It was beginning to rain outside now as the droplets of water could be heard hitting like small pellets upon the window pane gusting along in the windy night outside and the feeling of damp coldness setting in as winter had finally come to Millie and the other people in those parts, though the cold bringing all its reminders of past December months and the coming Holiday's and Christmas time spent with her parents.

For now, instead, all she could think of was the present though and what she could do at the moment as she readied herself for bed, and went to blow out the lantern light of the bedroom on the bureau afterwards as she lay in the dark, and the howling wind and rain now at the window. Opening her eyes for a moment she thought about the portrait again and the woman Wyatt had spoken of – Sarah Jordans – as her evident connection and meaning to him was something she could not possibly know, or to the extent to which she had affected him that was apparent. In her inquisitiveness, however, she knew she could not help herself, either, to find out more about her or what she had been to Wyatt, even if she would have to ask Evelynn the old and dedicated woman at her side to understand and know this – Perhaps, the first real desire and unabatingly curiosity for that matter to come into her mind in a long and well - requited time.

The sheriff had all the while been looking at and trying to make out the Spanish script and text of the map kept hidden away in his home or tucked away safe in a drawer by lock, though which was useless to him at the moment unless he could understand the Spanish notations and/or markings of the map it contained on the first few pages, but seemed to layout a place that looked much further south from Wyoming with a sketch of some mountains all over, and on the other pages a groupings of some valleys and passage ways that seemed to lead to a common destination. Only one word in all of it stuck out to him, or the name of a deposit of mountains that the area of interest seemed to be located in, but otherwise known as the, San Juan, which he knew, beforehand, were to be found somewhere in the South Westerly parts of Colorado, just below the Wyoming state itself.

This detail was encouraging though as he knew wherever the map led it could not be possibly too far off from where he was already, but still knew he would have be able to read the map better and its outlay upon the Spanish scripture underneath it, as he had so thriftily, gone ahead and done the duty of paying a small visit to the one roomed school house where he knew Mrs. Motts the town spinster school teacher herself taught, but to see if there might be a stray book upon her shelves that could help him better of finding this out, or for the teaching of Spanish that he could use in interpreting the map.

The youngish woman teacher had quietly been grading some of the weeks work at her desk during one mid evening and when school had finally been out for day when Jeff had knocked on the school house door to let himself in as she was more than surprised to the sheriffs presence and quite suspicious in her treatment towards him, far from a supporter of the local sheriff and his questionable office he held. Nonetheless, she helped him as best she could, after making his awkward request as to any book she might have in her shelves, or herself even, that was used for such.

Hesitant at first while he lingered on, Mrs. Motts eventually found one such book, old and outdated as it was, in the back where she kept most of her other books and texts entitled, "The Proper Grammars and their Pronunciations of Spanish to English Words," as she handed over the book kindly, though not before asking why he needed it. To this, however, he merely tipped his sheriff's hat and said that he could use it over at the precinct for some odd work he was doing and under some special circumstances, but certainly not giving her any definite answers and telling her that was all he could say about that for now.

He went on his way, regardless, and with the school teachers book in his hand, but tipping his hat to her again upon exiting the school house, and despite her questions or what reservations he suspected she had of him, or even in lending him the book itself, but remarking to her on his way out that he'd be sure to give it back to her as soon as possible.

It wasn't long from that though when he would look at the book he had borrowed from the school teacher's shelves and compare it to the notations of the hand written Spanish scripture of the map, and what he could make of some of the meanings behind the words.

He would keep at this inside his sheriffs home for the rest of that evening using the light of his kerosene lamp to do this, eventually, making some progress in learning some of the written words, though one which stood out from the rest and in more bold letters and almost ingrained into the paper itself among a long group, or sub set of sentences, but the particular Spanish word, "Oro" which by some intuition and estimate after looking it up seemed to be the word in his own English for "Gold". Upon making his discovery his face settled back into a brightened and gratifyingly grin, as he leaned into his chair only to light one of his cigars from out his pocket, but now knowing he had been right about the map, and that he would be leaving in a short enough time to get his hands on the very thing in front of him.

* * *

It was the next day since Millie had noticed the missing portrait in Wyatt's drawer as she was just then downstairs in the den doing some embroidering work with the old woman, or Evelynn, as she was trying to get Millie interested and busy herself with something, but Mrs. Jones able to knit almost just as exquisitely as Millie' own mother, although her old and fragile fingers barely nimble enough to let her do so or work the tiny needles, but the two sitting there in the arm chairs side by side quietly as they did.

Suddenly, however, Millie stopped at what she was doing which did not look hard for her to do as she was still in her acutely melancholy manner as she put down her sewing for the moment. Then, carefully looking over to the old woman or Mrs. Jones who did not notice her do this as her head was still down at her own sewing and wearing her older lady's glasses to see, Millie spoke up just then to ask the question that had been on her mind ever since.

"Mrs. Jones?" She said as the elderly woman removed her glasses from her face to answer seeing that something was on her mind.

"Yes, dear?"

"Do you know the picture of the woman in Wyatt's drawer?" Millie went on after a moment. Evelynn looked of thought trying to figure out what she was asking.

"Yes," she finally answered. "I do, dear."

"Do you know what happened to her?" Millie asked after some showing of effort as Evelynn looked away for a brief second to reply. Turning to her then, she answered.

"She had been one of my students up at the school house, a long time ago, when I had taught and when Wyatt had been one of my students. They had always been friends of one another." At first she looked to not go on as Evelynn looked back down into her lap at her embroidery, but lifted herself from her chair and setting her sewing off the side on the table as Millie sat there looking at her and listening to what she had to say.

"Later, after they were finished with their lessons and were ready to leave here Wyatt had asked her to marry him, but she was always ambivalent herself of taking his hand and I think deep down she did not want to marry him, but when she did it was more out of her own kindness for him than her own desires. I think for her marriage was something she could not understand, and the idea of it was more of Wyatt's notion of her, but love as they often say is a one sided carousel for the other, and Wyatt loved her almost knowing this I think, even if he knew she could not see him in the same way."

"But, what happened to her?" Millie asked insatiable of her curiosity to know the woman's fate.

"Wyatt and Sarah Jordans, my student and the woman you want to know of, had, by then, moved out to the east to live in the big city where Wyatt planned to write and settle down with her hoping to have a family, and become a more serious writer which in part I myself, if I am to be true was to blame for, as I had always regarded him as a special student of mine and could see, even perhaps like you Millie, the part of his eye and cheek that had been different from the rest, or all the others I had taught long after. As for Sarah it was not long until she was given to bearing a child. As for Wyatt he was struggling to make what little living he could, even working other jobs just to support themselves in his endeavor, but the winter had been harsh and she was stricken ill one night after going out in a storm trying to look for him. She was not a strong woman in much sense as even I could know this myself having been married to someone once who had died young. But, Wyatt stayed with her as she had gotten pneumonia shortly after the next several weeks trying to help her get better of whatever he could do though in the end she did not and having died shortly after with the child inside her."

Hearing this Millie's face turned to sorrow, but only thinking of Wyatt and what had happened, and now that she finally knew who the woman had been to him; but also, the truth that Mrs. Jones had spoken to her and confided in her as something she could accept as real, despite the obvious turmoil that it spelled for both Wyatt and the woman whom he had known.

"He has kept that portrait of her ever since, and tucked away in his drawer to take out," Evelynn continued as she could see Millie's face react to her own words she had spoken. "She had posed for it I believe just before the two had left for the east. She was very beautiful."

At that moment Wyatt himself had just come down wearing a wool coat he wore while making his way out the door in order to get some more wood for the fire that evening as Evelynn stood near the fireplace looking at Millie as she could see him pass by, though not before himself glimpsing back for an instant before opening and going out the door into the cold weather.

Millie, just then, seeing Mrs. Jones looking off as the girls eyes settled back inside of her asked if it would be alright if she could take a break from her sewing though Evelynn kindly letting her leave if she felt the need to, but seeing the girl rise from her chair and walk out of the room, as she looked about to go upstairs to her room, though instead, tucking her arms to her side and opening the front door where Wyatt had just gone out as Evelynn looked on.

As she went out onto the porch then in the cold weather Millie could see Wyatt over in the small wood shed near where the garden Mrs. Jones kept in the front as she stand there on the porch in the cold some more waiting for him to come back.

She could see Wyatt, then, come out from the shed with a stack of wood he had inside some noose for carrying the bundle as she went over to help him and coming to his side as she bent over to accompany him in lifting the small timbers though Wyatt replied, "Aren't you cold, ma'am?" but Millie saying nothing as they continued up the steps of the porch and inside.

Mrs. Jones was then in the same place as she had been in the den waiting for the two to come in as Wyatt took hold of the bundle carrying it over near the fireplace to put in the bin next to it. As he placed each timber inside Millie began helping him at this as Wyatt hesitated for a moment from her good gesture before continuing with her to do so, but Evelynn had went out of the den then into the kitchen to let them alone for the time being.

Once they had finished the task Wyatt was now standing with the girl alone in front of the fireplace that had some of its own wood inside burning and slowly dying as Wyatt looked then to leave the room, but Millie stopping him for a brief moment before himself turning away.

"Wyatt?" she said as he turned to her, though he said nothing.

"I'm sorry," she went on. "I mean, for that woman you married in the picture and what happened."

Wyatt just lowered his eyes upon this at hearing the woman's mention after Millie had spoken, but himself eventually replying.

"Thankyou – Millie," he said kindly to her condolence. Nevertheless, as the two stood there for a moment quietly Wyatt after saying this would only make his way out of the room while Millie watched him from the side of the fireplace.

Just then, Evelynn came back into the den though to see to the girl after having heard what she had said outside from behind the door, although she had been listening most of the time.

"Are you alright, dear?" she asked in her lightened tone, but Millie still looking off the where he had just left.

"Yes," she answered turning back to her. "I'm alright. I'd think I'd like to go to my room now."

"Well, of course, dear," Mrs. Jones replied as Millie went to do this then, and going out of the den as Wyatt had just done through the open sliding door and up the stairs after as she continued down the hall to her bedroom.

Inside his own room, or the one he now occupied, Wyatt could hear the girls steps go by as she stopped for a moment and continued as he sat there on his bed, though knowing now a new special girl had come into his life as if taking the place in some way of the girl or woman who had died, and somehow within her caring words a redemption to his past he could not ignore knowing Millie was herself alive, and would have a chance for a new life and beginning that he knew he was now a part, but for which he could not turn his back to, and for the better.

27

I t was another day at the precinct and Jeff McCormack had his feet up on the desk as habit, but rather than reading the paper as he would usually do he had his head bid down inside the book he had borrowed from Mrs. Motts and reading quite absorbedly at that while Joe Collins was the only other one inside the precinct at the moment as Will and Pat had gone out for their break now that it was lunch for them, but Joe Collins gazing at the sheriff from his vantage point, though, and oddly quiet himself.

"Hey Jeff," his partner suddenly spoke, but not sure what the sheriff was reading as he had never seen him ever once reading a book and thinking it strange to see him in such a way. "What's the name of that book you're readin' there?"

The sheriff did not look to answer at first, although he did eventually in a dismissive way without so much as lifting his head away either.

"Oh, nothin' that be interestin' you."

"Well, I don't know," Joe answered cockeyed as he got up from his seat to get closer. "Why don't you try me? Would you be readin' something racy now, sheriff?" he asked trying to get a lift out of the other.

"No, Joe," he answered his partner back short wordily as the sheriff's habit.

"Well, just was is it, then?" his partner went on asking.

The sheriff stopped reading for a moment again as he looked at Joe squarely.

'The Proper Grammars and their Pronunciations of Spanish to English Words,' he finally obliged him, "By E. M. Forster - Miguel."

Joe Collins face lit up then, at the sheriff's bluntness while Jeff put the book up to his face so he could see.

"Well, how 'bout that," Joe said trying to sound obtuse to the sheriffs intent, but hardly sure of himself or knowing why on earth Jeff would be wanting to read that of all things and having that same feeling of suspicion carrying over upon the sheriff's lament.

"They got a lot of Spanish words in there, now?" he asked trying to cajole on with the sheriff and acting benign the whole time, or at least looking like it.

"Seems that way, Joe," the sheriff leaned in.

"Well, no kiddin'," Joe went along candidly enough. Looking down towards the floor as he put his hands to the back of his denims he continued though still perplexed. "Well, in that case I think I'll be goin' out and feeding the horses just now." The sheriff said nothing to this as Joe went over to the door, but his partner suddenly looked as if about to turn to ask him something though faced forward again to let himself out.

"Be back in a little while there, sheriff," he said and continuing his way as he opened the precinct door.

On his way out though he could swear he heard something said to him by the sheriff, almost Spanish sounding, but just minded himself as he went on in back or near the side of the precinct where the horses were at the moment.

Despite this as he went around to give them their daily nourishment of hay and some Barley weed that they would eat the thought stuck out in his mind of what the sheriff had been reading and the coincidence of overhearing what he did about the Mexican as though having some ominous connection, but although he could not reconcile the thought he knew just the same the strange behavior from the sheriff and once again lost as to any previous notions he had had of him before.

28

The town's Mayor had been getting more and more fed up with the complaints or whatever had come his way in terms of the sheriff and growing tensions in the air, whether from outsiders words as to what had really happened down in Nebraska, or why Colby's body was said to have been shot by someone near the gang's own hideout, and by some mysterious person still unknown. The claims of this, however, would not entirely be accepted as concrete as the ones who had mostly passed this on being chiefly Colby's own nefarious set of men, but from others as well that had made their way up talking about it, and unreliable for the most part, themselves, as to have known what had really happened, and almost with as few scruples as Colby's own men.

Still, this talk perpetuated on and on from its source even now among respectable people as Mayor Whitcomb, finally, had gathered enough nerve during one later part of the day to visit the sheriff himself at the downtown precinct to make an interrogation.

Joe Collins and the others had all been inside when he had come in, although uninvited and surprised to see the Mayor come through the precinct door as the others all stood at his reception, but the Mayor quickly telling them to be at ease with no need to be cordial.

As for Jeff or the sheriff he just remained seated the whole time with his legs in the normal and assuming position on his desk and reading the dailies, though quickly removing them once the Mayor had made his reason for the visit known and hardly impressed nor intimidated from Whitcomb's presence either, needless to say.

"Jeff, I want to have some needed words with you," the Mayor bellowed out from the redly puckered lips.

"Well, just what is it you'd be wanting now?" The sheriff asked without flinching as the Mayor hesitated a moment before going on.

"Well, frankly, I'd been getting a lot of complaints of you back at Town Hall and my office 'bout what happened down there and you comin' up the way you did."

Removing his legs finally and setting the paper down in the way described before, the sheriff looked up at him to take out and light a cigar while the Mayor just stood there looking at him do this.

"Oh, I'm sorry Mayor," the sheriff said seeing Whitcomb eye the smoke. "Would you be carin' for one now for yourself?" He asked in his spiteful manner.

"No. That's quite, alright," the Mayor quickly retorted trying to look and sound stern with the sheriff, if it were even possible to do so.

"You were sayin' now Mayor Whitcomb?"

A moment went by as the Mayor shrugged back to continue.

"Well, as I was saying," he went on huffily, "There are a lot of stories gettin' around that you..."

"Now, now," the sheriff interrupted trying to look innocent as he could to the other. "Just what stories are all these bein'?" he asked from behind his desk.

"Well, frankly I'd rather not say just here now with your men and all being here," the Mayor carried on. "Maybe if we could talk alone, that is, it would be better for the moment."

Looking around at the other men the sheriff decided to comply with the Mayor at this knowing he had a few words of his own to share with him, but dismissing his men surely enough and as Mayor Whitcomb had suggested to let them speak.

"Alright, boy's," the sheriff said. "You heard the Mayor. You just take yourselves a little break so me and Mayor Whitcomb here can have our little chat. That is why you came, of course. Isn't it Whitcomb?"

"Well, certainly," the Mayor recapped on a lower clave of voice while the others stood by waiting for the sheriff's que to leave as he looked to Joe Collins for them to do this, but the sheriff just sitting back in his chair smoking on his cigar and calm as could be.

Once the others left though, and went out the precinct door the Mayor began speaking up again as to his concerns of the sheriff in front of him.

"Well, as I was saying," he went on. "There have been a lot of rumors going on about that business of yours with that Colby down in Nebraska. Some are saying now you weren't even around the time he was shot."

"Well, is that so," the sheriff said straightening himself back up into his own chair.

"Yes, it is," Whitcomb deposited, almost now suspecting the sheriff as much himself.

"And just what is it you want me to be doin' about it," the other spoke blowing out the rings of smoke with his cigar. "Well, I don't know," the Mayor said facing off to the side in his apprehension.

"Were you or weren't the one that killed Colby Jenkins?" He finally asked facing back at the sheriff, although the other hardly blinking an eye.

"What do you think Mayor?" The sheriff sneakily reciprocated the question while the Mayor stood there looking at him.

"No, of course, you had killed him," he said though after some unsure hesitation on his part.

"I just wanted to come here to make sure of it," the Mayor recapped still looking on helpless to the sheriff's lack of feeling, or knowing for sure what he said was right.

"Well, I guess that's that," Whitcomb went on blindly.

"I wouldn't be worrying about too much anyhow," the sheriff suddenly spoke from behind his desk as Whitcomb looked surprised to the sheriff's words or what he was hearing.

"And just what do you mean by that now," the Mayor asked almost more apprehensive than before.

"Well, it just so happens I'm not plannin' on staying on here as the town's sheriff. If that's alright with you Mr. Mayor?"

Whitcomb began looking flustered to the sheriff's statement, but unsure as to why he would be leaving.

"This certainly comes as a surprise," he said as Jeff got up from his chair to get his hat down from the other side of the precinct.

"It rather does me too," the sheriff said as he slipped on his hat.

"And just who do you think I'll get in here to replace you with?"

The sheriff turned to the Mayor looking to go for the door to make his way out but answered him just the same.

"Seems to me Joe Collins be the next one in line for the position," he replied to Whitcomb with the obvious suggestion. The Mayor just stood there looking back though, as the sheriff went to go out the door, but turning to him again the sheriff spoke.

"I'll be leavin' in a few weeks, or a month or two from now soon as I get what I need to where I'm goin'."

"And just where would that be out of curiosity?" asked Whitcomb.

Just before closing the precinct door behind him as the Mayor stood there he answered.

"Colorado," he said as Whitcomb looked down puzzlingly for a moment and back up to the closed door that had just been shut on him. As for the sheriff now out on the town veranda he went on passing his men who were hanging around and dressed now in the warmer clothes and coats as he bid, "Evening men," while Will Blake stood out on the side looking back, but the sheriff pretending not to notice as the other and the young deputy could see him walking down the rest of the boardwalk lit up with its torch light and others mingling around.

Just then, the Mayor himself popped out of the precinct door as the men could see this and Whitcomb looking on with the others, although having almost just as much enthusiasm of the sheriff as they did, but deciding then to give the good news over to Joe Collins about the sheriffs own leaving and his being promoted to official head deputy, or at least until the sheriff would finally depart and go his way. For regardless of what the others thought and even the Mayor as to his abrupt announcement to leave the Little Cavern town and abdicate himself of holding the office as town's sheriff, it was particular that in those days before car and automobile and among those mid - western parts when drifting and leaving someplace was something much more common among both men and their women, but all whom were in search of something, or a kind of freedom and promise that only the west was thought to give, and even, if only a chance at it.

29

Millie's parents had been at home as before, but waiting now to hear word from Doctor Treadwell about their daughter or anything Mrs. Jones might have passed to him about how she was doing, or anything at all knowing the coming holidays would soon be taking place and just wanting to see their daughter and spend the time with her during the holidays, and, of course, Christmas itself, but were bent on not taking no as an answer to this refusal or anything which might cause them not to be with her no matter what her ailments were, or what Treadwell thought.

Still, they knew they could not hinder their daughter any more than they or she had to herself already and just knowing that Millie was safe with the warm hearted and caringly Mrs. Jones whom had diligently in her selfless way been at Millie's side and helping her get through the day's without complaint which was and had been a relief in itself for the time being, and appeasing to themselves of any fearful thoughts of the alternative or Millie being in a faraway Institution, or an asylum during those early and deplorable times when such places were not given to good name or as to the fate of the patients they harvested, and moreover, without the benefit of ever hardly seeing their daughter for the duration of her stay, or knowing of her state of being without their own sight.

Instead, they were content enough now the way things were and Doctor Treadwell stopping by weekly to speak with them, though it had been some time since they had last seen him after having asked if their daughter could come home with them for the Christmas day as he had gone to Mrs. Jones to speak to Evelynn about this to find out if Millie had spoken herself about the coming holiday's or what she wanted.

In town by now the display of ornamental wreathes had been hung beneath the torch lights and the numerous shop windows also decked out for the Christmas time with shades of Holly wrapped and garnishing whatever displays and all the Knick knacks that one could associate or would imagine during those times in such a place and town, but also, when its own aforementioned Christian spirit and values shined and permeated the streets and its people the most. As it was the hopes for the new year and Christmas were long waited in the wake of all the past events that had come the towns way and in spite of the all hovering suspicions and scandal that had gone down to affect its own reputation and scruples that the town represented itself with as most now just wanted a new beginning for it and themselves as the chance for this was now ever promising and those who had come to live in, or near Little Cavern the New Year and Holiday a hope for a continuation as to this freedom and the redemption those drifting few now sought from other places before, or, as had been put before in alluding to the notion, if even for the chance of it.

This rapture and Holiday awe though far enough from Millie herself, at the moment, could still be felt within her and all that she knew in the past, or the town's reflections of it and her own parents.

As for Mrs. Jones she was not like most nor cared to live up to the time and place the year was at with the impending arrival of Christmas soon, but her and Wyatt were and always had been to themselves mostly, without any outside visits or need for celebration as to this or traditions they had towards it, with just Mrs. Jones putting out a few symbols here meant to acknowledge the spirit of the year, although for the most part and Wyatt, especially, was merely a reminder of things that once were and something they no longer were apart of in the sense of towns meaning of it, or any of the residents nearby similarly.

Millie herself, had, of course, noticed some of the décor of Mrs. Jones, or around the home and had even heard the old woman speaking to the doctor not more than a few days back about the idea of spending Christmas with her parents, or if they could even have it with her at her own home and Millie present with them, but they knew they would first have to ask Millie about how she felt of the whole thing as she stood their listening from the top of the stairs like before to the two, although inside her felt indifferently about the coming Holiday but deep down knowing she would want to be with her parents and spend it with them, regardless of how.

Therefore, she had taken it upon herself to go downstairs after listening the little bit she did to the doctor and Evelynn, in order, to express her want of this as the two could see her in the frame of the open door and calling her in to speak about the affair, but Millie coming forthright of her desire to spend the holiday with her parents as the final decision would be agreed upon by both Treadwell and Mrs. Jones that they would all, herself, Millie and her parents spend Christmas day at the old woman's quaintly home that year not only out of convenience, but also, out of necessity of the girl or Millie herself and not wanting to risk any possibility of any recurrence of past behavior. Nevertheless, this detail would be kept more to themselves, but only appropriate, as the Doctor himself was quick enough to get the final word back to the parents shortly after the talk they had, as the two parents, Benjamin and Kate, were more than compliant with the outcome and looking forward to spending the time they could with their daughter, even as she was.

Aside from all the ongoing hullabaloo, or what not in town and the Holiday festivities soon about to arrive to both Millie and the others around her, it was not long from this when Millie would have another chance encounter with Wyatt Cobb though one that would stand out from the rest and unlikely in any regard as its inevitable impact on both would be derived from the mutual and emotional constitutes that existed between, either, so as to heal of themselves what and could only be healed by their own bond to one another, in some way, or that which had been and the very consequence of their being together as though all energies around them and within them had brought them together for this purpose, and the same one that has been spoken about thus far as to Wyatt's salvation and the girls own desire for life that could come as result.

For all this had come to a common point now that was inevitable and a fate, to either, that would carry out the rest of their lives, whether for better or worse, this condition would only be up to the one looking at it and a perspective that is ultimately judged for all its efforts by others based on the good and the better in them more than the less.

As it was Millie had been sleeping in her bed, or Cobb's more accurately for that matter, and had gotten up in the middle of one night when it was late and in the early morning hours to go down and pour herself a glass of some left over milk in order to help her sleep and get through the night however she could aside from all the ambivalence of another day ahead and the current ruminations of her head that kept her at times from sleep or unconscious itself.

In those days Milk or perishables could not be kept cold for too long either, or in one's hands or pantry without going bad, but Evelynn would leave some out fresh she had gotten and leftover that morning before on the kitchen table every so often in a glass jar if Millie so desired the need to take some as she knew she would use it for this purpose or at night for herself.

After coming down the steps of the stairs by light of a candle she had lit to help her see she made her way slowly to the door of the den as she went through in the darkened room to get to the kitchen and then by opening the door that led into it she set the small candle and wick down on the table in front near the jar of milk set out and thereafter went over to get a glass from out one of the above cabinets to drink from.

It was another cold and gloomy night outside and had been almost the whole evening as she went to pour herself from out of the jar into her glass the milk while the December wind and rain continued to stir outside and lightning even showing through the far window as she stayed there for a moment inside and drinking her helping of milk from the glass and nothing or no one else around her.

Just then the flame of the candle went out for some reason though she was unsure why as the lightning from outside continued to pour in and cascading herself and the inside of the kitchen as well.

Now without clear sight she had stopped drinking the milk she had poured and set it down on the table in front of her, and in the helplessness and dark around her, though she knew she would have to get back to her room somehow and without guide of her Candle as she went on out of the kitchen holding its useless and blown out wick in her hand as she opened the door to the den.

At that moment, however, another flash of lightning distributed over herself and what was more, someone in front of her, as Wyatt Cobb's face suddenly came into view and lit up from the lightning coming through from outside as only his could, as Millie stood back almost out of a strange sort of shock from his sight, or having some kind of fear within her from his presence as she stood their momentarily looking back at him though his face was expressionless, but the girl as Wyatt came closer almost collapsing to the floor in a fainting manner as Wyatt seeing the distress in her eyes beforehand had caught her in time from the fall.

Bringing her inside the den then as he still had her in his arms he set her down on the nearest chair as he went over to get a candle down from the mantle place and lit it by using one of the fireplace matches from out of its canister.

For a few moments, he was afraid that he might have harmed the girl as she was still faint and not awake seeing her in the flame of the light he had just lit but some sounds coming from her, nonetheless.

Not sure what to do he went inside to dampen a kitchen rag he took of some water he used from a bucket or citadel they would use to keep it in after pumping it from the outside, as he came out with the rag and went over to her setting it to Millie's head and wetting her.

As he continued to do this in the light of the candle and seeing her face almost in the likeness he had mentioned to her on that same night in front of the fire he could not help but see the beauty of her skin and modest face and lightly colored hair, but an image becoming to him as, perhaps, few people or anyone else would see it.

Suddenly though Millie's eyes opened as he look back at her and she to Wyatt, but seeing the look on his face as he had just then removed the rag from her forehead.

For at that moment there seemed to be a conception for the both that was unmistakable to one another and an intimacy that had not come before as Millie sit there in the chair and as Wyatt continue to admire what he saw.

"Are you alright, ma'am?" he asked during this brief pause, and as Millie continue to look back now awake.

"Yes," she replied eventually. "I'm fine, now."

"I'm sorry I scared you ma'am," he went on. "I had thought I heard something before and came down, but..." he could see Millie begin to fret again in her face then. "Are you sure you're alright?"

"Yes," she answered again perking herself up to him. "I am."

Wyatt could see she was still apprehensive and vague in her eyes as he continue to look at her in the candlelight, but asked her if she was alright to walk or if she thought she could make it to her room.

"Would you be needin' any help upstairs ma'am," he said.

Getting up then from her chair after Wyatt had asked she rose to her feet without any help as Wyatt stood there overhead tall as he was as he could see this, though Millie beginning to fall again from her lightheadedness as he took her in his arms again to bring her up, taking the candle in one of his hands from its handle while exiting the den and then up the stairs down to the familiar room at the end of the hallway, setting her down on the bed after he had put the lit candle off onto the bureau.

As he went to tuck the sheets over her though he could not help but to look at her again like before helpless to her entrance and wondering if she had just felt as he while the girl opened her eyes again to him and closing them after.

But, just the same, a passion had just been crossed that inspired Wyatt in a way that had long been requited and a source of desire just as the girl had observed of him that would drive the writer and man inside him to commit the lost love he had always indebted himself to, and, once more, in her place cause him to take up the craft that would, perhaps, find meaning in his life as it had before and when he would pick up the pen to hand to finally express the passion he had just recovered – The truer of love's he had always known.

30

The wintry days passed along one to the next and the town buzzing with its normal flair, and busy crowd, at the moment, in the fuss of the present holidays as it was now on the Eve of Christmas Day itself and shop keepers staying open for the last bit of purchases and gift buying they could tally, although near the closing hour then when business would finally be out for the evening and the men and women and, more importantly, the many Santa hoping children of Little Cavern enjoying and ushering in all the promise and rejuvenation that the Lords Birthday could bring.

As for Benjamin and Kate they would not be seeing Millie herself until the next day, or on Christmas as they had agreed with the Doctor and physician on this as Millie was, now, instead, joined with Wyatt and Evelynn in the den by themselves with the mere presence of a rather unimposingly but decorative Christmas tree, and dressed with some of Mrs. Jones' stowed away decorations with silver linings and ribbons wrapped throughout, and even a few lit candles on some of the branches as they would do back then, or when such tradition was a formality rather than something that could be spared.

Millie herself had been looking and admiring the tree from her chair that was tucked away in the corner as Mrs. Jones and Wyatt stood aside as usual, but all in front of the Fireplace, warm and relaxed by the light of the all - consuming fire, and drinking a bit of some homemade eggnog Mrs. Jones had prepared specially for that evening, although no one speaking up and all very calm and serene looking.

Just then, Evelynn spoke up from her seat across from Millie as to ask the girl about tomorrows Christmas day but Millie replying as enthusiastically she could to the old woman after having taken another sip from the porcelain tea cup in her hands.

"Are you looking forward, dear, to seeing your parents tomorrow?" she asked in her softly tone to her.

"Yes, Mrs. Jones," Millie answered, after lowering her cup.

"I know they'll be glad to see you," Evelynn went on glancing down into her lap after taking a sip of the eggnog that she had made. "It has been a while."

Millie, of course, did not say anything afterward as Wyatt just looked over at the girl every now and again from his standing point next to the fireplace, although Millie hardly so much as looked at him herself, but instead, just minding the tree mostly that she had helped decorate along with Mrs. Jones some, or after Wyatt had sawed it down and brought it back for the purpose.

Mrs. Jones just looked back to Millie, then, though not saying anything as she rose from her seat to go somewhere after having set down her drink onto the nearby table. Nevertheless, making her way in back of the den to a cabinet as she open it herself, she would go to get something out while Millie and Wyatt just look at the fire, but still hardly acknowledging one another for that matter. It wound not be long, however, until the old woman would come back shortly and now holding whatever she had gotten in her hands but wrapped up in some bland and brownish kind of paper or lint, though held together with some string and small bow on top.

As she handed it over to Millie the girl took it into her hands while Mrs. Jones held onto her small cup and trivet for her, as the girl showed some lifting of her eyes to the gesture and gift she had just given her, but wondering what it could be as Mrs. Jones stood there looking on with Wyatt behind her.

"This is just something I thought you might like dear," she told Millie as she began unwrapping the paper and string with her hands, though the texture of the package was soft and could suggest attire of some kind.

As she did this she could finally see what it was as her eyes opened a little wider than before.

"They had belonged to my mother when she had been young," Evelynn went on as Millie held up what appeared to be two pair of finely silk knit evening gloves, though charming and nicely worn at that, even for their old age but befitting for that of a young lady such as Millie.

"Thank you, Mrs. Jones," the girl said holding onto the gloves in her palms as Evelynn smiled to her.

"You're quite welcome dear," she replied as Wyatt had then also went away to get something, but Millie going on to slip on one of the gloves to her hands to see how it felt, or, more than this how it looked.

"You have small hands just as my mother had," Evelynn remarked seeing how well the glove fit her.

"Mrs. Jones?" asked Millie, then, curiously.

"Yes, dear," the old woman replied in a plain tone.

"Was your mother from around here, or did she grow up someplace else?"

"No," she replied tipping her head slightly. "She had come from the east and had lived in the big city as a young woman, but had met my father some time shortly after that."

"I see," Millie said.

Just then Wyatt had returned again though holding something himself, strange as it was, but meant for the girl as she mirrored to him seeing the gift or thing in his hands she knew she was about to receive.

The object itself, however, was not wrapped like the gloves Mrs. Jones had just given her as by now she had removed the one from her hand, nor looked to be anything other than a scrolled and folded piece of some thinly paper, with just a mere red ribbon wrapped around it to hold it together as he handed it to her more plainly than anything, but Millie hardly sure of what it could be as Mrs. Jones was not completely without curiosity herself, and her face overcome with slight intrigue.

"This is for you, Millie," Wyatt said after he had handed it to her. As she would start to undo the ribbon around it though, noticing too that it looked to belong to a woman, she only look down to see the plain verse and hand written poem Wyatt had rendered for her and in his scriptive pen as she read it to herself in his presence.

The O'Leary Girl

There once was a girl
Who lived not far
In the mid - western town
Of Little Cavern.

Her name was Mildred
But to those who knew her
She went and liked to be called
The name of Millie; rather than Mildred.

Her face was lightly
And her grace was tritely

But to those who knew her
She was seldom to be called Mildred -
But just plainer than old Millie O'Leary.

She loved like all others
And fell lost one day like most lovers will do –
But, still would not have one of her own

And, perhaps, this is why
Whenever she shied of eye
She was always called, but dotingly Millie,
And not by her maidenly name
Of Miss Mildred O'Leary.

After having read the poem to herself she looked up to Wyatt standing next to her, but went on to read it out loud so as everyone to hear as she herself was both moved and charmed in her way by the subversive meaning of the ballade, or what she thought Wyatt had observed in her and his reflection, almost having the lightened affect to her face that he had alluded to, but, for a brief moment, the poem in its simplicity as he had written it for her allowing the girl to break, and distract her from all the esoteric worries going on within.

As for Evelynn she just looked over to Wyatt after Millie was finished reading, although surprised that Wyatt had written it, but also, in a sense, relieved for the time being that he had made the gesture in the form of his own writing to give to Millie as a gift, and, once more, almost seeing the promise in him she had once felt, or to know, that he had at least made the nigh attempt of writing again, even in the small token for the girl.

Going over to her, then, Mrs. Jones picked up the paper from Millie's lap as the girl let her do this, but wanted see for herself the prose as she put her glasses to her face to see, though after skimming it she quickly gave it back to Millie, just merely having bent over to look, as she glanced back to Wyatt now with his back turned to the fireplace almost.

As for Millie she stood to her feet shortly with the gifts she had received still in her hands to thank Mrs. Jones again for the lovely evening gloves she had given her as the old woman only returned one of her more gentler and tellingly smiles, but Millie, making her way then after to Wyatt as he turned to her.

"Thank you, Wyatt," she said as she looked up to him and curtly gave him an innocent kiss of her unto one his cheeks. Only after doing this with the delicate ribbon or bow still in her hands she asked, "Did this belong to the woman?"

Cobb simply bid his head to her as she went to open one of his hands and only gently giving back the ribbon as she closed it for him.

"You keep it, then..." she told him as Wyatt took back the lace or heirloom with almost as much grace as he had given it over, the brief moment in the form of her requital as though a restoration to a kind of faith Wyatt had long been without, and a distinct kindness from the girl that had all along inspired it. Turning back to Mrs. Jones then she only went to say, "I think I'll go put all this away now before I come back down," and as innocent in her tone and conduct as only Millie could be.

"Alight, dear," Evelynn replied as Millie continued on out of the room and up the stairs after while Mrs. Jones turned her attention back to Wyatt near her still, as she put her hand to his shoulder for a brief moment, before continuing into the kitchen to put away her cup and saucer.

After a little bit upon coming out Millie had already come back downstairs, now standing near and close to the Christmas tree in the corner and looking at it as she had, but Evelynn asking her then, if she was ready to have the cake that she had made as well for that evening, as they had already had their supper before, or some mutton Mrs. Jones had prepared, similarly, though Mille replying she would at that while Mrs. Jones went back inside to cut and place the some pieces out on a few plates to bring out for all to have.

As Millie and Wyatt stood alone for the short time she was in the kitchen Millie went over to talk to Wyatt and to tell him how she liked the poem he had written about her, as he stood their listening kindly enough, but hardly looking at her as she spoke.

Finally, though, he turned and said, "Thank you, ma'am," as Evelynn was just about to come out with the plates of cake in her hand. But, to this Millie would only playfully reply, "You mean *Millie -*" as Cobb's face reacted with a small jeer of smile.

As soon as Mrs. Jones had come into the den with the plates of cake in her hand she could see Wyatt and Millie close to one another, and noticing the nearness of the two but handing each off their plates as the three went on to have their dessert in front of the fire, and Millie remarking how good the cake was herself as Evelynn returned the courtesy.

Meanwhile outside snow had by then fallen onto the ground throughout the past days as small flakes could be seen blowing outside through the glass frosted panes of the window beside the tree though the Christmas Eve night would go by unlike most before it, except for that slight cheer and jingle in the air that seemed to come with the Holiday itself as if those that could only know so many young and youthful Christmas's before felt, even in the absence of being young or the passion of a child, or adolescent they had before. For Millie she had now definitely been among one of these people, and just as Christmas was being celebrated jovially in other parts, nearby, the distance felt to these other places was ever greater to her with only the memories of Christmas past and future to think of, but the present one that she was only trying to get through as best she could as her parents had also spent the evening quietly to themselves with the exception of Doctor Treadwell coming by earlier to make a small visit knowing their daughter was elsewhere and out of his own goodness that, as the saying goes, the very spirit of the season would permit.

Indeed, Christmas carolers composed of some of the small and straying children of Little Cavern dressed down in there mittens and long winter hats could be heard singing time to time and from house to house, or the ones they chose to visit with even the O'Leary's as one of these people as Benjamin briefly came outside to bid them a goodnight and with a small pocket of change to give them as tradition, but heading back in with Mrs. O'Leary soon afterward, now pent up near the fire and only thinking of her daughter.

Regardless, of the evening though whether Millie knew it or not by accepting Wyatt Cobb's poem as a gift for what it was she had taken her first step to getting better, or as to Treadwell's words of what he had said to her before pertaining to this, and what was more as she go on to disseminate the meaning behind it a realization in her own angst even if she could not voice it, but to know at least what the source of her worries were mainly at even for the time being of her reclusion from the rest of Little Cavern, and the one roomed school where she had gone every day in the sight of her own peers and her teacher Mrs. Motts up at the blackboard looking to her, perhaps, as Mrs. Jones had said of her before, or in the light of that one special student from the rest as she had seen this in Wyatt once herself.

Nevertheless, she would go on despite the obvious afflictions of her character and her temperance towards those that were hard for her to tolerate, or even those few mentioned closer to her, when one day, sooner than later, she would depart to the East to continue her education and as Mrs. Motts had envisioned for her, but not out of anyone's desire for this, or for the sake of her prideful parents and what they wanted, or even out of her teachers ambitions for her, but instead, out of her own blunt Will to do so, as now her landscape or that had transpired as a result of where she was then, was beginning to fall behind her with a new view and new way of sight she would have to force herself to reckon with in order to move past.

Therefore, she would see her parents the next Christmas day and spend the time with them to let them be with her, and, perhaps, in an even more lightened heart and frame of mind than they had seen of her so far, but to know they could see her as such only a furthering the confidence that she could get well again and fulfill her role as their daughter to higher purpose and that they knew for all her quietness and vague sense of self was well within her.

31

It was after the Christmas Holidays and the New Year had passed over to the new dawn and hopes of the town as though a fresh start to everything, and now that word had passed on that the sheriff himself would even be leaving bringing an end to any consternation's to do with his presence, or whatever fuss towards the Mayor and claims against his Chief Deputy abruptly pausing for the moment, but everyone feeling the new beginning for the town they once loved for its simple quality and aspect of peace that made it so. Still, others questioned if the town would indeed resume its normal pace as before as time would only tell.

Now that it was in the mid - later part of February this burgeoning for the town was near its peak as spring was shortly to be on the horizon and with the feeling of "Rebirth" that it brought for those who felt as in the latter.

As for Millie she had been staying with Mrs. Jones, naturally, for the past few months and weeks trying to find relief from her anxieties, however, or whenever she could throughout the cold winter months, as Mrs. Motts had paid her a visit time to time, or more than twice to talk about the possibility of resuming her place at the school house, or at least to finish out the year with the other children her age, although the idea of it to Millie was hardly something she wanted to think about with anticipation as she knew her previous friends such as Stella would be there and only gawking at her as they could, or at least the contentious images of her mind after having done what she had and after the visit paid from Doctor Kettle, but with all the talk she could imagine that had come from it.

Whether or not she would go back would inevitably be up to her, without say, but Mrs. Motts had merely suggested the notion without cause to upset her as she had also gone ahead (In spite of the view she would not finish out the school year) but had applied for the special grant or scholarship for her to study at a University in the East, and written a special letter to the board, or the ones endowing the fund, informing whomever of the girls special circumstances and her desire to further her education, as well, the distinction Millie had served her as one of her students, and requesting for them to at least to consider the girl's criteria for being selected as a candidate to receive the endowment.

Although Millie was ever apprehensive as to all of it, or what Mrs. Motts suggested she could neither help but feel her own Inner Being becoming more and more firm of the newer view of life she had taken on, and as it would be some time until she would be given word on the subject of her schooling, presumably, from Mrs. Motts own mouth, she could only wait anxiously as before on the decision, and then as to her own decisiveness or the swing and Pendulum as to her future, incongruent, and awkward as her present state seemed to it.

Aside her, or Millie's own dilemma, or what was now manifesting within, the sheriff about town had been busy making some of his own plans, likewise, in a sense, and getting ready to head off soon, and, once and for all, hopefully, never to return to the God fearing town of Little Cavern, Wyoming, undoubtingly distressed and misshaped about it as he could hardly be, but soon to be divested in his own riches and what good fortune would await him in the lustrous though idyll, San Juan mountains residing below in those lower parts of Colorado and Mid-Western states. For this undertaking he had now gotten together some tools and gear for the trip in order to find what Gold there was to be found in the nearby mountain range and that the sketchy map looked to show with just the borrowing of a donkey or two, perhaps, along his way to help him in this task, and by some of his own debauched and Black Blooded Luck find and haul back the gold he had found to some place quiet and private so as to begin the process of turning the cherished commodity into superfluous and highly stacked green dollar bills, some as high as a thousand dollars each and toppled over each other, but as many of them as he could imagine in his fantasy of greedily fortune.

Whether the towns quest in all of this contusion to Destiny, or the sheriff's own plotting or sordid scheming, or even bereft Millie at Mrs. Jones, there was what seemed to be another Puebloan, or Mexican looking man about town, similar to the one who had come up from some unknown place and who had asked Farnworth again about where it was the book that the sheriff was now the secret owner of, or as to what the town Undertaker had done with it, hardly shocked by now the lukewarm mortician was of anything to come his way and answering the man with his dullen face as to the third inquiry of, or about the Mexican's ragged book, but knowing that it could hardly be the useless text he had thought it. The man as himself though was hardly the beggar and toothless peasant that had come to Farnworth in the first place, but instead, more keen of eye and dressed slightly finer, but by no means a seemingly pugnacious character as to warrant fear in the town that rarely saw such people just keeping to himself for the most part as though trouble was the last thing he wanted, although the question like others posed before it or as to why he was there still unknown.

For many though the man was still a reminder of what had occurred earlier of that last year, but the town's own sense of Rejuvenation and Good Will overpowering for the most part any trepidations that could arise as far as his presence as the man had hardly spoke to anyone since his being their anyhow, and staying at Mrs. Ruford's Inn of all places, but signing his name in the registry – *Cortanado Juarez* – in plain ink with a slight air of charm and quietness so as hardly to be noticed.

Soon, however, despite the man's passiveness, and even disregarding the town's new outlook of the coming year and newer prospect set out for them, the overhung Ball of Fate that most thought had now stopped rolling towards their lovingly and redemptive town would be, no less, finally, at its doorstep only waiting to tumble over it from overhead, almost dwarfing the town itself in size, as the red skinned foreigner, or Spaniard, in fact, as it would turn out to be was no other than the leader cohort of a Mexican Bandit outfit, and who had come all the way up to the Mid - Western Wyoming town just for the waiting of being joined with the rest of his Mexican enslaves, or the fellow bandito's under him, but all with the common motive of coming there to recover the book the more clumsily named Juan Julius Pugliano had been buried with after Juarez had gotten word somehow himself of where the text was located, or perhaps, even by that other poor Mexican who had been there not so long ago himself, though never to be heard from or seen again for some mysterious reason still uncertain.

A once fellow bandito and traitor himself to Cortanado Juarez's certain cause of dignity, or merely the looting and vandalizing and even killing of his own people where he had come from, the presently dead, but loudly declarative Mexican, as when he had first come in Little Caverns drinking saloon on that night not long ago, had taken the initiative of stealing the book for himself after upon escaping the Juarez clan, or before and around the time he had arrived in small Little Cavern to avenge the death of his slain friend, as he knew or at least thought after having made sure with Farnworth that the book was then buried along with him in the graveyard, although had no intent of peacefully digging up his adversary.

Instead, Juarez's plan, in so many words, and was the custom of the Mexican horde he rode with, would be for his men to simply come in shooting all around with their pistols in the air and making a big show so as to make their presence quite obvious of why they were there, or what they had come for, hardly in the frame of mind or mentality of a person of Little Cavern, as force was something they used and vehemently to apprehend whatever it was they wanted, not just for themselves, but for those back in Mexico waiting for others alike to bring back the riches that the sequestered map and text would lead them to. For power, otherwise, or in their hands in this sense was only as good to serve them in their own homeland for this purpose, or as to the ones they who saw had taken this from them, and the upheld government that they saw as conflict to their cause, whether for good or for worse to this end, only a wizened and timeless judge will be able to tell.

The sheriff or Jeff McCormack had even taken notice of the man, on one occasion, or seeing him off in the distance a wee bit down one of the towns sorrowful and drudgingly inundated roads, or in the wake of the snow that had just fallen and now beginning to melt down to permeable frost, with small pockets and spits of wet and ice all around and even, of course, with the presence of the unmissed horse dropping's scattered around, a juxtaposition in their own setting that even then could not forewarn them of what was about to occur, and the sky overhead daunted with the same filth for that matter but still unobvious to all despite.

It would be no less the sheriff Jeff McCormack who of all people could feel this something about to happen, or that Black Cloud literally hanging overhead and with the presence of the Mexican an ominous feeling of his own deplorable self, that others like him were coming to lay claim on something, if not the very book and sought map he now had to himself.

In spite of his observance, though originally wanting to leave later than had planned or just after the colder winter months had passed to avoid the winter snows, he had gone ahead and taken the opportunity one day of going up the Mayor's office to inform Whitcomb that he would be taking off in the next coming days for sure, although Whitcomb even confessed he would be sorry to see the sheriff go, as even he knew of Joe Collins's own short comings,

and the one to assume the position. Like most officials though his small griev-
ance, despite the argument he had been given over the sheriff, was more out
of concern of task rather than popularity, always helpless, especially Mayor
Whitcomb, to the frailties of his own character, or who he thought should fill
the position whatever it be to represent the town he thought he knew. Still,
Mayor Whitcomb told Jeff that he could vacate so long as he stayed on as sheriff
until Sunday to finish out the week, of course having no way real way of making him stay, even so much as vainly proposing a weekly increase in salary if
he were to, but Jeff promptly declining the Mayor's feeble attempt to make him
stay, as only the sheriff knew what he was after, or, more appropriately put,
aside from those soon to be arriving bandito assassins and clan members coming up and closing in on the town Cortanado had already arrived in, but, expecting his men almost any day now.

Indeed, as the sheriff had come out of the Mayor's office he had seen again
the same Darker tinted man down the road some among the town's traffic during that slower paced part of the afternoon, but avoiding him as best he could
and without any real effort in this as he was still the town's official sheriff for
the next day or two, making his way back down to the precinct where Joe Collins and the others were inside waiting for the unconfuted and unvarnished
man of the hour, or Jeff McCormack to come in as he would and take his seat at
the sheriffs desk for the last few days he would be on. It was then, Thursday,
around half past three, but the sheriff had told Joe and the others upon making
one of his last showings around the precinct or when he had come back on that
same day that he would be taking off Sunday morning to wherever it was he
was going, and that Joe would thereafter be head as the towns sheriff and the
precinct they served.

No matter what else to come the final culmination or soon tossing of the
Ball out on the horizon would inevitably deplore itself and unto the town the
next few days of that chillier February month when a new chapter for Little
Cavern would be inspired, but not only out of the arrival of the Mexican Van-
dals and Bandits or others to come, but, also, out of the very nature that all
people and places are bounded to, regardless of what forefronts of rule's or
whatever tools and obstructs are implemented to fend them – But nature itself
hardened and unmasked as it can be, and the town of Little Cavern upon its
wake.

Craig Sholl

32

The few days had turned over to the next, or since the sheriff had announced his final departing as it was then the early morning of Saturday during the February month, as the clouds above hung overhead placid and with an emptiness to them that strewed the dismal and lachrymose sight it was. Also characteristic or in the wind was the odd feeling of a mild breeze all around that had seemed to sweep in during the latter part of the night, although of which had not abated since, nor levied in any way as those few who had woken up at the early hour of that morning when first equally faint light had dawn, and could notice themselves the distinct cloudy forecast and that strange stillness in the air as mentioned with its deadening aspect giving way to that part of the morning though a forecast of weather that was not entirely unfamiliar to those parts, and in those places or people before.

The sheriff had, indeed, gone to the office his last official day on the job, but did not plan on staying the latter part of that evening or into the night when Little Cavern would be at its peak or what crowds over at the saloon shuffling in, and any possible arrests which surely there would be, and on such a night with the rest of the towns barter or what complaints may come.

As for Mrs. Jones at her home and the others, or Wyatt and Millie, they would mostly keep inside, of course, and seeing the outer promise of a storm coming through at some point though of which never seemed to come, and Mrs. Jones herself taking notice as she looked out her bedroom window after having risen, but noticing the old turn wheel of her old wind silo more affected and indicative of the breeze than usual, almost having an erratic quality to it at times or when she would momentarily stop to look at it during that early part of the day. Shortly after having first seen it, in fact, the way she had she went out onto the landing of her porch, but could hear the squeaky turn wheel herself while the wind and breeze picked up around her, going on inside shortly after, but only to see to her young friend or Millie who would take stock as well of the stormy pattern of forecast overhead and waiting it out like the others for the anticipated rain and thunder and lightning to come, but which never did for some reason.

Those early morning hours of business in the town went on as usual and in the same hurried way of routine and conduct as all before them, and despite the bitter appeal of the weather, and, of course, without any regard towards the forecast than other days and mornings they had seen like it before, nor paying anymore mind to the sky than the cash registers that could be filled, or what chores needed to be done that day, and whatever else could be fulfilled for that matter.

Therefore, it was just Joe and the sheriff himself at the office that glumly, but uniquely felt Saturday morning when young deputy Will Blake and Pat Thomsen would be coming in themselves later on, or around high noon, but, both soon to be back under the command of their partner Joe Collins again in the next day or two, although anything as they saw it better than having Jeff McCormack in charge for that matter. Even the younger of the two or Will was thinking now of leaving the town to go elsewhere to find work, or perhaps, another line of job, with his growing disillusionment of the law he had sworn to upheld, but thus far not within the fame or mind or action he had started with, and after having his own friend been killed the way he did, but unsure either way what he would do in the time to come.

All had been going well, as stated, nonetheless, and fair in the town so far, but it would not be long until the impending chaos would, finally, erupt within the town's streets, and all to witness what would come as something they would not forget, nor would leave them with the same notion of the fortress of a town they thought Little Cavern to be or any place, ever again, but the attitudes they once had like this forever and brokenly tarnished even in the devout Christian spirit of triumph they had, at once, knowing how frail uncertainty could be for anyone, or anywhere.

But for now as this event was yet to come the faces and temperament of the people was common, regardless, of fate they would be given as Mr. Dixon took in his usual, weekend clientele or local town goers requests, and the tangy and taffy sweet shop of Mrs. Cannerville's down the road to be met with what children and women would come in for their morning treats, or cakes and pies she had prepared to be bought, and even, nervous and ever so ambivalent Farnworth himself now, at his own funeral and mortuary as the towns Undertaker getting ready for the next procession, little did he know a profession that may or was about to payoff greatly.

Still, in regards to the sky pockets of sunlight could be observed every so often, or off in the distance, with slightly distributed rays of visible clear sunlight pouring down below giving that ethereal and Angelic effect that happens at times, or for what few amount of time the display could be seen a ways off, as what Angels to come to the town, for that matter, or on that day would be few and far in between, with Juarez's men now just on the horizon of the town closing in any hour, though precisely when was still unknown.

"…Well, Jeff. I guess this'll bein' your last day here," Joe Collins foreboded to still head Sheriff Jeff McCormack at his desk thumping over some last details of paperwork, or what the Mayor had given over to him upon his departure to do with Joe's promotion to head chief.

"Yeah, I guess you're right, Joe," his boss talked down to him and keeping his head in the paperwork though, acting aloof, almost in some sense as poor Joe himself.

"Boy, sure has been a sight for sore eyes today outside," Joe went on looking out the window, but the sheriff quickly calling him over to his desk.

"Alright, Joe…" he said after signing or writing something down. "You just come over here now, and sign your regular John Hancock on the dotted line."

At this Joe did what he was told while the sheriff put out the paper on the desk in front of him almost in a hastened and abrupt way just wanting to move along with Joe's approval as head chief, or in the eyes of what meagre paperwork had to be done, but Joe going on to sign anyhow and with the sheriffs quick whip of smile into his seat after, knowing he was sooner to being on his way.

"Do you think I could be readin' any of that, their Jeff?" Joe asked his old partner and sheriff, as he looked over whatever he had signed and setting it back down on the desk.

"I don't think so, Joe," the sheriff replied uncaringly as he could. "Just a lot a paperwork gotta be done."

Nevertheless, Joe yielding as always to his sheriff stepped away from the desk in his unsure manner, but listening out for what the other had to say next, as Jeff took out his signature cigar and lit it with match, and resting his legs on top of the desk for the time being.

"Well, Joe," Jeff said almost sounding likeable. "Soon, you'll bein' the sheriff of this hometown," he went on in his imitating manner.

Joe not taking heed, of course, just went over to one of the cells in the near back to give a smoke to one the crusty and overnight inmates who was stagnating in his cell and sticking out his hands as they would do, or when in need of one.

As Joe handed over one of the rolled-up smokes from out of his shirt pocket, the inmate or whoever it was, some older man with a crinkled face, just looked at Joe as he lit it for him, but the deputy coming away from the cell thinking nothing of it as the inmate went on back to sit on his stool aside one of the bungalow cots of the jail.

As for the sheriff he had taken out a wallet full of cash, or a wad of the crisply thin and large type they carried back then, but making sure it was all there for what trip he was about to embark on as Joe had come over to his side again while the sheriff got up and slipped the wallet back into a small poncho hanging off the wall where his hat would usually be. Tucked away for that matter inside was also the Mexican's Text which he would keep well within his grizzly sight the whole day, or for whatever time he would be there at his office into that evening, but not wanting to take his chances with it otherwise.

"When was it old Pat Thomsen and his friend say there gonna gettin' on here today?" the sheriff asked Joe as he looked to him.

"Well, I don't know. Same as they usually get here I guess, around midday," Joe replied.

"That's good," the sheriff went on in more affable talk after sitting back down behind his desk. "Not planin' on stayin' here long today, matter of fact, Joe. Maybe leavin' soon as it gets on dusk."

"Won't be hard on a day like today," Joe spoke. "Darkest day I've seen out there so far. And windy as a bitch too."

Turning to the sheriff, then, with one his puzzled looks he asked in his charm of curiosity, "Where was it now you said you's was movin' on off to now, Jeff?" But to this the sheriff did not say anything as he only sat back down at his desk smoking the cigar, though just then the Mayor had popped into the precinct to interrupt in another surprising visit from him, or to retrieve the paper work he had given to the sheriff upon his last seeing him at his Mayor's office, and that Joe had just signed over on.

"Well, Mayor," Jeff said sitting upright. "So surprised to be seein' you on this weekend day off."

As for the Mayor he just shuffled to the desk where the sheriff was sitting, even in ignorance of the inconspicuous remark, though glancing at Joe for a moment before speaking up.

"I trust all the paper work has been done between you two men," he said as Jeff got it together and stacked it for the Mayor himself.

"Got it all right here for you Mr. Mayor, stacked and ready to go," the sheriff said as he was doing this while Mayor Whitcomb took it out of his hands to look it over. After this he just look back to Jeff, and then back to Joe, but then to the sheriff again as he spoke.

"Well, everything looks in order here," he said looking down to the paperwork in his hand.

"Sure does," the sheriff recapped sitting sideways in his seat and brandishing his cigar.

"Well, then, Gentleman," Whitcomb went on to excuse himself after nipping at his hat about to leave. Just about looking as if to do this and head to the door he spoke to the sheriff again, though stopping and turning slightly back to Jeff.

"There is one other thing I wanted to know sheriff," he said with a straight face at him.

"And just what would that be, now?" the sheriff asked unsure of what he had in mind.

"You had said that you had killed Colby, running towards you, before," the Mayor pondered.

"Yeah, I did," Jeff McCormack said after a moment.

"I'm just curious," the Mayor said looking away.

"What's that to you?" Jeff canted on still unsure.

"Nothing," Mayor Whitcomb replied, almost unconcernedly, as he went over to the door to let himself out. Only turning to the sheriff after as he opened the door half way he would finally reply to him as the two stared back.

"Just happens I had heard Colby was wounded, and shot, two rounds in the back, but with no wounds or gunshot to the front," he said and shutting the door behind him now leaving Joe and the sheriff alone in the precinct, as Joe looked through the window seeing the Mayor with the papers clutched and folded in his hands, but hardly enthusiastic about anything as he took off.

As for the sheriff he just sit there, seeing Joe and knowing sure as shit he was having more than second thoughts about him, but staying calm and collective as always he could be, even such as then. He could even see the slight expression of awkward fear in Joe's face as he turned to him trying to look obtuse and unreflective as to what observation the Mayor had given over, but carrying on anyway despite.

"I'll 'a just be goin' out now and checkin' in on the horses," he said in a nervous undertone and making his way to the back of the precinct, though the sheriff just quivered and scanned over him with his suspicious eyes of guilt, but knowing even old Joe would not think anything less of him, as he was quite accustomed to his natural timidity and looking up to his own authority and image, or at least the way he thought he had seen him.

Unlike for Joe though or what eternity of wait it seemed to be with the sheriff like that at the precinct it would not be long until noontime when young Will and Pat would interrupt the gap of time, and, finally, show up at the precinct themselves as Joe had predicted, although their partner in allusion to the later would not so much as share or either say what comment and word of mouth he had heard out of the Mayor, only trying to be nonchalant Joe Collins.

As for Deputies Will Blake and Pat Thomsen they would simply go on in their business, or daily routine at the precinct getting ready for the night crowd to overcome what left and spare jail cells they had for whatever petty infractions or busily drinkers they would be met with during the rowdy Saturday night, but not thinking anything of what to come.

Hour to hour would go by inside the sheriff's precinct though, as the weather outside had still not lightened, but in fact had only picked up even more so than the morning gone by now and the incessant winds still being lashed about, with road debris being tossed and shuffled about outside, and the sky itself above, darkening and becoming morose with the vengeance and catastrophe it would, eventually, come to spell.

Now nearly half passed four, and almost at the early hour of winters dusk the sheriff himself would soon be getting ready and tidying up to head out and back to his nearby sheriff's home, only, finally, a day closer to taking off as he planned to hop town the next morning after, without even bothering to come in his last day of duty, or as he had told the Mayor.

Indeed, it was so dark that Sonny Pickens had gone ahead and lit the torches one to the next, earlier than usual than he would normally, even, and in spite of the unpromising and dismal sky above, while over protecting the light or flame and wick with a specially glass ensconce given the conditions, or then by fitting the irregular bulb upon the lantern with another long stick or apparatus he would use for such.

In addition to the evening formality there were much fewer people out or roaming the shop windows, rare as it was, but hardly a couple or courtly man and woman side by side in sight or on any of Little Cavern's sidewalks, or crossing any of the roads, similarly, as Sonny Pickens went on lighting. As he look up and around him to the sky and over his shoulder the utterance even of a small and silent chant to himself might've of been heard and feeling of all others something was on the horizon, almost sure of it in his wise and common man's soul, and having the sense for death, and the insurmountable bloodshed he was certainly no stranger to.

As for the saloon crowd, this aspect would not be happening for a while yet, although the piano player and all others inside, at the moment, were routinely preparing and getting ready for the night to arrive, if anyone should even show up in such vile weather, but assuredly, no matter what strain of sky or wind, every single one of them or rancher finding a way to the settlement, no how, if they could.

All had been quiet so far and in the town moreover without trying not to sound too redundant, if possible, and down at the precinct and Sonny Pickens lighting the lanterns, or even Farnworth in his parlor, and even the town's unstated Barber, so far, or that of Carl Higgins and inside his shop trimming an older man's whitish thin hair like himself silent and driftily to themselves as the two could be, and never presuming that only down the road at a distance coming forth, were Cortanado's own men and bandits arriving as expected and about to intercept the town at any moment and railing their gun's up high, or rifles and trigger arms, but seven or eight of them in all headed straight for it.

All of a sudden upon the imperiling threat the few patrons that happened to be out on the street and sidewalk could, henceforth, see the bandito's entering the town, at once, and rummaging down the roads shortly pissing off a few rounds all over, each of them, and making their loud laudable presence known, and dressed in their bandito outfit and sombrero hats and tomatillo Mexican capes fitted over their chests and back, but continuing on their pace until reaching a destination in the town or which could be presumed the center of Little Cavern. Some had even come out, momentarily, or at least peeped their heads out to see the dangerous men passing by, even some just missing of being hit with a round and glass and store front windows shot in, including that of Carl Higgins' own Barber shop, but causing a ruckus of confusion among all and as described that could not be missed, with all in mortal fear of what to come.

Stopping for the duration at a standstill, but continuing to fire a few shots in the air, nonetheless, while all had fled the streets, or either, gone inside keeping clear of the Mexican and bandit filth that had come, Cortanado Juarez, notorious and ruthless leader of the bandito clan, descended out into the open road on foot even passing by Miss Purcell's own clothing shop and shot up shop window where the Parisian dress and gown maker could see the leader now herself, and hiding aside her cash register looking at him with her own snide and gossamer pair of eyes as she put the same prim spectacles up to see better, and squinting while he calmly walked along.

As for any judicial law and order, or at the Mayor's office, and at the precinct the Deputies at the other end of town had heard the burst of ongoing and were only then loading and getting ready their guns, hiding out in the office and jail but waiting for command by the sheriff who was more than disappointed and secretly downcast for the obvious reasons that the threat he had seen coming had finally come to his doorstep, though managing to keep his grip anyway, and see to the threat of Mexican's as best he could.

As for Cortanado he soon reached the others and his fellow bandits in the center of the dissembled and ravaged Wyoming town, as Mayor Whitcomb who as it just so happened had gone back to his office during that day off, perhaps only to go over some of the paperwork, but at that moment was so dissimilarly looking down through the frame of his second story office window of the Town Hall and with fearful and terrified eyes, not knowing what to do as he tried to see what Cortanado and his men were planning.

At first, they were merely talking in their plain Spanish with no one around hearing or possibly understanding what they were saying. After some time of speaking, however, the one bandit in front with his black hair and curl of a mustache would look of surprise to what Cortanado spoke and having a grim sort of expression to him, as he stretched back his neck momentarily with wide eyes and saying something.

It was not long though until the bandito's and leader all look up to the second story window of the Mayor's office, as Whitcomb himself could see this, but plunging and getting away from it as best he could and out of sight in his fear. At this two of Cortanado's men suddenly went into the Hall in order to retrieve the Mayor hoping he would be inside and to begin what it was they had come for.

As they went in to commit this minor additional act of lewdness, or of taking the town Mayor hostage, one of the Mexican bandito's would soon spot a lone clerk in fact hiding and shaking behind his desk and with his own clerks hat on top of his head wearing his own clerks uniform too as they forcefully stood him up and asked if the Mayor was anywhere inside with him. But to this he merely point his simple clerks finger up to the upstairs level, as the bandits looked to each other upon going up to find him wherever he was.

Making the flight of steps then, they looked side to side down the narrow hallway, but could see no one, as one of the Mexican's went into the closest office entrance and shouting to his other Hombre to come, though seeing Whitcomb plainly standing in sight in the open, nor hiding himself anywhere, as was his more emboldened intent, but his white hair in a slight mesh and almost shakenly nervous from the calamity that had just taken place outside. As to what was going on he was without any clue of why the vile men had come to his town of all others, though he could not help but think it would most certainly, or possibly, have something to do with the dead Mexican who had been formerly shot by the sheriffs own gun, either all come to avenge the death of their friend, or either rob and loot and pillar the town for whatever values they had after, but no matter what would come, a fear like no other he had felt inside him, and with, perhaps, the only sad but more comic relief should he even live through it all, that the ominous sheriff in all his pension for wreaking such trouble in the first instance, would assuredly be leaving the next God fearing Sunday off – And with all hopes of never coming back.

Mayor Whitcomb, for that matter, just went along with the Mexican's taking him arm by arm without saying anything at first and leading him down the stairs and outside onto the sidewalk, where the clerk was presently being held and a gun pointed at him with his arms raised, as the two men escorted Whitcomb over to the gang leader who was now upon one of the men's horses and talking down to him, or the Mayor, as he tugged away from the men's arms.

"What is the meaning of this now?" he rapt out to the leader as Cortanado's face gleamed of the torch light now almost completely dark and with the wind blowing around him.

"Hello, amigo, or Mäyer *Whitcomb*, I believe it is," Cortanado spoke in his Spaniard sounding voice.

"What is you want now?" the Mayor asked straight forwardly as the leader Bandito looked down to him. Nevertheless, Cortanado was almost as prompt in his reply.

"My hombre's – As to your question, Mäyer Whitcomb, have come for something that I was told had been buried in your church's graveyard with the man killed in this town not long ago, and that he had taken from myself and my fellow bandito's, and that I have come to take back for myself from the man that betrayed me."

Whitcomb thought for a moment before replying.

"Yes," he said looking up to Cortanado. "I suppose it could be. What are you going to do?" he asked nervously in his dread.

Suddenly all his bandito's started to laugh as Mayor Whitcomb was hardly sure of why, but Cortanado just had one of his men holding a shovel from on top of his horse throw it down to the Mayor while he petrifyingly gaped over it.

"You..." he said stuttering to Cortanado. "You don't plan on makin' me..."

"Yes," Cortanado replied. "To the Graveyard with you now!" he went on in his abrupt way of command while Whitcomb went to grimly pick up the shovel that had just been thrown his way.

Just then, one of the Hombre's of his horde noticed one of the sheriff's men up on the storefront roof, or Pat Thomsen as it turned out to be trying to get a shot off at the leader, although the single Mexican able to see the deputy plainly enough even in the dark, and irksome night it was, by just moving his eyes as he raised his gun or rifle to fire at him though Pat falling to the ground dead upon being hit at the sound of the shot, as he took down with him even a piece of one of the store signs laying on the ground next to his body.

Upon this the others and the leader began looking around for a moment or on top of the other storefronts looking for any other deputies to shoot at them, or snap a shot off, and the leader talking Spanish to his next in charge as he then looked to the Mayor with the two bandits still side by side holding onto him and as he held the shovel in hand.

"If anyone of my bandito's are killed we will burn and kill all the people of your village and town. Tell your deputies, now, Mäyer Whitcomb to put down their guns, if you want to live."

The Mayor now in his stunned affect just complied with Cortanado's demand and spoke out so the sheriff's men could hear him.

"Don't shoot!" He said looking to his rear though no one answered still as Cortanado waited but talked back to the Mayor after.

"It seems no one has listened," he went on. "Do your men not listen to you, Mäyer Whitcomb?"

"Well, I don't know..." Whitcomb answered anxiously. "Maybe it was just the one."

"I see," Cortanado exclaimed from on top of his horse.

"Then, where are the rest of your deputies?" He asked though Whitcomb was not sure how to answer.

"They could be down at the precinct. *I don't know...*" He said in an apprehensive sounding voice as the men took hold of him.

"Very well, then," the leader continued. "If they won't come to us as they say," he arrogantly went on. "Then, we will have to go to them."

Turning to his men on horseback right after he uttered the word, "*Andele!*" as several or rather two of his men set out upon his command to find where the other sheriffs men, or even Jeff McCormack himself could be at or down the road some on the opposite side they had entered the town before, but taking caution in their own stride as the bandits approached the darkened precinct with the only exception of some of the torch light that was glaring onto its side.

As for Will Blake and Joe Collins they had been busy inside and only getting ready for the bandits to come their way but had not tried their hand or chances as Pat Thomsen did at trying to go out and shoot at them though, instead, had remained in the precinct even boarding up and blockading some of the windows or where they could see in hoping to fend them off and praying hard for their lives, though they knew they were outnumbered by many.

As for the sheriff or Jeff McCormack, on the other hand, he was hardly in the mood to stay and fight out the bandito's that had come to lay claim on the very article he already had in his own satchel, but knew he would not be able to get away from the scene or the precinct without being spotted on his horse by either the deputies or bandito's encroaching in on them, and, in fact, had taken some higher ground like Pat in the meanwhile to try and see if he could set them up, somehow, hoping to use Joe and Will inside as decoy's in his attempt.

Having his satchel around him and with his usual sheriff's hat on he could see the two Mexican's gang up on the precinct from behind another one of the shop windows above it, as he tried to keep the two Mexican's in sight with his .45 moving his gun along at one of them or the closest ready to shoot, though a roaring shriek of lightning and thunder had just erupted from overhead lighting up the sheriff and all others, as the bandits looked up around them. One of them, however, had noticed Jeff on top of the store though as he went to hide himself, but telling his fellow bandit next to him to look out, as his friend slipped off to try and lure the sheriff out, although Jeff knew just as well he had been spotted as he tried to figure out what to do next.

In addition to the thunder and lightning that had just come about though, large bits of hale and ice and rain mixed with it, began, at once falling from the sky and with the tense wind picking up creating a most stormy scene as the rest out on the road took cover to its side with the Mayor still held up and clerk next to him, but more thunder and lightning continuing on, as the two bandits down the road went on trying to force the others out while Joe Collins was at that moment looking out the open precinct window to see if he could get a shot off. The bandito well-hidden though, and even, able to see the deputy from behind his horse dock, managed to fire a shot off at Joe Collins almost killing him, although missing by a hair as the glass of the window shattered from the strike of the bullet, while Will Blake stuck his gun out shooting towards where the shot had come from, but no luck for that matter in hitting or wounding the Mexican.

As for the other bandito he had, by then, gone around the store front to the back to try to close in on the sheriff, or to see where he was though Jeff had already taken the initiative of hiding himself so as to create a trap for the other, as the bandito crept up the ladder with his rifle and seeing what he thought to be the sheriff, but as it would turn out to be merely only his hat on top of a barrel that he had planted to make it look like himself.

As Cortanado's man looked to aim his gun or rifle finally, after nearly reaching the top of the ladder another flash of bright lightning had come over-head illuminating the point at which he thought the sheriff to be, but instead, to his grim surprise saw only the sheriff's hat or as he had placed it on top of the barrel and realizing he had been setup, as the sheriff from the other side aimed while the Mexican dreadfully turned to him, and shot the Bandito down to the ground falling with an audible thump as sheriffs face cascaded in grin.

Having heard the sound of the shot or what had been his friend, the other Mexican still hiding behind the horse dock yelled out, but could hear no re-sponse from his fellow bandit as his refugee face turned to petty shock, and Cortanado down the road with the others yelling out to his man having heard the shot himself. In response Cortanado would only wave his authorial arm to his bandits, aside, or to move forward while taking the Mayor and clerk with him as the bandits walked both down the road to the precinct or close to it, and while the hale and rain continued to pour onto them from the night sky.

"Ok, Mäyer Whitcomb," Cortanado said from on top his horse once they had finally reached the precinct. "Tell your men inside to stand down, now, or we will kill you and your clerk where you stand. It's up to you Mäyer Whitcomb if you want to live," he continued as he took out his pistol from his side and cocked it pointing his weapon at the Mayor and ready to shoot, as Whitcomb without hardly any hesitation made his plea.

"Alright, men," he said looking at the darkly lit precinct in front while the rest of the bandito's were off to the side looking around and searching up to the surrounding roof tops to whomever had just shot their comrade.

"Stand down, and come out or they'll kill us both."

Hearing the Mayor outside and looking through the window Joe Collins could see both Whitcomb and the clerk standing at the throws of the Mexicans as he looked over to his partner Will Blake though the two knowing now they would have to come out upon the Mayor's order as they sorely undid the blockade on the door and went out to the bandito's and Mayor as he told them to while raising their hands in the air.

Suddenly Cortanado's man, or the one he had sent with the other before spoke Spanish to him from below as Cortanado looked back to the Whitcomb afterward.

"Well, Mäyer," he said. "I believe there is one more of your men. Where is he?"

The Mayor just looked apprehensive in the face looking up towards the Mexican Leader, before answering in his beleaguered state.

"Well, I don't know. He must be somewhere around."

The Mexican's just kept turning their heads though looking out on top of the store front roofs all around for the loose deputy.

"Where are you?" Cortanado yelled out in a bemusing manner. All of sudden, however, one his men sharply pointed off into the distance, nearby, as the others and Cortanado took notice, but could see the sheriff trying to gallop across the road further up from where the town ended and into the hills, as the Mexican Leader rode in a quickened hurry and a hard kick to the stirrups to reach the lawman.

At first it was hard to catch him as he kept chasing him from behind through the open plains in the dark and thundersome night before them, but able to keep Jeff, or the sheriff well within reach on his fast Bandito's horse. Nevertheless, while trying to hastily jump over some heap of undergrowth Jeff's horse slipped taking off from the muddy and moistened ground, though winding him up on his side as his horse nearly pounded over him, but rising up to its feet shortly after as Jeff tried to get up then himself, though was quickly met with Cortanado looking down at him and pointing his gun.

"I see seignior, Sheriff," the Mexican leader said from above as Jeff was still laying there in the mud. "This is not your lucky night."

One of Cortanado's men catching up had just yelled out to him in Spanish, then, as the leader went to answer, although the sheriff took the opportunity of distraction while he had slightly turned his head to do this, as Jeff hurriedly whipped out his gun to fire a round off at him, though only wounding the Mexican's horse as it plummeted to the ground but Cortanado himself quickly getting back up to his feet and shooting Jeff in his left arm at that, as the sheriff slipped and only fell back down to the ground after having taken a few steps to his horse to make his getaway.

As Cortanado approached him cautiously with his gun in hand he sternly shouted the words, "On your feet, sheriff!" while one of Cortanado's men had come up next to him by then, but seeing the lawman holding his arm and where he had been wounded.

Pointing his gun at him Cortanado's man went to get him up from off the ground as the Mexican Leader kept at a distance between the two, but the one bandit seizing Jeff's bag and poncho from him as he slung it over his shoulder and digging his gun then a few times into the sheriff's side to make him walk as he approached Cortanado in front.

"Well sheriff," Cortanado said. "Now we will see what will become of you," he continued as the sheriff or Jeff McCormack kept his same straight face, not so much as squirming upon Cortanado's word of indemnity as Cortanado himself just uttered something then to his fellow bandit in Spanish, though Jeff submitting to the Mexican and knowing he could not possibly get away now with having the bandito's gun in his rib's and the wound in his arm, but Cortanado and his man taking control of both the sheriff and his horse as they proceeded to bring the two back to where the others and Cortanado's men had been keeping at or near in front of the precinct still and where the Mayor, his Clerk and Lawmen were presently still in their clutches.

Coming out from a distance then through the cold and blistering howling wind and shale still at their faces the bandito's could see their Leader, all of a sudden, or Cortanado returning on his horse with the sheriff on foot clutching his arm and the other bandit with the sheriffs poncho now, instead, around his shoulder, though he had not looked inside it yet, as only the sheriff knew with what unaccounted surprise for all would be met if he did.

Needless to say, Jeff's capturing in the light of his attempt to escape the bandito's while abandoning his own men and Mayor did not sit well with any of the lawmen or Whitcomb as the sheriff came up to the rest with Cortanado from behind and his other man pointing his gun at him as the sheriff could see Joe Collins looking at him with indicting eyes, though greeting him anyway in his own appalling wit.

"Howdy, there, Joe," he said as Joe Collins lowered his expression.

"I'll live to see you hang..." the Mayor uttered unto him while Jeff just grinned at this.

"Looks like you won't have to be waitin' long for that," the sheriff replied as Whitcomb looked up to Cortanado on his horse with a weary face. As this had been going on, however, the one bandito had been going through the sheriff's poncho as he noticed of all things the uncharacteristic book inside as he took it out and uttered something with a look of astonishing surprise to his leader.

Opening it up to the first few pages and handing it up to his leader hands Cortanado could make out the map even in the dim lantern and torch light coming off from the side.

"Well, Mäyer Whitcomb, it seems our friendly sheriff here has already done your digging for you," Cortanado said as the Mayor looked to the sheriff with ever deplorable eyes and his partners all in shock as well.

Just then, another heap of lightning and thunder came over head striking the top of one of the storefronts and creating some sparks that had fallen onto the road, or some burnt up pieces of wood from the sign that had been struck off by the bolt, as Cortanado's horse jumped up, momentarily, from the unexpected flair. One of his men just then said something to him in his Spanish, or the same bandito that had just handed over to his leader the book he had so desperately wanted back for himself, as Cortanado seemed to be in agreement with whatever it was he suggested, but Cortanado shouting jovially to his men afterwards, as all concurred back in uproar with equal enthusiasm and in their faces, proceeding then, to take the Mayor and the sheriff and his men by gunpoint down to the saloon to get out of the storm and squall around them and, perhaps, a good whiskey and soda, or a strong heaving of Spanish Tequila in celebration to their discovery of the book that they had come all the way from their Mexican homeland to acquire.

As they went down the road there was still no one in sight and all had well – fled by most of the imperiled town, although there were still some in Little Caverns Saloon, either above it in one of the rooms the concubines would have to themselves, or behind the bar like old Max Singleton nervously and shaking with fear and hoping like anything the bandits would not come in his drinking saloon, though he was about to be met with a nasty surprise, any moment, as the ominous night itself ahead would be unlike any other in the past and or to come.

All of sudden then, as Max was still behind his bar, and hearing the laughter of Mexican's just before making their entrance the saloon doors swung open as the faces and bandit men and Leader Cortanado came in quickly piling up at the bar like the hyenas they were and bringing inside the Mayor and his deputies and sheriff for the corral and drinking frenzy and orgy of wry and disdaining humor that was about to take place.

Max trying to act substantial enough to the crowd and men just asked in his nervous manner, "Well, what will it be?" As for the Mexicans they just laughed before one turning to the other to say something, as another one took out his gun and shot at the kegs and bottles behind the counter while the liquor poured out onto the floor.

"Whiskey, for all," Cortanado spoke for the men. "Straight up."

At this old Max went to get down a bottle off from the shelf as he reached, but Cortanado shooting it to pieces before he could grab at it.

"Not that one," he said eyeing a lusher looking bottle and one to his quenching taste that evening.

"The one on the top next to it," he went on as Max Singleton moved his hand along, to get it down almost shaking now, and placing it on the counter in front of the bandits.

"I'll think we'll be needing a few glasses my good Hombre," Cortanado added piteously to Max as he started putting out a bunch of shot glasses in both of his hands out onto the counter.

One by one the Mexican's started pouring shots of the liquor set out for themselves as Max and the other's held up by the bandits could see them hounding down there hardened drinks, as one of the Mexican's was holding up his rifle to them with their hands still raised, and Cortanado himself keeping an eye on all, in particular, the sheriff and Mayor next to him. Of course, in addition to this voracious drinking going on, one or two wandering Mexican's had even gone up to the above rooms to see what women were around, alas, finding a few about or in their rooms, terrifyingly waiting for the Mexican's to barge in as they did, and taking, or the few that were still around, this including the famous Miss Lena Perkins and down to festivities, even over their shoulders, as the women and Lena shouted kicking and gurgling the whole way, but only God knowing what would be next for them, if the Mexicans were to have their way – A certainty the women and occupants of the Saloon could count on.

The new Cattle owner, or that of the venerated John Simmons, by now, had even heard the bandito's arrival and the town having been shot up as it had with all the people evading and keeping clear now from the abominable place it had become as the wicked weather outside had also helped at this, but John Simmons gathering some of his ranchers, or the few one's that were not impartial to the attempt at dismantling the Mexican Bandits, as they got their guns together and made their way to the town during the heap of the storm to try to do this. Nevertheless, the winds by now had been so harsh making their way had not been easy, though they would arrive soon enough to the scene, seeing the horses of the Mexican Bandits parked outside near the front of the saloon, off the corner, but taking caution where they could as to not make their presence known.

In fact, at that moment, the bandit's had just gone on to play some of their Hombre games and lining up the Mayor with the sheriff and his deputies trying to shoot shot glasses off and around their heads, as Max was only so glad he was not in line, but also wondering what they might have in store for himself, although knowing full well he might be last in the present charade and trickery as their show of good shot so far was the only consolation in all of it.

Even the thunder and lightning still to be heard had not lightened as John Simmons and his men could see the scraps of charred wood upon the road from before, but waiting on their horses the good ranchers they were to assault the saloon as John Simmons tried next to figure out what to do, but one his ranchers suggesting then that they take them from the back and enter the saloon from the other side of town as he knew the circumstances would be tricky for all, and not wanting to endanger his men more than he wished, unsure of how sly the bandits would be at their surprise as he knew taking them from the front of the saloon would be an all-out duel and shootout between both his men and the trigger happy Mexican's, but unconfident, either way, though he knew he would have to act soon.

Suddenly, however, one of the more confiding of his Ranchers men on horseback along with some of the others thought he could see something way off in the distance and down the Little Cavern road on the opposite side coming towards them, but not sure of what it was as each of Simmons men including the Rancher himself eventually could see whatever man and drifter get closer and to the saloon in the slow stride and pace of his horse. Even as the harsh weather continued to come down the man did not look affected by the storm and rain and slurries of shale that were coming down all over and on top of John Simmons own men as they tried to keep warm and huddling their winter coats for warmth, as whoever it was did not seem to be from around those parts, only, however, seeing a mere shadow of a man with most of the torches and lantern lights vacant of their flames, either having been broken of their sconces, or put out from the torrent winds.

"Who is that, now?" One of the Ranchers men asked with a unrelenting curiosity, as they all could see the drifter get down from off his horse, which they could hardly make out either even in the dim light that the saloon was giving off inside, but baffled, all of them as to who the man himself could be, and nor why he would not be afraid to enter the obvious upheaval going on within, although he hardly looked to be one of their own, or the Mexican bandits, for that matter, still inside playing their games with the Mayor and his sheriffs men.

For at that very moment Cortanado himself was about to take his hand at shooting a glass or a pair of them from off the Mayors head and then one sitting on top of that of the clerks who served him, the two quenching with fear in anticipation of the first shot, though his opportunity to commit this foul prank was sorely interrupted from the swinging open of the Saloon doors, as one his bandits had turned his head, not even noticing the one who had come in yet. The Mexican's face, however, upon his inception, only turned from the arrogant and mean intent it had, to almost, opposite fear and acute anxiety, but seeing the tall and statured presence of what was a man dressed in all black with black gloves and a black hat and trousers, and, even black boots, and a black kerchief over his face as the bandit went to draw on the lone gunman upon his sight and from the obvious intent of look in his demeanor as he entered, knowing he had not come in to be merely poured a drink, but also, seeing the pair of six shooters he was carrying in his, similarly, black raw hide leather holsters.

The Mexican bandit, regardless of his fast and spontaneous draw, was quickly blown away four or six feet from his place, the stranger taking out the two pairs of pistols from his holster and beginning a chain of uproar and shooting frenzy in the whole saloon, as John Simmons and his men could barely believe the shots being heard and the frantic yells and shouts of the women inside who were taking cover themselves in the back with the others from the massacre going on. Some of the shots could even be seen exiting the establishment through the Saloon window and swinging doors, but all and John Simmons not knowing how the one man could stand a chance against the bandits inside singlehanded.

Going one from the next and so on down the line as the Mexican's all tried to draw or shoot at him, the gunman was almost hit a number of times as bullets were heard zipping past him, allover, but the stranger able to maintain his pace of shot without so much as being hit as he killed and had blown four or five of them away, by then, though Cortanado taking his own stab at this in all the bloodshed and carnage around him, and already having been hit in his left shoulder, beforehand, as he quickly redelivered fire from his side wounding the man in his leg one time, as the other quickly turned and shot him in his chest for good. As he did this one of Cortanado's men had shot him again, upon turning, only this time in his arm, as the gunman returned fire to him killing him and the man, or bandit next to him while a few moans could be heard in the aftermath, but the gunman still standing in all of it as the bandits were now killed or close to it. The others, however, including the sheriff and his men had immediately recognized who the lone gunman, or rather heroin was, or no other than the nameless stranger who Jeff McCormack had bludgeoned in the Saloon, prior, and who his entrusted lawmen had set on his way on the pathetic stag outside as they were in almost as much fear of him as they had just been of the Mexican's, though Jeff had taken clear sight of him the whole time, ever the loathsome and impenetrable sheriff he was.

"Well, I'll be damned, yet," the sheriff instigated from his place in the line with the others or those that were waiting for the Gunman's next victim, wondering who it would be as the young women and Lena just kept back, away from the lawmen and the smirking sheriff and Mayor, but with Max near the other end of the bar, and with scared eyes and faces, almost aghast from what they had just seen.

"If it isn't the grim reaper himself come back to this piss pot town to be reclaimin' his sanctity," the sheriff relented on without deference, never in fear, as seldom was his sheriff's nature. "Just what is it you'd be comin' back now for?" he asked with his hands still raised like the others.

To this, however, the man merely came a few steps forward waiting to make his reply as the others lifted their arms, putrid with fear, unlike the tepid sheriff.

"My Horse," he exclaimed from behind his kerchief as the sheriff looked to laugh from his reply, but the others hardly in a comic mood.

"Well," the sheriff said almost laughingly. "Just what might the name of this horse of yours be?" he asked still unflinching in his tone, though the man responded as the sheriff harped on the name with equal amusement.

"Bucephalus –" the Black Hooded stranger bequeathed in his low tone of voice as the sheriff near giggled.

"Well," Jeff said almost sounding gregarious as he spoke. "If isn't Alexander the Great and Greek of Macedonia returnin' all the way from Ancient Thebes to be gettin' back of his own horse named Bucephalus. Well, I'll just bein' damned on that!" he continued in his unnerving rant while the Mayor took notice of the talk, or as to the mention of the Gunman's familiar Black Stallion steed and that he come to the town riding upon the night before of what the sheriff had done to him, but knowing like the others that it was and had been kept all along in the towns horse shack and stable, or ever since the incident, and was being cared for by, Tom Hooley, the stable tenant and who would take care of those either staying the night in town, or as in the man's own.

"That horse of yours is just down the road some," the Mayor said trying to interrupt the sheriff's useless banter, in his own nervous tone of voice. "They've been keeping it inside the Town Stable all this time. He's there for you right now if you like Mister and, then, you can be gettin' on your way."

"Shut up, Whitcomb –" the sheriff interceded with coldly vigor. "This Greek of ours isn't goin' for his horse," he went on clutching his arm and coming a step forward, as the Mayor near grumbled to him, almost about to piss his pants, practically. As for the gunman he just kept standing there with both his pistols still aimed at him, although his wounds to his arm and leg were beginning to weaken his posture as he had not even so much as twitched, yet, while standing in the same place.

"He's goin' nowhere," the sheriff went on crazily. "Not until he kills all of us dead in cold blood just as he had these pig and Heathen of Mexican's here. Isn't that right you sorry sonuvabitch of a grim reaper you bein'."

All of sudden, as the others closed their eyes the masked Gunman went to shoot off his pistols from one to the other, but without luck of having a live round in either chamber and the click of empty guns heard from all in witness, as the sheriff took the opportunity of the misfire to go for a nearby pistol of one of the dead Mexican's, hoping it to be good and loaded and taking it with his unwounded arm. The Gunman had already dropped both of his, however, while the sheriff went to shoot at him, though before he could get the round off his partner Joe Collins had gone for the sheriff's arm to stop him at this, but well aware now of the villain he had thought him. As for the sheriff though he quickly retorted his efforts in his attempt, and raising his gun again to the lone gunman who had gone and ducked behind the bar during the skirmish, but Jeff shooting a few rounds, above and over the bar, as glass shattered and bottles broke bursting of the aberrant liquor within.

As he was shooting though, he had been making and rushing his whole way to his poncho now lying on the floor next to the dead Leader who had taken it from him in plain sight as he managed to pick it up, with a few more shots to the side of the bar, but making it through the saloon doors alright, and into the typhoid of weather outside that was still plaguing the stormily night. John Simmons himself and his men, for that matter, had already taken cover from the deploring winds outside, or between a small alley that went crosswise to the direction of the wind itself, and where it was less chaotic than out in the torrent road, though the bits of shale and pounding rain had already mysteriously lightened by then, as another burst of lightning and distant thunder came overhead.

One of the Ranchers still looking out towards the saloon from off his horse, and around the edge of the situated alley, indeed, had turned his head at one point, as the wind and rain swept his face and when the lightning had just taken place overhead, but, in the opposite direction as he could see to his terrified eyes what mother Nature had given over, only yelling to the others, "Holy incarnation!" before continuing with the words and pointing to what he saw in the far distance, "Tornado – Coming straight for us!"

Even the sheriff as he got up on his horse with the poncho and map inside he had wanted so much to give him the lustering riches he desired, had seen the Cyclone phenomena laying out in the distance, or in the hills of the Wyoming town passed the roads as the wind from all around blew his shirt and poncho about, as he still had the gun in hand and trying to face his horse forward, his face adorning the terror that wait down the road of the sin and hell he could inspire, as though the thinly hollowed Twister and Tornado coming out of the dark and thundering clouds above were of him in a different variant and alter form of evil itself.

For a moment, his eyes took in the sight as though he thought he could take on the Twister Tornado himself making its way to the town with its hullabaloo base smashing and grifting and sucking everything in its wake headed for the town soon, as it seemed to keep coming in that direction while John

Simmons and his men tried to get out of the area on their horses and make a run for it knowing they only had minutes or even seconds to get out of the area as they came out from the Alley while Jeff McCormack could see them himself, and down the road fleeing, as he could also see and make out the pitiless wrath coming his way and what they were fearfully running from.

Just then, as had been looking, the wounded gunman had come out of the Saloon doors, in order, to get back at the sheriff and man that had depraved and bludgeoned him on that horrid and speechless night not long ago, though so unlike the one happening now, and in front of the very establishment where it had happened, while the sheriff could see him out of the corner of his eye turning and firing a quick shot and actually wounding the lone gunman in his shoulder as he had not even risen his weapon, but just clutching one of the posts of the sidewalk after having been shot again.

Stretching his arm out, nonetheless, and holding one of his guns he pointed at the sheriff looking as if about to get away on his horse, and shot him in the back through his spine as the sheriff, shrieked momentarily, almost falling off his horse, but staying on at that and turning around after a few paces, although weak and sluggish looking.

Lifting his head up to the Tornado still in the far distance, though slightly closer than it had, his eyes gleamed of redness in their pupils and a reality he saw in the impending Chaos he could not replete, nor knew his nature was meant for earthly good or conduct, as he set out on his way kicking into his horse with as much strength he could muster from the gunshot that had bored him, while the nameless drifter continued to hold himself up by the post and looking on, the sheriff riding his horse down the Town's road almost barely holding on and into the natural obstruction that bared his name, if not only in soul.

As for the sheriff he kept riding straight for it as his horse buckled a few times from the unsurmountable winds coming off the twister, but making his way closer and closer, insane with his own sense of depredation, and almost laughing as he did in his foul prant to the Gods, preparing to be sucked up into the mammoth heap he was about to meet, and hence, finally, come face to face with his ultimatum.

Within distance of his intended point, and having the fatal intent he did, the sheriff's horse gave way and jumped up to its hind legs, knocking him down to the ground, but his horse running off loose after, although uncertain at that if it would even getaway, as the sheriff's fate was much less hopeful in this, needless to say, but the Tornado deftly approaching his wounded self while Jeff looked up to his master, and, with one last heinous laugh, consuming the sheriff whole sucking him up into the Cyclone, as he orbited around and around until he could not be seen anymore, disintegrating into the mound of tubular wind, as the thunder and lightning burst, once more.

All that was left now, however, was the town that lay ahead in its path as the Mayor and other lawmen remaining, along with, Max, and the few girls around and Lena, but all whom had taken caution, or cover for themselves down in the saloons brick and mortar cellar, after one of the lawmen, Will Blake, had stepped outside onto the porch trying to see what had become of the lone Gunman but, for some reason, seeing no sign of him anywhere as he turned his head then, only to see the Tornado out and down the road above the incoming horizon, surely to devour all in its path. As for what damage it would present remained still to be unseen, but the deputy had come back in to the others to inform them of what he had just witnessed as everyone almost scurried into a panic while quickly hurrying and following Max into the Saloons emptied cellar hoping it would be able to protect them sufficiently from what was about to be at their doorstep any moment.

As for all other people in the town, or whomever was still left after the Mexican's had come, they had by now either taken themselves cover to lower ground after seeing as well for themselves the funneling Cyclone about to come through, or who were either, instead, hiding in a store cellar down below like those over at the saloon, though it could not be guaranteed if all had seen the twister beforehand as that old feeling of the Freight Train effect with all its shims and shams was now being felt, and the walls beginning to nudge and buckle which was perceived, or either felt in one way or another, and while those in the Saloon Cellar, in particular, the girls holding onto to one another could be heard in their fear for the natural disorder outside. For even in a form unlike them it could not be certain in its inhuman composure and levity in force, of what damage it would impel, and even more terrifying the thought if they would be able to withstand the its absolution about to ensue.

Gradually, as the element of the Tornado took hold, a few of the liquor bottles fell off the shelves and could be heard spilling over in their vibrations, though the cellar proved to be quite strong at that in keeping those safe from whatever god knows what was happening above so far. Suddenly though, the upstairs of the saloon could be heard in an uproar of broken glass and chairs and nearby tables being spilled over, while even the flame of a lantern light that they'd brought down with them had gone out amid the racks of Liquor vibrating more and more, but, no one hardly making a sound, so overwrought with fear itself, and as the Tornado carried out of its wrath within, and no one knowing for how long the unsettling turbulence around would last but hoping it would be not much longer.

It would be only a few more seconds until the Tornado would pass over, as the quietness of this moving on could be felt by all kept safe inside the pitch black of the Cellar, with a complete deadening of affect in the abstinence of the gone Cyclone, and all beginning to breathe again knowing they had been spared from the Natural disarray that was so familiar to only them and the people in those places of the Mid-West, or, with as much force as it had come and the Power of God over them, unlike any other Force, they, or those alive and their children even now and then, would ever come to bear Witness.

Coming up the few steps from out of the tightly and snug Cellar as Max, finally, opened the door to see what was left of his bar and Town's drinking establishment the other lawmen, girls and Mayor and Clerk followed from be-hind as the bartender looked around to his astonished eyes and gawking at the mess that had ensued, but seeing that nearly one half, or the entire front of the Drinking man's bar and front wall of the Saloon being completely obliterated and taken off by the violent Nature observed, as everyone including the bereft Mayor of the Little Cavern Town looked around, almost self-condoling of his own grief, as he stepped out onto what had been the sidewalk, now twisted and in a mensch of wood with nails sticking out all over, and seeing what was left of what had been, once, a quaintly town no more, and the Store Front buildings torn off like the Saloon, and wagons turned upside down and the mess of the Store goods in the street piled and left broken up in the unspeakable mud and dirt that lain.

So unlike before, the rain coming down had ceased with the feeling of dry-ness in the air all around, but some faint and audible cries for help could be heard then, from down the town's road, as the two lawmen made their way out the nearly half dismantled Saloon, effortless as it was in this venue as they made their way from that point to see and try to find who it was doing the shouting in her higher pitched and womanly voice, or as it would turn out to be the French dressmaker Miss Purcell herself whose shop had been com-pletely torn out while she had taken cover in the wee back though with a pile and heap of some of her cloths and fabrics toppled upon her and hardly in the frivolous and gossamer mood she was given to.

Craig Sholl

Eventually as they looked throughout the rubble, or of whatever had been left of the French Lady's shop, both remaining deputies Will and Joe finally found and carefully took the Madame from the ruined fabrics and dresses all about her and that she lay under as Miss Purcell stood there for the moment looking around and almost in disbelief of it all. As for the two lawmen they just looked on then, as Miss Purcell spoke some incompressible French to herself, in her fit of shock and perplexed as to what had been her store, and even the Mayor coming by to try to offer his condolence as to her ruined clothes shop though making little impression unto her as she just kept fussing around and in her milieu of frantic excitement of the whole disastrous scene, but finally, the Mayor himself giving her a small smack to the cheek as she stopped her useless hysterics and would remain unusually silent for the next few hours, until others up and around in those parts near the Town and those who had not been effected by the Tornado as much would come by to help and see what was left of the place, especially in the case if anyone had gotten trapped during the horrendous event without being able call out for help, or if unconscious.

As for the Saloon and bar, the shot up bodies of the dead Mexican's were no longer inside and had been exhumed by the ferocity of the Cyclone as even their horses were not to be found or seen anywhere, for that matter, though it was uncertain if they had gotten away, or were either given to the fate of the latter, but with few store Fronts not being affected as such, and even Miss Ruford's Parlor slightly bashed up, and not as bad as most others, or even Mr. Dixon's own Stationary store on the other side of Town in the condition, similar, to that of the women's clothing shop or Miss Purcell's.

In fact, all in all, it was only a few places or storefronts of the Town that the storm had not been affected by to this detail, one of which under this exception was Farnworth's Parlor and Mortuary across but closer to the precinct and jail which was not too bad off, either, coincidentally, with just its front caved in, although no one had been inside or trapped in one of the cells which were all still intact of their steal and by all means ready to go, and in view of the stupendous calamity upholding the petty squabbles of the law that night or next were the last things on anyone's mind.

In fact the only body that remained of the recent blood shed was that of Law Man Pat Thomsen's which had been wound up and found in one of the stores nearby, and shortly taken over the next day to Farnworth getting ready for anyone else that might have to be buried, or at least, to be mourned as the Undertaker was just as discouraged as anyone else about what lay ahead, or as to what had become of the Christianly Haven of a Town, but preparing for more dead Folk to come his way regardless of his attitudes and in his own sense of obligation to those that would need the service.

Even Mr. and Mrs. O'Leary had heard themselves of the town's destruction and had come like most others the next day familiar to it as any and living like many others on its outskirts as to take part in the salvaging and moving of debris and destroyed stores and Little Cavern town over the next days and even weeks to come, but an effort that would take a long time to mend and in time rebuilding of the small Town they once knew and wanted for their own, even if they had not been as enamored or put on by its display as their neighbors had, but feeling a likened obligation to come partake in the painstaking effort as to repay all others for the caring and kindness they had been given so far after what had happened to them.

Of course, neither was this before having visited their own daughter at Mrs. Jones' to see how they had fared but the look of the homestead from their carriage as they approached quite intact for the most part with some minor windings around or blown decay about which had been endured by all really, and Glad that Millie and the others were out of harm's way similarly to themselves, an act of God that had actually spared them on this account.

For in the wake of all the devastation, perhaps, the redemption they had wanted was within this new and unexpected course as the Town after having been unmercifully Martyred and Scandalized, and then, ruined by a Force Larger than themselves or almost in any other way practically imaginable had finally tipped the rock to its bottom as they knew they would have to begin again without choice and, finally, realizing it was not for them to know all disasters that may come. Instead, for now it would be for those in witness only to greet whatever Toil with as much repent as they could gather in their revelation and the erudite message that had been learned and given over not by the finality of human hands but by Nature ravaging and Stark in all its forms and not to be defeated by any amount of Soldiering that any people could overthrow or gain a far advantage over – For it was Nature itself of all that defied the Town of Little old Cavern in the end, and with the once demonical sheriff himself residing it, never to be heard from again but only his sinister laugh blowing through the wind and waiting to come back to the land somewhere else below, or in some other Town far, far away and in his new Blazed Incarnated Form.

Therefore, in regards to the Town, or that of which has been told, perhaps, this notion of feeling was, finally, deplored no better than on the following Sunday of the Towns Crisis, and during the present demoralization as Father Coleridge went on his usual morning of Sunday worship without hardly any delay to the service, even, as all just wanted to be in the Lord's house to pray very long and rather hard for what was to come in the aftermath and for those who had lost some of their own homes, or that had not been spared the Colossus that had come down from the sky, contrarily clear on the February Morning with hardly a cloud to be seen and with the sun overhead as though tranquil in a kind of Peace brought forth.

It is also, noteworthy, that the Church itself had Hardly been touched with the exception of the commonly Church Bell that had hung in the Church's Steeple and that would ordinarily be rung, but which, instead, had been found by the parson as to be oddly detached from its scaffold, having a small crack on the inside as well, but soon to be reattached to its Mount to proceed the many Sunday Mornings to come during the Town's renovation as the Mayor or Whitcomb was sending for Relief in the meantime, in order, to press on with it, but like all things under the Circumstances, the Price of which had already been Paid.

Church, in consequence, was more full than it had been with some standing up over on the sides and all occupying the pews and Coleridge prophesizing for the new Hopes to come, and with Fervor.

The only few in fact not to be present was, of course, Millie with Mrs. Jones and the Somber mild Wyatt Cobb, although Millie and Wyatt had spent the day, or that part of the morning in such a more pleasanter way of themselves, or away from the Town and where it was He had originally found her near the Stone Wall, though the trees in contrast were Now much more empty looking in the cast of the early March sun as the two sat down for a few moments Upon the Wall to Take in their Surroundings and with clear sky above listen to Silence all around as Millie look to Wyatt with a Growing Fondness not only of the Writer he was but the man she had come to know and that had impressed her mind, unlike few others to come.

For even a brief Moment she had went to touch his hand, but Wyatt pulled back not out of distrust, but rather out of fear unable to accept the touch of another Woman in a long while as Millie took his hand, Wyatt finally, giving in and taking it above to her hair as he fondled the strands for as long as she kept it there, while Wyatt eventually retracted and rising up to legs as he went over and picked an early Spring Flower to give to her, a lone wild Rose that was not too withered from the Winter Sog, but blue and very familiar to those parts of the Mid – West.

She would keep the token for as long as she would go on after, and to remember the man she had mistook to be the thing and person she could relate to than any other, the outsiders and Misbegotten people they were, or would be.

There mere touch to one another, however, would not go any further than the intent of the gesture as Millie did not mean anything suggested by its possibly mistaken inference other than the simple kindness and showing of affection for Wyatt she meant, and what it was she thought he had had seen in her, although his impact would go on to influence her no doubt, even perhaps, herself at this time beginning to have notions of taking up the pen and writing as he had, not only to express her inner thoughts and feelings, but to tell of things she knew and saw unlike through and by others apart, so in a sense to find the beauty in these Creations as to make them live on, rather than die from forgetting. For in my own writing of the preceding's and the Obvious lyrical depiction of the Town I chose it is this element or idea of preservation of the past that is, perhaps, the most crucial of all and that has been discussed or rendered as to convey what it is or what I think is important, or what should be told rather than not.

Indeed, just as the Journals from which I had gotten the inspiration to write of a town I have never known and recorded by my Ancestor it is my use of wit and Character and Charm that bring the Town to life the Little While and survives its own inevitable end as the old West slowly Closed in those remaining years not to be seen Again, or under its Likeness.

For the Town of Little Cavern is now Gone like so many of its Kind since and a Chapter that has Closed on the American Way of Life – a Freedom deposed by its own Virtue and search for Redemption.

As for my Ancestor herself these writings or the recorded Journals, along with some of her other writings that were still kept hidden away in the attic and in the Same Metal Cabinet I had Absolved these but are only to serve the Story as mere Fragments of the reality I had set Forth, and my Interpretation of the Daily ongoing's between Herself and the others and Her Parents are merely a

Craig Sholl

Representation of the Reality I think Lingers on Today and Sets the Stage for Events even now occurring, Likewise, as they had then, and in the Same Light I have Spoken of.

For my Ancestor or Mildred would go on to fulfill what had been destined for her and get the Education to supply her with the knowledge and Will to flourish as the woman and Writer she would become as some of her myriad of works as mentioned had been spared the Fate of her own Human existence with a beginning and an end in place, though she would inevitably come back to the West to return to her Parents and join them to see the town that had been Rebuilt by then, but also, go on and have a family of her own after meeting the Gentleman that would eventually have her hand, or what might have been my Great, Great Grandfather who I was told From my Grandmother was given to the name of – Edward.

Her writings like her Journals are still Frail and quite old to the touch though one of which seems to have been a clipping removed from the Daily Newspaper where she had lived after marrying young Edward and that she had submitted in older age when her husband had by then, perhaps, passed on and her own children, or my Grandmother had moved to the East as she would stay here for most of her life and where I have resided for all of mine never once having seen the Western Country she had come from, with only her reminisces and the Journals and the only poem I had seen written by her Mother's mother or as it appears from the clipping:

"The Town of Little Cavern"
(1941 Drummond County)
By,
Mildred "Millie" O'Leary

I knew a Town Once
When I was Girl.

Its wheat was the Color
Of my Hair

And it's Beauty

NO GUN'S IN LITTLE CAVERN

Was uncommon –
One could not help but Stare

For in the Sky
Came out its Wrath
Of Despair

But in My Heart
Little Cavern will always
Forever,
Be There.

The Poem Plain and Simple Like Millie is Perhaps what made her so, and it is this use of her own works, or what little composites I have of her, or the things that she wrote of That I have used in my Portrait of her as a Young Lady, Compassionate and Caringly Millie.

For the Reality Of It is I had very little knowledge of her in the First place and what story I have woven is not just of the Characters I had chosen to Represent, some of Which, are Even a Figment of My own Imagination and are Just to Drive The Stories Points as best I could, though I think it is Just as Well that They were Written for this Purpose, and Purpose is what a Story should have if it is to be Told I Think in the First Place.

As I see it the past is what often feeds the present and so in the Telling of This Fable I Deploy all that I know Within as to make those remember the past in a way that can be appreciated for the mere idea and Folly of it, rather than what precisely was going on or whom was where or what happened to Who, all of which are better left to the interpreter most times. For what a man sees and Likes is often himself in others.

Now that I have told the way I have seen it, though, I cannot say that the things and devices I have used are not at times ridiculous or more often lauding than to write about a time and Town I could Hardly know myself, nor having lived Remotely in the era or Place, but I instead, Turn the Page to Move Forward.

For what Writing I have done and did is Hardly the Way of Life I Have Known as My own Life has been Almost the Opposite at times In Struggle, and my Neighbors are Hardly those that of Which Millie had, or what I Want and Have Lived for.

All I can do is offer the present Prose for now and wait for others to come as I watch the passing of the Day over to Night and Find what solace within. For there were many times I wanted to stop and not go on, but, perhaps, My Writing only serves me or in this Light.

A Light that I cannot put out nor give in to My Inner Voice of Doubt, and that I Surrender to when All Hope is Uncertain, just as Millie's own Fears and Desires were the Object of her Own Peril's and Ambiguities to Live – She Lives Now rather in me.

For as To the Aspect of my Ancestors Name and the Supposition of Mildred To Millie it is My Belief that although Millie Lived in Mildred it was Millie whom all Wanted to See out of her and the Name of Mildred that was given to Tradition; Whereas, Mildred is Old, Millie was Young and Vivacious, and Full of Life though Mildred serves Only as the Power over Tradition rather than what should or ought to be instead – But Tradition something that withers of Time until the next Generation borrows and wilts what it can, and then, to be lost until it is not heard anymore, and Finally, *Gone into the past...*

As for Millie's mother and father, or Benjamin and Kate and who rightfully are to be both the Grandparents of my Grandparents Parents, or just more shrewdly put my Great, Great, Great Grandparents, they, too, would live out the rest of their lives in the same home where Millie had left from to go East and where she would come back, eventually, in time after, but were contained to themselves mostly as to their daughters ways and as to her prior collapse, though were still able to see her soon grow more and more into the adulthood she would assume, but quietly and well cared for by both, regardless. For even Mrs. O'Leary, or Kate, had turned to her husband one slightly more subdued evening soon after the town's present misfortune and with other thoughts she had only to ask what Millie would ever have to come back to after all, but Benjamin without being too hard pressed and the word in his lightened voice as though an end to the saga that had gone on, but only replying with the one simple word, hesitant and ever enduringly as the word may really come to imply - "Us."

33

The Town of Little Cavern was, as said, eventually rebuilt and put in place the Store Fronts and Shops as Before, and with as much Pride in its Revival as when it had originally stood the Many Years before the Natural Impediment that had Claimed It, or as to the self-dubbed Ball of Fate that had All Along only been at its Gate to Open and Receive its Condemnation from above.

For no Town or Country for that matter can withstand the elements it surrounds or that which surrounds it for Too Long without Consequence of the other.

And the Rule that had made the Town different from others only served it in this way as to bring more Trouble than deserved, or would ascertain than other Towns that simply did not care for Such Dominion over Rule.

What makes Little Cavern different is what makes us all different whether in the face of Conquest or the Natural Elements above or below, but we cannot change this in any other way, so far.

Indeed, the talk and gossip of The Town was and went on in the Days to Come in the Wake of the behemoth Cyclone that had been brought on, with mention of the Sheriff and the questionable Spaniards Book with Its own Treasure Map woven within, and the Lone Gunman that had come to Finish him, though it was never certain of where the Sheriff had Gone with only the Reader to Indulge in my own Serving out of his Fate, or the Way I Have seen it to Be and maybe He really did Offer himself Up to the Storm or Cyclone as he had, and Shamelessly laughing as he Went but only serving the Reader as to what he Represented rather at least Through My Eyes.

For it is also my Interpretation of the Lone Gunman, whose Horse was Not to Be Found the Next day after, and, of Which had Never been Found Following its eviction though Whether it was Taken From its Kennel out of the Town's Horse Stable or Shack by the Gunman himself would be a matter of Contention, but most of The other Horses had Remained for the better Part in their Places, unlike the Black Stallion he Had Made His Entrance on and Bearing the Name Bucephalus, though the door to the Kennel had been Slightly Unloosened and Broken of its Latch, as, perhaps the Lone Gunman, Nameless as he Had Come, Only Rode off With His Valued Steed as Only the Spirit Form he had Become.

In time these Stories would Circle and come together in a rumoring Bind as Millie would note them and Collect what she had Heard in her Diaries, once more to Resume where she had Left off after her Initial Collapse, if You Like, but Ending around the time she Had gone off to School in the East as She would Come Back to Stay with her Parents Before her Departure, and Even Attend the Very Dance she had Become lessened in her Fear of and in the Same Outfit Her Mother had made for Her, and when That Inevitable Question of Womanhood Had First Beckoned.

Her Friends for that Matter Did not Seem to Her what She had Thought all Along, and Received her as Courteous as They Could, and even Her Friend Stella Saying Hello to her During the Young Persons Festivity and Town and County Gala, though Which had been Put off for the May Time in View of the present Towns Upheaval, and to Coordinate Better the Old Governors County Tradition as Even Wyatt Cobb had Made a Small Showing of Himself but To Dance with the Girl he Knew and Admired.

For she was Very Pleased in This and Not Put Off either, but Obliged From His Showing of Company not to Run from His offering in Hand, But to Accept it for What it was and as All Looked on, Without Saying anything But Observing the Two Shamelessly in their Ritual, and Peaceful Looking as They Did.

Even In Time Mrs. Taylor Herself, Would Come Back After her Partner Had Squabbled Away His Money On The last Bit of the Californian Gold With Empty Hands In All of It, But to Reclaim Her Estate Which Was Still rightfully Hers and Had Not been Occupied Since, though Had been Burnt to The Ground the Same Night That the Storm and Tornado Had Come; Mysterious as to How it Could Have happened, As John Simmons Had Been Occupying Another Shelter or a Much More Modest House of His Own Making He'd Built Alongside the ranch and Without the Need of Mrs. Taylors Chamber Maid or Nanny, as such, Whom She Had Brought with Her to the Golden State.

Having Hardly Any Money To Herself At The Moment She Could Not Possibly Hope to Buy Mr. Simmons Out of His Ranch Even if She Wanted to or if He would Accept which Would Inevitably Be On His Part, And Hardly As Easily Bought As She.

So, Instead, she Would Carry Off and Find Other Means of Living or Marry Another Well To Do Bidder Never To Come Back to the Town she Had so Ironically Come To Hate, Almost Comical In Contrast To The Other much Less Formidable People Around, And Unlike Those that Would Prove To Stay on and Endure Whatever Its Toil For Whatever Price of Themselves, So Different In Character to Shrewd Mrs. Taylor Herself wife of the Late Cattle Man.

The Cattle and Ranch Owner John Simmons would Also prove to Be a Great Help to the Rebuilding of the Town and go on to Make a Success of the Ranch he Had been Reunited with and the Townspeople more and more appreciative of his Good Conduct and, Eventually, becoming Just or as More Successful as the Man he Dethroned in this Venture, but Proud and Forefront of His Prospects as any Working Man of His Trade.

In Time Will Blake and Joe Collins would go on to continue to serve the Law as Will would inevitably make up his mind to serve at the Precinct upon the New Town's induction into the Future, oddly he thought even to himself, but the preceding's almost as if a precursor to his decision and the Destruction that he Observed only a Reminder that the Law and Justice is only as Good as the one's upholding it, as Joe Collins under this Action would eventually Step Down as Towns Chief Deputy to Pursue Other Interests, or To Make a Small Go at a Business. Although Joe would not Profit much; in contrast, the Law was something now unlike his Partner, that he could No Longer answer to or for now on without seeing Jeff's Cold eyes staring Him back. But, the Town would go On Like That For Years with more Deputies and Mayor's to Come until, eventually, it would Fade and Become another Ghost Town of the West and only the Fields and a few Shades or Scraps of wood to Mark what Once was, but Gone like everything Else.

As for the Brevity of Narrative itself, it has also once been Told, or at least Suggested: "Brevity Is The Soul Of Wit;" And Provides the Poetic Strands In Myself To Be Unleashed And Used To Proper Good And Just as the Distinguished Gentleman and Artist of The Woods Had Proclaimed His Take On The Sheriff It is My Intent To Spread Similar Notions Of What an Artist Should Be And Teach and Live For.

Craig Sholl

For Others May Too Have seen The Pale Faced Man Named to whatever, or
The Ghost on the Night that Would Forsake All Others In the Same Way When
the Moon Had Been Full, And Stories Made Up About Him of Who and Where
He Had Come From or This and That Of What He Said, But In the End Remain-
ing a Voice To All That Met His Whitely Face With a Caution They Would Not
Forget And His Presence Not To be Seen or missed For Long Periods Between
Each Sighting.

Was He who He said He was, or A Darkened Poet for All Time?

It is Also Notable; or That the Sheriff's own Hat and Pair Of Guns Was, As Well,
Found the Next days After that Unspeakable Day Or among Judd Mare's Own
Crop and Corn Field By the straw Hatted and Colored Man Himself, and that
Some Children Had Found Playing around In those Parts After He had come up
to Them To see What it was they had Found, But Seeing the Sheriff's Items
Distributed on the Ground Side By Side and Hardly Knowing Whom They Be-
longed To, Or Where They Had Come From Planted Their, Perhaps, By The Na-
ture that Had Took Him and Left as Jeff's Last Testament.

It May Not Be So Surprising Either that Scott's own Horse Had Come Back
After All and Within the Next Few Weeks Or During What Would Be the Next
Phase and Chapter of Little Cavern, but Discovered By the Same Judd Mare who
Had been Spared the Wrath of the Tornado Unlike Some, But Coming up to the
Cattle Ranchers Horse That Had Returned With His Own Eyes Slightly Less
Cynical in What He knew to Be Man's own Destruction Over Himself, A Notion
Judd the Colored Man He was Would Know Better Than Most.

* * *

But Just as Scott's Horse, or "Curtain" As he had Called Him, Would Come
Back to His Place Of Origin The Darkly Side of Little Cavern Would Close in on
its own Curtain When In time A New one would soon Begin Again, although
One That Would Know Better Than the Last Of What Could Happen In The Face
of Anything To Come, Or Which Had Already, and though Time Has Changed
Hands Since there Are Certain things That Have, Perhaps, Always Remained, A
Knowledge Learnt By those Of Little Cavern Harder Than Most.

As For the Town Itself No Rule Can Prevent A Place From the Rest Of The World For Too Long, And The Town Rule Only Served Itself To the Exception As Though A Wall To All Others Who Would Come Their Way. But No Wall Can Prevent From All Disasters Or From Those That Choose To Come In.

It Is Man's Very Desire That He Should Embark into the Unknown and Live to All Corners That He Should Find.

And, It Is This That Makes Him So To Live As He Wants Like Those That Are Kept Out Behind It In the First Place.

For in this Case Was The Town That Stood In All Its Glory, and With it A Shrine In the Form Of A Sign And Etched Or Written Upon it The Words – "No Gun's to Be Worn In Little Cavern" – A Simple Dream They Could Not Resist, Only To Be An Echo In the Wind.

The End.

Made in the USA
Middletown, DE
30 July 2022

70174646R00170